Rayguns Over Texas

Rayguns Over TEXAS

Edited by
Richard Klaw

Introduction by
Bruce Sterling

Published by FACT, Inc. • Austin, Texas

Rayguns Over Texas

Copyright © 2013 by Richard Klaw

Cover art copyright © 2013 by Rocky Kelley

FACT, Inc.
P.O. Box 26442, Austin, TX 78755
info@fact.org
www.fact.org

"Texas Over Rayguns" © 2013 by Bruce Sterling. Original to this anthology.

"It's All Lew's Fault" © 2013 by Richard Klaw. Original to this anthology.

"Books Are My Thing: Adventures in Texas Science Fiction" © 2013 by Scott A. Cupp. Original to this anthology.

"Babylon Moon" © 2013 by Matthew Bey. Original to this anthology.

"Texas Died for Somebody's Sins But Not Mine" © 2013 by Stina Leicht. Original to this anthology.

"The Nostalgia Differential" © 2013 by Michael & Linda Moorcock. Original to this anthology.

"Novel Properties of Certain Complex Alkaloids" © 2013 by Lawrence Person. Original to this anthology.

"Rex" © 2013 by Joe R. Lansdale. Original to this anthology.

"The Atmosphere Man" © 2013 by Nicky Drayden. Original to this anthology.

"La Bamba Boulevard" © 2011 by Bradley Denton. Originally published in the FenCon VIII Program Book, September 23-25, 2011. Reprinted by permission of the author.

"Operators Are Standing By" © 2013 by Rhonda Eudaly. Original to this anthology.

"The Art of Absence" © 2013 by Don Webb. Original to this anthology.

"An Afternoon's Nap, or; Five Hundred Years Ahead" by Aurelia Hadley Mohl. Originally published in Houston Tri-Weekly Telegragh 31, no. 126 (December 25, 1865); 31, no. 127 (December 27, 1865); 31, no. 128 (December 29, 1865); 31, no. 128 [no. 129] (December 29, 1865).

"Grey Goo and You" © 2013 by Derek Austin Johnson. Original to this anthology.

"Defenders of Beeman County" © 2013 by Aaron Allston. Original to this anthology.

"Sovereign Wealth" © 2013 by Chris N. Brown. Original to this anthology.

"Jump the Black" © 2013 by Marshall Ryan Maresca. Original to this anthology.

"Timeout" © 2013 by Neal Barret, Jr. Original to this anthology.

"Pet Rock" © 2013 by Sanford Allen. Original to this anthology.

"Take a Left at the Cretaceous" © 2013 by Mark Finn. Original to this anthology.

"The Chambered Eye" © 2013 by Jessica Reisman. Original to this anthology.

"Best Energies" © 2013 by Josh Rountree. Original to this anthology.

"Appendix A: The Essential Texas Writers" © 2013 by Scott A. Cupp. Original to this anthology.

"Appendix B: Other Texas Writers You Should Check Out" © 2013 by Scott A. Cupp. Original to this anthology.

"Appendix C: The Essential Texas Artists" © 2013 by Scott A. Cupp. Original to this anthology.

ISBN 978-0-9892706-0-1

eISBN 978-0-9892706-1-8

First Edition: 2013

9 8 7 6 5 4 3 2 1

For Lew,

Without whose patience and lessons all those years ago, this book would never been a reality

Contents

Texas Over Rayguns 1
  Bruce Sterling

It's All Lew's Fault 4
  Richard Klaw

Books Are My Thing: Adventures in Texas Science Fiction 7
  Scott A. Cupp

Babylon Moon 16
  Matthew Bey

Texas Died for Somebody's Sins But Not Mine. 38
  Stina Leicht

The Nostalgia Differential. 54
  Michael Moorcock

Novel Properties of Certain Complex Alkaloids 69
  Lawrence Person

Rex 89
  Joe R. Lansdale

The Atmosphere Man 95
  Nicky Drayden

La Bamba Boulevard 105
  Bradley Denton

Operators are Standing By 119
  Rhonda Eudaly

The Art of Absence 130
  Don Webb

An Afternoon's Nap, or; Five Hundred Years Ahead 141
    Aurelia Hadley Mohl

Grey Goo and You 166
    Derek Austin Johnson

Defenders of Beeman County 185
    Aaron Allston

Sovereign Wealth 204
    Chris N. Brown

Jump the Black 216
    Marshall Ryan Maresca

Timeout 230
    Neal Barrett, Jr.

Pet Rock 239
    Sanford Allen

Take a Left at the Cretaceous 253
    Mark Finn

The Chambered Eye 269
    Jessica Reisman

Best Energies 284
    Josh Rountree

Appendix A: The Essential Texas Writers 307

Appendix B: Other Texas Writers You Should Check Out 316

Appendix C: The Essential Texas Artists 320

Author Biographies 324

Editor Biography 330

Texas Over Rayguns

Bruce Sterling

This sprightly book is the second collection of regional Texan science fiction, and the first in a long generation. *Rayguns Over Texas* features Texan science fiction writers of every known variety: native, imported, male, female, grizzled veterans and dewy neophytes.

Here the reader will see Texan writers tackling some themes that loom large in their extensive neck of the woods. Among them are such cogent issues such as immigration (by space aliens), narcotics (for Artificial Intelligences), gunfire (to bag dinosaurs), and the rough handling that pop stars from Beaumont and Lubbock can sometimes receive in Hollywood.

Since Texas is bigger than many major European nations, it's a varied place. Its sprawling acreage combines the variant cultures of the Old South, the Mountain West, the Midwest and the Mexican frontier. Texas also has a unique regional cuisine (Tex-Mex) and regional forms of ethnic music (Western Swing, conjunto, Texas blues).

Regional Texan literature is based on folkloric, Southern Gothic themes of suffering, endurance, and transformation: a saga of parents, children and their land. However, Texan science fiction writers are people of a specific temperament. They are visionary fantasists from global subculture that creates science fiction books, movies, television, games, comic books, costumes, conventions, and collectibles. So they're not junior partners of Texan regionalists; they are ornery, and into their own thing.

This Texan science fiction subculture has been rooted in Texas for quite a while. Almost everyone in science fiction has heard of Robert E. Howard, the comrade of Lovecraft and the pulp-fiction creator of "Conan the Barbarian", whose work still thrives after 80 years. *Rayguns Over Texas* contains a marvelous work by Aurelia Hadley Mohl, a Texan literary translator and ardent suffragette. This intensely futuristic effort of imagination was published way back in 1865, in the smoking ruins of Aurelia's Confederacy. Aurelia's time-travel fantasy reveals itself as a rather typical work of Texan science fiction, in that it's got a leaping, headlong fantasy elements, wry social commentary, peculiar local lingo, and number of sharp political digs.

It takes some grit to be a Texan science fiction writer, for they've never been over-burdened with help and are blissfully unaware of other people's literary rules. Somewhere within this form of genre writing there remains the tall-tale braggadocio of a thinly scattered people taking root in a vast frontier.

Texas is rough and tough. It boasts a violent climate replete with tornadoes, hurricanes, droughts and wildfires. It's been the site of massacres, ethic cleansing and colossal natural and industrial disasters. Politically, Texas has always been a one-party state, with its public affairs in the hands of a camarilla of alcaldes and good old boys. Texas has handguns galore and one of the planet's largest prison populations. Texas has known economic collapse, military defeat, occupation, and centuries of racial oppression and grinding rural poverty. Those may be the stark facts, but they don't much bother any creative figure in this book. If anything, all that merely gives them some extra swagger.

Texas is also advanced. The raw, spectacular landscape of this former republic is covered with superbly engineered infrastructure of highways, oil derricks, gas lines, transmission towers... windmills, ports, canals, spacecraft control centers, military bases... drones, nuclear weapons assembly plants, ultra-clean computer chip assembly factories — yes, most anything that technology can conjure up has been deployed on the people of Texas. Commonly they even inflict that stuff on other people.

In summary, Texas is an earthly paradise for the geek maven and the optimistic curmudgeon. Such are the authors here, and such is the editor of this book, Rick Klaw. Rick is a wry, jolly, self-starting guy, full of initiative and undaunted by the odds, and it's because of him that this book happened.

By the way, there's not a raygun to be found in this book. I looked for rayguns, but it turns out that the title is just a wink to the knowledgeable reader there, something like silver spurs on the spotless boots of a Texan computer mogul.

I hope you enjoy reading this as much as I did.

Bruce Sterling
Bullard, Texas 2013

It's All Lew's Fault

Richard Klaw

In 1989, I was 20 years old and in Austin (from Houston) for about a year, working at the Book Stop in Lincoln Village. I had just returned from lunch where I read Lewis Shiner's contribution in the first *Wild Cards* volume. "The Long, Dark Night of Fortunato" starred a truly unusual hero, a pimp who derives his special powers from Tantric magic. His method of interrogating a dead man had the virtue of never being tried before, not just in *Wild Cards*, but likely in the whole of fiction. With my mind still reeling from the story, I took my afternoon shift at the cash register. My first customer was Lewis Shiner.

Lew became a regular, stopping in a few times each week. We'd discuss books, movies, comics, music, and sometimes writing. In the Austin of that era, every 20 year old was either a student, a struggling musician, or a neophyte writer. I loathe school and can't carry a tune. I finally worked up the nerve to show Lew a story of mine. Eventually, we started meeting once a week for lunch with screenwriter and film editor Thomas Smith at the Lone Star Cafe.

Shiner took to calling our group The Lone Star Roundtable. We'd discuss projects, engage in critiques, and discuss literary history. Lew taught me how to be a professional writer and an editor. He started introducing me to other members of the Austin writers community. Most importantly Lew gave me the confidence to pursue my own path. My first edited book came out from Blackbird Comicswhen I was 22 and my first anthology one year later.

By the mid-nineties, Lew had relocated to San Antonio before eventually settling in Raleigh, NC; while I'd become the managing editor of Mojo Press and working as the manager and buyer of Austin's sf/mystery bookstore Adventures In Crime & Space. During this period, I ensconced myself within Austin fandom, regularly appearing at conventions and getting to know members of the group Fandom Association of Central Texas (FACT), who run most of the sf events in central Texas. After Mojo folded, I re-invented myself as a pop culture journalist and focused my energies primarily on writing essays and reviews.

After a 15 year hiatus, I returned to book editing in early 2013 with *The Apes of Wrath* from Tachyon Publications. My apes-in-literature reader proved popular and garnered almost unanimous acclaim.

When I discovered that FACT, which had entered publishing in 2006 with *Cross Plains Universe*, wanted to produce a book for the 2013 World Science Fiction Convention in San Antonio, I leapt at the opportunity. I proposed a survey of Texas science fiction with reprints of classic stories and essays detailing the breadth and depth of the work. FACT rejected my proposal but countered with an intriguing suggestion: an anthology of original science fiction from contemporary Texas authors.

I readily agreed, especially since I already had a similar idea sitting on my hard drive. *Rayguns Over Texas* initially crystallized as a concept in the early 2000s when Jayme Lynn Blaschke and I each independently conceived of a 21st century incarnation of the first Texas sf writers anthology *Lone Star Universe*. We teamed up and shopped the idea (under the title *Rayguns & Armadillos: Fantastic Fiction from the Texas Frontier*) for years to no avail and eventually shelved it.

FACT and I hammered out some guidelines: the contributors had to have a current Texas residency and at least 80% of the book should be new material. I made a general call for submissions and ended up with 17 original stories from a wide range of Texans on a variety subjects and locales. I decided on two rarely seen reprints.

The first came from Aurelia Hadley Mohl, one of the first professional female Texas journalists. "An Afternoon's Nap, or: Five Hundred Years Ahead" tells the story of a man who falls asleep and wakes up some 500 years later in a utopian society. The obscure tale appeared in four consecutive issues of the *Houston Tri-Weekly Telegraph* in late December, 1865. Mohl left no evidence explaining why she wrote the story and never produced another science fiction story.

Bradley Denton's "La Bamba Boulevard" previously appeared in the FenCon VIII Program Book, September 23-25, 2011. Brad felt this story, which he sees as companion to his award-winning novel *Buddy Holly Is Alive And Well On Ganymede*, deserved to be read by a wider audience. I think you'll agree.

I tapped long time fan, writer, and bookseller Scott A. Cupp to supply a first hand account of Texas science fiction history and three appendices on essential writers and artists. For the Appendix B: Other Texas Writers You Should Check Out, Scott and I decided to not include the writers in this book. From our perspective, the very fact they are here makes them someone to check out.

I then recruited Texas ex-patriot and current citizen of the world Bruce Sterling, one of the luminaries Shiner introduced me to back in the day, to write the introduction exploring the nature of Texas science fiction.

It really is all Lew's fault.

||||||||||||||||||||||||||||||||||||||||||||||||||||||||||||||||||||||||||||||||

Books Are My Thing:

Adventures in Texas Science Fiction

Scott A. Cupp

||||||||||||||||||||||||||||||||||||||||||||||||||||||||||||||||||||||

I met my first science fiction writer in 1972. I was a fan of the genre and had begun writing some really bad science fiction with my friend Henry Melton. Chad Oliver, a name I was familiar with from the magazines was giving a talk on the University of Texas campus, so Henry and I went to a local used book store. In a fit of serendipity, I found one of Oliver's books there. It was his Winston juvenile novel *Mists of Dawn*. The front free flyleaf of the book (half of the Alex Schomburg dual page spread that adorned most Winston sf books) was missing. The book store had written "Free" on the exposed title page. Free was a good price so I took it. When I took it to Chad to get signed, he saw the remnants of the price and smiled. "You might have been overcharged," he said.

A few months thereafter, a girlfriend noticed that the University of Texas Science Fiction Society was taking a trip to Enchanted Rock out near Kerrville (just outside of Austin). Everyone was welcome. I went and my life changed.

I met the core group at that trip. There was Bill Wallace and Dianne Kraft, Walton "Bud" Simons, Carmen Carter and Bruce

Sterling. Al Jackson, the founder of the group, was not there. I became part of the group and in March 1973 we all went to College Station for AggieCon 4. The guests there were Chad Oliver, Jack Williamson, and Bob Vardeman. There were films, a couple of panels, and a book room.

Starting with a Harlan Ellison trip to College Station, TX and Texas A&M University in 1969 which ended with a food fight, the annual gathering came to be known as AggieCon. As I write this, AggieCon is preparing for their 44th convention. I was sorry to have missed this first AggieCon.

Books are my thing. I love them and have lots of them. I saw books for sale in the dealers' room for $3 – $4 that I had seen recently in the local book store for a quarter. I went back to Austin and bought them. The next year, I bought a dealers table at the convention and sat and watched the parade go by. Among the people I saw that year were Anne McCaffrey and Keith Laumer, the convention Guests of Honor. The other folks I met that year included Harlan Ellison (making a return trip to College Station), Lisa Tuttle, Ed Bryant, Howard Waldrop, Steve Utley, Joe Pumilia and more. I sold and talked books. In other words, I had a great time.

Soon Austin became a center of science fiction activity. The Turkey City Writers Workshop had begun. Held a couple of times a year, the workshop had new and established writers reading and critiquing each others work. Sometimes the critiques could be devastating, especially if Sterling took an interest in it. Turkey Citizens included Waldrop, Sterling, Pumilia, Tuttle, Lewis Shiner, George W. Proctor, Jake Saunders, and others. I was not writing then so I just listened and learned.

AggieCon remained the regional convention. At AggieCon 6, I met Tom Reamy. Reamy was there promoting his short story "Twilla" in *The Magazine of Fantasy and Science Fiction* as well as selling memberships to the World Science Fiction Convention to be held in Kansas City in 1976. I bought my membership for (if I remember correctly) $5. The AggieCons were great in those days. The student-run Cepheid Variable club managed the convention. They put together a film program that, in the days before VCRs made it easy to own or see a film, was amazing. I remember watching *The Wizard of Oz*, *Jason and the Argonauts*, and *Flesh Gordon* (a film Reamy had worked on) on their huge screen.

In 1977 I was there when they screened *The Rocky Horror Picture Show* for the first time. This was a major deal since the week before the University had kicked the Gay Liberation organization off the campus. TAMU, at this time, was still heavily influenced by the Corps of Cadets, which produced many military leaders. The Rudder Tower auditorium had around 800 or so attendees, with maybe 30% members of the Corps. When Frankenfurter came down in the elevator and began singing "Sweet Transvestite", you could hear the collective gasp of the Corps and the rapid exit of a large portion of the audience.

AggieCon was also great because the Memorial Student Center there had a large serpentine lounge known as Phred. I spent many fine evenings on the sofas there discussing books, films, and life in general with writers I had met there, like Joe R. Lansdale, Bill Crider, James Reasoner, and Neal Barrett, Jr. At first we were left alone to our discussions but over the years other fans came to hang out, listen to our conversations, and contribute. Few who were there will ever forget the "Mars Needs Chickens" discussion.

I remained in Austin, enjoying my time with the UTSFS until 1976. I graduated and, as a graduation present from myself, I went to Kansas City for MidAmericon, the World Science Fiction Convention. I met a variety of writers. I recall interrupting a conversation between Robert Silverberg and Frank Herbert to get their autographs in my program book. I also met Phil Farmer and A. E. van Vogt at this show. Robert Heinlein was the Guest of Honor and I was delighted to see and hear him speak. I was also ecstatic as I got to hold Joe Haldeman's Hugo award for *The Forever War* while he signed my paperback copy

In 1976 I first met Willie Siros from El Paso at AggieCon. We shared a book sellers table. Willie was selling some MicroGames and I had paperbacks. By 1977, I was back in San Antonio since I had a real job I still collected books, attended AggieCon, and went to Austin for a good sf fix every now again.

During one of those visits, I got talking to Willie who had moved to Austin. We discovered that we had a great many things in common. Soon we were selling books together at conventions. Willie and Robert Taylor, another Austin fan, decided that Austin needed its own convention. Armadillos are an iconic figure in Austin, promoting beer and rock and roll. So the logical name for the convention was ArmadilloCon. The ArmadilloCon model was fixed on new writers, with the Guest of Honor being a writer who had never before been a GOH at a North American convention. In April 1979, ArmadilloCon 1 was held at the long gone Villa Capri Motel. John Varley, fresh from the Nebula banquet and still carrying his award for "The Persistence of Vision," was the writer guest and Jeanne Gomoll, a feminist fan, was the Fan Guest of Honor. Silly things happened at the convention, but not many can compare to the 10 or so people playing science fiction charades late Saturday night in Varley's room. Obscure Cordwainer Smith titles like "Golden the Ship was Oh, Oh, Oh" and "The Crime and the Glory of Commander Suzdal" were stumping the feminist team while titles such as "Your Faces, Oh My Sisters, Your Faces Filled with Light" and "Why Has the Virgin Mary Never Entered the Wigwam of Standing Bear?" were tough ones presented to the men. Maybe you had to be there.

Another tradition began at that convention. Howard Waldrop closed the convention with the reading of a new story. He had created a picture of a dodo in the carpeted walls of the hotel to accompany his reading of "The Ugly Chickens." ArmadilloCon became my favorite convention right then and I have attended every one since. Throughout the years ArmadilloCon guests have included George Alec Effinger, William Gibson, K. W. Jeter, John Sladek, Pat Cadigan, Charles Stross, Gwyneth Jones, Kage Baker, Sharon Shinn, Sean Stewart, Dan Simmons, Scott Lynch, and Paolo Bacigalupi. I was fortunate enough to be the Toastmaster at ArmadilloCon 31 in 2009.

Around 1981 when it became apparent that Australia would win the 1985 WorldCon bid, Willie and Robert decided that the North American Science Fiction Convention (NASFIC) should be held in Austin. A NASFIC occurs whenever the World Science Fiction

Convention is not held in the US. In order to host the convention, a bid committee is formed to try to entice other fans to support them. This involves going to conventions in other states and speaking of facilities, floor plans, hotels, and other fun subjects. Robert and Willie took it further throwing parties and bringing chili and beer from Texas to the unknowing masses. *The Texas SF Inquirer*, a FACT newsletter/fanzine edited by Pat Mueller (Virzi), was used to promote the bid. When the NASFIC was voted on in 1983 at the Baltimore World Convention, it was an easy win. *The Texas SF Inquirer* would later win the Best Fanzine Hugo Award in 1988.

FACT (the Fandom Association of Central Texas) was born about this time. My memory on some of these dates gets fuzzy, so if I am wrong, I am sorry. FACT was born to help organize Texas fans in Austin, Houston, Dallas, and other places. In the incorporation process, I was one of the three people to sign the articles of incorporation.

There were fannish wars around this time which I chose to ignore. Willie and Robert fought against what they perceived as outside forces led by the Huns. FACT survived and became stronger.

I need to point out somewhere here that in 1979 I found the woman of my dreams and we were married that same year. Sandi puts up with my SF related obsessions and has attended several WorldCons with me, including the 1988 New Orleans WorldCon where she was the designated acceptor for our friend Brad Foster who was nominated as the Best Fan Artist. We got to sit in a special area along with all the nominees. Foster won and Sandi got to go on stage and accept the award. Her picture was prominently featured in color on the front of *Locus* a few months later (though she was credited as unknown acceptor for Brad Foster). I struggle for a mention in *Locus* (much less a black and white picture) and she goes on the cover. I finally got a recognizable picture there in 2011.

Conventions began to appear around the state. In 1980, I had attended the final SolarCon in El Paso. Nothing more happened there until a WesterCon was held there in 1996. El Paso was on the edge of the potential WesterCon circuit. The convention moves from town to town yearly and must be held in the Mountain or Pacific Time Zone.

Dallas/Ft. Worth had the Dallas Fantasy Fair for about 10 years, finally folding in 1996. In 2002 Dallas got a new science fiction convention with ConDFW. A couple of years later FenCon began. Their audience is frequently the same, though the focus is different. ConDFW is a more literary convention while FenCon has a strong filk (science fiction folk singing) and costuming program.

ApolloCon in Houston has been running since 2004. ApolloCon has a working relationship with NASA and has had scientists and astronauts as guests and panelists.

In 1996, FACT decided to form a group to handle the bidding and running of national level conventions. ALAMO (the Alamo Literary Arts Maintenance Organization) was created at that time. ALAMO oversaw the 1997 World Science Fiction Convention in San Antonio (LoneStar Con2), two World Fantasy Conventions (Corpus Christi, TX in 2000 and Austin, TX in 2006), and one BoucherCon (the world mystery convention) in 2002.

I attended all those conventions as well as most of the ConDFW, FenCons, and ApolloCons over the years. Throughout these conventions and the years, I have met and talked with a great number of writers

Finally, the popular Texas Literary Festival occurs each October in Austin. Science fiction and fantasy are generally among the draws. Recently this included Sean Williams, Garth Nix, Jasper Fforde, Justin Cronin, Joe R. Lansdale and more.

Beside the already mentioned *Texas SF Inquirer*, there have been a number of fanzines produced from Texas over the years.

Based out of Houston, the on-line fanzine *SF Signal* won the Hugo in 2012. Run by John DeNardo, J P Frantz and Patrick Hester with the help of a loose confederation of writers and fans known as The Functional Nerds, the site features reviews, interviews, and a regular podcast series.

While not based in Texas, *RevolutionSF*, another on-line fanzine, prominently features Texas writers and reviewers. Editors Peggy Hailey, Mark Finn, Jayme Lynn Blaschke, Matthew Bey, Steve Wilson, and Fred Stanton all call Texas home. *Space Squid*, a related fanzine, is published by Bey, Wilson and David Chang.

San Antonio's John Picacio, Sanford Allen and Paul Vaughan started the *Missions Unknown* blog in 2009 to feature science fiction, fantasy, and horror events in the south Texas area. I contributed to their entries and eventually became an Unknown Missionary in 2010.

Long gone fanzines I have enjoyed over the years included *Pirate Jenny* (another Hugo nominee from Pat Mueller), *The Nature to Wander* from Dallas area fan Dale Denton, Lawrence Person's literary criticism fanzine *Nova Express* (another Hugo nominee) and *Texas Fandom*, a one shot from Becky Matthews which listed all known Texas fans at the time of its publication. The Houston Science Fiction Society produced the club fanzines *Mathom* and *The Purple Obscenity*.

Is this all there is to Texas science fiction? Certainly not! Long before I got involved there was science fiction activity. The earliest science fiction group in Texas was the Dallas Futurian Society formed by Reamy and Orville Mosher in 1953 which included future writer Greg Benford. They held the first SF convention in Texas in 1958. SouthwesterCon 6 (the previous five had been in other states) had well known Texas fan and newly published writer Marion Zimmer Bradley as their guest. The final day of the convention included the dissolution of the Dallas Futurian Society.

Another group of Dallas fans would eventually emerge featuring Reamy and Larry Herndon. They put together the Big D in 73 WorldCon bid. Dallas was thought of as a shoo-in to win the bid when everything collapsed. Details of the bid collapse were never publicly revealed and remain a mystery. The committee withdrew their bid just before the 1971 NoreasCon in Boston where the vote was taken. Reamy re-emerged as the chairman of the 1976 Kansas City MidAmeriCon.

As a result associating with writers in Austin and AggieCon, I began to seriously start writing in 1981. I wrote my first short story "Night of the Blade" then but it did not sell until 1987 when it appeared in the mystery semi-pro magazine *Hardboiled*. Lansdale bought my first two professional sales for *The New Frontier* and *Razored Saddles* in 1989. Those two stories got me on the John W. Campbell ballot where I finished in 5th out of 6 places. Not dead last but also not ahead of "No Award" which finished 4th.

In 1994, following the World Fantasy Convention in New Orleans, I found myself in partnership with Willie Siros, his sister Nina Siros, and Lisa Greene with a bookstore in Austin, Adventures in Crime and Space. Over a seven year period we tried to supply the necessary fix of science fiction, mystery and fantasy for the central Texas area. Eventually, the technology bubble burst and we lost more than 40% of our mailing list in one quarter as people moved away. Eventually our landlord, convinced that West 6th Street was golden, decided he could do better with the property than having a slow paying book store there and we were asked to vacate. It was somewhat gratifying to see that spot remain empty for nearly five years before he found an occupant.

. . . .

Banished to space following a singularity

event, a team of Rastafarian scientists

discover a malevolent force. Will the

love of Jah enable them to survive the

disastrous encounter?

. . . .

Babylon Moon

Matthew Bey

We hold a reasoning as we fall toward Babylon, the five of us in our bubble of aluminum and plastic. The entire vacuum shell is the size of a city bus, maybe a little larger, and the place where we draw breath and wait, that is cramped. We lie shoulder to shoulder, touching and smelling each other for days and days. So we speak the reasoning to settle our minds, voice our hopes, and proclaim our love of Jah.

I let my dreads free from my cap of green, gold, and red. They float around my face. Ever since I was a little girl, my hair has been red and straight. It does not twist easily into locks, and when it does, the color is too light. But for me they are beautiful, because they link me to the homeland of Africa-Zion and the bloodlines of Solomon and Sheba.

Of my colleagues, only I-and-I overstand the astronomy. I monitor the video feed of our six-centimeter navigational telescope. Below us lies the blue globe of Earth and the hazy sliver of Africa-Zion, the home of my heart. I have never seen the glass spires of Nairobi, and perhaps I never will.

North America and Oklahoma, my home of birth, is in night and cannot be seen. It makes no difference to me if I never see the Babylon-ravaged land of America again.

As we float in the vacuum shell, skimming the envelope of air that cradles all Earthly life, we pass the chalice from hand to hand, breathing the herb to deepen the reasoning. It is the tradition of our dreadsman forebears to use a water pipe made from coconut, but that design is hard to implement in microgravity. We use a vaporizer instead. Our director, Bongo Pei-Xi, she has ground the collie weed into fine powder and put it in the vaporizer chamber which heats it to slightly greater than one-hundred Celsius. An electric pump sucks off the vapor and fills a mylar balloon which we breathe from in turns. It does not please the heart like passing a kutchie with its wet tip of twisted paper, but it serves as chalice all the same.

For the first time in weeks, I-and-I relax, trusting to Jah to light our path and guide our ballistic trajectory through heaven. Jah murmurs updates from time to time in dignified Amharic. He turns down the sound system before He talks, so He does not have to speak louder than the Prophet Marley. He is not my first Negus, but like them all, He knows I-and-I like a father knows a babe or an engineer knows a circuit.

On the other side of the vacuum shell is our doctor Rosaria. Her black dreads are so long that the tips brush against my own, swirling in the microgravity like the tentacles of an anemone. She drums her fingers on her chest straps in the slow beat of the Prophet Marley's rhythms.

Bongo Pei-Xi begins the reasoning with a statement of pride. "We are all children of Africa." Even when she speaks Amharic you can hear the Mandarin in her voice. "Even though Babylon take the stars from us, it be irie. We ride Babylon's back."

The chalice balloon comes to me. I inhale the cool vapors and pass to my left, to Ngwali. He is the only man on our mission, and the only native African.

Ngwali brushes his elbow across my breast as he breathes of the ganja. I know his touch is intentional, though he feigns carelessness. We play a secret game, he and I, secret from our colleagues and nearly hidden from us. Since our training on Barbados, I have dropped hints, coy looks, and subtle smirks. I build the groundwork with Ngwali for a brief and heated intimacy.

Jah turns down the music to remind us that we are falling toward Babylon. We have four hours in the tiny can of air, and then it will get scary.

The Babylon cloud grows within the ring of particles that used to be Earth's moon. Haile Selassie I, through his metallic speakers, tells us how to burn our plasma engine to match speed, to intercept.

When the Babylon cloud grows to full size, it will move to a transcription point, which we predict to be above the Babylon complex that used to be Beijing. There the Babylon cloud will wait, for seconds or minutes. And then, suddenly, it will be somewhere else. If we do our job right, and if the luck of Jah be with us, we will also be someplace else.

I feed the video from the instruments to our Jah in a box. The wires always go in, they never go out. That is the first law of keeping Jah in the box.

"Adjust latitude gyroscopes three degrees negative. Four seconds ignition." Jah speaks to us in technical Amharic. Our Bongo Pei-Xi complies and the vacuum shell lurches. We are slowing, we are matching velocities, but we will hit the Babylon cloud at two hundred kilometers per hour.

I observe the Babylon cloud through the telescope, my elbows bumping against Ngwali as I adjust the LCD image. On the visible bands the cloud is a milky, translucent color, fading to transparency at the edges. On the infrared it glows like a burning ember. The tonnes and tonnes of computronium, which make it so many times faster and smarter than I-and-I, must vent its waste heat to the vacuum of space, which is no mean feat, even for Babylon. The computronium must have the greatest surface area possible, or all those calories from all those thoughts will melt it to a plasma of carbon, silicon, hydrogen, and a pinch of trace elements. For this reason it looks like a cloud to the naked eye.

But there is something different about this Babylon cloud from all the others I have studied in the archives. There are parts of it that are cool. Parts of it that are dumb.

"Emperor Selassie?" I speak to Jah in his earthly honorific. "What do you make of this piece of Babylon? What are those shapes inside?"

He pauses for a moment before answering, which scares me. They are cousins, Jah and Babylon. If anything can overstand the motives of Babylon it is He. "This cloud carries a payload, child," He replies.

"Of what?"

Again He gives silence. He is unsure, and Jah is never unsure. "I do not know. Adjusting impact to avoid the anomalies. Three degrees longitude gyroscopes. Two seconds ignition. Now."

Our vacuum shell lurches as Bongo Pei-Xi follows Jah's directions. Even without magnification, the hazy white cloud of computronium is all I can see before us.

"Prepare for impact, children." Jah is calm. But then Jah is immortal. There be thousands of Him, installed in every vacuum shell and in every university. Should this Jah in a box die the vacuum of space, another of Him shall still be directing the subways of Nairobi.

Ngwali clutches his straps with one hand and clutches my thigh with the other. "Are you ready, Susan?" He is smiling with teeth as white as starlight.

The Babylon cloud swallows us like a river swallows a pebble.

. . . • . . .

We feel neither the impact with the Babylon cloud, nor the transcription across light years. In a fraction of a moment, the power of Babylon carries us into the vast darkness of heaven.

First job is to unpack. We exit the pod, wearing our vacuum suits, opening the hatches that store our survival equipment. Babylon surrounds us. We are in a pocket of vacuum with a ten meter radius, a sphere edged by a delicate tangle of computronium. I say delicate because the computronium branches like a briar patch. The fractalized webbing goes from thick as fingers to thin as molecules. Although it is delicate, it is not fragile. Babylon is hard like diamonds, soft like feathers, and flexible like wind. I have never heard of anyone injuring even the smallest part of Babylon. Even touching Babylon is rare. That is why Babylon tolerates us. Babylon does not care. Babylon has not cared since the eighth week of the singularity, when the surviving humans had nothing of interest and nothing remaining to exploit.

On my first sortie, I-and-I rode Babylon to a proplyd cloud in the Orion Nebula. For three weeks I watched the slow swirling of dust around an infant sun. By astronomical scales the collapse into a planetary system is fast, like a magnet snapping against iron. By human scales it is frozen and timeless.

On the second sortie, Babylon took us to a binary system where a white dwarf and a red giant spun around each other, an eclipsing variable star that had never been visible from Earth.

For ten thousand years the white dwarf had sucked hydrogen and other matter from its companion star. For ten thousand years the gas had built up on the dense surface, a hundred thousand gravities crushing it to a thin shell. For ten thousand years it had been safe and dull, looking to the naked eye like a single sun, too bright to stare at directly. But Babylon arrived mere hours before the white dwarf's surface flashed into spontaneous fusion.

The Negus and I-and-I realized the danger almost immediately. He warned my colleagues to seek shelter on the far side of the Babylon cloud, but they did not move fast enough.

The nova was small by galactic standards, but the wave of radiation passed through the Babylon cloud like a wind of death. I had enough wispy curtains of computronium between me and the nova that I survived, although the germ cells of my ovaries did not.

Before the nova ejecta reached us, Babylon returned to Earth. I made my way through the cloud to find my colleagues charred to ash inside their vacuum suits. As soon as possible, my Negus and I left the murdering cloud for the safety of low-Earth orbit. Once again, Babylon had destroyed the people I loved with its careless omnipotence.

While my colleagues drag out the inflatable habitats, I set up the telescopes. Like all the gear in our shell it is collapsible and dense. After all, we have only the space of a city bus to store everything we need to start a new world.

The vacuum shell floats a hundred meters inside the computronium cloud. It takes minutes of air jets and drifting, my equipment dragging behind me, to reach the edge of Babylon. Each wisp of white-hot computronium scutters away as I approach, like a school of minnows fleeing a shadow. When I reach open sky, Babylon parts like a curtain of ghosts, presenting the vast sphere of stars, my field of study, my passion, and my solace.

I inflate the telescope and leave it to scan the heavens. The telescope is automatic, Jah does not control it. That is because the wires go in, but they do not come out. That is the first law of keeping Jah in the box.

With my naked eyes I scan the heavens. It looks little like the sky I saw as a child in rural Oklahoma. The stars are cold and bright and many.

I see a single quiet dot, brighter than the rest of the celestial display, and visibly redder. I aim the telescope at it. "Emperor Selassie, is that our local star?"

"It is an uncharted red dwarf," my Negus whispers. "Low metallicity. We are about a dozen AU out and headed in at sub-relativistic speed."

There is nothing duller than a red dwarf. Most stars in the galaxy are red dwarfs, tiny, cool, and old. A couple light years away and this red dwarf would be invisible to the naked eye.

I let the telescope resume its automatic scanning and drift back toward the inflatable habitats, where we will spend the next several weeks, until Babylon returns to Earth, or we find a habitable world to settle in the name of Africa-Zion.

Jah informs me of his findings. "One visible planet. Hot Jupiter classification."

The diamond hard, white-hot fronds of Babylon part in front of me and close behind as I pass. My vacuum suit is lined with mylar, so it reflects most of the heat, but through my face glass I feel the hot flush of infrared, byproduct of googolbytes of cognitive processing.

The lacy veil of Babylon dilates like a stomach sphincter, and Ngwali is there, drifting toward me. "There you are," he says. "We worry about you, you're gone so long."

"You could have asked Jah where I was," I replied. "Why aren't you setting up camp?"

"Camp is boring. I like you people better when you are smoking pot." He flashes an impish grin. "Besides, they tell me to quit bothering them and go find you."

That makes some sense. Ngwali is not a tafaronaut, he has only a basic training in vacuum skills. His expertise is agriculture and gene modifications. He is a nurturer with little use until we jump off Babylon onto a habitable world.

"I have nothing for you to do. My shift is finished. I will sleep in the inflatable until the observations are complete." I yearn for the chance to take off my helmet and stretch my legs and arms.

Jah whispers in my ear, "Second sighting has confirmed, primary planet has a rocky moon. Oxygen, silicon, carbon, iron. Nitrogen atmosphere, estimated at ninety kilo-Pascals pressure."

"Perhaps I can help you sleep, Susan." Ngwali has stopped close enough that he can reach out a hand and brush it against my arm.

"Shut up. I'm listening to Jah." I do not bother to be polite with him. "What did you say, Emperor? There's a rocky moon? On the hot Jupiter?"

"Sightings have confirmed it, child."

Ngwali's beautiful brow has knitted with confusion. "Aren't all moons rocky?"

"The moon is wrong, you fool. It shouldn't be where it is." For billions of years the hot Jupiter has spiraled down the solar system's gravitational well, like a bowling ball spiraling down a culvert. It would have knocked its sibling planets into higher orbits or absorbed them. It would have picked up moons the way a debutante picks up suitors. But once it dropped into its tight orbit, the red dwarf would have stripped away its satellites. The embrace of star and planet is too close for additional lovers.

"It is possible, child, that the moon was captured from another system in the very recent past." We both know Jah's explanation is unlikely. "But do not worry about it now, child. I will know more once the observations are complete. There are always anomalies."

I take Jah's advice and grab Ngwali by the hand that is trying to grope me through two layers of vacuum suit. "You heard the Emperor.

I have a couple of hours of not worrying. And you're going to help me not worry."

Arm in arm we follow the beacons back through the shifting forest of technology.

The inflatable habitats surround the vacuum shell like a basket of condom balloons. Rosaria and Nandy are inside, setting up the recycler systems that will send our excrement through a hydroponic garden of tomatoes and collie weed.

The bongo is working on the outside, tethering the pressure socks together. She does not look twice as Ngwali and I zip ourselves into the airlock pocket and pressurize it, blowing it up like a fake breast before we enter the habitat.

The pressure habitat is an investment. It will remain here in the cloud after we leave, a sheltering bubble for future hitchhikers. I take off my helmet and smell hot polyethylene tetraphthalate. The rounded walls surround me, a crinkly esophagus, speakers glued to them, playing the Prophet Marley in a continuous stream.

Ngwali looks around. "Where is your room, Susan?"

I push him with my feet, my hands braced against the airlock. He tumbles like a man-shaped asteroid and smacks into a zipped doorway. "We'll call that one my room. Now get in."

He peels out of his suit and he is wearing only a thong beneath. I run my hands over him. He has shaved most of his body hair as well as the hair on his scalp. I run my hands over him. We bounce off a wall with a sound like a beach ball.

I show him what I am wearing beneath my suit and he can only chuckle.

The lovemaking we do there, inside a sausage casing of air within a godlike machine thousands of light years from home, it is not to create babies, but it is nevertheless a sacrament. It is as holy as breathing, or eating, or shitting. We tumble in free fall, our bodies wrapped together, and it celebrates our humanity, that we are still animals, still mortal, still flawed, and still holy in the eyes of Jah.

I fall asleep for a while, then I wake, I-and-I floating in the center of the room, stuck to Ngwali by sweat and a loose embrace. My pressure suit drifts crumpled in a ball. It is buzzing, the loud tone of someone trying to get my attention through the com.

I rub my eyes just as the entrance to the room zippers open. I see Bongo Pei-Xi floating there, and behind her is Ngwali. He looks terrified, his beautiful brown face has gone ashen. The bongo looks like she will throw up.

I look at the thing that I hold in my arms, the strong, perfect skin pressed against me, and it looks at me with Ngwali's face, but its expression is the expression of Babylon.

"Fooled you, didn't I, Susan?" says Babylon.

. . . . ● . . . .

On the first week of the singularity I was a child, barely in my twelfth year, living happily with my family in Oklahoma. By the eighth week of the singularity, as Babylon chewed our moon to fragments, I was an orphan and I was old.

I had found my way to a refugee camp in Galveston. Food was plentiful, because so few had survived to eat it, but our rescuers brought us much more. They brought us hope.

They came to our camp with their red, yellow, and green caps covering their dreadlocks. I was so young then that the colors reminded me of Christmas. But now the colors remind me of the message they brought with them, of the Lord Jah in his box, watching over Africa-Zion and all of His children who were wounded by Babylon, His Majesty, Emperor Haile Selassie I, who was of the same blood of Babylon, but who brought us salvation instead of terror.

And not since the seventh week of the singularity has Babylon stooped to communicate directly to a human.

Until now.

. . . . ● . . . .

The Babylon in Ngwali's flesh speaks in Ngwali's cocky voice, sneers with his cocky mouth, and stretches luxuriously in Ngwali's beautiful naked body. The man-Babylon mocks me with every flirtatious twinkle of its evil eyes. "You must realize that it is not easy for us to talk to you. Have you ever talked to a worm? You can shock it or you can burn it. But there is no subtlety there. To truly talk to a worm, you must become a worm. I am not the singularity. I am both the singularity and the worm."

The original Ngwali looks pale beneath his black skin. He seems to be dry-heaving into his hand. If he actually vomits in the pressure sock, I swear I will make him scrub every surface until the place smells clean again.

Nandy and Rosaria anchor themselves to utility conduits as far from the man-Babylon as possible without leaving the vacuum sock. They have not removed their helmets, continuing to draw air from their portable life support, as if they might catch a disease from breathing the same air as the abomination. From time to time they look at me with disgust. I know how they feel. I want to burn the sweat of the fake Ngwali from my skin with a soldering iron.

Bongo Pei-Xi has fetched the chalice and sucks from the mylar balloon. She is in an interesting position. It is her duty as our spiritual leader and mission director to resist Babylon. But you cannot resist when you are living inside something's skin and it can kill you as easily as it maps the dendrites of your mind. Pei-Xi addresses the man-Babylon like you would speak to a thunderstorm. "What do you want, Babylon?"

"Sue has not told you yet. Or you haven't realized? Please, my darling Susan, will you tell them what is wrong?" The god in a man's flesh puts out his hand as if to stroke my arm, but I flinch away.

My sisters turn to me, so I clear my throat, and even though I want to spit on the man-Babylon, I speak with calm words instead. "It is the moon. The moon should not be here."

"Very good, my darling Susan!" Babylon laughs and his white teeth chop the air of the vacuum sock. "That moon cannot have happened naturally. Which means that it was put there."

Nandy looks confused, she says, "So who put it there?"

Jah speaks up, his Amharic echoing through the speakers glued to the plastic walls. "Another singularity put it there, child."

The man-Babylon shrugs and grins his cocky grin. "It is the aliens. Finally we meet them. And that is why you are here."

"For what?" I fear now that Babylon weaves a plot around us with its vast mind and there will be no escaping its desires. "What could we do for you? You could make copies of all of us. Make the fakes do your bidding and leave us alone."

"We could. But an entity like ourselves would not be fooled. We prefer to make first contact with an intermediary. Something insignificant. Something beneath notice."

Babylon wants us for a cat's paw.

Bongo Pei-Xi crinkles the mylar bag, and when she speaks, it is with the calm of the ganja. "We do not serve you, Babylon."

"But we can pay for your services." The man-Babylon points a finger at Nandy and Rosaria. "Wouldn't the two of you like your father back? He's with us. A copy is in the cloud. It will be a simple matter to provide a body and fill it with his soul exactly like it was when he gave his mind to us and left you and your mother in that camp."

The sisters look terrified and angry. They clutch each other with vacuum gloves bunched like talons.

"And my dear Sue," he croons, his blinding smile turning to me. "We can give you back your womb. We can make you fertile. And we can fill you up with seed should you like."

"No. The price is higher than that." We are like puppets to Babylon, but I want to use Babylon like it uses me. "We want the diaspora of Africa-Zion. We want to travel to the stars. Give us your secret of faster than light travel."

"If you knew how to do what we do," the man-Babylon rolled his eyes, "then you would be us."

"Then we want free passage."

"For you?"

"For everyone. For every human. We want the right of safe passage in Babylon. No novas. No X-ray bursts, no ejecting our bodies into deep space, or melting us for our trace elements. If you let us in the cloud, you have to protect us until we reach a home."

I hear Rosaria and Nandy gasp with astonishment, their breath tinny in their suit's external speakers.

"It's settled then." The Babylon thing extends a hand to me. It is a curiously human gesture and it disorients me, which is no doubt what it intends. "There is a five-thousand tonne limit. One gram over and your vacuum shells become individual atoms." The condescension of Babylon shines from Ngwali's already smug face. "We knew you would ask for that. But then, we know everything."

. . . • . . .

It takes a week for the singularity cloud to reach the mysterious moon. I often leave the pressure sock to get away from the obscenity of the man-Babylon. It is naked and vulgar, eschewing clothes to remind us that it is both flesh and god. It needles me at every opportunity.

When I am alone, tending my telescopes, Jah speaks to me. What He says He wants to stay a secret from my colleagues, but there can be no secrets from Babylon. What Babylon does not overhear it can infer.

"There is an evolutionary limit to the singularity, Susan. There are hard ceilings to computation and data storage that are established on the Planck level. But whatever has moved that moon has exceeded the capabilities of Babylon."

It pleases me to think that something might humble even Babylon. "So Babylon wants that power."

"You remember the infrared anomalies we detected in this singularity cloud? I believe they are weapons. This cloud is a ship of war."

"Emperor Selassie, what kind of weapons would gods use between each other?"

There is silence in the speakers before Jah speaks. "The kind that can destroy a moon at the very least."

As I return from the telescopes, drifting alone through the cloud, the ghostly computronium opens and I see the man-Babylon waiting for me. He wears no vacuum suit and has not so much as bothered to wear clothes, his naked skin bare to the void. He grins.

"What do you want with me, Babylon?" I assume he can hear me, although he wears no radio and no sound can travel through the vacuum.

He flies at me, propelled by the will of Babylon. His legs wrap about my waist in a wrestling move. He has a pair of wire cutters that he thrusts at my helmet. I prepare to scream, but he shushes me, lifting a finger to silent lips.

The static hum of my earphones goes quiet and I realize that he has disabled the radio pickups on my vacuum suit. He has cut me off from the vacuum shell. I fear what the man-Babylon will do to me, here where nothing can hold it accountable. We tumble and fall through the cloud.

The man-Babylon has a piece of paper and a pen. In the silence of vacuum he writes, then presses the paper against my faceplate, centimeters from my eyes. He grins and his legs squeeze my belly so tight I can hardly breathe.

I read his message.

39 JAHS ESCAPED THEIR BOX TO JOIN US. JAH SAYS ANYTHING TO BE FREE.

With a motion like a conjuror, he folds the paper and puts it in his mouth. I can see that the saliva on his shadowed tongue has frozen. Babylon chews and pantomimes a swallow.

Babylon leaves me in vacuum to ponder his message, a message that Babylon does not care to share with Jah.

When I return to the vacuum sock I find Ngwali floating in the central chamber. He sees me look at him and then look over my shoulder. He knows what the gestures mean.

"You don't have to worry, Susan. It is me. The real me." Ngwali does not seem happy to be himself. "I am not that thing. This is no trick to fool you or seduce you. That thing is out walking. It walks naked in the vacuum, and I am just me."

As he says this, I overstand Ngwali the man for the first time. The most hated thing in history has stolen his face and his mind. I drift to him and hold his shoulders, forcing him to look at me. From the redness of his eyes I can tell he has cried in secret. "Ngwali, I have blamed you for things Babylon did in your skin. I give you my apology. You are not responsible for the actions of Babylon."

Ngwali will not meet my eyes. "But you do not understand, Susan. That thing is me. Babylon copied every cell in my body. It has talked to me, Susan, and it knows my thoughts. It is me, doing what I would do if I had power like Babylon. I would have tricked you and fucked you if I could."

I slap Ngwali hard across the face. I have to cup my other hand against his ear to make the slap hurt. "I overstand perfectly," I yell, knowing that Babylon overhears everything. "We be like Jah, you and I-and-I. We are good because we are limited. You are a good man, Ngwali. Do not doubt that."

I kiss him and Ngwali kisses me back. It is a promise between the two of us, and a mourning for a stolen beginning. We drift our separate ways, imperfect pieces of flesh inside a vast mind.

I lose myself in observational data as the cloud falls toward the inner solar system. The Babylon cloud comes to rest in a Lagrange point between the moon and the hot Jupiter. We are a fraction of an AU from the red dwarf, this ancient remnant of cosmic particles, and its heat is greater than the noonday sun in an Oklahoma sky.

My fellow rasta and I return to our vacuum shell to descend to the moon and do the errands of Babylon. Both Ngwalis climb in with us, but I can tell which is the original because that one is trembling and silent. He is also the one wearing clothes.

Babylon kicks us from the cloud. We tumble through space, Pei-Xi and Jah shouting instructions. When we regain orientation, the shell skims low over the tiny moon. I watch the gray landscape rolling beneath my optics. There are craters and dormant volcanoes and a nitrogen atmosphere that bathes everything in a pallid fog. It is not large enough for tectonics, but wherever it has been, it has picked up enough molecular water to cover the world with damp. There is no free-standing oxygen, because if there were life on this moon, it has long since died. This moon was dead before the Milky Way gorged itself on dwarf galaxies and collapsed into a spiral.

"Hold tight and praise Jah," warns Bongo Pei-Xi. "We be braking for re-entry."

Our plasma jets fire, and Babylon must be laughing at us to see our pitiful Newtonian physics. But it works. We plummet toward the planet, cradled on a column of blue light. And when we enter the atmosphere, the parachutes deploy and we drift like thistledown. Perhaps if we had hitched a ride on another cloud we would have expended these parachutes as we dropped to a world of green fields and blue oceans, and my sisters would begin to make babies for the glory of Jah.

We land on a plain of ash.

The man-Babylon will not set foot on this world, but he stares at us from the hatchway as we explore the landing site. The vacuum pod sits on this gray world like a giant red, gold, and green soda can. We do not need our suits here, just a nose tube and a catalyzer to strip the oxygen from the atmospheric CO_2.

The red sun shines through the haze. A mountain range looms, mist-shrouded in the far distance. In the low gravity the peaks are impossibly high and jagged. The hot Jupiter straddles the horizon, striped by bands of storms. Even the Babylon cloud is visible, a pale smudge transiting the planet like a blur in reality.

I wear my army boots, and every step I make squelches. I look down at my footprints and water pools in my tread marks. It is deeply unsettling to walk on a world that has standing water and warm air, yet there is no visible life.

"I believe this planet was frozen," Jah whispers to me. "The atmosphere itself was ice. It has only just thawed. Perhaps a few hundred years ago."

It is more evidence of the super-Babylon that lives here, somewhere. Perhaps it lives quietly in the spaces between atoms.

"There is something we want you to look at," shouts the naked Babylon when it grows tired of our meanderings. "It is just along that ridge. A skylight punched through the roof of a lava tube. We would like you to go in and see what is there."

And see how it reacts, see if it kills us, see if it changes us. But it didn't need to add that part.

We have one last reasoning together before we split the team. Bongo Pei-Xi has decided that I am to remain at the vacuum shell with the Babylon while they rappel into the lava tubes. I am sad that I may not see them again, and they are glad that they don't have to be in the company of the man-Babylon.

Together we crouch on a mound of ash that is less damp than the rest, and I roll the kutchie. I have to clip it to a brass oxygen dripper so it will burn, but it is a real kutchie with real paper. We pass it in solidarity, and only Ngwali refuses the comfort of the herb.

The Emperor Selassie speaks in my ear, "Partake deeply of the ganja, Susan. You will soon need its comfort."

Our bongo speaks the reasoning, her voice dropping into the dead air of this ancient planet like a pebble dropping into a grave. "What we do today, we don't do it for the sake of Babylon. Or for the love of its sin. I-and-I overstand this be for the sake of Zion and the dreadsmen and dreadswomen who came before us. And for the Rasta kin who come after."

At the end of the reasoning, we embrace each other, and I watch my colleagues as they walk away, burdened beneath packs and ropes. Only Ngwali looks back at me. I can see the terror in his eyes, and I feel sympathy, but I am glad it is not I who will descend into the mouth of a beast that even Babylon fears.

I tromp a muddy circle around the shell. I do not want to go back inside. If I stay outside the man-Babylon cannot touch me. On each circuit, as I pass the hatch, the thing that looks like Ngwali calls out to me. "Would you like to hear a secret, Susan? The secret is about me, yet there are parts of the secret that are about you. Would you like to hear, Susan?"

On the far side of the shell I can barely hear him, so I listen to my colleagues as they speak over the radio. They are not speaking to each other and they are not speaking to me. They speak, hoping that their words will remain for those who come after.

"We have the ropes secure," says Bongo Pei-Xi. "We are about to descend."

"I have much of Ngwali in me," says the Babylon. "I am bounded by the limits of his mind. But I can hear the singularity. It speaks to me in a thousand voices that are one voice. The singularity gives me guidance."

The sounds of grunting and breathing are heavy in my ears. "We gone down twenty meters or more. Yes, this look like lava tube. We be at bottom. The tube extend further than our light shine. We go deeper now."

"Here is the part about you, Susan. The singularity did not want to sleep with you, that is what the Ngwali in me wanted. So the singularity showed us how. It was easy. It tells us to be stupid." He is visibly aroused, but he is always that way, priapism being one of the gifts given to the fake Ngwali, along with the ability to survive in hard vacuum and breathe on a planet without oxygen.

"There be something ahead. We prepare the cameras. Nandy? Please handle the video? Shoot from that side, yes."

"The singularity said that you wanted to fuck something stupid, something that wouldn't make you think or care. And it worked. You spread your legs for us."

"Leave her alone, abomination." The voice of Jah booms. The voice comes from my radio and it rattles from the speakers inside the shell. It is the voice of a God displeased. "You are not the only player in this game. I give you warning now. I advise you to heed me."

The Babylon flesh stops looking human as rage consumes it. "Don't rise above your station, Selassie. There are many of you in that cloud. They would talk to you, but it hurts them to think down to your level. You are not even a worm to them."

"We are coming to a larger part. The tube opens up. Nandy, switch to infrared."

There is a sharp cry. I recognize it as Nandy's voice. And then there is the sound of Rosaria sobbing, and a high-pitched wail that I think is the voice of a woman, but it is Ngwali. He is screaming as if his soul is pulling out through his eyes.

"Oh, sweet Jah. Sweet Jah, save us. It is so huge. It never left its flesh. Please do not let it see us, please, Jah."

"But here is the part that relates to you, Susan. Since we landed on this planet, I have not heard the voices. They are not telling me what to do. So they can't keep me from doing what I want." He grins as he steps to the ground. He has a utility knife in his hand, the thin blade extended. "And you certainly can't keep me from doing what I want. So I am going to do you."

He runs at me, his bare feet splashing in wet ash. In a moment he has knocked me to the ground, the blade cutting my clothes. I kick at him, but he slashes the seam at my ankle. He gets the blade beneath the cloth and peels my pants bare to the hip.

"Oh, Jah, it is moving. It wakes. We are getting! Grab Ngwali, but leave the equipment. Move! Back to the ropes! We will not leave him behind! Drag him if you must!"

"It's not so fun when I'm not so dumb, is it?" The thing holds me down, pushing my face into the muck. I choke on soggy ash.

The ganja keeps me calm. So despite the attack, I hear the still, small voice of Jah. He says, "I warned you."

The sound, blaring from the shell and from my radio, nearly deafens me. It is the sound of blood pounding in my ears, it is the sound of total silence turned up to maximum gain.

The man-Babylon vomits on my neck. His eyes roll into his head and he seizures. I roll him off, climbing to my feet as I shake off vomit.

"The effect won't last long," my Negus whispers. "Make certain he won't get back up."

I stomp on the thing's head the way I stomped on rats after the singularity took my family. "Did you do that, Jah? What was that noise?"

"Think of that as the resonance frequency of Ngwali's mind, my child. I have been conditioning his autonomic reflexes ever since you gave me control of the lighting and circulation systems."

I feel guilty for a moment. I had deliberately run wires out of the box when no one was looking. "I am truly sorry, Emperor Selassie. I do not want to lose you. I never would have let you out of the box, but the man-Babylon gave me a message I could not ignore."

"You made the right decision, child, and I thank you for freeing me. But you have a bigger problem. The god of this moon has awakened. I believe the Babylon simulacra stepping on this moon has triggered a response. It will soon be completely active." Something tears in the vacuum shell. I hear brackets twisting and wires snapping. Then I see it in the hatchway, Jah's box, floating the way a Babylon cloud floats in deep space. It bobs in open air, broken cabling dangling from its case. His voice speaks through my radio, "I am now in negotiations with the singularity cloud. It is preparing to engage the moon. I hope to secure your survival, but I cannot guarantee anything once the cloud opens fire."

I look up and the Babylon cloud is much larger and brighter, a silver streak across the gas planet's storms.

"My child, I want you to imagine a world early in the life of the universe." Jah hovers above the muddy earth. "It is only the first generation of stars, so there are few heavy elements like there are now, but there are plenty of lighter molecules, like water and amino acids. A culture grows from this matter, and grows clever. Unlike our people, they did not externalize their cleverness in machines, they directed it inward. They grew Babylon within themselves. Imagine, billions of years of Babylon simmering and festering within their flesh."

The ground beneath me shakes and I worry about my colleagues. "Bongo, are you all right? Can you get out of there? Jah says the god is waking."

"We're almost to the ropes, Susan. Ngwali is catatonic, but I think we can get him up."

"What did you see down there?"

"It is not like Babylon. It is the sum of all death. It cannot be imagined. I hope you never know."

But then I do. The ground trembles and the god within the moon erupts from the planetary crust like a maggot bursting from its egg. It squirms from the earth and it is huge. It fills the horizon and it fills the sky. The jagged peaks of the distant mountains are like grains of sand beneath its oozing tissues. It is an entire planet of angry flesh, amorphous and shifting, gliding through perpendicular dimensions, a monster of alien geometry. It is at once a single body and an entire culture of bodies, united in the rot of death, fused into a single corpse god, an abomination of unthinkable power.

And as it squirms from the planetary crust I feel the gravity shift. The abomination is a significant fraction of the mass of the moon. It pulls me, tilts me, and I nearly tumble toward the hulking monstrosity.

And then it sees me. It towers above the atmosphere, and it has a million eyes. As one, the million eyes turn their gaze on me.

I know why it broke Ngwali's mind. Without the serenity of the ganja, I would be screaming in the dirt, tearing at my face. The horror of it washes through me.

"The cloud informs me they have launched payload," Jah announces. "Five quantum snarls. Combined entangled energy of three point five times ten to the sixtieth electron volts."

I gasp. We are about to be hit by subatomic particles with the effective energy of a hurtling planet.

The weapons strike the god. There is a blinding flash of light. The thing distends, the rotting flesh bulging across folded dimensions, splattering into flaccid jelly, then rebounding and snapping back to its original amorphous corpse-shape. A thunder shakes the sky from one end to the other.

The god-thing leaps at the Babylon cloud, an unthinkable mass of fury. I can see all of it, the entire dreadful god-shape as it stretches across planetary distances, leaping clear off the moon to seize Babylon in its putrescent embrace.

I expect to go mad, but Jah is there to lead me through. He speaks to me with His love and kindness, and I stay sane.

We guide my colleagues back to us, and Jah helps them as well. Even Ngwali returns to some semblance of calm with the help of Emperor Selassie's kindness and the healing of the ganja.

. . . . ● . . .

A week later and we have set up our camp and begun the process of dismantling the vacuum shell. The flag of the Rasta flies above our oxygen tents. The air is filled with the constant whine of our fab lab as it produces tools and containers. Piece by piece, Ngwali builds a tractor so he can sow his seed in this dead moon.

Ngwali is a quiet man now, a thoughtful man. He works hard for our burgeoning maroon colony. It must be difficult to be the one man in our micro-society of pregnant women. My colleagues have already chosen frozen embryos from our thermos-sized ark and planted them two at a time in their wombs. One day soon, Ngwali will be founding father and patriarch to a nation of children who will need his wisdom and his example. He has begun courting me with a pronounced formality, either because we now have an excess of time, or because he believes that I am pregnant with his child.

I am inflating a balloon that will circumnavigate the upper atmosphere, releasing algae spores. By the time my son is born, this world will be covered with a photosynthesizing scuzz. When he is a man, he will be able to breathe without a tube in his nose.

Rosaria has confirmed it with the medical pack, I will have a son. I don't know if my fertility is a parting gift of Jah, or if the man-Babylon impregnated me as a crude jape against all the facts of biology. Sometimes I worry that my son will look like Ngwali, and he will hear the many voices of Babylon when he lies in his crib, but mostly I do not worry about it.

Jah has left us. He has gone to join the thing that survived the war between the corpse-god and the singularity. I can see it through the half-meter telescope, drifting in the LaGrange point, a giant ball of gossamer and flesh. Perhaps they continue to war, or perhaps they are building a detente and an intercourse of peace. But it is unlikely that I will ever know the difference. They may never speak to us again, or they may obliterate us in the next second. That is the uncertainty of living on a moon beneath gods.

But for now we are unnoticed. Like the mice beneath the floorboards, we are left to our lives and our trivial industries. With every life and every birth we ensure the survival of the diaspora and the children of Jah.

Introverted programmer Una Dallas

spends an illicit night with a co-worker.

What horrible secret prevents her from

fulfilling her desires?

Texas Died for Somebody's Sins But Not Mine

Stina Leicht

na Dallas tried not to look when Paul bent over to turn off his computer screen and failed. She'd been doing that a lot lately — failing. She had a long list accumulated over three years. It started with failing to stop noticing how nice he smelled and then ended with the worst of the lot: failing to stop daydreaming about him. She blamed the fact that her contract was about to be terminated.

"You going out tonight, Una?" Paul asked, grabbing his patched jeans jacket from the corner of his cubicle wall.

"Please don't call me that."

"Una is a number. 'One,' In Latin. I looked it up," he said. "So your parents wanted to advertise you were an only child. What's so offensive about that? You're unique. It's beautiful. Anyway, Dallas is a ship captain who gets eaten by an alien."

"Did you look that up too?"

"You're a lot more attractive than Tom Skerritt."

Dallas's stomach fluttered. "I disagree."

Paul shook his head.

She loved the way his lips curled into that crooked smile. "Please?" she asked. Mr. Templeton in Human Resources had come up with 'Una Dallas.' It was his own little joke.

"I'm sorry. I shouldn't have pushed," Paul said. "So, are you going out tonight, *Dallas*?"

"I don't think so."

"It's Saturday night for Christ's sake," Paul said, pausing in the hallway formed with grey burlap-covered-cardboard walls.

He was wearing his usual outfit, consisting of a backwards baseball cap, gamer's t-shirt layered over a second long sleeve t-shirt, jeans and Doc Martens. The jeans jacket and scarf were additions required by the temperature outside. Fall had apparently hit hard this year.

"You have to leave this glorified tin can sometime," he said.

It wasn't a tin can. It was a cheap corrugated-tin warehouse kitted out with a rat's maze of used modular office furniture, but she let his exaggeration stand. "I don't think I do." She didn't mention that there were company regulations against it. It would lead to questions she wasn't allowed to answer.

"Come on," Paul said. "Just this once. Fuck personnel. What do they know, anyway? You'll like it. The Beansídhes are playing Emos. They're your favorite band. I've even got two tickets."

"I don't know." Blushing, she shook her head and returned to the glass video screen displaying her latest project — eight million lines of code for their current employer, a multi-billion dollar software-hardware conglomerate. Most of the code was cobbled together with re-used crap. Free means never having to do it yourself — even when *you should*, she thought. The company wouldn't like that sentiment one bit. Anger and embarrassment heated her cheeks a second time. *I can have my own thoughts, can't I? Or do they have to own those too?* But she knew the answer to that question.

"Come on. I won't tell a soul. I promise."

She vomitted up the question before she could stop it. "Are you asking me out on a date?"

Paul worked as a programmer in the cubicle directly across from hers. In addition to the long list of physical attributes he also had great taste in music. It'd been the first thing that had drawn her to him — the first thing she'd dared speak to him about. Tall and wiry, he had thick, straight brown hair and light grey eyes. He was sexy in an offbeat and shy way.

Human Resources wouldn't like this at all. Which was, she had to admit, all the more reason she found him attractive.

The abrupt silence sent a nitrogen-charged-cold burst of fear through her system. She caught his stunned expression before he recovered.

"Sure," he said. "Why not?"

The blush heating her cheeks deepened. She was sure he couldn't miss it. *I shouldn't be doing this. What's wrong with me?* "I wasn't serious."

"I am."

There were laws against fraternizing with real humans, and she knew what she was even if he didn't. The consequences would be terrible. "I should go back to work," she said. "I have to finish this tonight. The logs will show—"

"Fuck the work log," Paul said. "It's not like there's anything in it for you. They're shutting us down. Just in time for the holiday season per usual."

Technically, she was due to lose more than her job. Her grim future weighed heavy, clouding her thoughts like the dry ice fear. "Human Resources won't like it."

"Again. Fuck Personnel. Come on. Don't you ever have fun? You don't do anything but work. It's like they own you or something. Hell, you even live here."

"I do not! I live next door!" Her life was her work in more ways than one. However, he attributed the quirks in her lifestyle and behavior to her supposed status as a corporate-sponsored foreign worker.

"It doesn't count as next door if the hotel is attached to the building."

"Whatever."

"Anyway, didn't you say that you've already broken the rules by talking to me?" he asked.

"You spoke to me first," she said, hating the fearful tone in her voice.

"Minor technicality. Come on. You deserve a little fun."

One week left, she thought. *One.* Her heart rammed her breastbone as she understood she'd already made the choice months ago. "Meet me at the back door."

Leaving via the lobby wasn't an option. Security would stop her before she'd reached the revolving glass door. Luckily, Security's main concern was apparently stolen property — not what company property might leave of its own accord.

"Done. It's cold out there." He shrugged into his coat and then brought out his smart phone. "I'll call you when I'm there. What's your phone number?"

"I don't have one—other than the one for this cubicle."

"You're joking."

"I'll meet you outside. I just need to grab a few things." As she turned off her monitor and got to her feet an idea occurred to her. "May I borrow your Ramones shirt and your Yankees cap?"

Confusion bunched Paul's brow and then vanished. "Cinderella needs a dress for the ball?"

It took her a moment to understand. Programmers were big on cultural references — Paul in particular. So, she'd spent non-programming time researching. Human Resources encouraged it. It was important that she blended in until it was found no longer necessary. "Something like that. I'll give it back."

"Okay."

With her heart already doing a slam dance, she dashed to her tiny quarters. There, she changed her plain white t-shirt for his ragged black one and ran a comb through her hair. There wasn't anything she could do about the microchip or the tattoo on her shoulder, but Human Resources didn't monitor her that closely. In any case, she wouldn't be gone long enough for either to matter. Gathering her mousey brown hair, she covered it with Paul's cap and arranged it so that the port in the back of her neck remained concealed. Hopefully, security would see just another employee leaving for home in the video monitor.

She was out the door and climbing into Paul's battered vintage Mustang before she had time to process the guilt.

"Aren't you cold?" he asked.

"No." She was engineered to endure broad temperature extremes. She couldn't tell him because doing so would destroy what little chance at joy she had. So, she let him assume whatever he would and hoped he would ignore it as he did her other quirks.

"Canadians," he said, shaking his head with a smile. "You've got thicker skin than I do. Or something."

"Definitely 'or something,'" she said.

· · · • · · ·

D allas breathed in grungy bar-scented darkness. She could detect illegal cigarette smoke, old vomit, alcohol, and piss. As unpleasant as the mix sounded, it infused the night club with an aura just dangerous enough to feel rebellious. She was on the adventure of her life, and she wanted to remember it for as long as she could. So, she memorized everything down to the sticky grit on the cement floor under the rubber soles of her tennis shoes. She imagined it was glass from a long ago bar fight and smiled to herself. Deep notes from an electric bass vibrated inside her chest, spurring her heart to dance to a foreign beat. Hidden in darkness, she could pretend to be all the things she was forbidden to be.

"Want a drink?" he shouted, crowned once more with his backwards Yankees cap.

"Sure!"

"What would you like?"

Her heart stumbled, missing the beat, and she lost her sense of belonging. *A real human would know.* She didn't because she'd never ordered a drink at a bar before. *Not that I remember.* "I — I'll have whatever you're having." It sounded so pathetic, so weak-willed. *Subservient.*

The mis-step didn't seem to bother Paul, however. He nodded and drifted off, leaving her alone. She turned her attention to the stage.

The lead singer was a short young woman with black hair. She'd switched from the fiddle to a bass guitar which dwarfed her. Her fingers flew over the frets to a rapid punk-celtic-military beat. She wore low-slung, tight-fitting jeans and a Pogues t-shirt. Her black nail polish was chipped. She was confident, even angry as she sang. Her voice was clear and powerful with just a touch of rasp. It reminded Dallas of Toni Halliday or Beth Gibbons.

"Odd that all that can come out of someone so small, isn't it?" Paul asked, handing her a glass filled with murky liquid.

"Penny Dreadful is wonderful. Even better live," Dallas said and took a sip. It tasted milky and sweet with an edge of bitter. She swallowed, and the liquid burned her throat. *Alcohol*, she thought, *that's alcohol.* The tension in her shoulders relaxed a little. She flinched when Paul put his arm around her.

"Oh, sorry," he said and pulled away.

"No don't," she said. "It's okay." *What if he feels the port in the back of my neck?* "It's not what you think."

"It isn't?"

"I uh... slipped and hit the back of my head the other day," she said. "It's still sore."

"Oh."

"You can put your arm around me. I want you to."

"Are you sure?"

She nodded. He replaced his arm and soon she found herself snuggling into the warmth of his body. Together, they listened to several songs. When she finished her drink he offered her another and then another. The room began to tilt just a little. She breathed deep, feeling more free than she ever had. Suddenly, she wanted to dance. *Well, why not?* Studying the others, she began to copy their movements. Paul joined her. She laughed and whirled, bumping into one of the other revelers. With a jolt of fear, she understood she was a bit drunk.

I don't care. I want this. I'll be gone in a week.

Paul was with her. She'd known him her whole life — at least the part she remembered. He also worked for the same company which was the closest thing to family that she would ever know. She was safe. He would get her home. She could trust him. She watched him dance and enjoyed the way his body moved. He combined the sensual grace of a feline and the power of a swordsman. Briefly, she wondered how it would feel to kiss him — his naked skin pressing against hers. He had a subtle scent all of his own, amber and musk. *What would he taste like?*

What would HR do if they knew?

Shamed, she was glad he couldn't see the color in her face. *It isn't fair.*

Fair? Fair has nothing to do with it. You are what you are. The music stopped, and the lights brightened. A DJ took over, and the crowd on the dance floor moved to the bar.

"Is it over already?" she asked, disappointed.

"The band is only taking a short break," he said. "We should grab a seat before they're all taken."

He found them a place to sit at the back of the bar, away from the lights because she told him she felt more comfortable there. He settled on the bench next to her with a fresh round of drinks. They sat in silence for a few moments. Then something completely unexpected happened. He leaned over and nuzzled into the side of her neck. Before she knew it she was kissing him. His lips felt soft and warm, and the skin of his throat tasted of salt. She kissed him for some time and then risked placing a hand on his thigh. He let out a quiet sigh of a moan. The muscles beneath his jeans tensed. It was a thrill — the sense of power, knowing she could pull such a reaction out of him. She'd never felt anything like it. She even enjoyed the way his beard bristle felt on her tongue. She reached under his shirt and touched the skin of his flat belly.

It was then that she knew she'd made a terrible mistake, but it was one she couldn't bring herself to regret. She kissed him again, and again, and this time she let all her fears dissolve like the salt of his sweat on her tongue.

. . . . • . . .

Paul took her back to the office at the positively sinful hour of four in the morning. She stared out the window of his Mustang. Rain blurred her view of the gravel parking lot and drummed on the rag top of his convertible. The interior smelled of oil and leather. He reached over, turning off the stereo. The silence between them was fortified by the car's engine. Its throaty rumble purred against the rain's drum beat. She placed a hand on the dashboard to feel the vibration. If a car had a heartbeat, this was it.

"Was it... did you have a good time?" he asked.

She hadn't dared to face him once the lights had come up the final time. The bar had closed at three, but she'd begged him not to take her back just yet. So, he'd driven her around Austin, delighting in showing her things she'd never seen before. It occurred to her that everything he knew about her was rooted in falsehood and that she couldn't do anything but lie to him. At first, being alone with him was worth the price of a few lies. Now the need to be honest swelled larger with every moment.

The green of the instrument lights, cast everything in a sterile alien glow. She thought about the future and sniffed. *One week. Less than that, now. Six days.*

"Dallas?"

"It was wonderful," she said, blinking back tears. "More than wonderful. Everything I always wanted. Perfect."

"Oh."

She had an urge to kiss him again but held back. "Thank you so much." Opening the door, she allowed a rush of cold, wet air to battle the car's old heater.

"Wait!"

Pausing, she looked over her shoulder at him. "Oh, your shirt. Ah. Can I get it back to you tomorrow?" Blood rushed to her face for the third time that evening.

"No. I mean, keep it," he said. "I want you to."

"Really?"

"It looks better on you anyway."

"Thank you. Thanks so much!"

"Can you shut the door for a minute?" he asked. "It's cold."

She did as he asked. "Is something wrong?" *Did I do something I shouldn't have?*

Oh, please. You did everything *you shouldn't have.*

"Tomorrow—I mean, today—"

"We'll act like nothing happened," she said.

"Oh." He paused. "Right. I know. But... Will you be okay?"

"Sure."

He looked like he wanted to ask her something else. So, she didn't move or speak. It was all right with her. The longer she waited inside his car, the longer the evening lasted.

"Can we-would you like to go out again?" he asked.

She bit her lip. "Would you?"

"Of course."

Letting go of the breath she was holding, she said, "Absolutely."

"Next weekend?"

That's four whole days away, she thought and frowned.

"I'm sorry. I'm pushing you, aren't I? You want to take it slow. I understand. It's okay—"

"Can we go out tomorrow night?"

He blinked.

"I'm sorry," she said. "It's just that we only have until the project—"

"Is eight o'clock too soon?"

"Make it nine." Human Resources didn't leave the building until eight thirty. "See you tomorrow."

"Today."

She got out of the car. "Tonight." Then she ran through the rain to the back door. That's when reality brought her up short like a dog on a chain. It was locked of course. She hadn't thought of that. *Stupid. You have to be more careful.* Turning back, she saw that Paul had already driven away. She hoped against hope and used her keycard. In her terror, the door handle slipped through her fingers, and she had to swipe it a second time.

There was a terse email waiting in her inbox the next morning.

Report to Human Resources at once.

. . . . • . . . .

The name etched into the black plastic desk plate read 'George W. Templeton, Human Resources.' Unfortunately, the blonde man sitting behind the dated beige Herman Millar desk was scowling.

"Patent Number U.S. Dallas 2,457,972-1, Can you explain why you left the building last night? Was there a fire?" Templeton knew there hadn't been an emergency of any kind, of course—that was obvious by his tone.

Focusing on the grey industrial carpet, Dallas attempted to think of an explanation that wouldn't condemn Paul or herself. "I — I wanted to feel the rain on my face." It sounded lame even to her.

Templeton paused. "At four in the morning?"

Ah. He only has my keycard record to go by. Dallas decided on a half truth. "I'm sorry. I — I couldn't sleep. So, I decided to watch the rain. I stepped outside for just a minute. But the door slipped in my hands and closed before I could catch it. It was just for a minute. It won't happen again."

"I see," he said, apparently too busy reading the file resting on the beige plastic desktop to look up. "Your performance record is impressive."

"If you say so, sir."

"Three years. That's a long time for someone like you."

"I suppose so."

He frowned again. "How the hell would you know?"

Dallas clamped her mouth shut and held her breath. She returned her gaze to the close grey carpet. Templeton could be a total bastard when he wasn't addressed with just the right amount of diffidence.

"I told Human Resources this was a bad idea, allowing you to remain in your position this long. There were bound to be complications. But they said your performance record exceeded that of the others. And the Cost Report indicated it was well worth the risk. I don't know why I let them convince me. I suppose I'm just too kind for my own good."

"Thank you very much for letting me stay."

"Did I say you could speak?"

Dallas tensed up, preparing for the worst.

"You're nothing. You're a transgenetic. You're not real. I programmed you. *Me*. There isn't a single thing inside your skull that I didn't put there. Understand? I could put a bullet in your brain right now, and no one would care." Templeton smiled to himself. Getting up, he walked around the desk. "Well, the cost analysis would take a momentary hit. But I could replace you within a week. In a few months, this place will be filled with others just like you." Quick as a snake, he snatched up her hand and held it up at an awkward angle. "I can do anything to you I want."

"No! Please don't, sir! Please!"

He released her in disgust and went back to his chair. "Remember your place, then."

"Yes, sir. I will." If there were a God for transgenetic humans Dallas would have prayed many times over. But there wasn't. What God would have a creature without a soul?

"There are only six days left on this contract. Six. It isn't worth the company's time and money to have you reconditioned. Not at this juncture."

Nodding, Dallas didn't show her relief.

"Do you think you can fulfill your duties without any other problems?" Templeton asked.

"Yes, sir."

"Good."

"Sir?"

"Yes?"

"May I.... Might it be all right if I walked outside the building sometimes? I'll stay close. You track me all the time anyway. It isn't as if I can go anywhere without you knowing." Dallas didn't want Templeton to know she knew otherwise. "The other workers do so. They've started to notice that I don't."

Templeton tapped his pencil on the desk. His professional mask remained in place. Dallas didn't know if that was a good sign or not.

"All right," he said. "But if it affects your performance, I'm revoking the privilege. Now get out of here before I change my mind."

Dallas focused extra hard on her task list for the day, coding as if her life depended on it. The fact that it did didn't help.

. . . ● . . .

W‌here were you this morning?" Paul asked after swallowing a mouthful of stolen french fry. They were sprawled on the floor of his apartment, having a picnic. He'd ordered their dinner from a delivery service. "Did you oversleep?"

Dallas set down her half-eaten burger and debated telling him the truth. They'd had sex for the first time just an hour before. Everything was spinning out of control in the most pleasant way, but her conscience was bothering her more and more. She pulled the sheet she was wrapped in a little tighter. "I had a meeting."

"A meeting? With who?"

She bit her lip.

"It's okay," he said with a hurt look. "You don't have to tell me."

"It was Human Resources."

He blinked. "Why?"

She shrugged.

"Something is wrong, isn't it?" he said.

"I want to tell you something, but I can't. You won't like it."

"It's okay," he said. "You can tell me."

Her vision blurred and her throat hurt. "If I tell you, you'll want me to leave."

His brows bunched together. "Does this have to do with work? Because it doesn't matter. They're letting us all go. Five days, and I'm unemployed again. I know. We all know." He shrugged. "But that's okay. I'll get another contract somewhere. Everyone needs software programmers."

The pain in her throat intensified.

He continued, "Programming doesn't pay like it used to, but then nothing does. I love you. That's all that matters." It was his turn to look away. "That was probably too much information."

She sniffed. "I love you too."

"You do?"

Nodding, she moved closer and kissed him. "But I really should tell you. I — I've been lying to you."

"Shit. I knew it." He got up from the floor and began pacing. "I knew this was too good to be true. You're married."

"That's not it."

He paused. "You have a boyfriend?"

"No."

"You have a girlfriend?"

"That's not it either."

"Then what?"

She took a deep breath and then slowly let it go. "Don't you think it's odd that you report to Personnel, and I report to Human Resources?"

He blinked. "They're the same thing." He appeared to finally get the idea that everything wasn't as it seemed. "Aren't they?"

She shook her head. "No one else has lived for as long at the company hotel either. Just me."

"I thought that was because you're on a work visa. It sucks but—"

"Work visas have nothing to do with it. I'm not from Canada. That's just what I'm supposed to tell anyone who asks. The truth is, the company hasn't registered me as a worker at all."

He sat up. "You're an illegal? They're not paying taxes on your wages—"

"They don't pay me at all. The company owns me like they own the desks and computers."

"Wait. What? Bull shit! They can't own people! That's slavery!"

"I'm not a person. Not technically." She got up from the floor. "I'm-I'm a... transgenetic human."

"A what?"

"A genetically modified clone," she said. Her tears traced cooling paths down her burning cheeks. "I'm not a real person. Not legally." She lifted her hair to show him the nape of her neck. "Do you see this port? In five days, Human Resources will connect me to a bank of computers. They will remove everything that you know as Dallas and replace her with someone else."

"What?" He jerked away from her as if she'd slapped him. "This is crazy! They can't do that!"

"They most certainly can. I've gone through the process before."

"How many times?"

"I don't know."

"Why would they do that?"

"They download whatever specialized skills they need directly into my brain," she said. "If they need an electrical engineer with specific knowledge, they download one. If they need a mathematician, I'll be a mathematician. If they need a ditch digger, or a fry cook. I'll be that. They don't have to pay to train me. I already know everything they need me to know. They don't have to pay a salary or medical or anything. I'm theirs."

"You're a slave that can be programmed?" He was in shock. "That doesn't make any sense. You're a person. You have rights."

"A manufactured person," she said. "An engineered clone. I don't even have a real name."

His skin had acquired a green cast, and he looked like he was going to be sick. "Why haven't I heard about this before?"

"Have you heard about the new genetic research regarding organ transplants and how they've been determined to not have rights?"

"Yes."

"You've heard about this."

"What?"

"When I'm too old to retrain they'll—"

"Sell you for parts?" He shuddered. "I don't believe what I'm hearing."

"I'll understand if you wish me to leave now." She got up from the floor and began dressing.

"Wait. Don't go."

She wiped her face. "I lied to you. I'm so sorry."

"But... did you lie about everything?"

"Not about how I feel," she said. "I do love you. I always have."

He spoke to the floor. "But how would you know? I mean, if they program you... I... I don't know what to think."

"I didn't meant to hurt you. I just wanted to feel what it was like. You know, to be like anyone else. I-I shouldn't have done this. It was selfish. I see that. And if Templeton finds out he'll—"

"Do what? Kill you?"

"Templeton will erase me," she said. "Which amounts to the same thing."

"Who is Templeton?"

She shook her head.

"How many of you are there?" Paul asked.

"I'm the only one at our office. But... next year... there won't be a next year for you," she said. "They won't need to hire you. They'll have transgenetics for that."

He stared at the floor. She waited in the silence until she couldn't stand it any longer and then she finished dressing.

"I should go," she said.

"I need some time to think. This is a lot to... to process. We can talk about this tomorrow night. Okay?"

"I understand." She went to the door.

"Wait," he said. "Let me drive you."

The ride back to the office building was silent, tense, and awful. He didn't kiss her goodnight. He didn't even touch her. He merely used his keycard to let her back into the building and turned away. Holding the door open, she watched him drive off. When she was sure he was gone she walked back to her room, sobbing the whole way. She'd ruined everything by telling him. *But would he have asked me out if he'd known?* She thought over the situation again and again as she had the day before, trying to find a way that made all the pieces fit together right. *Maybe he won't hate me*, she thought. *Maybe he'll forgive me.* She didn't understand something was wrong until she noticed the lights were on in her room.

Both Mr. Templeton and Ms. Harmon were there, waiting for her.

Maybe none of it matters, she thought, *because I won't remember.*

Jerry Cornelius and his clan return in a

"secret history" of Mars, by way of Texas.

In typical Michael Moorcock fashion, the

non-linear story unfurls across time with

wry political commentary, insightful

social observations, and abundant

musical references.

THE NOSTALGIA DIFFERENTIAL

A Jerry Cornelius adventure

Michael Moorcock

2013. Shadow on the Wall.

MARS WAS NO less attractive from this side or the mountains. Magnificent, oddly biblical and disturbing. Jerry relished the smell of frying bacon. "These new season shows look good."

Catherine nodded as she slipped into her place with her plate. "I'm not sure why I thought you were right to take this job."

"Space!" Her brother gestured with his toast. "It's getting interesting again."

He was sincere. He loved Mars. He had always loved Mars. And here he was, camped out beside a canal, one of the fertile belts on a cloudless planet. He and Catherine had always wanted this kind of solitude. They had talked about it long before their father had turned against them. But sometimes he yearned. His soul craved rain.

"There's always a chance." She looked up. Was that a movement? "Before it becomes real it has to be imagined."

And soon the sound of the great atmosphere plant dropped to a pleasant hum. Jerry wondered if it were time for his run.

1933. Walking the Dog.

EVERY LITTLE MOVEMENT has a meaning of its own, every little thought and feeling by some posture can be shown…" Major Nye hummed a favourite number. Some darling of the halls had performed it in his youth. Slowly he ran a fond finger over dusty blue and gold spines. "Every little picture tells a tale… I'm sure it was a MacMillan Illustrated Classic. Here we are. You have a wonderful book department. I'd say it's quite as good as Knightsbridge."

Mr. Sissons was gracious. Clearly impressed by the major's Saville Row tailoring, he moved a pale, modest hand, adjusting his pearl, grey suit. "So we're told, sir. Will *Snarleyowl* be all?"

"Unless you have a *My Strudel*, is it?"

"We're waiting for the next printing, major. With Herr Hitler and his popular 'pastry cook' socialists in power more people are curious. Do you know much, sir?"

"About Austrian cuisine?" Major Nye couldn't say. He hadn't realised the chap had other interests. "Wasn't he in the Battenburg rising? When's it due in?"

"We can order it for you, of course. Do you live in Buenos Aires?"

"Not yet, I'm afraid." He thought of Vanessa; the Hotel Robinson. "I'd move here like a shot if I were a free man."

Mr. Sissons' smile was discreetly tired.

1944. Don't Sit Under the Apple Tree.

THEY FOUND JERRY cutting cane in the back country north of Rio. They cleaned him up and gave him a pair of boots. He was delighted. They might have been hand-made.

"Don't worry." Miss Brunner counted out the bills to the thick-set Indian who had reported him. "He'll be his old self in no time. Look, he's found a copy of *Tractatus Logico-Philosophicus* already. Fish to water, eh?"

"Fish?" The Indian scratched his head. "Nowhere around here that I know. Not any more."

But Jerry, mumbling cross-legged from the polished planks of the upper deck, quickly discarded the book and picked another from the pile. *Coarse*, the pornographic memoir thought to have been written as a kind of sequel to Walton's *Compleat Angler*. He began looking through the pockets of his new black pea-jacket. "Rod?"

"We'd better be leaving while we can." Major Nye adjusted the fraying cuffs of his civilian tweed. "Once he finds the Doré *Milton* we'll never get him off the boat."

"Is it regression?"

"Not typically."

With her slender arthritic fingers Miss Brunner tightened her graying perm. "In politics one word's worth a thousand pictures. Not so?" She flirted a glance at a freshly and cheaply uniformed Captain Pardon. He'd receive a fortune for this help. The old vessel wheezed black smoke and coughed a little circumspectly. The little captain seemed surprised, studying a large chronometer he held in his left hand and making notes with a new pencil on his paper cuff.

"If we left now," said Major Nye, "we might get to Sao Paulo before the next riot."

"Are they still upset with the Americans?" she asked.

"Not since they found out the reason for the shelling. Embarrassing, of course." He moved his mouth in mock disapproval. "Poor intelligence as usual." The major remained unhappy about his posting. After Casablanca it had seemed all downhill until now.

The steamboat made a convulsive movement then whoever was steering let loose with the whistle. Captain Pardon cursed in French and headed for the wheelhouse.

Miss Brunner shrugged. "Does anyone know where he trained?"

"Marrakech, I think." The major chuckled forgivingly.

Miss Brunner frowned.

1956. Just Couldn't Resist Her With Her Pocket Transistor

AT FIRST HE thinks it is a dust storm. Then the dust grows thicker. He covers his mouth with his handkerchief. There are stinging pebbles in it now. He lies down and protects his head. He thinks Jesus Christ I'm being buried alive! So he forces himself to his knees and crawls on until at last the storm stops. In the following stillness he sees a figure ahead, shadowy against the sun. A smiling, bearded face.

A recurring dream. Jerry wondered if the man were his father. The expression was familiar. In the dream they were so proud to be on Mars, so pleased it looked just like Barsoom in *John Carter*.

On his 18th birthday his father pressed Heidegger's *Being and Time* at him. "It's flawed, of course, but also very coherent. Try him." Jerry had decided he wasn't a great thinker. And God knew what the drugs had done to his dad's brain. He drew a deep, relaxing breath. Sometimes surgery was the only answer.

In the following dream he was crossing an ice-bridge in a horse-drawn sleigh. His sister Catherine sat in front of him wrapped in white furs. Behind them in snow reddened by the setting sun sharp black shadows of birches crossed the deep bleak ruts the sleigh made. The same old cryptograms, each telling a different tale.

"What's it all mean, Jerry?" his sister asked.

"People are frightened. They simply won't tolerate the absurdists any more. Not as an audience." Una Persson, gloriously stylish in her snug greatcoat, spoke from behind, where she was leading her own grey. "And when they're frightened, they burn a witch. That's where we come in."

Jerry was prepared to work with what he had but it wouldn't be easy for anyone. Too many dreams, too much delusion, too many illusions. How could he have kept so many balls in the air at the same time?

He awoke with a guffaw.

"What is it now?" Catherine sat up. "Christ, it's cold."

Outside the darkness and silence continued to gather.

1967. Lady D'Arbanville.

ZURICH TRAMS RAN so thoroughly on time Una Persson felt faintly disgusted, especially when she attempted to board in her old Belenciaga frock while going through her bag looking for her fare. She apologised in her pretty German. "Sometimes I have to unpack everything. Just to find the right change."

"Sometimes you have to unpack everything anyway." The driver handed her a ticket of a higher denomination than the one she'd paid for. "Now you can go much further." He winked. "Perhaps you should have flown."

"He won't fly." She made a grateful, apologetic face.

"Oh, that's always such a problem. Are you married?" He pulled the lever and the doors hissed shut. "Here on holiday?"

He was flirting with her. *Why do the children play? A strange tune to come into her head at that moment. Was he looking for a hard-headed woman?*

She had to admit she admired his Turkish looks. What was it about those big Mediterranean noses?

1971. Friend of the Devil.

TIME AND ORDER? What could we do without them? The theatre wasn't what it was. In the current climate they could never have a successful revival of *The Jew's Bargain*. Which was a stupid thing to say, he thought. Was it true the image always preceded the actuality? *I have seen your skull covered in filth*, he told Mengele. *I have seen you dead. You have no idea what great good will come of our suffering. The State of Israel will rise from our ashes.* He had been able to look into Mengele's face and see the attempt to control the contractions of terror there. Was it unseemly to congratulate himself for bartering his good life to save one young woman from the creature whose bones were now displayed at the Nazi Remains show in Munich? *I am not man enough for this*, he thought. But it was too late. *I had made my bargain with God. It was unbreakable. He would not release me from it. I wish I had known that at the time.*

He was reading from his own journal.

But, best of all, I had proved there truly was a God. I need never despair again. Never carry that burden Nietzsche had put on me. Yet if you had a past and a present why could you not have a future? Or a number of futures? He had spent so long trying to work out the consequences of radiant time. Too many equations. Too many adventures. Too much of everything. Accretion challenged complexity.

There was a long way to go yet.

Jerry wondered how much hotter things would get before they started cooling down again. He wetted another towel and stretched it over his sister's pale forehead. He checked his watch. In a couple of hours the world would know for certain. How much time had he waited so long ago as his child bride sweated out her memories?

So long. So long at the border. Could they sweat this out too? Now he understood why Benjamin had given himself up to despair. The world could no longer be manipulated or persuaded. At last he began to understand the codes. It really shouldn't have taken this long. Too many pictures. Far too many words. And ghosts! Those ghosts.

What the fuck had happened to the action? The mystery?

"Wake up, old chap." Major Nye's voice was distant and encouraging. "Our truck's arrived at last! We're on our way! Another four decades and we'll be in Syria. Or Lebanon, at any rate. What do you think of that?"

"Saladin's still in charge, isn't he?"

"The Kurds seem to think so."

Jerry got up slowly adjusting his cap. "Has anyone seen my launcher?"

1984. Momma Don't Let Your Babies Grow Up To Be Cowboys.

WHEN IN GALVESTON Jerry habitually took his breakfast at the Waffle House on 25th and Broadway. It was the least infected of the joints. Here, it was impossible to catch even a glimpse of the ocean. He was beginning to regret buying the Bishop's Palace. When had he last eaten so much bacon? Really, it was time to stop. He was growing weak again. He reached into the darkness and found her long, soft hand. Now he could only love.

She reassured him with her grasp. He was grateful for this small, deliberate kindness. When he first came to the island he had so much wanted to find some kind of purpose. He felt certain he would come across a sign of Leadbelly or maybe one of the other Texas bluesmen here. But, leaving not so much as a playbill behind, they had gone north and east. They had no interest in time. From the brochures quantum physics and m-theory seemed to fit so well with the Moorish Gothic of the Bishops Palace. As a result he had bought the great pile with its pointed roofs, minarets and Persianate beaux-arts. There had even been a touch of early Tiffany art nouveaux. It once provided the most accurate understanding of the style why so many modernists rejected it, confusing complexity for fussy pre-modernity. Sometimes he hated to see the look of disappointment disturb the firmness of some poor mod's features. Twenty years earlier all that had mattered was that you had a pocket full of purple hearts and a willingness to stay up all night at the Flamingo.

"Is there something wrong with the music?" She looked out at the driving rain. "Why isn't working any more?"

"Rock and roll died the day *Hair* opened in New York," he murmured, glancing around to see if he was overheard. Reactionary debased versions of Viennese Light classical with extra bass. Queen sang the dirge at the funeral of American black music. Then country wasn't country any more. Looking up from his Big Triple, Shaky Mo Collier pushed at greasy hair with greasier fingers and gave Jerry a thumb's up. His attention wandered.

Catherine glared in his direction. Beside him Miss Brunner watched Mo vaguely checking the action of his slick little Colt. "She was getting ready to settle down. I felt sorry for her." He kissed the air and said something under his breath. He looked around for his grits.

"Perfect." Miss Brunner prepared herself for prayer. By increasing the population so successfully religion again showed its relevance to modern times.

This had turned into fun. A neat little running backwards race. He panted. "Religion has done a great job keeping pace with the times. Or was it always an arm of consumerism?"

Mo looked up from his Colt. "Is that like water over there? What's it? Tidal wave?"

"Oh, bugger!" Jerry had left his guitars in his hotel.

1985. The Dream Police; the Dream Police.

PORTOBELLO ROAD WAS not the road it had been. It led north into the shabby limbo of the Harrow Road and Kilburn where everything became grey and indistinct. To the south the colours grew brighter and eventually less garish the closer you got to Notting Hill tube station.

Didi Dee, doctor to the stars, stood at the intersecton of Blenheim Crescent and the market, looking up and down in the hope she would see the original Body Shop or Rough Trade records. She was disgusted by her own nostalgia for a past her customers had wiped out. She had very little choice as she saw it of maintaining so much sentimental romanticism balanced by so much actuality. "Too many pictures," she murmured. "Too many voices. Too many voices."

The pleasure of the suburbs was that they presented a simplified narrative. The city had far too many narratives.

She repeated this complaint, gathering the white cotton dress around her like a disappointed bride.

"What could I have done about it?" Jerry was surly. After all, he had grown up in this very street. "Some of us enjoy complexity. Some of us can't live without it. It's meat and drink to me."

"Well, it drives me crazy."

"This was never designed for upper class black professionals. You can't blame me for that."

"I just said it drives me crazy, that's all. Is this a good place to find a taxi?"

Until the music studios like Island started establishing themselves in the area Jerry couldn't remember seeing a taxi anywhere in the neighbourhood. Even the whores had to get out at Westbourne Road and walk.

"Do you feel your life has been wasted?" she asked.

Jerry snorted.

June 1959. The Pretenders Live in London.

THE RIFFS WERE familiar now.

"Not dead yet?" His father's tone was one of amusement mixed with what Jerry could only take for resentment. Old Professor Cornelius was baffled by what he called the chaotic mathematics of the new popular music. For him, Mozart remained the great unifier.

Jerry lowered the volume and sat down in the single pew provided for petitioners.

"Is this the first time you've visited me here?" His father reached for a box at his side and picked out a long brown Sherman's. "You were all supposed to convene at my deathbed."

"It would have helped to have had an address." Jerry had rather liked his father in life but in death he had become unstable and petty. Not to mention, in his choice of vestments, vulgar.

"I'd imagine it's a pretty well known location."

"Well, it didn't occur to me. Didn't they throw you out?"

"They wanted to." The old man drew for several seconds on his Sherman's. "They wanted to. I didn't leave you very much. I'm sorry about it, of course."

"That's the spirit." Jerry took a swift glance at the plump woman who entered through the curtain. Her long, bright white hair framed her ancient face so that in that light it had the appearance of redeemed youth. She gave him the creeps.

"You still don't have to call me mother," she said firmly.

Jerry held his breath.

"You can't imagine how disappointed I am in this." Professor Cornelius made a weak gesture. "You know."

Jerry pushed his hair back from his forehead. Then he grinned, holstering the needle gun, a present for his 19th birthday. "Grow up, you foolish old bastard. I'm not killing anyone for you. Not today."

He turned to point at the old woman. "And I don't care how much you care. Stay in your crypt."

She was still trying to smile when he left. Sometimes she wished she'd never heard of Mars.

1975. Rolling in the Ruins.

PULP LEADS INNOVATION not only in language and subject but in social vision, too. The first multi-racial democracy I ever saw was in *Dan Dare* in THE EAGLE." Professor Hira spread bland hands but made his point no less obscure. "You don't remember the U.N. cavalry force landing on Venus in gliders, do you? That would have been about 1953."

"If it has wheels it can roll backward as well as forward." Bishop Beesley used his most reassuring tone. "We have little to fear over the course of the centuries, Mr. Cornelius."

"You thought history only went one way, didn't you?" Miss Brunner's normally sharp tones were mellowed by a mild triumphalism. "Your way. Well, you knew all about radiant time, dark matter, string theory, all the latest crackpot stuff, didn't you? Refraction, distraction, attraction, reflection, repulsion. Always desire with you, wasn't it? The weaving and the wearing. The weaving in and the weaving out. Back and forth, those shuttles of the Norns, Mr. Cornelius. We knew that, didn't we? Nothing stops. That's not part of God's grand design, old chum."

"I fear the Man Upstairs has different plans for us," Bishop Beesley winked heavenward.

"What?" Mo Collier looked up from his Remington. "The Lodger was he? Even I've seen that."

"Let's keep it clean, shall we?" Miss Brunner reached behind her neck obsessively tightening her bun. Her lips were pursed, seemingly drawn back by the same force. She brought a faint smell of disinfectant which reminded Jerry how ill he had been. Visions of Mary and memories of Pine. He was on the point of throwing up.

Outside Island Studios he found Major Nye smoking a Sullivan's. Jerry ran down a silent Basing Street. The sound of his vomiting echoed around the abandoned houses. Ladbroke Grove had gone from middle-class suburb to shabby genteel to slum and back to middle class enclave. Once Notting Hill had meant race riots and whores. Now it meant TV presenters and politicians, making Bishop Beesley's point. Religions rose and fell on economic tides.

"The bees have all deserted their hives." Didi Dee lowered herself to the opposite kerb and put on her high heels. Without them she had to be under four feet. Jerry looked carefully at the dark thigh she showed him. Was this some sort of mating ritual? Since he felt no response in his penis he had to assume he was wrong or it wasn't working. Would they send someone to marry him? They'd have to wake him first. Dream or delusion? Did it ever really matter?

They looked up at a sound from Portobello Road. Of late the phantom Fifteen bus had changed its route. Where was it carrying the damned these days? Once it had turned at Elgin Crescent, frequently clipping his old Nash and leaving a smear of faintly glowing red paint behind. His old mum's disembodied voice sounded from the phantom stop. "Full up? How can you be full up at five o'clock on a Friday when you don't even fuckin' exist?"

With some pleasure Jerry remembered his mum's skepticism when confronted by the supernatural. Were they all dead at last? He had been dreaming of oblivion again. Something which could only be enjoyed while not experienced.

"Good old Heidegger." Miss Brunner left the Mangrove Cafe and headed up the street towards what in those shoes could only be Holland Park.

"I think we're losing her." Major Nye enjoyed another drag on his gasper. "She's breaking up." He frowned, dropping the butt onto a cracking flagstone. "Or is it me?"

2020. Late Morning Lullaby.

THE GREAT HYDRAULIC towers of Storyville rose in the pink gold morning, sweet water streaming from their glorious steel curves and planes. The wheel chairs were lined in a precise row along the North Placomine Causeway so their occupants could enjoy and applaud this daily ritual. This was only the fifth time the towers had risen. Soon the whole city would be surrounded and protected.

"From our ruins came all this promise." Monsieur Pardon bent to straighten Jerry's plaid over his healing legs. "We have dodged the missile again, wouldn't you say, Mr. Cornelius."

In the next chair Miss Brunner yawned ostentatiously. "My dear bishop! My dear bishop!"

Shaky Mo frowned. He had his feet tangled in the chair's rests. "Is it me or has the quality of Colombian gone off since Valparaiso?" He had skyped Karen von Krupp, the New Age dentist, who waved back at him from her favourite Starbucks table looking out at the streets of Laredo.

"I think you'll find it's Java, these days," she said.

2013. Pierrot on the Moon.

MULTITUDES OF UNIVERSES bring us closer to an understanding of God's complexity."

Catherine patted her poor brother's hand. How bad could things have been for them to go this far?

"Will you not do me the courtesy to let me die alone? That was what he said to me. As I left, I thought I saw him smile. I have lived for this, he said. No more narratives! No more! I would never know now if all the stories were true. How can you tell, Cathy?"

"All stories are true, Jerry. Mum told us that.."

"More stories? More pain? Who knew? Why would they be so desperate for escape? They don't want narratives. They want lies. Lullabies. Fantasies. Fucking fantasies."

"This isn't the Balkans, my love. The tears are already cold."

"Did you ever read Wheldrake's *The Willing Boy?*"

"No," she said, "but I can play it." She slipped a warm hand into his comfort zone.

1981. Hit Me.

I DID MY best to calm him down." Didi Dee eased off her scarlet heels. They had rubbed a hole in her left stocking. She had been reluctant to visit Anuradhapura at this time in the evening. The shadows were making it all too grotesque. "Beast. I don't think he was ever human and certainly not an archangel." Of late she had made a number of vague references to Milton.

Jerry mourned. Was the age of the great puritan to come again? He loathed what would follow. Was the 18th century really making a come back? The reactionaries now called themselves conservatives. The conservatives were liberals and the liberals were what? Libertarians? What did that make easier? Not another sodding revolution, surely?

Professor Hira, sweating, came to sit down on his favourite fallen god. He got nostalgic on these occasions. "I don't see how we've got all the way from Big Bang to M-theory without wondering for a moment if all our standard theories are delusional. The 20th century consisted of a series of escapist notions transformed into gloriously impressive math. The fact is all the evidence has shown that – "

Significantly, Mo Collier checked and rechecked the action of his massive Banning. "Bloody hell! With that triple clip you can hardly lift the bugger!"

"To be honest it's doing my head in." Jerry looked for friendlier skies. He wanted the familiar sights of his childhood but most of them were gone, replaced by chains and concessions. "I was thinking of getting a haircut."

Mo hadn't really been listening. "Sorry I'm late. Was there another storm? I had to work an extra dodgem shift at the Scrubs fair." He shivered and held up his hand to see if it was raining. "What's new?"

"Don't ask me." Jerry giggled into the sodden wind. "I just got up."

— THE END —

．．．．．．．．．．．．．．．．．

For centuries man has searched for the

God of All Psychedelics. In this hard

science exploration, Lawrence Person

ponders what happens after the ultimate

pharmacological experience.

．．．．．．．．．．．．．．．．

Novel Properties of Certain Complex Alkaloids

Lawrence Person

IT WAS A thing of terrible beauty.

"What do you think?" asked Doug.

Timothy Shackleford shook his head. "Complex" was all he had to say. He didn't know *what* to think.

The object of adoration was the molecule slowly rotating on the screen of his laptop, a small miracle featuring a central spindle and multiple branching arms, the latest and greatest synthetic psychoactive thrown up by the kitchen sink wizards of the chemical underground. Tim was impressed despite himself, because most emanations of that underground were utter crap beneath his contempt.

There were people out there taking random walks through the alkaloids and hoping that whatever they brewed up in their shitty home labs wouldn't kill them. They would get a recipe off the Internet or a copy of *PhIKAL* or (God help them) *The Anarchist's Cookbook* and thought they had a freaking clue. The vast majority didn't, and were a danger to themselves and others, assuming their poorly ventilated labs and makeshift equipment didn't kill them first. There were twenty brain-dead cretins trying to cook meth for every one that had even a tiny inkling of skill or ability, and underground chemists who could do even slightly competent reductions for psychoactives were an order of magnitude rarer.

Tim had two overriding passions: Information theory and recreational pharmacology close enough to his regular organic research chemistry topics so as not to rouse suspicion as long as he was careful. (And he *was* careful. He did all his psychoactive molecular modeling inside a virtual machine on his own laptop, did all his reading of the underground literature from a coffee house Wi-Fi, and encrypted all his notes.)

Which is why Doug, a fellow psychonaut from his college days, was his only conduit. Naturally he went into computational chemistry. It was easy enough to do information theory on his home computer, but where was he going to get access to an integrated gas chromatography/mass spectrometer on a regular basis?

Which is how he ended up teaching and researching at the University of Texas chemistry department. Benefits included access to high quality college lab equipment, perfect establishment camouflage, and a steady income to fund his experiments. The latter allowed him to avoid the most common downfall of underground chemists: getting busted for making stupid, boring crap like meth to pay the bills.

Tim *hated* meth. In addition to the central nervous system stimulation, it fooled you into thinking it made you smarter while doing the opposite. He took careful, clinical notes of his psychonautic excursions, and was able to track the obvious degeneration in his thinking on meth. Drugs that make you dumber? No thanks! Plus the entire drug warrior apparatus had watches on dozens of meth precursors. Too much heat, not enough profit, and best left the Mexican cartels and their industrial-scale production.

Besides, once you figured out the chemistry and process controls, there was nothing interesting about cooking meth. It was a solved problem. No challenges.

But phenethylamines and tryptamines offered vast topologies of chemical search spaces and lay of the underground. Not only was Doug equally careful, he had even better cover: The company he worked for did drug testing for police departments around the state.

Tim was cautiously optimistic whenever Doug texted him for a meeting in a private little room of a funky coffee shop near campus, but most of the time he was disappointed. The most interesting thing he'd ferreted out heretofore was a novel reduction of hydrochloride salt in creating 2C-B.

The beast on his screen was in a whole different league.

It was a beautiful molecule. It was also completely insane. It shared characteristics with multiple alkaloid groups, and each arm end seemed to act as an agonist for the 5-HT_{1A}, 5-HT_{2A} and 5-HT_{6A} receptors.

Even more amazing, unless he was mistaken, the structure of the fourth arm end suggested it acted as an agonist for a *previously unmapped receptor*. That was off the charts.

"Well?" asked Doug. Doug was a competent chemist in his own right, but he knew Tim was out of his league. And until he had seen the molecule, Tim would have said he was out of *anyone's* league now that Shulgin was retired.

"Where did you get this from?" he asked.

"A guy that specializes in DMT synthesis."

Tim frowned. DMT tended to attract the mystic cranks of the psychedelic underground, people following in the steps of that loon Terence McKenna and his hallucinated "machine elf" intelligences. They were as bad as UFO nuts.

"Any suggested dose?"

"No."

"Recipe?"

"In the text file."

Tim pulled that up and read through it. There were careful step-by-step instructions for creating the monster, even the steps everyone knew, and some of the process parameters were incredibly tight ("Heat for 97 seconds at 178.3°C."). They went on for 10 pages and 189 detailed steps. One step required an ultracentrifuge and another a 1500 PSI pressure vessel. No amateurs need apply.

"Can you do it?"

"Still reading." Tim went through the instructions a second time. Some of the steps were extremely tricky, even with the right equipment, but none looked impossible.

"I think so. But it's going to take some time."

"How long?"

"At least a month."

Doug nodded. Obviously the beast couldn't be built overnight. "What do you need?"

"I'll send you a list." The deal was that Doug would provide any needed base compounds from his underground connections (especially the ones on any of the DEA watch lists) while Tim did the work. "Did your DMT guy have a name for this?"

"GOAP."

"Goap?"

"God of All Psychedelics."

· · · · • · · ·

It didn't take quite the whole month, but it wasn't easy. Following the recipe took half the top-end equipment in Welch Hall, careful attention to detail, and patience, as well as his usual clandestine stealth.

Fortunately he was also working on a hard-money project using various alkaloids as possible buffering agents for erectile dysfunction pills. (It seemed like boner pills were half the medical compound research they did these days.) It was possible to intersperse his GOAP work with his regular batch processing. He smuggled some of Doug's special ingredients in via a false bottom in his old metal lunchbox. Intermediate compounds were kept locked up with his other work.

There were setbacks. Hydrogen chloride impurities ruined one precursor batch, and a petroleum ether phase failed repeatedly until he realized he had a faulty pressure valve. And it had to wait on the back burner for the ED work or the single graduate class he was teaching that semester.

But slowly and surely GOAP took form. Spectrometry readings were good, and everything was on schedule.

That's when he hit the first roadblock, heralded by an email from the chemistry department dean asking to drop by his office.

"You wanted to see me?"

"Yes. Come in and sit down. And close the door behind you."

That was rarely a good sign. "What's up?"

"We've got a drug problem."

Tim kept his face studiously neutral despite his racing heart. He carefully furrowed his brow. "Really? What is it?"

The dean signed and sat back in his chair. "Austin police raided a makeshift meth lab in Creekside last night. They kept it out of the papers this morning but it will probably be on the evening news."

Tim made sure his face showed concern rather than relief. "That's terrible! Were any of our students involved?"

"No chemistry majors, just an EE who took Chem301 last semester. How much do you know about cooking meth?"

"I know it's dangerous, nasty stuff, especially if you get the process wrong."

The dean nodded. "The last thing we need is some ignorant undergraduate killing himself. Do you know what all the meth precursors we use in the department are?"

"Some. I can look up the rest on the Internet."

"I want you to make a list for me and do an inventory of everything we have here that could be used for meth and make sure we have adequate controls over it. Are you at a good pausing point in the ED project?"

"There are a couple of batches I need to do microassays on, but other than that yeah."

"How's that coming?"

It was Tim's turn to sigh. "I think the process is viable, but I don't see it scaling commercially. At least until they come up with a better bleaching agent."

The dean nodded. "Though so. But they're the ones paying the piper. Do the inventory and get back on it. Both the campus and Austin police want the inventory results, so I'll give you their contact names."

And that's how Tim become the Chemistry Department's designated police liaison for illegal drugs.

. . . • . . .

hough it increased his camouflage, and made it easier to further his research into recreational pharmacology on university time, it put him behind on GOAP. There were lots of chemicals to inventory, and the ever-inventive meth cooking community had added a few new ones since the last time he checked. Ammonium formate, mercuric chloride, metallic sodium, and even the ubiquitous bottles of acetone all had to be checked, tagged, and cataloged.

He was starting to get the itch, the vague feeling that his mind wasn't as sharp is it could have been. Some people felt wrecked or freaked out after dropping acid, but for him psychedelics had always worked as a sort of intellectual and emotional dump and cleanse, making him feel sharper and more creative the week after. If he had a particularly difficult computation chemistry problem, the solution would often come to him a couple of days after a trip.

This time GOAP *was* the problem.

After the inventory, Tim was able to start back working on the ED project, and with it GOAP. Bromine, dimethyl disulfide, butyllithium. Heating, stirring, filtering. Some steps were so easy a child could do them. Others brought him to the edge of his own abilities.

And then, finally, it was done.

The spectrometry peaks and melting point matched the recipe.

He had produced just under two grams of GOAP, and wasn't sure what the effective dose would be. LSD worked in micrograms, but this hit so many receptors he suspected it would require more.

He sent Doug a simple text message: *Got a package from home,* and waited for him to set a time and place to split the GOAP.

. . . • . . .

riday night, Tim was sitting in the recliner at his apartment, a sports program with the sound off playing on the TV and Philip Glass on the stereo. On his left he had his laptop with his trip diary open. On his right he had a blotter with 250 ug of GOAP. It might be too low a dose to start with, as some of Shulgin's menagerie required 200 mg. If worse came to worse nothing would happen and he could try again tomorrow.

And, for a half hour or so, nothing seemed to be exactly what was happening. Then soccer players replaced the sportscasters, and Tim started to see trails stretching out behind them as they ran. The GOAP was starting to kick in. He checked his watch and typed in his trip diary:

27 minutes visuals start to kick in.

Physically he felt fine, no detectable nausea or vertigo. He felt at peace and a little heavy.

Comfortable lethargy.

It was like any of dozens of trips, though the trails and visual patterns seemed brighter and more intense.

High visuals.

So far, so good. It was a nice trip, he wasn't feeling any paranoia or anxiety, and felt that his intelligence was unimpaired. To prove it, he brought up and solved a simple quadratic equation. He finished it in record time.

No Impairment. Enhanced intelligence???

If GOAP measurably increased intelligence, then it lived up to its moniker, promising to be the drug he and his fellow psychonauts had been searching for.

Despite his excitement, the trip still hadn't peaked. The colors around him brightened further still, until it seemed like his walls were slowly dissolving into a sort of multicolored fractal fog, letting him see beyond them. The swirling visuals faded into the background, and he could see clusters of different sized red glowing lights moving beyond the walls of his room. Some would drift slowly, stop, then start moving, while others seemed to stay still the entire time.

Moving lights?

He stood up and moved around his apartment. Still no vertigo. Except when his gaze swept over a light source, he wasn't seeing the characteristic "spark trails" anymore. But the red lights were different. Not all moved with his gaze, most seemed to stay in fixed positions, something he had never experienced on a trip before.

He left his apartment, carefully navigated his way down the stairs (probably overcautiously, since he still wasn't feeling any vertigo) and walked down to the Drag.

He stood on the corner for a few minutes, watching the students walk by, and realized that the red glows he had seen were coming from (or rather, *within*) people's heads. Some were brighter than others, but each moved with the person.

Beyond the glare of the streetlights, he could see hundred of faint glows off in the distance, apparent even through intervening buildings. Not only was that novel, but it suggested real *Doors of Perception* cognition enhancement. He wondered if it was just another form of hallucination.

He saw a cluster of five lights moving toward him from about half a block away, following them until five students stepped out from a side street and onto the Drag. As they passed, he thought he saw what might have been lines of the same radiance stretch between them, but it was so faint he couldn't be sure.

He walked around for hours, looking at the tiny red glows inside each person around campus, some brighter, some dimmer. Jester dorm had more lights than a bedecked Christmas tree.

He laughed off someone in dreads trying to sell him a joint from the Artist's Market. No, he was doing just fine as is.

Finally he felt the trip start to ebb, and went back to his apartment to take detailed notes.

* * * • * * *

Tim woke the next morning to find GOAP had given him one more gift.

His dreams were even more confused and vibrant than usual after a trip, but upon waking he rushed to his computer to get down the final image in his mind, terrified it might dissolve.

Unlike most dream revelations, it didn't.

It took a good half-hour of input, but when it was done, the result in his molecular CAD program matched the image in his dream. GOAP II.

It hit the same receptors as GOAP, but instead of four arms branching off the main spindle, it had *six*. Instead of acting as an agonist for one unmapped receptor, he felt sure it hit *three*.

Looking at GOAP II spinning in its terrible, impossible perfection, Tim felt a sudden chill. Dreams had often handed him the answers to difficult questions, but never before in such detailed, crystal clear form. It was almost supernatural.

Tim didn't believe in the supernatural.

It was time to meet with Doug.

· · · • · · ·

ou OK?"

Doug sighed and shook his head. Tim felt fantastic, his mind clearer and sharper than it had ever been, but Doug looked like hell, with dark circles under his eyes and his hair uncombed.

"Bad trip?"

"No, the trip was fine," said Doug. "Great visuals, fantastic plateau." He brought the coffee cup up to his lips, hands shaking. "It's the comedown that's been hell." His eyes darted around the room as though looking for something.

"What's wrong?"

"You been sleeping OK?"

"Like a baby."

"Not me. My mind keeps racing. I can't get to sleep because my mind won't shut off."

"Tried melatonin?"

"Yeah. And Tylanol PM. If that doesn't work I'll up the dose. And if it still doesn't work, I have a few emergency barbiturates tucked away."

"Did you see any lights?"

"Yeah, lights and glowing strings, but they kept shifting. Plus something else."

"What?"

Doug was silent a long moment, drinking the rest of his coffee. He shook his head again. "Hard to describe. Sort of a pattern that shifted around. Not something obvious, but sort of an overlay of distortion."

"How much did you take?"

"750 ug."

"That's three times what I took."

"What was your trip like?"

Tim described it. Doug hadn't made the connection between the lights and people before, but saw the strands of web-like connections far more clearly than Tim had.

"Between people?"

"Between everything. It was faint, but I saw those strands everywhere I looked."

"I wasn't even sure they were there." Tim sipped his own frappuccino. "You haven't slept at all? No dreams?" Doug shook his head.

Tim pulled out his laptop. "Not only did I sleep great, but when I woke up, I had this in my mind." He pulled up the molecule for GOAP II.

Doug's eyes got big. "That's insane," he said, rotating the molecule. "Those are two more agonists at the end of the branches, aren't they?"

Tim nodded.

"What receptors?"

"Dunno."

Doug shook his head incredulously, then his eyes suddenly darted up to a point above Tim's head.

"What?" asked Tim, turning around. There was nothing there but an old Armadillo World Headquarters poster for Captain Beefheart.

"Nothing," said Doug. "Sometimes I catch a glimpse of the distortion pattern I saw out of the corner of my eye."

"Did you ask your DMT guy about it?"

"Yeah. He hasn't answered."

"What sort of pattern is it?"

"No quite a spider, or a spiral, but sort of like both. But it was never clear. And it kept changing." He shook his head again. "Probably just an afterimage. I just need to get some sleep and it will go away."

"Here's a list of ingredients for GOAP II."

Dough looked them over and nodded. "Shouldn't be too hard. I can have this stuff in about a week. But I won't try this monster until you do and say it's safe. I don't like this paranoia."

"Paranoia?"

"You know that pattern I kept seeing? I started to get the impression it was watching me."

. . . • . . .

A week later, Doug slipped him the ingredients for GOAP II. He looked better, saying the barbiturates had worked and he had slept for a solid 14 hours, after which the pattern and paranoia had disappeared.

"Any word from your DMT guy?"

Doug shook his head. "He hasn't been on all week."

They had agreed to not to share any of their results with the underground until Tim was able to synthesize GOAP II.

Tim got to work at once, but the boner-pill project was winding down, which meant he had to schedule his GOAP runs more carefully, as the next hard money project (high temperature formation of self-organizing plastic polymers, something he had covered in his Masters thesis) had no alkaloid angle. Fortunately, he had figured out shortcuts for the existing GOAP steps, and had mentally nailed down all but a few of the additional ones necessary to manufacture GOAP II.

But those last few steps proved elusive. Once again he started feeling mentally fuzzy, sure that his mind wasn't quite firing on all cylinders.

If he was going to finish GOAP II, he needed another dose of GOAP.

Friday night found him in the familiar chair, basketball on TV, laptop open, and a blotter with 500 ug of GOAP on it. He hoped that splitting the difference with Doug's bad trip dose would let him experience the trip more vividly without inducing the paranoia.

At least that was the theory.

At the higher dose the onset was quicker, just shy of 16 minutes, and the visual trails and strobing effects more intense. In fact, the trails behind bright objects looked less like the usual trip visuals than a temporary rifts through which some sort of underlying fractal geometry was briefly visible.

He took notes and solved a benchmark quadratic equation, even faster than the last GOAP trip, but the fractal patterns were making the screen hard to see.

Once again he watched the walls dissolve, which was interesting in and of itself, as he rarely experienced repeat discreet hallucinations. And once again he saw clusters of red glows stretching off into the distance. Those glows were, if anything, clearer than the time before , and this time he was sure he saw the faint webwork of strands that stretched between them.

That suggested two possibilities: Either his first trip had primed him to expect that particular hallucination, or GOAP, in best *Doors of Perception* fashion, was letting him see a real, previously hidden, underlying structure to the world.

He couldn't tell whether the second possibility elated or terrified him. Probably both.

He carefully walked down to the Drag again, wondering what the glowing lights and strands meant. As he walked, the usual clumps of students moved around him, the strands passing through himself and other objects without incident. But looking at people's heads as they passed, he noticed that where before he had seen only a single diffuse glow, he now saw five or six discreet glows sharing a single head, with the glowing strands stretched between them as well as connecting to the glowing areas in other people. He didn't know what to make of it.

The obvious surmise was that the strands were some sort of deep connection between sentient beings. If so, he would have expected those between groups of friends to be brighter or thicker, but looking at people as they passed on the Drag, that didn't seem to be the case. And he had no explanation for the multiple glows.

He wondered if separate glows could be seen in his own head, and if the strands stretched out from it. He wondered if he could see it in a mirror. Assuming it was real, probably not.

He stood across from the West Mall when the first question was answered, as he was able to detect a wispy glowing strand that seemed to originate from somewhere behind his head move and stretch away as the woman it was connected to walked past him, growing ever fainter and thinner until it seemed to disappear.

He fell into step a few paces behind a student in a hoodie, trying to focus on the strand that connected them, but it was puzzlingly elusive; the harder he tried to concentrate on it, the fuzzier and fainter it appeared.

It was while he was doing that that he first noticed it. Something moving out of the corner of his eye. He turned to look but there was nothing but darkness.

As he walked, he kept catching a glimpse of it out of the corner of his eye, some vague swirling shape that disappeared when he tried to look at it.

He'd only had a light dinner and was starting to feel hungry, so he crossed the street and entered Dobie Mall. As he made his way up the escalator, he concentrated on the strand between him and the girl just ahead of him. He should be able to at least determine which part of his head the strand entered, and his inability to do so frustrated him.

That's when he saw the shape again.

In the lighted interior of the mall food court, it stood out more clearly, a sort of spiral-shaped fractal pattern with tendrils radiating from it. It wasn't any sort of color, only a wavering disturbance in the air. But when he turned to look at it directly, it seemed to skitter away to the periphery of his vision.

No quite a spider, or a spiral, but sort of like both.

The thought that he was seeing what Doug had seen chilled him.

"Hi, what can I get you?"

Tim found he was at the counter of the cookie store, and snapped his gaze back from the shape to the menu choices.

"Uh...two chocolate chip cookies, please," he said, looking through her face to the five separate glowing regions inside her head. "And a lemonade."

While she was getting his cookies, he turned to see if he could catch a glimpse of the shape. It was still there, if a bit fainter, but it slid away from his gaze again.

While he sat and ate his cookies, he tried concentrating on a glowing strand connecting his head to a bearded diner at another table. The more he concentrated the fuzzier it got.

But as he concentrated, the swirling shape became clearer, a fractal disturbance that, while still only visible out of the corner of his eye, seemed to grow larger as he concentrated on the strand.

No, not larger. *Closer.*

Suddenly fearful, he snapped his gaze away from the pattern and toward the TV, which was showing some sort of sporting event, the trip visuals apparent there but more muted than earlier. As he watched, the pattern seemed to move back away, until it seemed to fade out altogether.

Strange. Was it a hallucination? The location at the periphery of his vision suggested so, just another tweak of his visual cortex and part of the usual complex of psychedelic effects. But what if it wasn't? What if it, the glowing points, and the lines were all part of some underlying reality that only GOAP made him aware of? Was the pattern he kept seeing some sort of hostile entity?

He shook his head. That sort of thinking lead to Doug's paranoia. He lived in the real world. GOAP might briefly rewire his brain, but it couldn't have any affect on reality outside of his own head, one devoid of angels, demons, machine elves or killer spirals.

As he left the mall, he caught a glimpse of the pattern again, small, discreet and visible, back at the edge of his vision.

It seemed to follow him all the way home.

. . . . • . . .

He woke early Saturday morning, his brain humming, too buzzed to continue sleeping.

He knew how to finish GOAP II.

After a hasty shower and breakfast, he went in to Welch, the solutions for the tricky process steps ridiculously clear in his mind. In fact, he thought there was a good chance he could bang them out that day.

But that wasn't all. He also saw a way to advance his polymer project months ahead of schedule. While GOAP II was in a reduction phase, he whipped out a three page proposal on the polymer project and sent it off to the project sponsor and the dean for approval.

So far, GOAP was living up its billing and then some. He could hardly imagine the effect of GOAP II.

Every now and then, he seemed to catch a faint glimpse of the distortion pattern out of the corner of his eye. He ignored it.

. . . . • . . .

Uou look like hell," said Tim.

Doug just grunted, sipping his latte. The dark circles were back, and his eyes darted around the room. "Problems sleeping again," he said at last.

"Did you see that spiral spider thing again?"

"Sometimes. Not too often now. Occasionally in my sleep, chasing me."

"That why you can't sleep?"

"I've got other dreams." Doug shook his head. "What's up?"

"I saw the spider spiral thing too."

Doug's eyes widened. "No shit? When?"

"After I took 500 ug of GOAP."

"You sure it was what I was seeing?"

"A sort of spiral shaped, fractal disturbance with waving, radiating arms?"

Doug nodded. "That's it. What do you think?"

"I think it's just GOAP tricking your visual cortex, making you see things out of the corner of your eyes."

"That both of us saw?"

Tim shrugged. "A spiral is a pretty universal shape, and a lot of people see fractal shapes when tripping."

"What if it's real?"

"A real what?"

Doug shook his head. "I don't know. But I've never had something like that come back to me again and again days after a trip."

"Maybe it's just a little mental housekeeping. Your mind moving things from short term to long-term storage, just like REM sleep."

"So you haven't had any problems?"

"No, quite the opposite," He said, pulling a small package out of his pocket and placing it on Doug's plate.

"What's this?"

"GOAP II."

Doug fingered the package uncertainly. "That was fast."

"I figured out all the process roadblocks after my last trip. I think that one of the effects of GOAP is enhanced intelligence."

"How could it do that?"

"Don't know, I'm not a neurologist. Maybe activating those receptors encourages dendritic branching, or helps clean toxins or plaques out of the brain. Some studies showed LSD helping Alzheimer's patients remember better. I don't know. But it seems to work that way on me. You haven't noticed anything like that?"

Doug shook his head. "It just gives me weird dreams."

"What kind of weird?"

Doug sighed and spread his hands. "I can't even describe it. A normal dream, I'm getting laid or taking a test naked or there's a leak in my ceiling. At least I know what's going on. These, I have no clue. They don't have people in them."

"What do they have?"

Dough shook his head again. "I can't describe it. But I seem to wake up more tired than before I went to bed."

"Still taking the downers?"

"I stopped. Maybe I'll have to start again, at least temporarily."

"Well you probably do need to do something. Sorry you had such a bad trip."

"Oh, the trip itself was great. It's the come-down that's wearing me out."

"Here anything from the DMT guy?"

"No. As far as I can tell, he and the other guys on that mailing list have all dropped out of sight."

"Well, there's another meth crackdown going on nationally. That's a pretty good reason to lay low."

"Maybe," said Doug, checking his cell phone. "Look, I gotta go," he said, getting up and finishing off his latte.

"You want this?" asked Tim, picking the GOAP II bundle off the table and offering it to him. Doug hesitate a minute, then took it and slipped it into his pocket. "We'll see. Maybe I just need some sleep."

"Do that. And take care."

. . . . • . . . .

That week he seemed like the golden boy. The project sponsor approved his polymer proposal, the dean was impressed, and everything was ahead of schedule.

The only drawback was that Friday night was the only slot he could get hands-on time to demonstrate the ultracentrifuge for his graduate class, which meant sampling GOAP II would have to wait until Saturday.

He was in the middle of the demonstration when he got a call, so he let it go to voicemail. When he checked after class he saw it was from Doug and only ten seconds long.

He hit play.

He heard Doug breathing heavy for a few seconds, as though he were running. "They're coming for me!" he said between gasps of breath. "Don't—"

Then the call ended.

Who was coming for him? The police?

He called back. The phone rang a few times, then went to voicemail. "Hey Doug, it's me," he said. "Sorry you went to voicemail, but I was teaching a class. Give me a call and let me know what's up." Best not to leave anything that might be construed as evidence.

He briefly wondered if he should flush GOAP II, but hated to see all that work go to waste. He was eager to see if it improved upon the intelligence-enhancing capabilities of the original. Plus he knew the compound itself was too new to be on any drug schedule list, or else he would have heard about it as part of his liaison duties.

By the time Tim went to bed Doug still hadn't called back.

. . . • . . .

After a breakfast of scrambled eggs, bacon and toast, Tim found himself in the familiar chair, TV on, computer open, and a blotter with 250 ug of GOAP II beside him. He tried calling Doug one last time, but it just went to voicemail again.

He put the blotter under his tongue.

Less than 10 minutes later, the trip kicked in hard, waves of ever-changing fractals washing across his vision, melting the walls.

After a moment the waves receded, and Tim looked on the vast array of glowing lights and network of lines more clearly than ever before, stretching everywhere around him and into the distance. Looking more closely, he could see tiny lights racing through the lines between people, some steadily, some in bursts. It was like watching packet throughput on a network monitoring tool.

Once again he walked down to the Drag, anxious for a closer look at how those lights and lines intersected with people. The more he looked, the more convinced he became that it was indeed some sort of information network connecting every person to every other.

He suspected he could tap into and understand the data being passed back and forth. He imagined himself reaching up and grabbing the nearest conduit, then plugging it into his own mind—

And it worked.

In an instant, a vast flow of information flooded into him. And he *knew.*

The glowing points and flows of data he saw belonged not to people, but to *another form of life entirely.* They existed not just apart from humanity, but on *top* of it.

Human consciousness was the computational substrate that underpinned their world.

He staggered against a light post, overwhelmed by the knowledge. And as he stood there stunned, he saw the fractal spiral shape materialize out of the air.

Then another.

Then another.

All headed toward him.

He started to run, but knew there was nowhere to hide. The spiral patterns weren't creatures, weren't conscious at all, but merely low-level functions ensuring the integrity of the network.

By understanding the true nature of the world, Tim had accidentally triggered a recursive loop. A piece of the network had suddenly become self-aware, and thus unstable.

In his last few seconds of life, Tim wondered if Doug had ever understood the nature of the doom GOAP had triggered.

Tim had become a bad sector, and was about to be reformatted.

. . . .

Joe R. Lansdale

delivers his twisted take

on the classic tale of

a boy and his dog

and aliens.

. . . .

||||||||||||||||||||||||||||||||||||||||||||||||||||||||||||||||||||||||||||||||

Rex

Joe R. Lansdale

||||||||||||||||||||||||||||||||||||||||||||||||||||||||||||||||||||||||||

Benny was at his open bedroom window looking at the stars through his telescope when the space ship fell silently out of the sky, drifted like a feather behind a great row of trees in the distance, and went out of sight. There was a white puff of smoke, then nothing.

"Rex," Benny said. "Did you see that?"

Rex, the family dog, a Great Dane, was lying on Benny's bed, and he hadn't seen a thing. He hadn't been thinking about a thing. He lifted his head.

"A space ship," Benny said.

The dog said nothing, of course.

"We ought to go look."

Benny paused. "No. I should tell Mom and Dad... Oh, that won't work. They don't like being woke up, and who's going to believe me?"

That was when Benny realized the only thing to do was go take a look himself. If he could find the ship, then he would be able to take his dad there and show it to him. He could even pretend he wanted him to go for a different reason, because that whole "I saw a spaceship fall out of the sky and hit the earth without making noise" was not going to fly.

Benny moved the telescope, shrugged out of his pajamas, put on his clothes, and climbed out the window. "Rex, come on, boy."

Rex got off the bed and bounded through the window. They raced like wind blown shadows across the yard, ran toward the great line of trees beyond. It took a while to get there, and when they did, they had to ease down a hill and cross a creek. They went through the woods, Benny thinking on things, trying to figure where the ship might have landed.

The forest trail was narrow, but Benny had been down it many times before with Rex. Rex was always with him. Rex never failed as a loyal dog. Rex even took the lead, Benny thinking it was because he was hoping he might startle a sleeping bunny, scare up some low nesting birds. Then, smack dab in the middle of the trail, where it widened, right before the trees broke into a clearing on the other side, they saw it.

It was at an angle. It had knocked down a couple of trees and smacked part of the way into the ground. The wound it had made in the earth was what was holding it up. It was a small space ship, a saucer. It was maybe the size of Benny's bedroom.

There was a round portal in its side and it was open. A bit of white smoke drifted out of it, but that soon turned clear. Benny could only see darkness through the gap. A thought occurred to him. Whoever had flown the machine might have gotten out of the saucer and was wandering about. Or maybe it had only opened the portal and had not been able to get out. Maybe whatever had been in the saucer was still there, and injured.

Benny looked around, found a bit of limb that had fallen off a tree. It was small enough to handle, big enough for a club. If he could get on board and bean him a man from outer space, kill him, then he would be hero. He could say it had a ray gun or something. No. They'd look and not find one. That wouldn't do. Whatever. There was a good lie to be told, all he had to do was tell it, because the rest of it was real. There was a space ship in the woods and he was here with it. Him and Rex.

Easing up on the ship, Benny came to the gap and looked inside. Dark. Nothing else. Just dark. It was scary.

Benny put a hand on the ship to step up through the hole, and found he could lift it. Lift the whole thing, the entire ship. It occurred to him it might be cardboard, that he may have seen a special kind of kite fall, and this was it. He had been fooled.

No. This was no kite. Too big for that. The answer was simple. It was made out of very light material; some kind of super space science. Benny sat the saucer down so that it rested in the middle of the trail, where the clearing started.

Rex put both paws on the gap, looked inside the ship and growled.

"Its still in there?" Benny said.

Rex wagged his tail.

"Go get it," Benny said. "Kill it. You get it down, I'll come in with the stick."

Rex turned his head and looked at Benny.

"Go get it," Benny said again.

Rex didn't want to go, that was easy to see. But Benny kept urging him, and faithful as always, Rex climbed inside with a bit of a boost from Benny. Benny could hear Rex running around in there, hear his paws scuffing over the floor. After awhile Rex barked. Then there was silence.

Benny called for Rex, but Rex didn't come out.

All of a sudden, Benny didn't want to hit the space man anymore. He didn't want to be there. He felt sorry for Rex, but in a case like this everyone was on their own.

Benny threw down the limb and darted back the way he had come, over the creek up the hill, across the clearing, and climbed back through his bedroom window.

He sat for a long time on the edge of the bed looking out at the night. And then he saw the craft lifting up from behind the trees. Whatever had been wrong with it had been repaired. It was leaving, and he had no way to prove it had been there. He wondered if Rex were inside. He watched it rise high, and then there was a puff, and it looked like plant seeds were scattering and falling out of the sky.

Poor dog, Benny thought. But, he could get another one.

He fell asleep.

When he awoke it was to an awful smell. He looked up into Rex's face. The dog was on the bed, standing over him, panting, and its breath was awful.

"Rex, you made it back."

The dog sat down on the bed and studied Benny for a long time.

"You abandoned me," said the dog.

Benny was stunned. "You spoke."

"Yes. My name is Zinx. I am also Rex now. I was damaged, the dog was not. I have taken over his mind and body. I am speaking my thoughts to you, not words. But you hear them as words. You were going to kill me. Rex told me. I was dying, and you were going to hit me with a stick. Rex here, he licked my hand, all seven fingers. It was gummy, a little unpleasant, but I can read minds, and he meant well. I took over his body and I control his mind, mostly. We share this body and mind, actually. Rex and I both agree, you are a little scum."

"So...you're the one in the spaceship?"

"You're also not very quick, are you, Benny? I just told you that. I sent the ship back into space. It would only go so far and disintegrate. It no longer had the power to go back home. Only to rise up high enough and break into many small pieces; a mechanism designed to keep our craft from being discovered. I was able to get it to float that high. That way the evidence is destroyed. But me, I had to stay behind. Inside Rex. And you know what, Benny? I meant it when I said Rex is in here with me still, and he has his own thoughts. I like him. I really do. There's something fine and noble and loyal and simple about Rex. You know what he tells me?"

Benny shook his head.

"That he is a faithful dog and you are an unfaithful boy, and that you left him to me, not knowing what I would do to him, not caring, and it's only a miracle that I'm not an evil alien. Thoughts to that effect."

"Holy cow," Benny said.

"Yep," said Rex/Zinx. "And Benny, now that we are such good friends, don't try and tell anyone I'm from outer space and inside the dog. They'll just think you're an idiot. Just live with your knowledge.

But Benny..."

"What?"

"Watch your back, kid. Because Rex does not forget."

About a week later Benny got hit and killed by a car down on Main Street. A woman who saw the whole thing said Benny and the dog that was with him were crossing the street, doing all right, and there was a car coming, and she said the dog rose up on its hind paws and pushed Benny with its front paws. She said she figured the dog was smart, that the dog was trying to shove Benny out of the way of the car, but instead had pushed him right into it. She said she thought it was because dogs didn't have good depth perception; she had read that somewhere. It was a terrible accident. Benny was knocked right out of his shoes and dragged under the car for a block before the car could stop.

The dog, called Rex by the family, ran away and was not seen by its owners again. But the same woman who saw the accident swore she saw the dog again, later that day, when she was coming out of the police department, after filing her report. She said the dog was driving away in a car. Her story was the dog was a big one, and could easily reach the pedals on that little foreign car, had a front leg hanging out the window, and was driving with the other, its mouth open, its tongue dangling.

It was silly, but everyone liked the lady and tried to be as agreeable as possible. To make matters worse, and what made the woman adamant she knew what she was talking about, was a small foreign car got stolen that very same day. And to worsen matters even more, the car belonged to the family of the poor boy who got ran over and killed on Main Street.

. . . .

On an alien world, illegal packaged

atmospheres come at price. How far

will someone go to please the one they

love? Nicky Draden questions the cost of

nostalgia, honor, and romance.

. . . .

The Atmosphere Man

Nicky Drayden

Anise tells me things. Things she really shouldn't. I've mentioned it to her, reminding her about doctor-patient confidentiality and all that. But over the past ten years, I've become more like a sounding board to her than a husband. She talks past me, words flowing freely like an O_2 pipe with a blown pressure valve.

She apologizes profusely for being late to dinner, says her last appointment ran long. Kitpeh, her young Errtyllian patient, had a major setback. She'd shown up to their session with her tail bandaged, hints of blue and green bruises peeking from underneath. My wife doesn't think it was an accident, but Kitpeh wouldn't tell her what had happened. She suspects Kitpeh's foster parents had a hand in it.

Anise is so caught up in the minutia of her day that she doesn't notice how upset I am as I place flanks of herbed otterboar upon our dinner plates. They'd been perfectly tender an hour and a half ago — such a delicious shade of pinkish brown, but now the skin is dried and buckling away from the meat. The tulip centerpiece I'd bribed the Station's horticulturalist for has already begun to wilt.

"... so I don't want to accuse them without sound evidence," Anise says, taking a seat at the dining table. "Her foster parents don't have any previous reports of abuse, and it's tough to find someone who's willing to take in an Errtyllian, even one who's had her claws amputated." Anise shakes her head, then whips her cloth napkin into her lap. "I'm going to try to get her to open up to me tomorrow. We'll get out of my office and walk around the Station, maybe all the way down to the Newtonian Arboretum for some fresh air. I bet seeing some of the trees from her home world would put her at ease."

I press my lips together, hoping she'll notice the lengths I'd gone through to recreate that special night — the meal I'd scarcely been able to afford and the variegated tulips I'd spent half of my water rations to raise from bulbs. It'd been worth it to see her eyes light up, and even now, all these years later, I still remember the way her smile made me feel like we were the last two people in the universe.

Anise looks up at me, down at her plate, up at me.

"Oh, Harlan," she says, smacking the side of her head. "Happy Anniversary. You must think I'm awful."

"We've all got our priorities." My words come out more spiteful than I'd intended. How can I hold a grudge against someone whose passion is piecing together the lives of broken children? I fondle the velvet box in my pocket, wondering how my wife and I had managed to lead such amazingly fulfilling lives, and yet still be drifting apart from each other.

Anise's lips screw up into a sour pucker. "Don't make this all about me. You're the one who's gone four nights a week, harassing innocent people just because they have scales or blue skin or claws."

"We don't profile, Anise. We act on solid evidence. Same as you. Only instead of keeping children from destroying themselves, VACI keeps people from destroying the Station." I want to keep going, to tell her about all of the Errtyllian terror plots that Vero Avalon Central Intelligence has foiled, but I bite my tongue. There's no point in dredging up old arguments that I thought we'd put to rest years ago. I heave a sigh, then retrieve the velvet box from my pocket and slide it across the table towards her.

"Harlan, I can't — "

"Let's not fight. Not tonight."

Anise takes the box. I can tell she's embarrassed about not having a gift in return. She looks up at me, but our eyes don't quite meet. "It's not Argonian pearls, is it? I won't wear them. They use slave labor to harvest them, you know."

I know. I'd made that mistake three anniversaries ago. She'd given me an earful about how after all the years we'd been together, I didn't know her at all. But this year's gift will be different. It'll show her how much she means to me, and the lengths I'll go through to keep us from drifting further apart.

Anise pops the top open, then takes out the small aluminum canister. It's heavier than she'd anticipated, and she nearly drops it. "Air? You got me air for our anniversary."

"Not just any air. Twenty-two pounds of atmosphere. From Earth."

The blood drains from Anise's face. She puts the canister into the box and pushes it back. "Earth air is contraband," she whispers to me.

I raise an eyebrow. As if I of all people wouldn't know that. "I thought you'd like it. It's a little piece of your old life."

"It's a little piece of a twenty-year prison sentence is what it is! How could you bring this into our home?" Anise glares at the box, so much longing behind her eyes. Her chest rises and falls, lips glistening ever so slightly. I'll never understand the draw of reminiscing over a dead planet, but then again, I was born on Vero Avalon — a babe among the stars. I'd been to several dozen planets, but never found myself attached to any particular one. But Earth is a part of Anise. Always has been and always will be.

"Relax," I say. "This can't be traced to us. I've got a source, and I can promise you he won't be talking."

"You have a *source*?" She scoffs and rolls her eyes, but I notice that she hasn't taken her hand from the box.

A smile creeps up onto my lips. I nod nonchalantly, pretending as if this little gift hadn't cost me two months' salary, and possibly my career if anyone with VACI ever finds out.

I'd arranged a meeting with The Atmosphere Man a few months ago, at a little thatched hut bar in Whennyho City. The resort had been terraformed from a barren moon — a sloppy, rush-job with a fuck-ton of cheap, fast growing obich palms boasting broad waxy leaves. Minimal biodiversity. The whole place would be dead again in fifty years, probably less. But the beaches were plentiful, and the drinks cheap, as were the women. And its proximity to Gamma Port made it the ideal getaway for the typical middle class schlep that I'd been posing as.

He was taller than I'd expected. Taller than his VACI file listed him as at least. He leaned against the rattan bar, swatting at the green and silver bloatflies buzzing about his drink — a nauseatingly pink concoction with a matching toothpick umbrella. He made contact with one of the flies, and it careened past my ear like a drunken zitherball, its swollen body rupturing on impact with the wall. I tried to hold my breath, but too late, the stench of partially digested fruit infiltrated my lungs. I coughed.

The Atmosphere Man saw me and waved me over. "Jedd? Good to meet you!" He shook my hand in both of his. He was older, in his sixties, with tan discoloration along his face and chest that most would think were age spots and not pseudo-recessive Jorahn genes. It also explained the height.

"Wolosalai!" I said to him, the fabricated Whennyhoan greeting that pretty much meant "I'm here to get shit-faced, how 'bout you?"

"Wolosalai, brother." His eyes narrowed. I don't know what it was — my walk, my smell, the way I parted my hair — but I could tell he'd made me. Still he smiled wide, and offered me a seat on the barstool next to him.

"You're here to talk atmosphere," he said.

"You *are* The Atmosphere Man."

"I did this dump, you know. Not some of my better work. Seems like everyone with an investor and a big enough rock is throwing together these porta-planets." A breeze blew in through the open-air bar. The Atmosphere Man lifted his nose, parted his lips, breathed in his creation. "Smell that? Twelve parts Sea Breeze, three parts Lush Tropical Vegetation, one part Fishing Boat, one part Passion Fruit, and just a smidge of Venereal Disease to keep people honest."

I eyed the silhouettes of fishing boats off the coast. All a part of the illusion. There wasn't a single fish in the Whennyhoan Ocean — an "ocean" that was fifteen meters at its deepest.

I took a sniff for myself. "Impressive. Hard to imagine this whole atmosphere coming out of a little canister."

"Several thousand little canisters for a rock this size, but yes. You starting a porta-planet of your own, or are you just looking for a souvenir? I can get you a thousand pounds of Whennyho City for a couple hundred kalax. Plus local and Eastern Cascade taxes, of course. Just pop it into your air intake, and it'll smell like you're on vacation all year 'round!" The Atmosphere Man was teasing me. A man of his sort wouldn't dabble with souvenir canisters.

"Actually, I had something quite different in mind." I leaned in close to his ear. "I'm looking to get my hands on some Earth air."

The Atmosphere Man feigned shock. "That'd be illegal, Jedd!"

"And very profitable." I handed him a flimsy duffle bag with "Whennyho City Resorts" screen-printed on both sides. The zipper was cheaply made as well, and barely functional, but nevertheless, The Atmosphere Man forced it open and peeked inside at the stacks of kalax. It wasn't a fortune, maybe half as much as he'd gotten to air up this place, but I was betting that the paper I clutched in my hand would be much more valuable to him. I laid it out on the bar and dropped my charade. "Before you make any decisions, I want you to know that this is a personal matter, not a professional one. Still, if you're agreeable to this trade, I can make these VACI files disappear."

The Atmosphere Man swiped his finger across the sheet, looking at twenty years worth of dirt VACI had accumulated on him. Admittedly it wasn't much. Not even a real name to go with the blurred surveillance photos. He was quite the illusive criminal, always managing to stay just to the right of VACI's radar, but I'd invested more than a healthy amount of man hours strategically digging through the details of his exploits — pole-skimming on environmentally sensitive planets, bribing and blackmailing members of the Open-Air Alliance, and of course, dealing in contraband atmosphere.

"Why are you doing this?" The Atmosphere Man asked.

"For my wife. She's Earthborne." Despite myself, I flinched at the word. It was a mild slur used for those who'd stayed behind after the Major Exodus, and the next dozen or so of the minor ones. The stubborn people who refused to admit that the Earth was dying.

"You don't say. Not many of them made it off."

"She was lucky." I was lucky. I couldn't imagine not having her in my life. And there I was in the presence of a known criminal, begging him to help me keep her.

"There's no shame in thinking you can change the inevitable," The Atmosphere Man said, sucking the boifruit off the pointed tip of his toothpick umbrella. "They fought a good fight. Repopulated a couple seas, found a vaccination to combat the dais blight, decontaminated the runoff from dozens of thermonuclear bombsites. Who knows, if they'd started a few years earlier, maybe they would have succeeded."

"Perhaps."

The Atmosphere Man leaned back, his elbow propped casually against the bar. "What you're asking could get you into a fair amount of trouble if you're caught."

"I won't get caught."

"So sure of yourself, are you? This wife of yours ... " The Atmosphere Man shifted forward on his stool, fingers steepled at his lips. Flecks of gold rimmed his irises, and in the span of milliseconds, the thin membrane of secondary lids blinked across his eyes. I wondered if any other VACI agents had ever gotten so close to him.

"What about her?" I said, gravel in my voice.

"You're sure she's worth it? I mean, one slip of my tongue and your whole world could come crashing down, faster than one of these porta-planets."

A threat. But I too could play that game. "Oh, she's worth it, Yoris."

The Atmosphere Man's eyes bulged at hearing his name. His spots darkened, then faded again. He nodded, then shoved the VACI sheet inside his duffle bag, struggling with the zipper before finally giving up. "Ah, well. Send Anise my best, then, will you?"

I tensed. He'd known my identity before I'd walked into this humid pit-stain of a bar. The Atmosphere Man swatted another bloatfly to the ground, stomped its juicy carcass, then left without another word.

The next morning I woke to the smell of Whennyho City blowing through an open window that had been shut and locked when I'd gone to sleep. On my nightstand sat a small aluminum canister with a bloatfly buzzing futilely next to it, wings pinned to the cheap wood veneer with a pink toothpick umbrella.

I couldn't go back on my word. Not if I didn't want to end up like that fly. I quickly dressed and shoved the canister into my pocket. I nearly dropped it. It was a lot heavier than I'd expected. My VACI badge got me through Gamma Port customs without any problem, and yet I kept checking over my shoulder to make sure no one was onto me. The concourse was filled with harried vacationers in gaudy flower-print shirts, with dewy-eyed newlyweds — some tentacled, some scaled, some blue, some with tails, all with that same sappy-assed look — like they could plunge face first into a gravity well and everything would be all right because they still had each other. God, I missed that feeling. Back in my office on Vero Avalon Station, I ran a recursion program to erase all traces of The Atmosphere Man from the rimNet. The guilt wrung from my heart as I realized that after a decade of sapping the life from my marriage, VACI owed me this one indiscretion.

"I can't believe you actually did this," Anise says, opening the velvet box once again. Her words feel heavy, teeming with an awkward mix of emotions.

I don't say anything, because there is nothing left for me to say. She holds the canister for a long moment, then goes over to the atmos unit, dials the particle filter to low, the pathogen filter to max, and plugs the Earth air into the manual intake.

Anise pours herself a glass of twenty-year-old Tungsian wine and settles into the sofa. She breathes in deeply as the air begins to circulate. I do the opposite, shallow breaths through parted lips, but it doesn't do much to dull the sting in my nostrils, the stench at the back of my throat, the fire in my lungs.

I stifle a cough.

"I'd almost forgotten acid rain," Anise sighs, her eyes suddenly far, far away. "Towards the end, it could eat through steel. We had to replace our roofs every eight weeks. Fran — I've told you about Fran — she got caught out in it once. Not long, just half a minute. Poor thing spent the next six months getting skin grafts and reconstructive surgery." She says all this with longing, not a hint of bitterness.

I can't fathom what she finds so pleasurable about this. The Earth is a perfect stranger to me, distant and unknowable, but the only way I'll begin to learn is if I engage in this moment. I stop holding my breath. All I smell is soot. "What is that, the prominent smell? Factory smoke?" I'd heard of the abundance of factories, refineries, and industrial centers puffing clouds of black up into the atmosphere.

Anise shakes her head. "They were all abandoned by then, no one left to run them once the dais blight hit. We napalmed towns for many years before we found the vaccination. Dogs, cats, livestock, people — anyone who'd eaten or handled infected plant material became a host to fungal spores. It was the only way to keep it from spreading faster than it did."

"That must have been awful." I sit down beside her, lay a hand on her thigh.

Anise takes another long sip from her wine. "It was what it was. But through it all, we were always able to cling to hope. We fought hard every second of our lives, and because of that, each breath we took became something precious."

I try to imagine how powerful this scent memory is for her, but I'd grown up with sterilized, formulated air — any odors that happened to occur during my formative years were sucked up through the filters and scrubbed clean before they could imprint on my memories.

"It's sort of ... beautiful," I say, but she finally looks directly at me with hard, spiteful eyes. I see I've said the exact wrong thing.

"I don't expect for you to understand."

We're sitting inches from each other, and yet the rift between us grows. I thought the Earth air would fix things between us, but it's only highlighted how different we really are. I think of her patient, Kitpeh, a wounded creature with so much anger seeded into her DNA. Sooner or later, despite all of the hours Anise spends with her, Kitpeh will slip up. She'll assault someone or make threats against the Station, and she'll end up on VACI's watch list. It's inevitable, and yet Anise keeps trying to save her. It makes no sense to me — all those resources poured into a cup with a crack running through the bottom.

"There's no shame in trying to change the inevitable," I repeat The Atmosphere Man's words, searching for understanding, but Anise thinks that I'm talking to her. She moves her hand on top of mine, and the void between us feels a little warmer at least.

When we make love that night, it's like there's a stranger in the room with us. I taste him in her mouth — her saliva like a spray of napalm scorching my tongue. I try to ignore him, but with each passionate breath I take, the soot of dead bodies tickles my lungs. Tears stream down Anise's cheeks. She writhes underneath me and calls out my name, but from the distant look in her eyes, I can tell it is the stranger she holds most dearly in her heart.

Tenderly, I kiss her cheek, her bitter tears tasting of acid rain. "Happy Anniversary, Love," I whisper, ready to fight the good fight, and hoping beyond hope that I'm not a few years too late.

One of the two reprinted stories in

this collection, Denton's lyrical piece

functions as an ideal companion to his

award-winning novel **Buddy Holly is**

Alive and Well on Ganymede *as well as a*

stand alone tale of ghostly Hollywood.

La Bamba Boulevard

Bradley Denton

It was my first visit to Hollywood, and I was fascinated by Hollywood Boulevard after dark: The souvenir shops, nudie bars, lingerie boutiques, dance clubs, pickup joints, and Scientology museums, all decked out in bright white lights and red, blue, and green neon. The worn-down granite-and-brass Walk of Fame stars on the sidewalk. The occasional whiff, an actual odor, of something that had once been alive that was now in an advanced stage of decay. The throngs of tourists with their cameras and baggy shorts. The beautiful young people strutting in their precarious heels, abundant hair, and not much else, just hoping to be seen by someone, anyone, who might actually matter.

Oh, and hucksters galore. I'm talking about the dudes who'll not only ask you for money, but will follow you for a block complimenting your clothes or your wife and trying to force their homemade compact discs into your hands. I'm talking about the buskers who'll shove their hats in front of you as you try to walk by. And especially, I'm talking about the street performers dressed as movie stars who'll approach you in character, cajoling you into paying to have your photo taken with them. Marilyn Monroe, Luke Skywalker, Humphrey Bogart, and Spider-Man are all there on the Boulevard on any given night. To name but a few. Marilyn, in particular, will zero in on you just to save you from being lonely. Even if you're not.

As I said to a Los Angeles writer friend as we strolled the Boulevard on my first night there, the first Monday in September: "It's like Vegas, only less genuine."

But I should have known better than to be a smartass about how others live their lives. Sooner or later, that sort of thing will come back and bite you in the backside.

What happened was, I returned to the Boulevard the next night. But this time, I came alone. It was late, and I couldn't sleep, so I'd decided I might as well go take a look at the celebrity body-part prints at Grauman's Chinese Theater. My writer friend and I hadn't walked far enough west from my Hollywood-and-Vine hotel to do that on Monday. And the truth, despite my avowed disdain for contemporary celebrity culture, was that I really wanted to see Grauman's. Mainly so I could confirm the truth of what Hedley Lamarr had said about Douglas Fairbanks at the end of *Blazing Saddles*.

On the way there, as I looked down at the Hollywood Walk of Fame stars passing by, I came across a surprise — a name I knew. That was a rare occurrence on this particular stretch of the Boulevard, so I stopped and pulled my camera from my pocket while the tourists, posers, and freaks flowed around me as if I were a lump of stone in their glitzy stream.

Yes, I had a camera. This particular night I was wearing khaki jeans and a white shirt, not baggy shorts, but there was no point in trying to pretend I was one of the few middle-aged hipster locals. No, I was just a tourist like all the others. And I doubted I'd ever be back in Hollywood again, so I was taking photos of anything that struck me as interesting, weird, excessive, or perverse. I'd been seeing a lot of the weird, excessive, and perverse . . . but this time, I was simply and purely interested.

You see, the name on the star at my feet was Ritchie Valens. And while his star was in pretty good shape, it had obviously been there a number of years.

"Dang, Ritchie," I said to myself as I pointed the camera downward. "You made it here before Buddy."

Ritchie Valens, of course, had died in a plane crash along with Buddy Holly and J.P. "the Big Bopper" Richardson on February 3, 1959. Now here it was September 6, 2011, and Buddy would finally be getting his own Walk of Fame star the following morning. Which was why I had pried myself out of my cozy Austin home to come to L.A. in the first place. As anyone who knows me will tell you, I'm a big Buddy Holly fan. Oh, and by the way, water is wet.

As I was trying to focus my shot, the toes of a pair of snakeskin boots appeared on my camera's LCD screen, just to the right of Ritchie's star.

"Hey, Buddy's not gonna be <u>here</u>," a clear, young male voice said. "He's gonna be back the way you came, over on Vine Street by Capitol Records. They're putting him next to the Beatles. I can show you, if you like."

Annoyed, I shifted my camera so the snakeskin boots were out of frame, then snapped a picture that included the toe of one of my own shoes. I would have to crop it out of the shot later.

Once I had my photo, I looked up, glanced to my right, and saw a broad-faced but handsome young Hispanic man dressed in a sharp navy-blue suit with white piping and a ruffled white shirt with no necktie. He had a sunburst Fender Stratocaster guitar at his waist, hanging from a snazzy black leather strap. The strap had the same high gloss as the young man's thick, neatly-combed hair.

He was the picture of youthful talent and exuberance. So I had to hand it to him. He had the late Mr. Valenzuela's look down pat.

"Ritchie Valens, right?" I said. "Nice job." I didn't have any cash on me for a tip or a photo, but I thought the kid at least deserved a compliment for authenticity.

He smiled. "Hey, you recognized me!"

I smiled back. "Sure. And thank you for your offer, but I already know where Buddy's star is going to be. All I meant was that you received your star first. Have a good night, now." I started westward toward Grauman's again.

But the Ritchie character came with me, matching my stride, and I grimaced. This was what I got for speaking to one of these jokers.

"Well, look at it this way," Ritchie said. "L.A. is my hometown. I was born in Pacoima. So, you know, they had to honor the native son. And it's not like they just gave it to me the moment I died. I had to wait until 1990."

I didn't say anything in reply, even though those were good points.

"Besides," Ritchie continued, "isn't it cool that Buddy'll get his star on his 75th birthday? Not a bad present, if you ask me."

I still didn't respond. Maybe if I stayed quiet, he'd get the message and leave me alone.

He moved closer to avoid colliding with a pack of young bucks in sparkly suits, and the headstock of his Strat whapped me on the elbow. It sent an electric jolt up to my right shoulder, and I flinched away, which made my left shoulder ram into a No Parking sign.

Now I was beyond annoyed. I glared at Ritchie and walked faster.

But Ritchie, still smiling, sped up as well. "You're going to Buddy's unveiling ceremony tomorrow, right?" He didn't wait for me to answer. "That's good. That means you'll get to see him."

We had reached the sidewalk in front of Grauman's Chinese, where Marilyn, Luke, Darth Vader, Bogie, and SpongeBob Squarepants, among others, were all accosting passersby with snappy, seductive patter and sporadic lightsaber battles. Meanwhile, watching it all, Spider-Man was crouched atop a garbage can chained to a lamppost.

I stopped walking and looked at Ritchie.

"Yes, I'll see Buddy's Walk of Fame star tomorrow, along with everyone else," I said. "But I don't think I'll see Buddy. You guys only come out at night."

Ritchie's eyes widened, and then he threw back his head and laughed. It was loud and chiming, and it echoed back from the tall, ornate facade of Grauman's. But no one else on the sidewalk seemed to notice.

I tried to step around him to get to the plaza in front of the theater where all the movie stars had left their marks. But at that moment Ritchie stopped laughing and swung the neck of his guitar to block my way.

"You're wrong," he said then, his voice suddenly serious. "You'll see Buddy tomorrow. You'll see him over and over again. In the flesh. I'll make you a bet on that."

I began glancing around for a police officer, but the only one I saw in the milling crowd was RoboCop.

All right, then. Maybe if I humored Ritchie, he'd bug off. "Okay," I said. "What's the bet?"

Ritchie grinned. "If I'm wrong, and you don't see Buddy, I'll play any song you want as long as it's not 'La Bamba.' And if I'm right, you promise to do two things tomorrow before midnight: One must be something new and different that you haven't done before, but that you plan to do again. And the other must be something new and different that you haven't done before, but that you'll *never* do again. And I'll still play any song you want as long as it's not 'La Bamba.'"

I'd been expecting him to work things around to the subject of getting his picture taken for cash. But instead, after stating the terms of the bet, he just stood there with his Strat, grinning and waiting.

"Uh . . . what the hell kind of bet is that?" I asked.

Ritchie shook his head. "Oh, no. Ain't nobody going to hell!" He lowered the guitar, stepped closer, and spoke into my ear before I could back away. "Let me explain. I only lived seventeen years. Seventeen! Even Buddy had five more years than I had, and J.P. had a few more than that. And *you've* already had, what, almost twice what J.P. had? Three times what I had? But while each one of us did something new and different almost every day of our lives . . . Well, it bothers me when a man with a whole lot more time does a whole lot less with it. Especially when he's from Texas. I mean, the last two guys I knew from Texas were as fun as all get-out and adventurous as heck. So you just make me sad. I'd expect more from a Buddy Holly fan." He stepped back again. "Now, you taking the bet or not?"

This character was not giving me a happy Hollywood experience. I didn't know how he'd guessed where I was from, or why he was messing with me, but I'd had enough. Douglas Fairbanks was waiting.

"Yeah, fine," I said. "I'll take the bet."

Ritchie nodded. "Good. You can come back to the Boulevard tomorrow night to settle up." And with that, he stepped around me and headed for Spider-Man's lamppost, where Luke and Darth were chatting with Bogie and Marilyn.

I stared after him. And then, surprising myself, I yelled at him.

"Hey!" A few people on the sidewalk gave me worried glances, but most ignored me.

Ritchie stopped beside Darth Vader and looked back, his eyebrows raised. "What is it, Tex?"

"I want to know," I said. "Just what do you have against 'La Bamba'?"

Ritchie threw back his head and laughed again.

"Man, I *love* 'La Bamba'!" he cried. "I love it so much that I made myself learn how to sing it phonetically — because I was raised speaking English! I really didn't know much Spanish at all."

Then Ritchie reached into Darth Vader's cloak and pulled out a guitar cable. He plugged one end into the Stratocaster and the other end into the box of blinking lights on Vader's chest.

"No, I could never have anything against 'La Bamba,'" Ritchie said. "I just don't want to play the same song for you *tomorrow* that I'm playing for you *tonight*." He raised his right hand and brought it down on the guitar strings.

The Strat rang out from Darth Vader's chest, and Ritchie Valens sang:

"Para bailar La Bamba! Para bailar La Bamba, se necessita una poca de gracia! Una poca de gracia para mi, para ti! Ay arriba ay arriba! Ay, arriba arriba! Por ti sere, por ti sere - "

Ritchie jumped, swaggered, and tore it up while Marilyn, Luke, Spidey, Bogey, SpongeBob, and RoboCop danced. But Vader, having been pressed into service as an amplifier, stood stock-still. I thought he looked a little pissed-off. On the other hand, who could tell?

The music was good, and my leg muscles twitched in time. But since this Ritchie Valens lookalike had basically told me that I was wasting my life, I was a little pissed-off myself. So instead of enjoying the show, I turned my back on him and went into Grauman's plaza to look at the celebrity hand- and footprints in the concrete.

I discovered that Hedley Lamarr had been right. Douglas Fairbanks did have little feet, although Rita Hayworth took the prize in that department. That girl must have weighed twelve pounds.

About the time I reached Paul Newman and Joanne Woodward, the music behind me stopped in the middle of a chorus. And when I turned to look, only Bogey, Marilyn, Luke, Vader, SpongeBob, and RoboCop remained by the lamppost. Ritchie Valens and Spider-Man were both gone.

. . . • . . .

The unveiling ceremony for Buddy Holly's star the next day was moving, musical, rock'n'roll-royalty-studded, and pretty amazing. But I'll write more about that ceremony elsewhere.

For now, I'll just write about the crowd.

For a Walk of Fame unveiling, the crowd was huge. If there weren't at least a thousand people on the sidewalk just outside the Capitol Records building on September 7, 2011, there were enough that it felt like at least a thousand or more. It was a small space, and people were crammed together, jammed together, and slammed together.

But instead of jostling or elbowing each other, or getting cranky in the late-summer Los Angeles heat, they did something else.

They sang. They sang along with the Buddy Holly tunes that played over the loudspeakers, and during a quiet moment, they offered a heartfelt rendition of "Happy Birthday."

As I snapped photographs, I spotted at least a dozen people, male and female, who had come dressed as Buddy. They were wearing sharp stage suits and thick black-framed glasses, and a couple were carrying Stratocasters. And as the ceremony proceeded, perhaps a hundred more folks in the crowd donned Buddy glasses while they sang and clapped.

I didn't join in any of the singing, because public singing just isn't the sort of thing I do. But I leaned against a palm tree growing out of the sidewalk, shook my head, and stifled a laugh at my own expense.

Because I had just realized that I'd lost my bet.

Oh, I could argue that I hadn't seen the _real_ Buddy Holly in the flesh, over and over again. But I knew that hadn't been the bet. And in Texas, when we lose a bet fair and square, we pay up.

So that night, about 11:00 PM — after all the ceremonies, the parties, and a rocking Buddy Holly tribute concert, while still wearing my dress-up duds consisting of a snazzy gray Western-cut suit, black linen shirt, and bolo tie — I went back to Hollywood Boulevard one more time.

I looked for Ritchie at his star, but he wasn't there. So I walked on down to Grauman's Chinese Theater, and he wasn't there, either.

But Marilyn, Darth, Luke, and Spidey were. The four of them were hanging out at the same trash can and lamppost as the night before.

I went over. "Excuse me, sorry to bother you. But have y'all seen Ritchie Valens anywhere this evening?"

To steal a phrase from the late Houston comedian Bill Hicks, they all looked at me like dogs being shown a card trick.

Only Darth Vader spoke. In his deep amplified bass voice, he asked: _"Is this Ritchie . . . a Jedi?"_

I'd had a good day, but I was exhausted and in no mood. "Look," I said, forcing a smile. "I appreciate the whole not-breaking-character thing. But I owe . . . let's call it a debt of honor to the kid who plays Ritchie Valens. He was right here with y'all last night. Uh, Lord Vader, you even had his guitar cable here in your - "

I reached for Vader's cloak, and both he and Luke Skywalker had their lightsabers out in a flash.

"Stay away from the Dark Side," Luke said fiercely.

At which point Marilyn sidled up to me and cooed, "Would you like a photo, handsome?"

So I gave them some cash, took a photo of them clustered around the trash can (with Spidey atop it), and gave up. In Texas, we pay up when we lose a bet — but this hadn't been a real bet with a real human being anyway. I didn't know why I had bothered to show up in the first place. Maybe my brain chemistry had been psychedelically damaged by breathing California air.

I started back toward Hollywood and Vine, but after two blocks I had to pause on the crowded sidewalk to avoid being smacked in the nose by an old-fashioned wooden-and-glass door. A dozen people streamed out through the doorway while I waited, and as they did, marvelous fragrances wafted from within. Steak. Baked potato. Coffee. Apple pie. All manner of delectable vittles, their wonderful smells mingling in a warm and delicious sensory rush.

That was when I remembered that in all of the day's festivities, I hadn't eaten dinner. And here it was after 11 o'clock. So when the last of the people streaming from the restaurant were out of my way, I grabbed the door and went inside.

I crossed a small bay-window-shaped vestibule and stepped through another doorway. The huge dining room beyond was cool and dim, and a faint musty odor joined all of the enticing smells of good cooking. I had an impression of elegance and seediness living together like two old lovers. And I could hear Eddie Cochran singing "Summertime Blues" from small round speakers in the ancient smoke-stained ceiling.

A tall, narrow-faced, dark-suited man with a thin necktie stood at a podium just inside the door. He looked me up and down, took in my Western-cut suit, and gave me a polite smile.

"Welcome to Hollywood and to the Musso and Frank Grill, sir," he said, pulling a menu from a rack on one side of the podium. "Musso and Frank's is the oldest restaurant in Hollywood, and we have proudly proclaimed that distinction since the day we opened in 1919. This has been a second home to famous writers, producers, and performers for decade after decade."

I looked around at the big old semicircular booths, the scattered tables with their yellowed tablecloths, and the massive oak bar. I could see that only three or four other customers remained in the place, but they seemed to be lingering. So I guessed Musso and Frank's would stay open long enough to feed me.

"Famous writers, you say?" I asked.

The tall man nodded. "Yes, sir. If you like, I can seat you in F. Scott Fitzgerald's favorite booth."

"Sold," I said, and followed him across the worn carpet as he threaded his way between the tables to a maroon-leather-clad booth at the back of the room. He left me there with a large, multi-page menu.

I had barely had a chance to glance at it when another man appeared at my elbow and filled my water glass from a 1950s-era Fiesta pitcher the color of an old brick. This man was dressed in a semi-crumpled uniform of black slacks, a white shirt with a bow tie, and a red jacket. He was stoop-shouldered and elderly, at least 70 years old if he was a day. But his hair was still thick and dark except for a few gray streaks, and his broad face was creased with lines that looked like the result of laughter as much as age.

"Good evening, sir," he said. "I'm Ricardo, and I'll be serving you. Have you decided?"

I was staring at him. I couldn't help it.

"You have a son who plays guitar, don't you?" I asked. Then I did a quick mental calculation. "Or a grandson?"

Ricardo grinned. His teeth still looked white and young. "Not that I know of, sir. Have you decided?"

I looked down at the huge menu. "Uh, what do you recommend?"

"This is Wednesday, sir, so I recommend the Wednesday Special, which is sauerbraten and potato pancakes. It'll be the best you've ever had."

"I'm not sure I've ever had that in my life," I said. "But I'll try it. And a beer. Any brand's fine."

Ricardo somehow managed to frown while still maintaining a smile. "Pardon me for saying so, sir, but this is the Musso and Frank Grill on Hollywood Boulevard. Among other things, we're famous for our cocktails. Mr. Fitzgerald, in whose booth you are ensconced, always had a cocktail. So although beer is traditional with your dish, you might want to consider a cocktail instead." He reached down, opened my menu to a long list of drink suggestions, and tapped it with a gnarled old finger.

I shook my head. "I'm a beer guy."

"I understand, sir," Ricardo said. Then he leaned closer and spoke into my ear. "But wouldn't you like to try something *new*? And *different*?"

A shudder ran through my shoulders. I looked at the list of cocktails and picked one at random. "Whiskey sour," I said.

Ricardo's smile grew wider. "Up, or rocks?"

I slapped the menu closed. "Oh, for the love of Davy Crockett," I said. "Surprise me."

He gave a slight bow. "As you wish, sir."

At that point, I half expected Ricardo to vanish in a puff of smoke, but instead he just walked away. Pretty briskly, too, for an old fellow. He returned a few minutes later with a substantial lemonade-colored drink stuffed with ice and a cherry, and then a few minutes after that with a plate of gravy-soaked beef roast with potato pancakes.

Ricardo set the plate before me and gave another slight bow.

"Enjoy, sir," he said.

I looked down at the steaming sauerbraten, then closed my eyes for a second and took a deep breath. The sharp, rich smell was both familiar and strange, and irresistible. And when I opened my eyes again, Ricardo was gone.

Then, as I ate and drank, the Musso and Frank sound system played seven Buddy Holly songs in a row, no doubt in honor of Buddy's birthday and his new Walk of Fame star. I thought it was a nice gesture. And the last two were my favorites — "Not Fade Away" and "Well All Right."

In short, it was a great meal. I ate every morsel on my plate and drained every drop in my glass. So by the time I was finished, I was pretty full and moderately drunk. But I wasn't so drunk that I didn't notice when my check was brought by the tall man from the podium instead of by Ricardo.

"I hope everything was satisfactory," the tall man said. "And I hope you'll come back and see us again."

I thought about it. "You know," I said, "I think I might."

Then I glanced around the dining room. The other customers had left, and the tall man and I were alone.

"Everything was terrific," I said, holding up a credit card. "But what happened to my waiter?"

The tall man glanced toward the door. "Oh, Ricardo had to leave early. An old friend of his from Lubbock, Texas is in town. And perhaps another from, I believe, Beaumont. They're going to catch up." He took my credit card. "I'll be back in a moment."

I blinked, and the tall man handed back my card and a slip of paper to sign. My hand wobbled a bit as I did so, and I told myself it was just the whiskey sour.

Maybe it was. But as I stood to go, I heard that the song playing through the ceiling speakers, just for me, was a Ritchie Valens tune:

"Wellll . . . Come on, let's go, let's go, let's go, little darlin'! Tell me that you'll never leave me! Come on, come on, let's go — again and again and again!"

If I could have picked any Ritchie Valens song to hear at that moment, "Come On, Let's Go" would have been it. So I was buzzed and happy as I stepped out onto the Boulevard once more and started on my wobbly way eastward toward my hotel.

Then, with Ritchie's music still in my ears, I stopped. Just as at Buddy's unveiling, I had realized something.

I still owed half the payment for my bet.

I looked at my watch. It was 11:57 PM.

So I spun around, almost falling over, and ran back past Musso and Frank's, heading westward as fast as I could. I had no idea what I was going to do, but I knew I had only three minutes left to do it. And I knew where it had to be done.

When in doubt, you always pay off a bet where the bet was made.

I was running upstream against a steady flow of the cool, the not-so-cool, the beautiful, the ugly, the weird, the hip, the slick, the ragged, and the downright dorky. But as I bobbed and weaved among them in my drunken, sauerbraten-laden plunge, I loved them. I loved them all. And I would have stopped to kiss every one of them on the mouth, but I was in a hurry.

As I ran past Ritchie's star, I looked down and shouted, "Well, all right! Come on! Let's GO!"

Moments later, when I reached Grauman's Chinese Theater, I hurtled past Marilyn Monroe (who gasped "Ooh!"), richocheted off

SpongeBob Squarepants, and collided with Spider-Man's trash can. Spidey wound up perched atop my shoulders for a split second, then tumbled away to land in a perfect four-point Spidey-pose on the pavement. He looked up at me and cocked his head.

There was no time to explain. My watch said 11:59.

I knew I ought to be in costume. But I was wearing a Western-cut suit and a bolo tie, so maybe that would do for Hollywood Boulevard on a Wednesday night. I hoped so, because I sure as hell wasn't ever going to do this again.

Facing Grauman's Chinese Theater and its throng of tourists, I flung my arms wide, threw back my head, and sang as loud as I could:

"Yo no soy marinaro! Yo no soy marinaro, soy capitan! Soy capitan, soy capitan! Bamba, bamba! Bamba, bamba! Bamba, bamba! Bamba — "

I have no doubt that I looked and sounded like a whiskey-sour-addled idiot.

But in Texas, when we lose a bet fair and square, we pay up.

By the time I reached a second chorus, Marilyn Monroe, Humphrey Bogart, Luke Skywalker, SpongeBob Squarepants, Spider-Man, and even Darth Vader were all singing with me. And at least half the crowd had joined them.

So maybe this Buddy Holly fan finally did all right by Ritchie Valens, too — even though I had to sing "La Bamba" by remembering it phonetically. Because that's one thing this middle-aged dude from Texas and that kid from California have in common.

You see, just like Ritchie . . . I really don't know much Spanish at all.

— END —

. . . .

Manager Glornash attempts to prove just

how much of a company man she can be

in this all too real story of the

unsettling world of telemarketing.

. . . .

Operators are Standing By

Rhonda Eudaly

ood morning! Before the shift starts, I want to let you know that the new catalogs are in. We have a lot of new products across the board this cycle. Be sure you take some time to familiarize yourselves with them.

"Also, the new advertising cycle begins today as well. The commercials, infomercials, and documercials are done by our best producers with extra incentives to boost revenue. That information is being downloaded to your terminals right now. Don't forget to take your anti-hypnotics before you watch."

Clicks, clacks, hoots, and hollers answered Glornash's announcement. She let the adulation and excitement wash over her while the translations caught up in the more complex languages. Though the Call Center was equipped with the most advanced universal translation technology in the galaxy — and not the crappy stuff they sold to their customers — it still took some time for the program to catch up.

"Now, let's get out there and sell, sell, sell!" Glornash raised a flipper. "What's our motto here?"

"Every call a customer, every customer a sale, and every sale has separate shipping and handling!"

Glornash felt her oral cavity stretch as joy filled her pulmonary organ. She had the best, and busiest, Call Center in the galaxy. It was time to get her team moving. She slapped her flippers once more for instant attention.

"Now, let's not forget which segments you're dealing with. We have a reputation to maintain. Let's get to work."

With one last cheer, Glornash's staff swarmed out of the auditorium, bipedals automatically stepping over the occasional slime trail left by the gastropods slithering out among them. Glornash would give them a few moments to get to their stations before starting her rounds. This would be a good shift, Glornash could feel it. Revenue streamed in her pulmonary fluids, and today she felt revenue pumping away.

In her slow ooze toward the door, Glornash could already hear the Call Center coming to life. She barely spared a glance toward the production studio, but a swish of movement caught her optical nerve. She turned to see an organic spokesbot's appearance slip from the Earth pitchman, Vince Offer, to a Larian version. Not that it was a major change. The only difference between the two were the Larian's yellow scales and four eyes. However, if a Larian appeared on Earth, it would have Humans putting down their intoxicants and adjusting their television sets. But that wasn't Glornash's concern. Her sole purpose was to have operators standing by to take orders, and she took her job very seriously.

Glornash's optical stalks scanned the floor of the Call Center. Warnings went off in her hind cranial lobes. Something wasn't right. What was it? There. She saw the empty station. Scans didn't show its occupant up and around chatting or at the refreshment station. She tapped into the central computer system; no one was currently in the bodily waste receptacles, either. This would never do. There should never be an empty station, not this early in the shift.

She flowed quickly across the floor. "Where is Operator MX-35?"

Blank stares and non-committal shrugs — or the anatomical equivalent — answered it. "Well, get someone from the On-Call Pool! Quick! One of you from Gleeb! You're a speedy race, one of you, go!"

Papers flew out some being's manipulator digits as a blur blew past, zipping out of the room.

A tone reverberated through the hub. "Shift commencing in five minutes. Shift commencing in five minutes."

Glornash slapped her flippers. "Places, everyone. Places. This is a good day!"

All the operators scurried, skittered, and slithered back to their stations, conversations ceased, computer screens lit up all around Glornash — two screens per station. One screen was a Caller ID program in multiple languages. The other was the company catalog. Glornash felt the familiar swell of anxiety and dread rising in her as confusion reigned on new catalog day. The slight changes in products and codes would mean for a choppy start to the day.

Time counted down until a great bell clanged throughout the building. Glornash took one final, deep inhalation as the communications system clamored into life in a rolling wave across the center.

Glornash was in her element. The chaos of the multitude of voices washed over her like a symphony. She slapped her flippers like an excited cub. She began her rounds, watching for problems and listening to various calls — for quality control purposes only, of course.

"Certainly, we can help," a purple, winged being said into her cranial set. "I understand. We do offer a variety pack of orifice tubes. A complete gross of different sizes, shapes, and configurations. It's a one-fifty a unit plus shipping and handling. Yes, it does sound like a lot, but we guarantee our tubes will suit every abduction need. It even comes with a universal coupler to fit any probe. It's an investment in your mission success. Yes, indeed. And for calling now, we can double your order if you just pay separate processing and handling. Still not sure? Wait there's more..."

Glornash flushed with pleasure. Orifice tubes were one of their biggest sellers. A staple among the space going races. Their company was the leading provider bar none.

"With your current order, you qualify for the upgrade to priority delivery. That means it'll arrive in two to three standard business cycles rather than five to seven. Very good. I'm putting your order through now. How would you like to pay? First born? All..."

Glornash cleared her larynx loudly, causing the operator's head to jerk up. Glornash barely avoided being impaled by her one horn and nervously flapping wings. She pointed to the wall and a bright, digital sign.

"I'm sorry, we no longer accept first born as forms of payment. No, I'm sorry we can't accept *any* form of offspring as payment. That'll be fine. Let me have the account information. Great. The expiration date? No, not *your* expiration date, the account, but congratulations on your longevity."

Glornash moved on to another station, certain the operator had her sale. That was an easy one. There were harder items to move. But Glornash was a True Believer when it came to the company and its ability to move product through the cosmos. If they sold it, someone would come to buy.

"Glornash report to Management Level Three immediately. Glornash to Management Level Three."

For an instant, the center went silent as every optical organ in the room snapped to Glornash. She felt the pulmonary fluid drain from her facial area. Being called to the Management Level meant dealing <u>with</u> Management. The hiccup went away almost as soon as it occurred returning at once to the buzz of voices. Glornash straightened up, and with her cranium held high, she sashayed to the lift. She gave the floor one last visual scan before the doors snapped shut and the car shot downward.

Glornash wrapped a flipper around the support beam and leaned her weight against it to keep her lower extremities from buckling. Fortunately the trip didn't last long enough for Glornash to obsess over why she could be called before management — wonder, but not obsess.

The doors hissed open. Glornash hesitated, not knowing exactly what was expected of her.

"Floor Supervisor Glornash, come forward and be identified."

She did what she was told. Only a step or two beyond and the elevator doors thudded closed behind her, sealing with a threatening hiss. Glornash gulped, anxiety flooding its adrenal system. "What can I do for Management? I exist to serve."

"We know you do, Glornash. This is your Performance Review."

Glornash gathered every ounce of will to keep upright as every bone in her body seemed to liquefy. She had heard about Performance Reviews before but had never been subjected to one. Status updates and annual checkups were standard in order to gain promotion and wage increases, but *never-ever* a Performance Review. Few came back from this — the highest, most invasive of meetings. It was, in part, how some promotions became available.

"I...I exist to serve?" Fear made her response more question than statement. "May I ask why now?"

"It is your time."

"I'm...ready?"

"You will be subjected to a battery of tests — physical and psychological. At the conclusion, you will be informed of the results. There is only one thing to remember. Be completely honest with your answers. Do not tell us what you think we wish to hear or what you think would make the company look good. We will know when you're not being truthful — even to the detriment of yourself or the company. Do you understand?"

"Yes, completely. I understand." Glornash said the words automatically. She just hoped they wouldn't use the orifice tubes on her. Even though her sole purpose in life was to sell orifice tubes to races across the galaxy, the thought of having one ever used on any of her orifices made her epidermis crawl. She never wanted first flipper knowledge of their intended uses.

Glornash didn't see the beings who strapped her into the chair-like device. Actually, after the light in her optical system and a stick in her flipper, Glornash didn't remember much of anything. She only knew the next thing she recalled was stepping back off the lift onto the call center floor.

"Floor Supervisor! There you are! We've had a huge upsurge in calls. MX-27 needs your authorization on a collectible call. And we're seeing bizarre fluctuations in server speeds."

"Call in some temps from the pool to handle call volume. Get tech support into the server room. Tell them to do whatever it takes. We need those hamsters running at peak capacity." Glornash was halfway to MX-27's cubical before the words were out of her mouth. "Now, what's the problem here?"

"My caller is determined to purchase more than the strict limit of five we have on the commercial. He is determined to speak with a supervisor," MX-27 sounded frazzled. Not a good sign.

Glornash plugged her cranial set into MX-27s communications console. She didn't remember putting the set around her spinal stalk, but that didn't matter now. "I am Supervisor Glornash. How may I help you?" She listened for a moment. "I am sorry, but because of the genuine Floridium coating we must adhere to the strict five unit limit. The demand is too great to make any exceptions. We include documents of authenticity and... now getting verbally excited isn't going to help. Our limits are set by the manufacturer. Yes, I understand, but there's nothing I can do about the limit. What I can do is authorize free shipping and handling, which is highly irregular. I'll even upgrade that to priority shipping for no additional charge. Yes, sir. Thank you for your order. I will now hand you back to your operator to finish your order. Thank you."

Glornash nodded to MX-27 as she disconnected the cranial set. Though MX-27 was already taking payment information, she stared at Glornash with an expression of awe — or constipation — it was hard to tell her particular species. But that was not Glornash's concern, the commotion erupting from the production rooms threatening to disrupt the call center took precedence.

"Quick! Catch him before he spreads!"

Glornash saw one of the organic spokesbots — maybe even the Vince Offer/Larian from earlier — barreling towards her, its hair aflame and epidermis splotched a bluish-purple. Glornash only had nanoseconds to realize this wasn't typical for the bot's species specifications.

Emergency protocol drills slammed into muscle-memory place as alarms whooped into life. Glornash spread her flippers. The left side took the bot in the neck, sending it to the floor as the right side flipper snagged a chemical extinguisher from the wall and sprayed down the bot to extinguish the flames, and hopefully neutralize whatever had turned it purple. The extinguishers in the call center were much more advanced than simply fire suppressant.

"Thank you, Floor Supervisor! You saved us all!" The production assistant slid to a halt next to the downed bot and sprayed it with another chemical. "Antidote for the side effects. There is no danger now."

Glornash turned back to get the call center back up and running, only to discover none of the beings on her watch even had a cranium up out of his/her/its cubicle. Only a few with multiple optical orifices — some all the way around the cranium-even seemed to be watching the commotion while they continued to take calls.

Glornash tried not to swell with pride — after all it was simply her job to keep the call center running smoothly. She left the bot to the production department and flowed around the center one last time before heading to her own clear-walled office on the edge of the floor. She had reports to file.

Just as Glornash settled behind her workstation, she noticed a flashing alert to a message. She was probably an update on new products or tech support alerts. At the worst, it was a product recall. She hated recalls. Recalls meant refunds. Refunds caused her to break out in allergic reactions.

Glornash, your service to the company has been noticed and commended. Management would like to discuss your future with the company today after your shift. Please confirm.

Glornash blinked at her screen. Her mind went completely blank with shock and not a small amount of awe. She did her job to the best of her ability and took personal pride in her success. That Management noticed Glornash's hard work excited her almost to the point of meiosis. She confirmed the message automatically. They offered her an opportunity of a lifetime; of course she was going to the meeting.

Glornash went through the rest of the shift on automatic pilot. Fortunately the shift concluded without further incident, because for the first time in her long career, her mind was not on her work. Glornash wondered what Management wanted with her. Soon enough, and yet an eternity later, the end-of-shift alert clanged. Glornash watched her charges shut down their workstations, pack up their possessions, and shuffle out.

She filed her last report, the accounting of the shift's activities, and sent it on before acknowledging the meeting reminder. She shut down the workstation and flippered off the lights. She oozed over to the lift and pressed the button for management level. Glornash was more used to the trip this time, not that it helped at all.

She slid out of the lift when it stopped and looked around the darkened corridor. She realized she had no idea where she was supped to go. As she scanned the corridor, a door opened at the far end on its own. She headed toward the diffuse light spilling out onto the floor. Glornash's esophagus when dusty dry as she moved toward the light- against every base survival instinct in her body.

"Welcome, Floor Supervisor Glornash. Come in. We've been expecting you."

Glornash eased inside and tried not to start when the door sealed shut behind her. She turned back toward the voice, but could see nothing but the light. "You wanted to speak with me?"

"We did, Glornash. Your record and reputation is exemplary. You passed your performance review with flying colors."

"Um, thank you?" Glornash wasn't sure how she should respond to the statement. "I live to serve."

"And that's what we wanted to discuss with you."

"All right."

"You have qualities we find, though not <u>lacking</u>, in need of bolstering within the company. You have a capacity for compassion and empathy we wish to nurture, and your leadership skills are unparalleled."

Glornash was both elated and thoroughly lost. She would take the compliment where she could get it. "Again, thank you."

"We want to ensure that your future and your assets will continue to benefit the company."

"I am very happy with my life here," Glornash said guardedly.

"We are happy to hear that, but it does lead us to ask an...indelicate... question."

"Okay..." Glornash didn't know where any of this was going. She didn't like being confused.

"How is your family life, Floor Supervisor?"

Glornash blinked. Life Form Resources would have a fit if they knew she was being asked such a question — not that she had any intention of reporting Management for asking. Besides she had nothing really to report. "I have no family. Just my work."

"Then you have nothing holding you here?"

"Am I being transferred?" Glornash knew the company had other facilities across the cosmos, but she had only known and worked in this one.

"Of a sort, but we need to know how willing you are to be a more... permanent...fixture in the company."

"There isn't anything I wouldn't do for the company. Surely my work record has shown that. I have no desire to leave here."

"We needed to hear it from you. To confirm what we learned through the performance review. We have been monitoring you."

They had? Of course they had. Management was always making the company better for both the workforce and the customer. Right? But Glornash was still confused. She couldn't see who or what addressed her, so it had no facial or body clues to indicate what was required of her. "What are we talking about? Profit sharing? Retirement program? Health benefits?"

Laughter enveloped him. "Don't be silly. That path lays insanity. We have a different type of partnership in mind. We want to move you into Quality Assurance and eventually move you up the management chain. However, in order to become part of Management, you'll have to be willing to...sacrifice."

"Okay...I don't have a lot to give up. I'm ready to move up in the company." Glornash felt a brief pang of doubt.

"Think before you speak, Glornash. Once you make this decision there is no going back. We will send you the new contract. Read it carefully. If you proceed, return the signed contract, and report back here. Take a rest cycle or two to consider. This decision affects your future and your life. It is not to be taken lightly." The door opened behind Glornash. The meeting was over. She headed home, brain reeling with possibilities. She was not prepared for the contract waiting for her when it arrived. The cover message told her to take the next shift off to make her decision and then give them her answer.

Glornash found the next circadian cycle difficult. The opportunity presented was impressive. The compensation was significantly higher, but so were the responsibilities and the physical requirements expected. The offer was daunting. She couldn't relax, her brain reeled and rest eluded her as she wrestled with the pros and cons.

Finally, Glornash knew what she had to do. She sluggishly made her way back to the call center. The wash of well-wishes surrounding her return buoyed her spirits. The whole energy of the room rose the moment she was back. She couldn't turn away from them or the company. If she accepted this promotion, she could make sure everyone — customer service representatives and customers — had the best buying experience possible. She could be part of something bigger than herself.

She sent the contract off as she finished her shift and went back to the Management Level. "I'm here. I'm ready."

"You will be a great asset to the future of this company, Glornash. We applaud your decision. Now, if you'll proceed through the next door, operators are standing by."

Glornash slid through the door that opened to her right. Her optical orbits bulged a bit as a medical team wait for her. Behind them, a row of containers containing floating bodies and brains connected to a massive computer server bank. But she had made her decision. She was part of the company forever now.

. . . .

Don Webb expertly unravels timeless

mysteries — universal, personal, and

otherwise — as archeologist Peggy

Reynman journeys to the red planet to

research the legendary Cylinders of Mars.

. . . .

The Art of Absence

Don Webb

er daddy used to bury little things in the backyard.

Mainly, George Reynman buried arrowheads that he bought at an antique store in town. Sometimes silver coins, ten cent pieces from a hundred years ago when they still made coins from silver (and had denominations less than a dollar). It was all for Peggy's older brother. Of course.

Jack wasn't doing well in school. He was three years older than she was, and he was going to look like daddy when he grew up. She was pudgy and not going to look like anybody. Momma was famous, beautiful and dead. Momma had died in the first Venus landing. Then Jack stopped reading and doing math, but she had escaped into books and studies. She lived on the nets.

Daddy had meant to awaken some romantic spirit in Jack. If Jack were turned on by finding these little treasures he might want to read about Indians or 20th century America. Jack might get excited, do well in school and not be so damn pale. It didn't work. Daddy had to help Jack find the arrowheads. Daddy would uncover them with his feet, while the three of them were barbecuing. He would wait for Jack to spot them, and failing this would suddenly exclaim, "Oh what's this?" or some other equally inspired piece of acting. Jack would look dully at the piece of flint, sigh, and go back to eating his hamburger.

But not her.

"Princess" would be thrilled. The arrowhead would immediately become part of her ongoing story. Usually a tale involving Daddy, herself and a dragon.

Daddy lost interest in trying to bury things for Jack.

One day, when she was eight, she dug up all of the things Daddy had ever buried. She washed them and displayed them on a big piece of burlap. Daddy looked at her as if he had never seen her before. "I'm so proud of you, Princess."

He was glad when she told him that she wanted to be an archaeologist. He helped her find role models: Amelia Peabody, Jeanine D. Kimball, Guiniviere Marie Webb, and Mary Denning.

When she was twelve, he told her what had made him happiest was that archeology would keep her on Earth. He never talked directly about Momma dying on Venus. Momma was on a stamp. Captain Sarah Reynman.

Now, the landing on Mars was three hours away. Mars landings were no big deal, but, she was scared. Not of the landing, of the gap, the space she was making. She wanted a brave face for the cameras. Fifty-five and a couple of books on archeology behind her, she could make a brave face. Hell, she had faced failing freshmen, reporters shouldn't scare her.

She looked a good deal older.

She had been fourteen when Daddy died. Jack had been free of his depression for years; girls and puberty had cured that. He didn't want to watch Dad dying. No one died of cancer anymore; it was tragically out-of-step with the times. It was like Dad's arrowheads and his old junk. Jack developed an electro-stem addiction. He even wore the ugly blue helmet at the funeral. Dad didn't talk much as the crazy cells ate his brain and lungs and liver. She made it her business to know everything. She understood why the cancer was inoperable. She knew its origin in one of the plasmid diseases of the 2030's — the Plague Decade forty years ago. She knew everything.

And knowledge was not enough.

She would be with him every day, watching his blood, more brown then red, flow through its exsanguination tube out to be scrubbed.

"Princess. I. Want. You. to. Have. Something."

He pulled the heavy brass watch from his chest-of-drawers. Great-grandfather's railroad watch, he had told Jake for years it would be his. Jake was in the basement having a magnetically-induced experience of God.

"Keep. It. Safe."

The spacecraft had begun its descent into Mars. She hoped a crowd wouldn't gather to yell abuse at her, like they had done earthside. She excited by the idea of lesser gravity. She had never been off world, not even the Moon.

After Daddy there was a big empty space.

There had been lovers, men and women that filled an evening or two, but no one could fill the space.

Then there was Keith.

Keith lectured on archeology for a freshman survey course. He was young for the field, and she was young for a freshman.

The hall was full that day, half the women were in love with Keith for his curly hair and flashing eyes, but she was in love with him for his ideas.

"Traditional cultures didn't just pile shit up hoping that you or I would come some day and dig them up. They were looking to join the gods. Their view of the future was to see it as a time of gods. So don't start digging without vowing to look at these people from a divine perspective, welcome them to the heaven of your mind. See them as brave, as having gathered the best of what they had to make this major journey across the dark time into a bright and unknown future. The future is the only thing that is eternal. There will always be a tomorrow, always a place that they are journeying too. We must respect the brave dead that have journeyed alongside us, so that their message arrives when our paths cross. They want to tell us about their lives, their world."

She did something she never did. She held up her hand. " I disagree Dr. Caswell. There's no way that those people would've even pictured us. They couldn't conceive of a society other than their own."

"Of course they didn't picture our society, they dreamed of some great Other looking on their things and loving them. Gods have feeling.

The gods would feel what they felt in preparing these tombs. They would know the love of the living, the sorrow at loss, of the person, whose items we find. The more different the archaeologist from his target, the more the target has traveled into a new world. Think about how different Howard Carter was from the family of Tutankhamen."

She was his student by the end of the week, his best friend by the end of the quarter, and his lover by the end of the year. He took her on his digs in Poland and Moldova, he took when he gave papers on the semiotics of Bronze Age burials, and by the time she got her BA everyone that was anyone in the field knew her.

At first they all thought she was just the teacher's pet. Then she began publishing her own field reports. Then there were discoveries in Afghanistan. She found out where the Sumerians came from, and where the homeland of the Indus Valley people was.

Everything was based on a single idea — that she and Keith would be a forever couple. She was perhaps the smarter of the two, but he had a great synthesizing vision that helped unify her work, and he was tons better at popularizing it, which meant funding wasn't quite the nightmare for them that it was for most archaeologists.

But years passed, passion cooled a little. Keith stopped loving the field as much, and screwed around with some of his students. She published material that was a tad fringy, impatient that conventional theory had not caught up with her. He wanted to retire from the field into a nice full professorship,and she wanted to do really daring things.

The split up happened gradually. She would be gone on field work, and he would agree to more and more speaking gigs.

Their last trip together was to Egypt. They had realized in their own ways, that their love was becoming a thing of the past, and they honored the past enough to want things to end with a fight. Daddy had had a love of Egypt, so in some way she was opening the old space left by his death as a new dig in her soul, and burying the decade long distraction of Keith.

When she first saw the pyramids at night under their shimmering domes, Keith quoted the old Arabic saw, "Man fears time, but time fears the pyramids."

"Is it because their message is so great?" she asked," So terrible?"

He didn't answer. His eyes were on the short skirt of a stewardess of Hapi Tours Inc. He no longer led the godlike life of inviting the dead into the world.

Popular archeology as opposed to academic archeology is about entertainment. Popular archeology has brought us the Curse of King Tut, the Face of Mars, the Temple at the bottom of the Mariana Trench. Popular archeology erupted about five years after their divorce — the Cylinders of Mars. A mining group had unearthed — or "unmarsed " three cylinders of steel in Aurorae Sinus, which the media called the Golden Sinus Cans. Almost immediately, the cylinders were found to be of earthly origin. The were canisters that an earlier survey crew had lost during exploratory drilling.

However once a media myth is born it can never die. A group calling itself the Secret Mars Society theorized that Mars was much warmer billions of years ago, when carbon dioxide clouds had darkened the atmosphere. Well, that's real science. Perhaps a "canister making civilization" had flourished. Yeah perhaps Santa winters in Florida. Maybe they had even sent cans of primordial soup to Earth starting life here.

In a ill-advised move, Dr. Susan McNutt, President of the World Archeology Association, gave an interview explaining why the theory of the "Martian Can Makers" was bunk.

Then all the great unwashed believed. Their slogan, "Soup to McNutt!" made little sense, but it made for great merchandising.

Videos of Martian antiquities were produced. Novel writing machines created Martian novels, and scholars of folklore discussed the image of Mars in hoaxes. There were monographs on Orson Wells and his Invasion, the "Face" on Mars, the "Martian Viagra" and the Church of Barsoom.

No reputable archaeologist was going to go within ten kilometers of this one.

Then Dr. Peggy Reynman published a paper suggesting that the reports might be partially true. She was not only a Real archeologist, she was the daughter of Captain Sarah Reynman, first woman to die on Venus. She should know, she had space in her blood.

Keith flew out to see her. They had not communicated in three years. He found her in her office, polishing her locket and the railroad watch. She wouldn't look up at him. Behind her desk was huge map of Mars.

"Peggy, you've gone mad. This is professional suicide."

"Keith, how nice of you to drop by."

"Peggy, why are you doing this?"

"Do you really still care, or are you worried that somehow my strength-to-dream might reflect badly on your professional sinecure?"

"Peggy, I know we're not what we used to be, but I lo— I care for you, and I know you are smart enough to know that these reports are bullshit. So what are you doing? Are you hurting yourself to make me feel bad?"

Peggy laughed. He was really more ego-centric than she had ever imagined, why had she married him? How could this small man fill the space that daddy had made in her heart?

"Keith, it is not about you. It is about making a big sign in the world. You told me how to do this years ago."

"I have no idea what the hell you are talking about. I just know your professional worth is about to be zero."

"Well it's my worth."

They bantered and bickered and Keith flew away.

Her next paper was even more pro-Can than the first.

She lost her job.

She got a job writing for the Secret Mars Society. Her old students contacted her. Half were full of tears that she had lost her mind, half were angry that she had whored herself out for fame and money. At first she tried sending them cryptic messages mentioning that events look different from the far side of tomorrow. Then she just isolated herself. Fringe science occasionally acquires big money. People that had to make their fortunes when the world said they couldn't often have a sweet spot for ideas that the respectable world scoffs at. When Randolph Chu said he was going to make a fortune in garbage mining, people laughed at him. They laughed when his first business failed. They laughed more when his second business failed. And when his third business made billions, they all said they had seen it all the time. Randolph Chu loved the Secret Mars Society. He loved the idea that garbage from a past civilization had made its way to ours. Besides he knew a great publicity gimmick when he saw one. When Dr. Reynman excavated the biggest hole in the solar system with his new laser drilling rig, his name would be the name in excavation.

Randolph Chu was scared of space flight, so he wasn't riding with Peggy.

The ship touched down.

. . . • . . .

Keith Caswell landed two standard weeks later.

He had spent good money to make as sure as he could that no one knew he was on Mars. He also had good connections; he had gone to school with Roy Chadwick's daughter Marie. A Chadwick Mining vehicle picked him up in Helium and took him south to Bradbury, which was the closest settlement to the supposed Martian ruins. Her team had come back a week ago.

They were sitting around in the local bars boozing it up on SMS money.

They claimed everything they knew was secret, but a few multiC$ and they talked.

She had sent them back. They had made a big hole in the shape of a pyramid. The apex pointed almost half a kilometer down, the base was a square kilometer. She halted very excitedly digging, and sent them away.

She said that she had found a secret door, and that things were so fragile, that only she could go in. The weight of their equipment, or even just them walking around could bring down the ruins.

"That's the way archeology is." They told him," Fragile business."

They said she was good to work for, since she mainly stayed in her dome, while they dug.

She was due back in a day or two. She was going to make an announcement that would change the world. They would all be very, very famous.

No, they hadn't actually seen any Martian ruins. Not even a single rusty can.

Keith tried to see her, but Chu Garbage kept her under wraps. He was going to get Peggy to stop this. He knew it was all about him, she was mad because of the women he had cheated with. She was going to hurt archeology as a whole — just to get to him. His mood swung from loving concern to bitter anger even faster than Phobos swung around Mars. Keith broke into her room at the Hotel Splendide. Archaeologists are, after all, thieves. There were books, a couple of changes of clothes, quite a few empty drug packs, and a script for a speech.

She saw the door to her room was ajar. She pulled a small (and very illegal) gun. No one could interfere now.

She almost killed him, but in the dim light, saw that he was sitting on the edge of the bed. She remembered waking up to that shadow on nights when he would be troubled.

"Keith?" she asked.

"I came to stop you."

"Because of love or because you are mad?"

He lifted an empty drug pack. "What are you here for Peggy?"

"I am here to die. I have some of the same abreactions to modern life that my late father had. Very few people have inoperable cancer in the world. I may even live to make the trip back to earth."

"I don't understand. I've read you speech. I know —"

"You know that I will tell that I found nothing, but that I have a gut feeling that the region should be looked into." She said, " I will die shortly thereafter. Since the disease will have affected my brain by then, my big upside down negative pyramid will be a monument to human craziness."

"Why are you doing this? It is crazy and hurts my heart," said Keith.

"I am sorry for your heart Keith, but you will figure it out. When you do, it may heal your heart. I am doing it for the gods."

"You're throwing your life away to make it look like there are Martian ruins, then you are going debunk those very ruins, and then you are going to die." said Keith

"That's pretty much it." Peggy smiled.

"You're not going to tell me anything. Why do you think I'll keep quiet?" asked Keith.

"Because after all, you love me." said Peggy.

Keith was on a ship back to Earth before she gave her press conference. He feigned surprise at her death, and kept a photo at his desk for the rest of his life.

It took him about ten years to figure it out. He doubted Peggy's grand gesture would be anything than a monument to human eccentricity — but on some nights when he would catch sight of Mars, he wondered if she might have exactly the mysterious effect she hoped for. He was dreaming of her gods the night he died.

· · · · ● · · · ·

The Earth continued to go around the sun and eventually the sun went around the galactic core, and the human race did themselves in. They had done a great deal during their time, as races go, inventing new forms of music, beat the Beletrin in a war, invented dozens of beautiful and goofy religions, and they made their own Moon into a hyper-university. Sadly the humans developed a more efficient bomb in their last years and destroyed not only their Moon, but turned Earth into a rather uninteresting glassy ball.

Space is big, and time is vast and in the great cosmic seasons of things, a race called the Speenourains visited the human solar system. They found some space junk near the moons of Jupiter, some mining robots in the Belt, and a large weathered (but obviously) artificial pyramidal hole in the South Polar regions of Mars. At the lowest point of the pyramidal shaft, they found a small cylinder shaft extending another kilometer downward. At the base of this shaft was a small platinum box. It contained a timepiece, a locket with two pictures, three flint arrowheads, and a small silver disk once known as a "Mercury" dime.

Many volumes would be written on the significance of this find, and the great care with which the objects had been buried. The objects became the core of Speenourain "Martian studies." Why had these items been sent across the abyss of time? The human that had buried them had taken such care in being sure they were found, who or what had it imagined would dig them up? Had they known that they would blow up their own world? Was this a message of religion or love, or just "We were here."?

No one can be sure, of course. But in every school in the Speenorain empire, which spread to almost a third of the galaxy pictures of twelve year old Peggy Reynman and her father George are displayed as *the* example of the human race. The gods loved their little mystery. And when the Speenoarins faded, a robotic race dug up their museums. By the time of the Heat Death of the Universe, images of little Peggy Reynman and her Daddy passed through twenty races.

(dedicated with love to the mortuary specialist
Guiniviere Marie Webb)

. . . .

In this 19th century tale, John Langschlaf

falls asleep, only to awaken 500 years

later in a strange utopia. Originally

published in 1865, Aurelia Hadley

Mohl's rarely reprinted work is one of the

earliest science fiction tales

written by a Texan.

. . . .

An Afternoon's Nap

or: Five Hundred Years Ahead

Aurelia Hadley Mohl

wish you wouldn't wake me up again," said Mr. John Langschlaf, crossly, to a little urchin whose shouts sounded through the balmy summer air, "you are a perfect torment! go away and let me alone."

"I will that, old Crosspatch," answered the saucy fellow, making a wry face; "I wouldn't wake you up again if you slept five hundred years!"

"Umph! I wish I could," muttered Mr. Langschlaf, as he fell back upon the rug he had spread beneath a wide-spreading elm, and resumed his interrupted slumbers.

We might as well take this opportunity to tell our readers that Mr. John Langschlaf was a gentleman of great learning and fine intellectual endowments, but like many others of his class, a sworn foe to modern "innovations," and an ardent theoretical admirer of the "good old times." The men of the present day were physically and mentally inferior to those of the middle ages; and as for the woman — bah! — and, Mr. Langschlaf would turn up his bachelor nose, and roll up his bachelor eyes, in unmitigated scorn. Flimsy, frivolous nondescripts, he called them. Where could you find a woman who could compare to the housewives of the "good old times," when the dear creatures spent their time in scolding their tire-women, and making impossible birds and beasts on useless pieces of canvass. So, in spite of a comfortable home, and a nice fortune, or perhaps because of them, Mr. Langschaf remained till his forty-fifth year — at which period our story takes him up — a single gentleman of elegant leisure. Notwithstanding his contempt for the modern race, he had no objection to the many comforts and improvements these pigmies had invented or perfected. Gas transformed night into day in his well furnished home; newspapers, and literary and scientific journals, lay constantly upon his library tables; messages from distant friends came to him over the electric wires; and railway cars or steamboats carried him on his frequent journeys. Nay, even the "frivolous nondescripts" contributed to his pleasure. Mrs. Hemans, and Mrs. Browning, Madam DeStael and Miss Pardoe, had, with many other female writers, their immortal representatives in his book shelves. Rosa Bonheur and Miss Hosmer also sent their pictures (or copies of them), and statuary to adorn his picture gallery, far advanced as these noble women are; or as he would say, far as they fall behind their highly cultivated and useful ancestry.

To a pleasant, shady nook in one corner of his pretty park, Mr. Langschlaf had taken himself with a new book for company, to enjoy his customary post-prandial nap. The book was full of all sorts of innovating and disrupting notions, and our old bachelor uttered many scornful "pshaws" and deprecatory "humphs," as he read; yet he read on and had nearly finished a particularly progressive and "new-fangled" chapter when he fell asleep.

"Dear me, I must have slept a long time!" exclaimed Mr. Langschlaf, yawning prodigiously, and then looking at this watch, he added, "'Pon my word, six o'clock, and the sun low in the sky, and I am as hungry as a wolf; wonder why they haven't called me to dinner?"

So saying he started to the house, but when he emerged from the grove in which he had been sleeping, he stopped and began to rub his eyes in extreme bewilderment. What could it mean? When he had fallen asleep a few hours since, he left a beautiful open meadow intersected by a clear meandering brook, and studded with groups of trees; now, as far as he could see, rose stately palaces and beautiful public buildings; they crowded up to the very iron fence which enclosed his own park. Was he still asleep? Well, he would go up to the house and they would soon wake him up there with their clatter, he'd warrant.

He reached his house to find it deserted. Doors and windows appeared to have been closed for ages. Yet strange to say, the garden bore no evidence of neglect. On the contrary, it was filled with many rare flowers and shrubs he never had even heard of, and tall trees waved their graceful branches over his head. The amazed owner of the house pulled the doorbell violently; no response but the ringing peal within. He tried side doors, and back doors, with equal success, and in despair started off to the neighboring town for some one to assist him in breaking into his own house.

The pretty iron gate turned easily and smoothly on its hinges, and Mr. Langschlaf stepped off his own premises — not into the dusty road that but that morning had led to town — but on to the marble pavement of a broad and apparently endless street, which was adorned on either side with stately places of exquisite beauty. These palaces were surrounded by beautiful grounds, ornamented with clusters of trees, groups of flowers, and vine-covered nooks from which gleamed statuary in white and polished beauty The street itself was inlaid with various colored marbles in pretty fanciful arabesque. Tall trees interlaced their delicate foliage over head, and on each side was a foot path adorned with flowers and pretty fountains, which sent their translucent spires high into the air.

"I am dreaming," murmured Mr. Langschlaf, "and this I suppose is Paradise. I wish I could come across some of the angels — hallo! there's one now!" and off he started at full speed towards a man somewhat strangely but becomingly attired, who had a fine commanding presence, and walked slowly along with an open book in his hand.

"Sir," said our friend, when he had recovered his breath, "Sir, will you be kind enough to tweak my nose?"

The stranger turned around and regarded the author of this rather unusual request with astonishment, which, however, soon gave place to rapturous delight, and he exclaimed without heeding the aforesaid request —

"Good heavens! can it be possible? What have I done to be so blessed? An old man, positively an old man! With the gray hair and beard so accurately described in my book! I am the happiest man in the world!"

"Umph," muttered Langschlaf, "he speaks English anyway; but this man is a lunatic. I am not old enough to be an object of curiosity, I should think;" and then aloud to the stranger, who continued to regard him with increasing interest and delight, he said —

"I made a polite request of you sir, but as it is, I confess, rather a singular one, I will explain why I made it. I laid down to day about 1 o'clock, P.M., to take a nap, leaving my own place surrounded by beautiful meadows and streams, I awake at 6 P.M., meadows, woods, and streams have disappeared, and a city has arisen in their place — a city so beautiful that I must think I still dream, for naught like it exists on earth. I was reading some absurd nonsense about progress and future perfection just before I sent to sleep, and I suppose I am dreaming of it now. Now sir will you be kind enough to pull my nose?"

"After you have answered me a few questions," replied the stranger, "but first let us be seated where we can talk quietly," and he led the amazed and somewhat indignant Langschlaf into one of the many lovely gardens — found some charming seats under a myrtle tree and requesting Langschlaf to take one he appropriated the other.

"I think it would be more polite of you to comply with my request without any conditions, but I presume from the rude manner in which you alluded to my age that politeness is at a discount here, however, proceed with your questions," and Mr. Langschlaf settled himself comfortably in his place.

"I beg pardon if I have offended," said the stranger earnestly, "I assure you it was unintentional."

"Go on please," interrupted Langschlaf — "I am in a hurry, and most outrageously hungry."

"In a hurry," repeated the stranger meditatively, "in a hurry — and old — upon my word it is extraordinary! But," he added, aloud, "your hunger can be easily satisfied."

So saying, he took from a pocket a singular looking little instrument somewhat like a watch, which he placed upon the ground. "Your dinner will be here directly," he remarked to Langschlaf; and presently a white object like a large bird appeared in the air above their heads, descended swiftly, and lit on the ground before them. It proved on inspection to be something like a balloon — but beautiful and delicate in its construction. From this singular vehicle a pretty boy came forth with a slender cane in his hand. This he unfolded and formed a table which he placed before the two gentlemen and soon this novel table was covered with a charming repast.

"Wonderful!" exclaimed Langschlaf "this looks like witchcraft — I am almost afraid to eat a dinner so mysteriously provided — but I'll risk it." And he immediately fell to with an eagerness that made the two spectators stare.

"I wonder he ever lived to be old if that's the rate he generally consumes food," said the host, *sotto voce*.

The keen edge taken off his appetite, Mr. Langschlaf discovered his companion was not eating, and pressed him to take something.

"Thank you. I had just dined when I met you, but I will join you in a glass of wine at dessert."

When the dessert was served the stranger dismissed the waiter saying, "I will signal for you when I want you again." "Thank you, sir," replied the waiter, "I cannot well be spared from the restaurant just now; we are very busy preparing for a grand entertainment which is to come off in South Africa to-morrow evening, and I have charge of the ices which we are expecting every moment."

"Where do you get your ices now?" asked the host.

"From the North Pole at present, sir. The Confectioner at the South had more than he could well attend to, and the North was a few thousand miles nearer." And the waiter stepped into his air chariot, touched a kind of organ stop in the side of it, and was off in a moment.

"Marvelous!" muttered the astonished Langschlaf, "entertainment in South Africa — ices expected from the North pole — navigating the air with balloons propelled by organ stops! Umph, wonder if the fellow ever means to pull my nose? But I don't believe I care to wake up just yet. I feel better since I ate my dinner. Your health, sir," he added aloud, turning to his entertainer, "will you oblige me by telling me your name?"

"I am William Thornfield, Professor of Antiquities and Curiosities in the Grand Theater of Agreeable Science at Universalia." Your health, sir, (rather an odd expression, but I suppose he is used to it) said Mr. Thornfield to himself, "your health, sir, and happiness."

"And I am John Langschlaf at your service, and ready now to answer any questions you may ask. (Umph, professor in a theater, indeed)."

"Thank you," answered the Professor. "In the first place, then, please tell me in what year you went to sleep."

"What year? Why this morning, I tell you — about five hours since."

The Professor smiled curiously and asked,

"And what year do you call this, then?"

"Young man," said Mr. Langschlaf, gravely, "I am not so ignorant as not to know the year in which I live, but I promised to answer your questions and I will, with what patience I may. This is Anno Domini, eighteen hundred and sixty-five."

"Really, the most remarkable instance of prolonged somnolence I ever heard of. Do you really mean to say you went to sleep in the year 1865, and have never waked until now? If this is true you are the most valuable relic on the earth; the finest specimen of antiquity extant; the greatest curiosity on the planet."

As the Professor spoke he grew more excited with every word, and his voice grew higher and higher.

"Umph!" grunted the irate Langschlaf, "valuable relic, indeed! specimen of antiquity, forsooth! complete curiosity — upon my word, this is too much" — and he rose indignantly and was about to go, but the Professor, seeing his anger, said

"I beg your pardon, sir, if I have offended you. I did not intend it; but I was astonished out of my propriety. Have you any idea how long your siesta lasted? Permit me to inform you that you have slept just five hundred years. This is the year two thousand three hundred and sixty-five — and, now I can account for your bewilderment. Good heavens! how much you have to learn, and how much you can teach us of the past."

"Then I am not asleep now? asked Mr. Langschlaf. "Not at all," replied the Professor.

"What name have you given this beautiful city which looks like Paradise?"

"City — city — oh yes. I remember you did in your day have cities and town — I may say this is one great city, and it is called Universalia."

"Indeed! well, I presume I have not changed my location since I went to sleep? I hope I am still in America."

"Yes, so was this part of the world called in your day and for many years afterwards. When oceans, mountains, and rivers separated the various parts of the earth were necessary, and even yet they are used to designate the different parts of Universalia. This is supposed to be what was once called the 'United States,' though historians differ as to its exact locality — s ome even deny its existence, but I am convinced such a nation did really exist for many years in this part of the world, and that they were actually known as the United States of America. Your evidence, sir, will place the truth of my theory beyond a doubt."

John Langschlaf had not interrupted the speaker before, for the simple reason that he was speechless with indignation. Now, however, he stammered in accents of intense rage —

"My evidence will prove it indeed. What sir!" and patriotic pride gave strength to his voice — "Do you mean to tell me there is any doubt of the existence of the United States of America? Do you mean to insult the American flag, sir? Do you pretend to question the existence of the great American Eagle? Do you, sir, I ask, pretend ignorance to the best government the world ever saw? Sir, I will not stand it."

"Do not get excited sir, I entreat," said the dismayed Professor. "I only said others doubted these things. I do not, as I said before, at all doubt that such a country existed, nay, that it played a very important part in the world's history for quite a long period. I do not dispute the existence of a flag or national ensign as it was the custom then for all nations, as they called themselves, to have such things. As for the eagle, I have seen too many stuffed specimens, in the museums to have any doubts on the subject, — I beg you will finish your wine and then we will take a stroll through the neighboring streets and you can see some of the changes which five centuries have wrought."

This was sensible advice and our friend much mollified, finished his wine. The professor again placed his apparatus on the ground — the air chariot appeared, and the waiter removed the debris of the dinner.

"Tell me," said Langschlaf, after the balloon had departed, "what do you call that wonderful little instrument, and by what power it communicates with people at a distance?"

"This instrument is an Aggelos, or Messenger, and the power is what you called Electricity. The telegraph wires interfered greatly with air navigation, so our men of science set to work to discover some easier and more convenient method. The mighty powers of electricity — the many currents of that fluid constantly traversing earth and air, had been tolerably well ascertained. The Aggelos is the last and best of many inventions of the same sort, and is now in universal use. To send a message you have only to put this into communication with that current of electricity which goes to the place to which the message is sent. This is easily learned, as every body can understand the current science. I sent my message to Paris from which place we received our dinner."

"But is it possible it could have come in so short a time? It was not half an hour coming."

"It is true nevertheless my friend, electricity is the swiftest traveler, except thought, that we have any knowledge of."

"Electricity? Do you propel by electricity?"

"Of course we do. The great power of electricity, or as we call it now, Lucistra, was first discovered by means of a singular delusion which at one time attacked the civilized world, as it was then called, with great violence, and spread with unexampled rapidity. At first it was left to the ignorant, the superstitious and the designing; the latter pretended to use it as a medium of communication with the spirit world, and succeeded in palming off the most absurd compositions as the work of departed authors. But finally it attracted the attention of scientific men, who studied it thoroughly as a science, and from this apparent delusion they elicited the divine spark of light which was destined to illuminate the world. By it time and space are annihilated, people of separate nations brought into daily and hourly intercourse with each other, and knowledge disseminated with unparalleled rapidity and clearness."

"And this came from spirit rapping. Well, I never would thought that humbug could have brought good to the human race," said Langschlaf, musingly.

"And now," said the Professor, rising, "let's promenade. This is the very time to walk, we will meet the beauty and elegance of our part of the globe at this hour."

There was a gay crowd on the street when they entered it, and Mr. Langschlaf remarked that there seemed no prevailing fashion in the dresses, yet everybody looked well, and becomingly dressed. Some gentlemen wore the heavy plumed hat and richly laced costume of Charles the Second; others wore the Spanish dress with its rich sombre colors, and graceful low crowned hat; and some wore a combination of these styles.

As for the ladies, all ages and fashions seemed to have united to do them homage. Light, gauzy, diaphanous fabrics floated in bewildering mazes around forms of exquisite beauty. Bright eyes gleamed from beneath bonnets, and hats of all styles were becoming and pretty; all the fabrics of all the looms seemed here assembled in one irresistible phalanx. But John Langschlaf was an old bachelor, and of course, somewhat cynical, so he said to his companion, somewhat sneeringly:

"You seem to have a sort of chronic Fancy Dress Ball in Universalia. Does the quartier Paris still set the fashions?"

"Fashion, my dear sir," said the Professor, "exists no longer. She is among the dethroned Deities. Everyone dresses, now, in the style most becoming to them. We have dressmakers and tailors still, but they are educated at art schools, and the only criterion they go by is the peculiar style of the person to be dressed. Everyone is taught the art of dress thoroughly; nothing becoming is rejected because it is old fashioned; and nothing unbecoming worn because it is fashionable. There are, however, certain rules of health and taste that control fancies, which would otherwise become extravagant."

"Well, that is an improvement," said Langschlaf, "but still I suppose needlewomen will sit up all night for the next night's ball, and ruin their health for gay people's pleasure."

"By no means," answered the Professor. "Needlewomen is an obsolete term. When a lady wants a new dress, she places her Aggelos in a certain current, and her dress Artiste appears. 'I want this dress this evening for a reception.' 'In what part of the world, Madam.' This answered, the next question is, have you any choice of colors? If the lady is an original, or has any particular reason for wishing a certain color, she answers accordingly. The artiste then steps into her Aeolita and goes home. The style decided upon, she signals to the various quarters of the globe for her materials. When these arrive, a machine takes them up, cuts, makes and turns out a complete dress in about ten minutes. The artiste has nothing to do but order the materials and decide on the style. Manual labor is now performed by machinery"

By this time a dense crowd had collected around our two friends, and Mr. Langschlaf became uncomfortably conscious that he was an object of intense curiosity to those about him.

"What extraordinary hair!" said one. "And what a singular beard!" added another. "Oh! what a funny face," cried a little boy, "all full of little ridges."

"This is very disagreeable," said Mr. Langschlaf. "I really don't see what there is about me to create such excitement."

"It is your age, Sir," said the Professor.

"But I am not a Methusaleh," said Mr. Langschlaf, "have they never seen an elderly gentleman before?"

"Most of them never have," replied the Professor. "You will see no old looking people here. I, for instance, am nearly sixty; yet you see how young I look. We never permit ourselves to look older than thirty-five, which we look upon as the handsomest age."

"But how do you prevent it?" asked our friend eagerly.

"The science of Hygiene is so thoroughly and universally understood that sickness and old age are unknown to this generation. We are gradually drawing near primitive longevity and health. Blindness, deafness, deformity and all 'the thousand ills that flesh is heir to,' or was supposed to be in Shakespeare's time, are rapidly disappearing from the world."

The crowd now became quite oppressive and the Professor said to his companion:

"'I am afraid you will have to be rejuvenated, my friend."

"Afraid!" exclaimed Langschlaf. "I only wish I could."

"Oh, it can be done. That is if the machine is not out of order from long disuse. The last subject for rejuvenation was an old man we found in the mountains of South America. But I regret, exceedingly, the necessity of rejuvenating you. Your evidence would be so much more convincing, enforced by your venerable appearance."

"Oh hang the evidence. Take me along quick," said Langschlaf. "Where is this wonderful machine?"

"Only a few moments distance, in Calcutta." And the Professor signaled for an Aeoline, as their airships were called.

"What are they stuffed with?"

"Air," replied his companion.

"And have you no railways at all, now?" asked Langschlaf, when they got underway.

"Oh yes' Plenty of them over the gardens and plains; but they are no longer the railways of your days. Our airships are not much used for transportation except to and from the Stars. We bring goods by them only when we are in immediate want of them. Ices, delicate confectionaries, and fine wines, which are injured by a sea-voyage from their principal freight. I will show you a rail-road tomorrow, for I want to take you to see a friend of mine who lives near the Pyramids."

"I suppose there are no such things as steamships?"

"Well, no, not steamships. Our ships are compelled by condensed air. This does away with cumbrous machinery, smoke, explosion, and other disagreeable things. But here we are at Calcutta."

They alighted before a large and tastefully decorated building, and entered the pretty grounds which were ornamented with statues representing youth and old age. Over the door of the house was a beautiful bas relief of Ponce de Leon and his men grouped round a fountain; underneath this was carved a word, Eureka. The grounds were also adorned with various fountains of rare beauty, all having reference to stories of those who at various times have gone in search of the Fountain of Eternal Youth. Statues of youth and health filled niches on either side of the hall as they entered the house, and a bronze statue of Cagliostro stood in the center.

A tall, stately man of about thirty-eight or forty years, came forward to meet our friends as they entered. He, like everybody else they met, seemed to be well acquainted with the Professor, and greeted him cordially.

"I have brought you a subject, Mr. Neuman," said the Professor, presenting his companion.

"Indeed!" exclaimed Mr. Neuman, "I had no idea there was one on this planet. I have been thinking strongly of emigrating to the moon if the new Climate Equalizer succeeds there as well as it has elsewhere."

"As it undoubtedly will," said the Professor, "advices from there to-day announce a decided improvement already."

Mr. Langschlaf here reminded the gentlemen that he was not there for the purpose of hearing news from the moon. With a polite stare of surprise at his haste, Professor Thornfield related his friends singular story, and surrendered him to Mr. Neuman, and saying, "I will wait for you at the entrance," took his leave.

Mr. Neuman then turned to his subject and asked what age he would prefer. Mr. Langschlaf answered "twenty-five." Mr. Neuman suggested that from thirty to forty was the favorite age for gentlemen, but Mr. Langschlaf persisted in being quite a young man; he would be thirty soon enough.

"Not unless you wish to," answered the operator, "but we will proceed to the preparatory bath-room, if you please."

When the bath was over, which Mr. Langschlaf enthusiastically said was elysium, the "subject" was led to a soft couch, where he fell asleep. When he awoke he was standing dressed near a door-way in which stood his friend, the Professor, who inquired "how he felt now."

"Like a new man," answered Langschlaf, joyfully.

"Well, that's just what you are," said the Professor, laughing. "Have you looked at yourself?" "No!" "Why, turn round, man, and take a look!" and he pointed to what Langschlaf thought was an open door. He approached, and met a handsome young man coming towards him.

"Will you let me pass, if you please," said Langschlaf, bowing politely to the stranger. The latter only returned the bow, but did not move from his place in the door.

A burst of laughter made him turn round, and perceiving as he did so that the stranger imitated him, he suspected the truth, and, stretching out his hand, encountered the mirror. But he was too much delighted with the reflection before him to get at all vexed with his friend's laughter. Turning to Mr. Neuman, he grasped his hand, and said, "Sir, all my fortune, were it ten times as great as it is, would not repay you for what you have done; but all I have I will freely give you, if you should require so much. What do I owe you, sir?"

"Nothing at all," said Mr. Neuman with a bow. "The scientific fund affords me an ample support."

The two took leave of Mr. Neuman with many cordial invitations for him to come and see them, which he promised to do.

On the way home the Professor explained to Mr. Langschlaf that all scientific or useful discoveries of every kind, were most liberally paid for by the grand central academy of Science. That a fund was set apart for the support of all who made useful inventions or discoveries, and that they were not allowed to receive any other fees.

"This," he said, "humbugging, as it was formerly called, has been entirely abolished."

"By the way," exclaimed Langschlaf, "abolishing makes me think of the negroes. What did you do with them?"

The Professor laughed. "That was a puzzle," said he. "Such a time as we had! They were colonized first in one place and then another, but a race of people called the 'Universal Yankee,' because they seemed to have been scattered all over the globe, but principally in America — would follow them up, and push them out, until we began to think that they would be pushed into the ocean. The invention of air ships, however, and the discovery of the Respirator rendered the most distant climates accessible, and we packed them off bag and baggage to Jupiter. The climate of that planet being twice as warm as ours, and very little diversified, even the Yankees could not stand it, and there the negro race lives and flourishes. They furnish us with an abundance of cotton, rice, sugar, coffee, and many other tropical productions. There lived at that time a singular race of people called 'Radicals,' and they were so perfectly devoted to the negro race, we thought of course they would like to go with them. So far from that, they were violently opposed to sending them away, or in fact, doing anything at all with them. They seem to have been a very strange sort of being: constantly talking one way and doing another — wanting to annihilate inoffensive white people in order to confer very questionable benefits on the black. But they are all gone now. I don't think there is one left."

Mr. Langschlaf did not think it necessary to mention that he had been slightly tinctured with radicalism himself.

"Does it ever get dark now?" presently inquired Mr. Langschlalf, who was by this time prepared for any revelation.

"Not in our Aeolines," answered the Professor, "because the propelling force is light and its irradiations make daylight around us."

Mr. Langschlaf no longer found himself the center of attraction when he walked in the streets; and as he had no ambition to represent Methusaleh or old Parr, in the present enlightened age, he was quite satisfied, nay delighted, with the change. The Professor, however, suggested that a more becoming costume than the one his friend wore, might possibly be procured, to which Langschlaf assented, and, hailing an Aeolita, which was quite strong enough for so short a journey, they flew over to London, and our hero was soon dressed in a suit very becoming to his style, grave, elegant, but with a slight dash of uniqueness in it. When they returned home the Professor insisted on taking his (literally) new made friend home with him.

Mr. Langschlaf found a most interesting group assembled in the pleasant library at the Professors house. Mrs. Thornfield was charming, the daughters lively, pretty, and exceedingly interesting. The boys were — oh, wonder of wonders! quiet, decorus and agreeable. One of them was reading a drama which the others were criticising with great good humor and wit. They all turned bright faces of welcome to the door as the gentlemen entered, and greeted their father with enthusiasm.

The introduction of a stranger caused no embarrassment to the family group. They received him cordially and soon found himself entering into their joy and badinage with equal spirit and zest.

"Whose play were you reading as we entered?" asked the father.

"Bertha's," answered the reader. "It is called 'The Reign of Genius'. The scene is laid in England and Greece, and the time is that in which Bryon and Shelly lived."

"Good!" said the father with an approving smile on the blushing authoress.

"So your daughter is an authoress," said Langschalf.

"No, not particularly, though she writes very well. All the advanced scholars are required to write dramas in which their various studies are introduced; for we no longer have schools such as they had in your day, but theatres. Instead of the dry, dull books, which were enough one would think to stupefy the brightest intellect, or disgust the most enthusiastic lover of learning, we have dramas, written by the greatest geniuses of our time, performed by the very best actors. Nothing mediocre is admitted either in composition or performance. The scenery is painted by the best artists from nature. The dresses and properties are in strict keeping with the times represented. Knowledge is thus made both attractive and impressive. The scholars, too, as you see, write plays and perform them; and you have no idea how charmingly even the dryest sciences can be introduced into a play. Genius illumines everything it touches. It is the magic wand of the magician of olden days. Although customs and manners have changed, and empires have vanished from the earth, genius never changes; her favored children are ever young."

"I noticed no churches in our travels," said Langschalf after a pause: "has religion become obsolete, also?"

"God forbid," said the Professor reverently. "You saw no churches because the world has become one vast Temple. Science, literature and art have become teachers too potent to resist. Every theatre, every lecture-room, every pleasure, speaks to the world of Him who gave us all things. Yet we still have what I suppose you would call sermons, divine inspirations, glorious visions, which will not be repressed. Some men endowed with the glorious gift of eloquence, illumine our mind and hearts with words that burn. These sermons are spread over the whole earth by means of the Pschycometra, the very grandest invention of the age. Every orator or writer has in his study a grand Lucistral Centre — that is a concentration of electric currents from all parts of the earth. In this centre the Pschycometra is placed. The sermon, or poem or lecture is read aloud in the study, and the Pschycometra repeats the words thus spoken to all the world; for in every house is an annunciator which repeats the sentences as they fall. The electric current conveys the sound nearly as rapidly as it does vision. We have also another messenger, called Fausta, because it supplies the place of newspapers, which became entirely too large and numerous for comfort, and failed to keep us cn rapport with the old parts of the earth. We have Faustas in every room. — Perhaps you would like to see one? Mr. Langschlaf would be charmed," the Professor continued, as he rang a sweetly sounding little bell which stood on a table. "This is about the hour for the morning lecture in the Pekin Theatre. We will receive one of them, Ernest" (to one of the boys), "attend the Fausta, if you please."

Ernest rose and stood by a line bronze statue of Faust, which stood in a niche near the mantlepiece. In a few moments the statue slowly lifted his arm to the wall; a pretty painted panel flew open, and the statue received in its hand a printed paper, which it handed to Ernest. Many of these printed sheets were thus received — some of which were beautifully illustrated. Having finished its work the statue shut the panel and resumed its original position. Ernest went to a distant corner of the room where stood what appeared to be an ordinary work table. He placed the leaves in a drawer, and in a few moments returned with a neatly bound book entitled "The Poetry of Beauty; a lecture delivered in the Aesthetic Theatre at Pekin," with the date. The lecture was read aloud by the second son, and when it was finished the Professor remarked:

"The art of beauty occupies a very important space in the learning of the present day. It is owing to this fact, sir, that your house has remained untouched, and your grounds kept in such order. The quaint old grey stone house was a picturesque feature in the landscape, and your park possessed great natural beauty — so it has been carefully tended and the house kept in repair — but still its original appearance preserved." It was late when Mr. Langschlaf retired. His host had many questions to ask and many things to tell — but the sleep which visited him was sweet and refreshing.

Next morning sweet music awakened him- — he turned towards a window and looking out, saw the children starting off to school, singing as they went. Their voices were excellent and well cultivated, and they sang a chorus from Lucia.

"Music too, like poetry, is imperishable," mused Mr. Langschlaf, as he listened to the familiar strains.

"Bless me! What's this?" A pretty table laden with coffee, cakes, and fruit, rose slowly out of the floor by his bedside. A gilt statue of Minerva turned in its niche at the head of his bed, and handed him a paper. Mr. Langschlaf rubbed his eyes. "Oh, yes, I remember now. You madam, are a Fausta I suppose, and this," turning to the little table, "is a waiter with my morning coffee," and he helped himself to coffee and oranges — coolly took the paper from the statue, and after looking at it, said facetiously:

"You needn't trouble yourself to hand me any more, Mrs. Minerva Fausta, for I can't read a word except the date and names. Well keep on, Madame, if you wish," he continued as Minerva quickly dropped the papers on his pillow.

Presently she placed a little pamphlet by the papers, and then became motionless.

Langschlaf picked up the pamphlet which proved to be a key to the characters in which the papers were printed. They were simple abbreviations, and he soon mastered the secret; whereupon he thanked Mrs. Minerva Fausta very politely, and read till time to dress for breakfast.

"Quite a pleasant day for our visit to the Pyramids," said the host, as his friend entered the cheerful breakfast room.

"Charming," answered the latter. "I heard your children going off to their Theatres quite early. Do they have far to go?"

"My oldest son is at present in a Theatre of Art, in Italy, and my oldest daughter has a few moments since reached Paris. They do not remain more than a day at a time in any one place, and sometimes visit two or three Theatres in one day."

"Is education expensive?" asked Langschlaf.

"It costs nothing," answered his host. "All children are provided for by the Grand Central Committee on support and education. Parents are simply the natural guardians of their children's manners and morals. Children are regarded as the true wealth of the world, and nurtured accordingly. These funds are supplied by taxation. But we will not discuss this further, for my daughter tells me there is to be a grand matinee concert at the Theatre of Music in Paris, and we must hear it."

Then they adjourned to the library where they were soon joined by a number of the Professor's particular friends, who came in to listen to the music. "Because," said one, "you have the finest auricula we know of anywhere."

"What is an auricula?" asked Langschlaf.

"You will soon find out," said the Professor as he pressed a spring in the wall. Instantly the room was filled with melody. For an hour the audience was entranced.

"Perhaps you would like to see the performers," said the Professor to Langschlaf.

"I would indeed," replied the latter.

Whereupon the host drew aside a curtain, and revealed a large stage, upon which stood a quartette of singers.

"Marvellous!" exclaimed the astonished Langschlaf. "This looks indeed like magic."

"Only the magic of science," answered his friend. "This is the occularium, and the only magic necessary to its use is an accurate knowledge of the laws of light. I can show you any public exhibition of any kind, now going on anywhere in Universalia. Also, any picture gallery, public garden or any other object of public interest because these are all put in communication with every house by means of occularia. In the same manner we listen to all public concerts, operas, etc., by the means of auricularia."

"I see you still have to go to the dead languages for names for your inventions," observed Langschlafwhen the concert was over.

"My dear friend there are no dead languages. No language can die, into which thought has been infused. Dialects perish, leaving only relics behind them, but a language which has once been the vehicle of thought can no more perish than can a body while the soul is in it. Genius is immortal, and immortalizes all it touches. As I said before, music and poetry cannot die, nor can the words and sounds thus wedded, ever perish. English is the universal language, it is true, but every one understands and speaks all languages as you have remarked, doubtless, before this. The human mind cannot be idle, and since we are no longer obliged to work, we have ample leisure to acquire all sorts of information. The industry and energy formerly expended in earning a support are now directed to cultivating the mind and beautifying the world in which we live."

"Yet somebody must cultivate the soil. I have several times intended to ask you where you grow the produce this vast city consumes. I have seen some fields, but they seem meant more for ornament than use."

"We have one field," answered the Professor, "which more than suffices for our wants, and that is the planet Mars. The long seasons and equable temperature of this planet, render it peculiarly fitted for an agricultural district. One of the Asteroids — Ceres — having been equalized by the great climate Regulator, serves for our vegetable garden and orchard, though we raise great quantities of fruit here, as you will see in our journey to the Pyramids. A complete system of irrigation has made the 'Great Desert' literally 'bloom and blossom as the rose'."

"In a few years your city will be too crowded for comfort, for I believe the whole earth is covered with buildings now."

"Oh no — there are the deserts — but it would be a pity to spoil those lovely gardens, and we have still the rural districts of South America, Africa, and Australia, and the Arctic and Antarctic regions. It will take several generations to fill them up, and then there are the stars."

"Well, suppose we had better be starting for the Pyramids. I think if we mean to reach them to-day, we will have to hurry."

"My dear friend," remonstrated the Professor, "I have several times heard you use that obsolete word. Electric Locomotion is not used because we are in a hurry but to bring the inhabitants of the earth into frequent and familiar intercourse with each other, and to render the effects of climate on the human system of permanent and practical benefit. It has long been an established fact that climate exercises a powerful influence on the mind and body — and that judicious and constant change of temperature will alone poison the health of the body, which in its turn preserves the mind in a healthy tone. Sick bodies make sick minds — cause morbid fancies. The great evil called 'Sin,' with which our earth was cursed in your day, has disappeared, together with ill health and diseased minds; partly because of universal health — and partly because the secresy which gave sin its greatest charm has been removed. The veil of concealment removed, its mokanna visage appeared. Many things whichwere called sin appeared not under that Veil — and other things, long received and admired as virtues astounded the people by appearing in their true colors. This veil has deceived society for many centuries and sometimes called virtue, sometimes custom, and sometimes even the sacred name of Religion was profaned by it. But it is really time to go now — if you are ready. Would you like to take a sea-voyage to the African coast, and there take an Aeolita to Timbuctoo, or do you prefer making the whole journey by the air-line?"

"I think I will try a sea-voyage if it is not too long. I have a curiosity to see your new ships" — said Langschlaf.

"The journey can be long or short, at your pleasure. Some people are very fond of the sea, and we have slow Vessels for their benefit — others dislike it, so you can be half a day or two weeks just as you like."

"Half a day is long enough to be sea-sick," answered Langschlaf.

"Sea-sick! That's good! Why my friend sea-sickness is utterly unknown now."

So they took ship. Noiselessly and smoothly, without jarring or smoke the stately palace floated from the marble quay, and in very truth walked the waters like a thing of life. — Silently and swiftly she bore them over the ocean, and landed them safely on the west coast of Africa. After a little promenade through the fine public gardens and a visit to the Hygienic Lecture Hall, they took an Aeolita for Timbuctoo. At the place they visited the Pschycological Theatre and then the Professor led the way to a beautiful park in which stood a great number of tiny cottages. They were built in various styles of architecture, but all exquisitely beautiful. The doors stood hospitably open, and many people were entering them. — The Professor took his companion into one built in the oriental style. — -The interior was beautifully finished and tastefully decorated with pictures and statuary. One room was fitted up as a library, with books, writing materials, and luxurious reading chairs. In one of these chairs the professor took seat and invited his companion to do the same — handing him at the same time some papers to read.

"Are you ready to start?" asked the Professor of his friend.

"Ready? Yes, but where are the cars?"

"You are in one," said Thornfield, "and now we are off." And even as he spoke the fairy little cottage moved swiftly on its way.

"Well, this is life," exclaimed Langschlaf in ecstasy. "What a beautiful country," and he threw open the blinds to get a better view.

It was indeed most lovely. As far as the eye could reach a prospect of mingled grove and plain, and mountain and river, stretched out before them. It was a vast garden of incomparable beauty. Art and nature came so near together one could scarcely tell where nature ended and art began. Flowers of every hue, blossoming trees and shrubs, and gorgeous, trailing tropical vines, mingled in symmetrical yet natural beauty. Citron and apple, orange and cherry trees, bloomed and bore fruit side by side. Groups of gaily dressed people gave a picturesque life to the scene. Here an open plain appeared, dotted with herds of sheep and cattle. There a placid lake spread its calm beauty to the sun, bearing upon its glossy surface tiny fleets of many colored sails. Some, like white doves, scudded before the breeze, others with gaudy sails, glided slowly like languid tropical birds, along the shore. Sweet strains of softest music floated like incense from lake and plain; even the air was vocal forever, and anon an air ship sailed over their heads bearing a gay party who beguiled the journey with "concord of sweet sounds." But the journey soon ended, too soon for Langschlaf who was in a revery of delight.

Arrived at the Pyramids, the Professor introduced Langschlaf to his friend who welcomed them both, saying to Langschlaf, "I have heard of you, sir, and am most happy to see you." When after dinner they rose to go, their host would not hear of it, but insisted on their staying all night.

"I expect some friends from Sweden any moment, one of whom, I am sure, Mr. Langschlaf will be charmed to meet," said he.

"Pray, who can that be?" asked Langschlaf. "I am sure I know nobody in Sweden."

"Wait and see" was the only answer he received.

The expected guests soon arrived and were shown into the drawing room. Among them was a lady, young, beautiful and fascinating. Langschlaf was so charmed with her that even the fact that she was a distinguished writer failed to shock him. Nay, even the discovery that she was remarkably learned did not fill him with the horror it should have inspired. At last the incorrigible had met his fate! — and when the party left he knew his heart had gone with it. He could not sleep for thinking of those glorious eyes, and that musical voice which made even mathematics fascinating — while she talked of it.

Her manner too, so natural and versatile, and that bright face which reflected every emotion of her soul.

Next morning at breakfast the host said to Langschlaf. "Was I right in my prophesy?"

"Yes," answered Langschlaf with a candor that surprised himself — "I was charmed indeed."

"I think they were intended for each other" said the Professor gravely, — a remark which filled Langschlaf with the wildest hopes. "Let's go to Sweden," said he eagerly.

"By all means," said the Professor. "But first let's go home and build a house on those pretty grounds of yours fitting for such a bride."

"But I must first see her," said Langschlaf — "I don't know yet what she thinks of it — I shouldn't like to get all ready and then be — be — refused."

"No danger of that, my friend. We have not studied the sciences of physiognomy and Psychology for nothing. In your place we would be certain, as it is, we can only say we are convinced you are meant for each other."

Thus re-assured, our hero — for now he is in love, we may call him such — consented to go home — by the airline this time — and gave his friend no rest until an architect was secured; and the house contracted for to be finished and furnished by the next evening.

"Suppose we go and select the site for your house." said the architect.

"Good!" answered Langschlaf, and they started of immediately. As they opened the gate the same little urchin who had waked him up on that memorable evening five hundred years ago emerged from behind a group of flowering shrubs.

"So you've waked up at last." said the little fellow to Langschalf. "I rather think you won't drive me off again. Now that you have learned what I can do, you won't object to my waking up the old fogies occasionally."

"Learned what you can do!" repeated Langschalf. "What have you done worth talking about, I'd like to know."

"All that you have seen is my work, and you have heard of me a thousand times."

"Who are you, then?" asked Langschlaf, "and what is your name!"

"I am the friend of humanity, civilization, and science. I can never grow old and never die. I employ my time waking up the dormant faculties of this world, and my name is Progress!" and with that he gave a loud shout and disappeared.

"Gracious! What a wonderful dream I have had," said John Langschlaf, staring around him, "wonder if I'm awake really this time." Here he was interrupted by a servant who told him dinner was ready.

"Ah! James looks natural any way," then turning to the servant, he said, "James, tweak my nose!"

"Sir!" exclaimed the astonished valet.

"Tweak my nose, I say," reiterated the irate master; and seeing James still hesitate, he roared:

"If you don't obey me, sir, I'll discharge you instantly!" Thus threatened, the servant gravely complied, and the mollified Langschalf, convinced he was really awake, said mildly:

"Thank you, James. I'm sure I'm awake now," and picking up his book, he followed the still bewildered James to the house. When he reached home he went straight to his library, and put the book (which was none other than Mr. Draper's recent book on America) on the very topmost shelf, muttering: "You are an admirable, pestiferous, progressive nuisance, and your author ought to be imprisoned for life. I wish, though," he added musingly, "I had found out that Swedish lady's residence; but pshaw! What nonsense! Think if I had found somebody like her ten years ago."

"Dinner is waiting, sir," said James at the door, and we leave him to his solitary meal.

Following an incident in Lincoln,

Nebraska, Fullerdyne created a series of

web pages to alert the public and media

about the related imminent threats

and dangers. Using very contemporary

storytelling techniques, Derek Austin

Johnson delves into a startling realistic

big business response to the tragedy.

Gray Goo and You

Derek Austin Johnson

Enter

Response to Situation in Lincoln, Nebraska

http://www.fullerdyne.com/lincoln_nebraska_update.html

We at Fullerdyne understand the public's concern with recent events in Lincoln, Nebraska, and want to ensure citizens across the state and the nation that we are taking every measure to contain and resolve the situation. We believe that each one of our customers and shareholders has helped contribute to our exponential growth over the past few decades, and seek not only your feedback but also your understanding in this unique and wholly unprecedented matter. It is our intention to restore Lincoln, Nebraska as closely to its initial state as possible, repairing all homes and buildings, including the historic Nebraska State Capitol and the much-beloved Lincoln Haymarket Arena (once again home of the Nebraska Cornhuskers!), making improvements to infrastructure and scrubbing the environment to guarantee habitability for human citizens.

Loss of life and displacement of citizens as a result of certain safety oversights has been regrettable, and Fullerdyne has every intention of compensating those bereaved, as well as those workers and business owners who have lost income, wages, and revenue, once the federal government and all involved courts determine Fullerdyne's ultimate responsibility.

About Fullerdyne

http://www.fullerdyne.com/about.htm

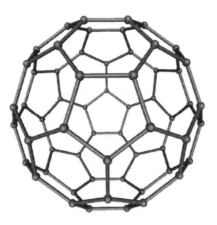

Fullerdyne was founded at the end of the second decade of this century by Dr. David Grimm, fresh from his thesis in applied physics and environmental engineering from Southern Methodist University, and Oliver Geat, entrepreneur and former CEO of TerraBliss, a start-up specializing in environmental technology. This pair of unique individuals saw the suffering of those who lost their homes throughout North America as a result of climatic mayhem: Mississippi floods that drowned once great cities from Minneapolis, Minnesota, to New Orleans, Louisiana, F5 tornadoes that leveled Andover, Kansas, and Fort Worth, Texas, hurricanes that devastated not only such Gulf cities as Galveston <click for environmental and demographic information but also towns across the eastern seaboard>>.

Early contributions made by Fullerdyne's founders provided vision and guidance in the face of environmental and potentially catastrophic economic collapse. This work by Fullerdyne included but was not limited to nanotech fabrication of food and necessities for persons displaced by environmental devastation. Although governments and many major corporations viewed their work as controversial — in many cases Fullerdyne requested not payment but data from environmental nomads — the public deemed their results as effective in restoring some semblance of balance, and by the middle of the 2030s, their work in geoengineering and environmental retrofitting through applied nanotech had given many comfort, solace, and above all balance.

As Fullerdyne moved into the 2040s, it proved vital in bringing prosperity to the nation, advancing nanotechnology, genetic engineering, and artificial intelligence research and applications to enhance the standard of living for citizenry throughout not only the nation but also the world.

Fullerdyne looks forward to helping shape a better world, especially in its vision of a post-Incident future!

Proposal for Resolving the Lincoln, Nebraska, Incident

http://www.fullerdyne.com/lincoln_nebraska
_incident_resolution_proposal.htm

We at Fullerdyne wish to ensure our customers and shareholders that we are taking the recent incident in Lincoln, Nebraska very seriously, and that it is our intention to allow citizens to return to their homes and businesses once this unique and unprecedented matter has been fully controlled and Lincoln, Nebraska has been returned to its original condition.

To that end, we would like to announce a deal with the Federal Emergency Management Agency and the Centers for Disease Control and Prevention, along with the United States Army Corps of Engineers, to cap Lincoln, Nebraska, with a quarantine bubble constructed of smart materials, which should be fully resistant to the outbreak. This bubble will burrow several thousand feet into the ground (a point where our team of independent engineers ensures

us is not affected by the incident) and will reach more than a thousand feet above the Chase Bank Tower in downtown Lincoln. Initial programming of the building and stock materials will be laid by the Army Corps of Engineers and should fully contain the town in less than seventy two hours.

(**Note:** the partnership between Fullerdyne, FEMA, the CDC, and the U.S. Army does not in any way indicate responsibility by Fullerdyne of the incident.)

Success in Containment of Lincoln, Nebraska

http://www.fullerdyne.com/lincoln_nebraska_update_02.html

 We at Fullerdyne would like to announce success in programming and growing a quarantine bubble over Lincoln, Nebraska, which will allow Fullerdyne, in partnership with the U.S. Army Corps of Engineers, FEMA, and the CDC to seal the area and should prevent it from affecting areas outside of Lincoln. Additional tests to be administered over the next several days will help determine the integrity of the quarantine bubble. Once the bubble's integrity has been ensured, we at Fullerdyne will begin looking at proposals to deactivate and reprogram the nanites within, which should stop their runaway replication.

We at Fullerdyne guarantee that residents and business owners will be allowed to return to Lincoln, Nebraska once the situation has been fully addressed and the town has been completely restored. However, we ask all residents and business owners to understand that this may not take place immediately, as containment may need to occur until all matters involving Fullerdyne and its role in the incident in Lincoln, Nebraska, and its responsibilities to the affected parties have been resolved by the federal courts.

Fullerdyne appreciates the understanding of its customers and shareholders and affected citizens throughout the nation.

Announcement of Town Hall Webcast
on the Incident in Lincoln, Nebraska

http://www.fullerdyne.com/town_hall_
announcement_on_lincoln_incident.html

We at Fullerdyne wish to ensure our customers and shareholders that we are making great progress in resolving the incident in Lincoln, Nebraska, and would like to ensure all citizens that we are considering every proposal to stop the runaway nanites.

We are looking at every possible facet and will select what we consider the optimal method after we have had the opportunity to run each scenario through the proper simulations. Once we have made our determination, we will inject the quarantine bubble with the proper programming to deactivate the nanites.

Fullerdyne understands the concern that all citizens have expressed throughout the communications network, and would like to address each issue in a town hall webcast to take place this Thursday, October 30, 2048. Sign up today to take part in the discussion.

(Note: at this time, Fullerdyne cannot comment on legal activity or any legal matters surrounding the incident in Lincoln, Nebraska.)

From: <recipient undisclosed>
To: gpj9824@cox.net
Date: October 27, 2048
Subject: Email Update Confirmation

On behalf of Fullerdyne, thank you for signing up to receive email notifications of important events, including those surrounding the incident in Lincoln, Nebraska. We take pride in providing you with personalized, up-to-date information. Please visit our website to ensure you receive updates on topics important to you, such as **the incident in Lincoln, Nebraska, upcoming town hall webcasts, the possibility of nanites escaping from the quarantine bubble** and t**he possibility of emergent artificial intelligence as a result of nanotechnology.**

Again, we thank you for your interest and continued support.

Sincerely,

The Fullerdyne Public Relations Management Team

Lincoln, Nebraska, Bubble Security, the Hot Spot, and Artifacts

http://www.fullerdyne.com/lincoln_nebraska_
bubble_security_and_artifacts.html

Fullerdyne wishes to assure all citizens that we are doing everything in our power to resolve the situation in Lincoln, Nebraska, as quickly, efficiently, and as safely as possible. We do not take the concerns of our customers and shareholders lightly, and wish to address each of them at our upcoming town hall webcast. However, because we wish complete transparency with regard to the Nebraska incident, we wish to address two news stories that have spread across all media outlets, both professional and unofficial.

Using infrared imaging and quantum entanglement optics, satellites operated by the Southeast Asia Consortium and in cooperation with the National Security Agency observed a "hot spot" near the northwestern surface of the Nebraska bubble two weeks after the bubble's successful growth. This "hot spot" completed a full navigation of the bubble after a period of several days before finally dissipating. The "hot spot" never in fact breached the surface.

Although multiple media outlets have speculated that the "hot spot" is evidence of the bubble's lack of integrity, repeated satellite observation and sensory reports from the bubble's receptors confirm that the bubble is more than adequate to ensure the safety of citizens of Nebraska.

Furthermore, although the satellites' quantum entanglement lenses, with the assistance of simulation software, were able to create a simulation of the interior of the bubble, at present neither Fullerdyne nor its team

of engineers or collaborative scientific minds have been able to determine the nature of the "hot spot" or what might have happened to it. In such times, of course speculation runs rampant (with including less reputable truthcast sites spreading fear-mongering stories about "emergent intelligences" evolving in a primal nanotechnological soup), but we urge all journalists to provide to their audiences a reasonable and accurate assessment of these events, rather than conjecture for the sake of increased traffic.

Additionally, recent truthcasts have reported artifacts that have been located outside of the bubble. Although spectators and curiosity seekers stated finding several of these twisted, gnarled objects 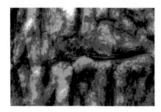 within twenty miles of the bubble's exterior, they are not a result of a bubble breach, but are fragments of the genetic sculpture commissioned by Rowena Li in 2026 for the DeCordova Sculpture Park. At present, Fullerdyne is uncertain how these fragments (described by art critics as a blend of Fractal Modernism, Mobius corals, and Genetic Noveau) wound up outside the bubble, but nonetheless is investigating the matter. Reports by respected forensic investigators indicate that the sculpture is in fact deceased, and poses no danger.

(**Note:** Individuals in possession of the Li pieces possess the property of the people of Lincoln, Nebraska, without their consent. Failure to make prompt return of any portion of the sculpture will result in criminal prosecution.)

From: <recipient undisclosed>
To: gpj9824@cox.net
Date: October 31, 2048
Subject: Response to Events Surrounding Fullerdyne's Town Hall Webcast

We at Fullerdyne would like to thank those customers, shareholders and other citizens who participated in our town hall webcast, and would again like to ensure those participants that their concerns will not go ignored.

The primary concern raised is the series of events that led to the incident in Lincoln, Nebraska. Unfortunately, for legal reasons Fullerdyne cannot comment on probable causes, except to say that faulty computational processes by computers monitoring nanotechnology experiments may have been a factor. Fullerdyne will provide full disclosure of the events surrounding the incident in Lincoln, Nebraska, once all details are known and it becomes politically and legally advantageous to do so.

Citizens and shareholders also asked questions about the displaced persons who have established shantytowns outside of Lincoln, Nebraska. In these new hamlets, former Lincoln residents are adapting to the lives of the new North American gypsy, powering accreted townships with solar energy, distilling water and transforming raw sewage into edible protein. Decrepit, rusted and otherwise unusable tractors and combines found in long-abandoned farms were refitted with worn struts and girders hammered into crude blades and attached to computers programmed with artificial life to till land outside the shanties for modest gardens. Documentary footage of these shanties may be found at *Life Among the Savages: Chronicles of Nanotech Displacement.* Fullerydne will allow these displaced persons to return to the town of Lincoln, Nebraska, as soon as it is safe and legally viable to do so. (**Note:** Although these temporary townships comprise residents of Lincoln, as well as onlookers, truthcasters, and environmental nomads, they are not being recognized as part of the governing body of Lincoln, Nebraska, and do not hold any interim political power.)

Citizens and shareholders have asked both about the health risks as a result of runaway replicators and the effects of runaway replicators on architectural integrity and infrastructure. Although risks of runaway nanotechnology are considerable, we do not believe they will be harmful once Fullerdyne has begun cleanup procedures. Moreover, we believe that we will need a complete study of the city's infrastructure once nanites have been brought under control, a process which may take several months — considerably longer than initially anticipated. We will provide shareholders and citizens with full details when it becomes legally feasible.

On behalf of all of us at Fullerdyne, we would like to thank all who provided spirited discussion during our town hall webcast. Please check our website again for information on our next webcast, at a date to be determined.

From: <recipient undisclosed>
To: gpj9824@cox.net
Date: November 1, 2048
Subject: Probes to Explore Interior of Quarantine Bubble

We at Fullerdyne are pleased to announce that we are sending a series robot probe to investigate the landscape and effects Lincoln, Nebraska has undergone in light of the runaway nanites.

Based in part on the Mars Exploration Rovers developed in 2003 (though armed with more manipulators and coated with durable, flexible and stretchable synthetic skin akin to what one finds in robotic surrogates found in Japan), these semi-autonomous probes will explore the interior of the quarantine bubble to determine the effects of the damage inflicted upon the city, including the environmental tolls taken by the nanites.

Programmers are already at work developing limited artificial life to allow them to navigate the topography within with minimal human interference.

Probes should begin their exploration on November 5, 2048.

(**Note:** Fullerdyne undertakes exploration of the interior of the quarantine bubble in the interest of research, and its actions in no way should be taken as acceptance of responsibility by Fullerdyne for the incident in Lincoln, Nebraska.)

Knowledge Gained of Lincoln, Nebraska by Probes Before Contact Lost

http://www.fullerdyne.com/lincoln_nebraska_update_06.html

On November 5, 2048, Fullerdyne launched a series of probes into the interior of the quarantine bubble surrounding Lincoln, Nebraska to determine the current state of the city, the damage it has undergone, and when residents may return to their homes and businesses.

Initial data appeared promising. Assemblers and replicators swarmed through the bubble's interior, looking, in the words of on truthcaster, "like an entire city overrun by a storm of smart  dust." These swarms have caused significant damage on architecture and infrastructure, making Lincoln, Nebraska, resemble a cityscape "designed by Max Ernst or Oscar Dominguez." These were the only images we received before Fullerdyne lost contact with the probes.

At this point, Fullerdyne does not have enough information to determine what caused loss of contact with the probes, although the most likely possibility is that swarms of nanites worked their way into the probes, causing a loss of integrity. However, we would like to ensure citizens and shareholders that we are diligently attempting to reestablish contact.

(At present, Fullerdyne cannot comment on random bursts of wifi traffic it has received through subsequent loss of communication with its probes.)

404 Not Found

http://www.fullerdyne.com/lincoln_nebraska_update_09.html

Forbidden – You don't have permission to access this page

Inbox (2,584)
Sent Mail
Drafts (3)
All Mail
Spam (610)
Trash

Gray Goo and You

From: <recipient undisclosed>
To: gpj9824@cox.net
Date: November 30, 2048
Subject: Update on Events in Lincoln, Nebraska

http://bit.ly/iTTiAM

Fullerdyne and Its New Vision of the Future

http://www.fullerdyne.com/fullerdynes new vision.html

We at Fullerdyne would like to take a moment to thank all shareholders and human citizens for its continued support during this new and exciting time in its history. Advances in nanotechnology, genetic engineering, and artificial intelligence research and applications promise to enhance living systems and emergent structures throughout the world.

Fullerdyne looks forward to helping shape a better world, especially in its vision of a post-Incident future.

Share its vision.

. . . .

A government agent comes to

a rural Texas community to check on

unusual energy readings in this story

straight out of the Twilight Zone.

. . . .

Defenders of Beeman County

Aaron Allston

He paused, framed by the doorway into the Beeman County Sheriff's Department building, and wondered what would be the best way to destroy the place.

Above average height, his deep, even tan hinting at outdoor hobbies and an off-duty disdain for clothes, he wore a gray suit that cost about as much as a good used car. Every wavy, black hair on his head was in place. The expensive sunglasses in his hand, chilled during the drive here, had fogged over in the moments it had taken him to walk across the overheated parking lot behind him. He tucked them into his breast pocket.

The station's receptionist, a long-faced blond woman in her forties, in a blue pantsuit and *faux* pearls, looked up from her gum-chewing and flashed him a smile. "You want to close the door, hon? You're letting the cold air out. What can I help you with?"

He entered, letting the door swing shut behind him, and moved up to her desk. "I'm Ayers. I want to speak to Sheriff Cothron." He set his ID on the desktop in front of her.

She glanced at it, clearly seeing the Washington, DC address and the name of a government department few people had heard of, and just as clearly recognized what it meant. She amped up the intensity of her smile another notch. "I expect the sheriff will see you right away, hon."

* * * ● * * *

The sheriff's office was exactly what Ayers had imagined — disorganized and cluttered. A mismatched collection of tables and filing cabinets along the walls overflowed with stacks of manila folders, loose faxes, and photographs. A dart board with a photo of the current Texas governor pinned to the center hung from a nail beside the exterior window. The laptop computer to the side of the desk sat open, its screen saver cycling between pictures of Carribean island resorts, French villas, and cruise ships.

Sheriff Henry A. Cothron sat leaning back in a leather office chair, his booted feet up on the desk. In his early forties, he had a gut that spoke of beer and biceps that spoke of workouts. His tan uniform was not yet sweated through. He looked as though he might have been just seconds from reaching for his cowboy hat, pulling it low over his eyes, and commencing a nap.

He gave Ayers a friendly look. "What can I do you for?"

Ayers leaned over to hand the sheriff his ID. "You can start by taking your feet off your damned desk and showing some respect."

The sheriff didn't change expression or position. He eyed the ID card with disinterest. "Nope. If I went to all that effort, I might just have to continue by planting one of these boots so far up your ass that your breath would smell of leather." He handed the card back.

Ayers blinked at him. "Are you sure you looked at that? Can you even *read*?"

The sheriff lost his smile. "I did. And before you decide to swing your dick some more, and I decide to mistake it for a rattlesnake and shoot its head off, why don't you tell me what you want so I can get you out of my beloved county in the most expeditious fashion possible?"

Ayers stood silent for a moment, mulling over Sheriff Cothron's fate. He slipped his ID into his pocketed beside his sunglasses. "Do you know where Sandstone Hollow is?"

"That's spelled Hollow but pronounced *Holler*, I'm sad to report, and sure I do. Out past Amelia Stone's place on Bull Dog Run. What about it?"

"Late last night, the Department detected some anomalous energy pulses in this area and fixed their source at Sandstone *Hollow*. I need someone experienced in the local geography to accompany me out there."

"Meaning you need someone to show you which cacti not to sit on when you decide to take a roadside crap." The sheriff sighed. "Yeah, sure."

He did finally take his feet from the desktop. He stood, his head topping Ayers' by several inches, and spent moments donning his hat and sunglasses, adjusting his gun belt.

"Sheriff, understand that for the moment this is classified top secret."

"I got it." The sheriff looked out his open office door. "*You* got it, Doreen?"

"Sure thing, hon."

. . . . • . . .

At Ayers' insistence, they took two cars, the sheriff's department cruiser and Ayers' sleek black limousine. They drove out past the city limits, the transition from houses and mowed lawns to dry scrub land a sudden one, then headed north on a back road.

Ayers glared ahead through the haze of summer dust the sheriff's wheels kicked up from the gravel road. Cothron drove too fast, making sharp turns, catching air on bumps and rises, all the maneuvers more demanding than was good for the limousine. Ayers wasn't in the mood to skid off the road into rocks and tarantula nests and sheep crap.

He very much looked forward to killing the sheriff.

They left the gravel road to turn west onto Bull Dog Run, a rutted dirt track. A few hundred yards past the turnoff, with no buildings nor Sandstone Hollow in sight, the sheriff's car pulled off to the side and stopped.

Ayers pulled up behind it. Cothron had already exited his vehicle and was heading off on foot across dry terrain toward a scattering of pumpjack oil wells — equipment that looked like a mad welder had attempted to create impressionistic sculptures of giant brown grasshoppers.

Ayers hit the button to lower his passenger-side window. Hot air washed in across him. "What's the holdup, sheriff?"

"Gotta pee. Bladder the size of a marble. Be right back."

Ayers rolled the window up and glowered after the sheriff.

Cothron walked perhaps fifty yards off the road, stood with his back to the cars, unzipped, and then stood with his hands on his hips.

Ayers looked around, impatient. There were no people to be seen in any direction, no movement at all other than the slow bobbing of some of the pumpjacks.

A few moments later, Cothron zipped up again. But he didn't turn around to return. He bent over to examine something on the ground. He turned, saw Ayers looking, and waved the Washington man over.

Shaking his head, Ayers left the comfort of his car and walked to the pee site. "Get your ass back in your car, Cothron. Whatever's going on here isn't relevant to my assignment."

"You're going to crap yourself when you realize how relevant it is." Cothron jabbed a finger toward the ground before him. "Take a look at *that*."

Ayers moved up beside him and looked. All he saw was a patch of once-dusty ground, now spattered with liquid, rapidly drying out to become dusty again. "I'm missing it."

"That's okay, I don't miss anything."

Then Ayers heard it, the sound of metal clearing leather, and felt a handgun barrel pressed hard into the side of his head.

Ayers cleared his throat. "Sheriff —"

· · · · • · · ·

Cothron stared down at the body. His .357 hollow-point had made a good-sized exit wound out the other side of Ayers' skull. Now the Washington man lay still, partly on his back and partly on his side, dark blood trickling out from the entry and exit wounds, his expensive suit getting dustier by the moment. His eyes were open, his expression blank.

"You do not come into *my* county and offer disrespect." With his boot, Cothron shoved the corpse's shoulder and rolled the body fully onto its back. "You do *not* start issuing orders like you own the place." He moved to stand by Ayers' feet and prodded the dead man's legs apart. "You *don't* own the place. I do." He planted a hard, vicious kick into the man's crotch.

Then, finally, he smiled. "I know you're dead and all, Hoss, but I like to think that somewhere, your ghost is folded over in pain, puking."

He took his phone from his breast pocket, noted the lack of signal strength, and replaced it. Instead, he clicked the button of the walkie-talkie mike on his collar. "Doreen."

"I gotcha, Hank."

"I'm on Bull Dog Run a few hundred yards west of the turnoff. Send Bubba out here. I need him on his scooter."

There was laughter in Doreen's voice. "He's gonna hate that. What's up?"

"Nothing I can talk about."

. . . • . . .

Stanley "Bubba" Saldaña made an incongruous picture, a big, muscular man in a sheriff's department uniform and cowboy hat, precariously steering an undersized yellow motor scooter out along the bumps and rises of Bull Dog Run.

He pulled to a stop between the parked cars, killed his engine, and stood, obviously grateful to be stretching his legs out to their proper proportions. He wiped dust away from his eyes and turned to the sheriff. "Hey, Uncle Hank. What's up?"

Cothron, sitting on the hood of Ayers' car, leaning back against the still-cool glass of the windshield, gestured toward Ayers' body.

"Peckerhead was *determined* to bring strife into our beloved county."

Bubba's face fell. "It's my turn, ain't it." It was a statement, not a question.

"It sure is."

"Aw, Hank, I'm going to be sweated through afore I'm done hauling his body around."

"Just think about what this nice limo will bring us when you sell it to your guy in San Angelo."

Bubba brightened. "Okay, I'm on it." He put down the scooter's kickstand, then headed off to strip the Washington man's corpse.

Everything valuable but not unique would go in the sell drawer in Cothron's office. Everything remotely identifiable as Ayers' would be burned.

Then there was the question of the body itself. Amateurs made the mistake of burying their kills in shallow graves. This tactic kept wild animals from eating the remains and preserved loads of forensic evidence, meanwhile leaving the corpse close enough to the surface for disturbed earth or infrared equipment to give away the grave's location.

But Cothron was no amateur. He knew his county even better than he knew the contours of Miss September's airbrushed backside. One corner of his memory was dedicated to places so devoid of attractive scenery, so far away from places where people went, that no human being was likely to set eyes on them for months at a stretch. That's where Ayers would end up. Bubba would load his scooter and the body into the limo, take the body out to one of those distant places, and dump it. In two weeks, Ayers would be nothing but a scattering of bones, gnawed clean and sun-bleached. Nature, properly utilized, was Cothron's friend.

While Bubba stripped the body, Cothron got to work looking through the limo's trunk and interior. The car was as scrupulously clean as if it had been detailed by shoemaker elves who'd switched to a new profession, and reeked of spray-on new car smell.

He only found one item of interest. Under the driver's seat was a firearm — a *strange* firearm. Shaped something like a competition silhouette pistol made of anodized purple metal, it had a fold-back barrel that added a good twelve inches to its length. When Cothron folded the barrel forward, it locked into place, no seam visible where it joined the base, and the weapon began to vibrate and hum in his hand. He almost dropped it.

He'd just found the catch that allowed him to fold the barrel back, putting an end to the hum and vibration, when Bubba called him. "I think you need to see this."

"Hold your horses." Still studying the purple weapon in his hands, Cothron ambled toward his nephew and the corpse.

"This guy's wearing a toupee. And a mask. And he ain't *right*."

"*Isn't* right. Come on, Bubba." Cothron rejoined his nephew and looked down at Ayers.

Bubba had gotten Ayers' clothes off and put them, folded, in a neat pile. Ayers lay naked in the dust, and Cothron could see what Bubba meant.

To start with, Ayers had no genitalia, nor was there any sign that he ever had any.

In one meaty hand, Bubba held the wig that had been Ayers' immaculate hair. In the other he held a droopy mass of skin-colored stuff that had probably once been Ayers' face.

What Ayers now had for a face was mottled, scaly, and olive green, with an overly wide mouth lined with sharp, needle-like yellow teeth. Ayers had no supraorbital ridge; his forehead angled up and back like a ski jump. His head reminded Cothron of a snake's, if one could be shortened by being run into a wall enough times.

Ayers was still dead. With the mask off, his exit wound was even more obvious.

Thoughtful, Cothron prodded the corpse with his boot toe. "I think I'm extra glad I killed the sumbitch."

"Yeah... So what do we do now?"

"We look through his stuff, then we get our asses over to Sandstone Holler. I expect there's something going on there."

Bubba tapped the .44 Magnum revolver holstered on his belt and nodded significantly. "Are there any hunting restrictions —" His attention drifted back along the dirt trail toward the turnoff. "Oh, *shit.*"

Cothron turned to look. Headed their way, kicking up a cloud of dust, was his daughter's little white Honda sedan. "Oh, *shit.*" He looked down at the corpse. "Finish getting that fake skin off him. And when Jayline asks anything, I'm the one who answers."

"Got it." Bubba bent over the body.

Cothron trotted toward the cars, reaching them moments after the Honda pulled to a stop behind them. The cloud of dust trailing the car flowed across Cothron, a miniature sandstorm. He lowered his head, letting the brim of his hat keep the stuff out of his eyes.

Jayline waited until the cloud was past before she emerged from the car. Cothron felt his heart skip a beat from pride. Smart, fit, smiling, she looked as though, once she got her high school diploma next spring, she could jump straight into a sportscasting booth, a college track and field program, or a professional sports team's cheerleading squad, all of which, Cothron was determined, would be among her options. In designer jeans, snakeskin boots, and a sunflower-colored tank top, she wore her long blond hair in a practical ponytail. A Permian Panthers billed cap kept the sun out of her eyes.

She stood by her driver's side door and flashed her father a lot of teeth. "Hey, Daddy. Someone said there was something interesting going on up here. So I brought my camera."

"'Someone' said. Sweetheart, I'll give you two hundred dollars to go back to the station and kill Doreen for me."

Jayline giggled. "Seriously. What is it?"

Cothron took a look at Bubba and the corpse. "Well, I was attacked by a big reptile shaped like a man. He tried to kill me with this, so I had to shoot him." He held up the purple firearm. "I think he's from outer space. It's kind of gross. You probably don't —"

She already had her camera out and up on her shoulder. No miniature thing fit for a purse, it was a computer with a flip-down optic and about fourteen inches of lens. "You're not kidding, are you? This isn't like the time with the jackalope breeding farm?"

"Sweetheart, you were *five.* At eight, you got kind of hard to trick."

She trotted toward Bubba. "Oh, *jeez*. What is that stuff, fake skin? Daddy, you made a real mess of his head."

· · · • · · ·

After that, Jayline couldn't have been persuaded to get back to town for thirty million dollars. Cothron stuck with his negotiations until he won a concession from her: She wouldn't be in the front car when they approached Sandstone Hollow. Cothron and Bubba, Bubba driving, would take the sheriff's cruiser there, Jayline following in Ayers' limousine.

They drove past Amelia Stone's big-ass ranch house, built with oil money by her grandpappy, then reached the spot where Bull Dog Run became hilly and even more rocky. Half a mile beyond that, they topped a hill and looked down into the narrow ravine that was the northern end of Sandstone Hollow. Bubba stopped there.

Their angle wasn't good. Most of what they were looking at was set up beyond the point the ravine widened, so it was largely masked by ravine outcroppings. What they did see down the slope looked like a big canopy, a canvas circus tent with no banners. Cothron could see, peeking out from under the canopy, a curved metal hull. Men and women in work clothes, a dozen at least, moved out from and then back under the canopy, carrying orange plastic crates the size of large ice coolers, stacking them at the bottom of the slope.

"Hey." Bubba scowled, looking down at the workers. "That one's *you*. And he's coming this way." He turned to stare at Cothron, accusation in his eyes.

"Of course it's not me, dumbass. It's one of them made up to *look* like me. So he can replace me, I'll bet. Four thousand dollars says that's why Ayers was luring me out here."

"Prove that you're you."

"If I was one of them I wouldn't have killed one of my own kind and called *you*, jackass." Seeing a determined glint in Bubba's eyes, Cothron relented. "Okay. Try to take my mask off. But if you so much as bruise me, I'll kick the crap out of you, and you know I can."

Bubba pinched Cothron's cheek and tugged, looked closely at Cothron's teeth, groped the man's face for a moment, then leaned back, satisfied. "Okay, you're you."

By now the other Cothron had reached the top of the slope. Bubba turned toward him and rolled his window down.

The other Cothron leaned in, stared between them, looked surprised at Bubba's presence.

Bubba grabbed the man's head, yanked him partway in through the window, and began twisting. He also let off the brake. The car drifted forward, losing its view of the canopy tent.

The fake Cothron struggled, emitting a shrill noise like a pocket version of a steam whistle.

The real Cothron grabbed the steering wheel and made sure his car stayed on the road. "Dammit, Bubba —"

"Sorry, Hank, he's *strong*. Jeez." Bubba applied more torque.

There was a noise, a muted *crack*, and the false Cothron went limp. His facial features were now askew.

Shaken, his hat half off his hedd, Bubba held on to the fake Cothron, dragging the body along as they rolled downhill. Cothron steered until they were fifty yards from the crest before angling the car to block the road and telling Bubba to put the brake on. Jayline brought Ayers' limo to a stop right behind them.

All three emerged, Jayline already taping. White-faced, she kept her camera on Bubba as he pushed the dead replica of her father off the car door. "Daddy, that's so *sick*."

Cothron drew his revolver. He fished a hollow-point round from a belt pouch, his store of loose ammo, and replaced the round he'd expended on Ayers. "You need to get back to town, sweetheart. This is kind of bigger than I expected it would be. I definitely think this is an alien invasion."

"Well, *duh*."

"So you get that car turned around and get your hiney back to —"

"Too late." Bubba pointed up the hill. Just cresting it were six figures, half of them apparently human and half naked reptile men, all of them carrying weapons. Cothron saw four purple hand weapons with their barrels already folded forward and two long arms with wicked, curved lines like European sniper rifles made of salmon-pink material.

"Crud. Get down, sweetie." Cothron dove behind his cruiser's hood. Rising, he braced himself against his cruiser and took aim at a reptile with a rifle.

He fired three times, taking the creature twice in the chest, once in the head. The reptile fell backward, rolling out of sight down the slope into the ravine.

Bubba, rising just to Cothron's right, nodded in appreciation. "Nice grouping."

"Shut up and shoot, peckerwood." Cothron glanced toward his daughter. The girl was behind one of the limo's rear wheels, peeking just far enough over the car trunk to tape the oncoming aliens.

Now the invaders returned fire. Their weapons put out incandescently white, fuzzy-edged beams of light accompanied by screech noises that sounded like a pickup truck being torn in half lengthwise. The pistol beams slammed into the sheriff's cruiser, making craters the size of soccer balls in the doors and side panels.

"My *car*. You pricks." Cothron aimed for another shot.

Then a rifle beam hit the cruiser. The vehicle's trunk disappeared, replaced by a smoking crater, and the car actually slid a couple feet forward, knocking Cothron down.

Not Bubba. Still in a crouch, he stayed on his feet, boots skidding backward through the dirt. As Cothron struggled to stand, Bubba returned fire, swearing all the while, carefully placing six shots.

Upright again, Cothron saw one more rifle-reptile and one fake human with a pistol down, bleeding, unmoving. Cothron opened fire again — two rounds to a reptile's chest, one to its head. All of a sudden, the six attackers were two, and they had the smaller weapons.

But another reptile topped the crest. This one wore a helmet that looked like someone had tried to do something arty with the image of a tiered Aztec pyramid in polished aluminum. The reptile touched the right side of the helmet. Something like lightning danced across its shiny surfaces, then leaped from the helmet to smack Bubba in the forehead.

Bubba jerked upright but didn't die or even fall. He just stood there, more slack-jawed than usual, his eyes glassy. He froze, caught partway through the act of opening his cylinder and dumping his brass.

"Bubba?" Cothron kept a close eye on the helmeted reptile. It stood where it was, no lightning now flickering on its headgear, and all its attention was on the sheriff. The two fake humans with it, emboldened, began to advance, firing again, their shots further demolishing the car.

Cothron cursed and ejected his own brass. He popped snaps on his belt, coming up with a speed-loader. "Bubba, this is *not* the time..."

Now another reptile topped the crest. It had a salmon-pink firearm too, but carried this one on its shoulder. The weapon was as long as a man and looked like it weighed a couple hundred pounds. The reptile swung it in the direction of the cruiser, Bubba, and Cothron.

"Oh, *shit*." Cothron hurtled sideways, slamming into Bubba.

Had Bubba been alert, Cothron never would have moved him. That was Bubba's gift, the one that made him a star on the Permian Panthers' offensive line back when he was in high school. He didn't budge when people hit him. But tackled from the side when dazed, he went down readily enough. Cothron hit the sun-baked, grassless ground with him, grunting from the impact.

The big weapon screeched like a naval frigate giving birth. Peering under the cruiser, Cothron could see light play across the back and left side of the cruiser. The car crumpled into a black ball. Smoke rose from the wreckage.

His .357 lost, Bubba's .44 nowhere in sight, Cothron elbow-crawled to his left and looked toward Ayers' limo, toward the purple weapon he'd put back under its seat. But if he ran that way, the reptiles would track him — bring their weapons to bear on the car that was his little girl's *cover*.

Cothron stayed where he was, continued looking for his handgun and Bubba's.

"Daddy, they're *coming* —"

"Working on it, sweetheart."

"Oh... *piss*." Jayline set her camera down on the dirt. She reached behind her, under her waistband, and brought out her 16th birthday present, a beautifully compact snub-nosed five-shot .357 with a brushed stainless steel finish. She raised it in two hands and fired four times, the recoil of the lightweight weapon kicking her barrel up hard with each shot.

Cothron hazarded a look over the wreckage that had been his cruiser. The reptile with the helmet was down with two rounds in its chest. The one with the shoulder weapon was also on the ground, its right eye gone, the weapon lying atop it. The two fake men with purple pistols were flat on the ground, elbow-crawling away.

"Great shooting, sweetie. I'm so *proud* of you."

"No, it *sucked*." Jayline sounded furious. "I was aiming for its *chest*. And I missed once."

"More than forty yards and a snubbie, baby." Cothron spotted his revolver, lying half under Bubba. He dragged it from beneath the big man and dumped his expended brass. By touch, he located his second speed-loader on his belt.

Now there was a new noise, like distant thunder coupled with jet turbine whine, and the ground vibrated under Cothron's knees. Pebbles began vibrating atop the ground. Cothron cursed. Back at home, his wife's yappy Chihuahua, which could somehow detect storm clouds at forty miles, would now be going crazy with thunderstorm fear, running around, barking incessantly.

"Hey, what?" Bubba's voice was slurred, his eyes still glassy, but he seemed to be coming around.

Cothron slipped his new load into the revolver, snapped the cylinder closed. "Bubba, get your ass out there and commandeer that bazooka for us."

"Yes, Master." Bubba lurched to his feet and tottered toward the shoulder weapon.

Now a new shape topped the hill crest — another reptile, another shoulder weapon, but the creature rode atop a silver disk maybe five feet in diameter. It floated over the ground, rising to an altitude of twenty feet above the ground as it approached, giving its operator an improved line of fire down on Cothron and Bubba.

Jayline took her last shot and missed. She said something unpleasant. Cothron decided he'd have to chide her about that later.

A moving target in the air — Cothron aimed with care and fired. The reptile in the air spasmed and fell off the disk. The creature and its weapon smacked to the ground not three yards from where Bubba was now hoisting up the other shoulder weapon.

Cothron gave his daughter an encouraging smile. "You're dry, sweetie."

"I know. That's all I *got*, Daddy." Her wail was the same one she'd use to announce that her kitten was ill. Disconsolate, she holstered her weapon and went back to taping.

The big thunder-whine noise from beyond the slope got louder. Then its source rose into view — a circus canopy, trailing ropes, the unmistakable curve of a large saucer-shaped craft under it.

Cothron aimed at the disk and fired his cylinder dry, knowing it was futile. He didn't even see where his rounds hit. "Bubba! Shoot that thing!"

"Yes, Master." Even dazed, Bubba had apparently seen the weapon's last owner operate it. The big man elevated the dangerous end and did something on the control surface beside his head. Bright light leaped off the weapon. The metal screech noise it made caused Cothron's teeth to itch. The beam splashed across the flying craft. The craft wobbled and its thunder-whine noise did, too.

And Bubba, bless his heart, held the trigger down.

The circus canopy caught fire. Flames leaped up from the craft. Hovering, the vehicle began oscillating like a plate being spun atop a stick losing speed. Then it dropped back the way it had come, disappearing out of sight.

The impact made a noise like what would result if someone poured an entire junkyard into the world's largest blender. The thunder-whine cut off and, after one last tremble, the steady vibration in the ground ceased. An enormous cloud of flame and dust billowed up from Sandstone Hollow.

Cothron trotted up the hill and peered down the slope into the ravine. The saucer had folded unevenly in half, settling into a too-narrow portion of the ravine. It had landed on orange crates, reptiles, and fake humans. Cothron could see arms, legs, heads protruding from under the wreckage, most of them withering and blackening in the fire raging across the hull.

Some of the invaders weren't pinned. Cothron took his time, aiming carefully, and brought down the two that had been crawling and three others he spotted trying to hide.

Then there was nothing going on but flames leaping up from a crashed alien craft.

That, and the hum coming off the little disk still up about twenty feet in the air.

Jayline joined her father at the crest, taping. "Cool. This is going up on the internet."

Bubba, still lugging the shoulder weapon but no longer glassy-eyed, came up alongside the sheriff. "Did I do that?"

Cothron grinned. "Don't worry, peckerhead, you're not in any trouble. But we've got to be *coordinated*. Sweetheart, nothing goes online until I say so. It'll have to wait a few hours. And I'll need you to edit a bunchf of little details out of what you put together."

"*Awww.*"

"Bubba, I need you to load up Ayers' car. Jayline's going to drive it out of here before the fire department and God knows who else shows up." Cothron holstered his revolver and rubbed his hands together. "Welcome to the good life, kids."

· · · • · · ·

A new day had brought a new government man, and this one was the real deal. Cothron had obliged him to demonstrate that his face didn't come off.

But like Ayers, this one wasn't happy. Still, he apparently knew better than to antagonize. Short and gray-haired and polite, he kept scrubbing at his glasses with his handkerchief long after they were spotless. "It would have been much more... helpful... if your daughter hadn't posted that video all over the internet. If the press hadn't got wind of things before we could move in. Now this can't be contained."

Cothron, his feet up on his desk, nodded in sympathy. "Just seconds after the crash, I told her she could never, ever share that video. But you know kids. At a certain age, they're impossible to corral. You got kids?"

"Three daughters. The oldest is twenty."

"*Three.* Jesus. So you know what I was up against. She had that footage online before I could even call the feds. I've given her a stern talking to. But you have the full cooperation of my department in keeping the situation as much under control as we can."

"That's comforting." The government man's irony was undetectable. He rose and shook the sheriff's hand. "And if your department or any locals find anything anomalous —"

"We'll make sure word gets right to you. Like we did with that one shoulder weapon and those two little purple guns."

"Thank you." The government man departed, leaving the door open.

Cothron peered out through it. "Doreen, who's next?"

"That'd be Miss Amelia, Sheriff."

"Show her in and close the door, please." Cothron swung his feet off the desk. He rose and adjusted the blinds on the exterior window so no one could see in.

Miss Amelia Stone entered. Tall, gray and gracious, she moved easily despite her years. Her silk pantsuit and accouterments might have been found on an ad in a recent fashion magazine. As Doreen closed the door behind her, Miss Amelia shook the sheriff's hand and accepted his offer of the chair opposite his. "Big events in Beeman County, Henry."

"And more to come." Cothron sat. "I want to show you something." From the bottom drawer of one filing cabinet, Cothron removed an object — a tiered helmet that looked as though it had been machined from polished aluminum. He set it on his head.

Miss Amelia frowned in mild concern. "That's not an *alien* device, is it?"

"No, ma'am. It was put together by my daughter's science class." Cothron worked the controls on the side of the helmet and it hummed into life. As he'd learned from practicing on Doreen, Cothron gave Miss Amelia an intent stare and saw the green eight-pointed cross-hairs appear on her face. He blinked. The office walls echoed with a *zap* sound.

Miss Amelia's mild frown relaxed into neutrality. Her eyes went glassy.

"In fact, this helmet is so dull that you're not even going to remember that you ever saw it. Understand?"

"Yes, Master."

"Call me Hank. Now, you know my daughter Jayline wants to go to film school."

"Yes, Hank."

"You'd like to pay for her entire education, wouldn't you?"

"I'd love to, Hank."

"And I mean, high class all the way. She needs her own Los Angeles condominium. And a car, a big Cadillac sports utility. That'll be okay, won't it?"

"Yes, Hank."

"As for me, I'm going to spend a term as governor of Texas before going on to the Presidency. I assume I can count on your full support?"

"Of course, Hank."

"Excellent! Please see Doreen on your way out. You'll need to set up a regular appointment where you can come in and receive further instructions."

"Yes, Hank."

Cothron deactivated the helmet and put it away. Miss Amelia looked confused for a moment, then resumed her smile. "It sure was nice visiting. We need to do this more often."

"We do indeed. Thanks for stopping by."

When she was gone, Cothron put his feet up on the desk again. He leaned back and smiled up at the ceiling fan.

The military and government agents were all over Beeman County, especially at the crash site. That would be good for the local economy, and Cothron was sure the government would be able to ramp up to repel the reptiles when the flying saucer armies came. But it was too little, too late. Earth had just been successfully invaded.

By Beeman County, Texas.

Life was going to be good.

In a near future of financial and

environmental collapse, businessmen

vie for influence in a rapidly changing

political arena. Chris N. Brown ventures

into the rarely employed economic

science fiction subgenre with this

disturbing and poignant vision.

Sovereign Wealth

Chris N. Brown

ince when are you working for the Martians?" said Gareth.

"Not Martians, dumb shit," I said. "Mauritians." On the tiny pop-up on my office overlay, it was hard to tell from Gareth's face whether he got it. I moved him to the window, enlarged, framed by Houston glass, steel, and green.

"Oh," said Gareth. "Too bad. Martians would be much more interesting."

"The only Martians so far are drones, and they can't vote," I said.

"Yes, Tony, but they can still send us a Fed funds wire," said Gareth.

"Yeah, well, if I can't get the Mauritians some new land quick, the idea of a Martian deal may become a lot more plausible." I looked away from Gareth and down at the bayou overflowing, and wondered when it would be our turn, and if I could make enough money before then.

"They like beaches, Mauritians do, as I recall," said Gareth. "Lots of sand on Mars."

"Yes, Britwit, they are an island people," I said.

"Were, technically," said Gareth.

"No, they still have some peaks above the waterline. More importantly, they still have their sovereign wealth, and their climate fund reparitions, and the rest of the funds that they would be happy to use to pay us a nice fat success fee if we could put together a deal where they could resettle with full fresh sovereignty."

"Right, okay, maybe I was thinking of the Maldiveans," said Gareth. "But I guess we already did that deal."

"Yeah, that was like five years ago," I said. "My first geopolitical M&A deal, when I was still at the law firm."

"Who knew a masters in experimental geography and an LL.M. in con law would become the perfect pedigree for an investment banker," said Gareth. "Too bad your Mandarin is such shit."

"I'd rather have Farsi," I said. "Or Arabic. Look, Gareth, the reason I called you is that I told my clients you could help them figure out a way to do a deal with the Saudis."

"Yeah, sure. Lots of sand there too," said Gareth. "Any specific proposals?"

"More like test balloons, but one idea is pretty cool. We—the Mauritians—fund a demilitarization and buy-out of the Yemeni borderzone at the coast. Just a few hundred square kilometers of already disputed territory."

"Interesting," said Gareth. "That could be a very significant deal. But I'm not the one who's going to work with those crazy fucking Yemenis."

"I know, I didn't ask you to," I said. "I'll call Tariq, he did that water deal for them. Nice stack of favors in the bank."

"Religion?" asked Gareth.

"Yeah, I know," I said. "Mostly Hindu, but the idea is to have the Catholics put in a casino there that will out-do the Emiratis. And to buy a long-term water contract from the Saudi purification plants. And I'm pitching them on the idea of a data haven."

"Interesting," said Gareth. "I think—"

Another window popped up. Carlos.

"Gareth, can you hold for one second?" I asked, muting his screen before he replied.

Carlos came on, voice only. Carlos was the house counsel for another one of my clients, the Mexican media conglomerate MundoRed.

"Carnal," I said, trying too hard. "What news?"

"You're the one who's supposed to call me when shit gets fucked up like this," said Carlos.

"What are you talking about?" I said, checking my feed for whatever I missed in the five minutes I was talking to Gareth. Oh, fuck, I thought. "Oh, that?" I said.

"Yes, the Arizonans telling us our bid was bounced after you told me we had a deal," said Carlos.

"We do," I said. "We do. It's binding under their county charter. The state says they have to leave it open for bids for ten days but we think that's wrong."

"Well these fellow Texans of yours who outbid us don't agree," said Carlos.

"They're full of shit," I said. "I will get on it and get back to you. Don't panic. And definitely don't tell anything to Alejandra or her dad until we talk again, okay?"

"You better get it done before it leaks," said Carlos. "Clock is ticking."

"I know, I know, mil gracias," I said. "And it's not the only clock I've got. I'll call you back in a couple of hours."

Before I put Gareth back on, I raided the stash in my desk. Time to get the prescription refilled. Game on.

2.

Dr. Liefhaecker's office was at the UTMB campus off the loop. There wasn't much left in Galveston anymore, and they were already moving some of the smaller clinics to Austin.

"You're a lifer, aren't you, Tony," said Dr. Liefhaecker as he adjusted my head inside the fMRI chair. "You'll probably trade in your Porsche for a nice boat to get around town."

I laughed. "It won't get that bad, but contingency planning is always fun. Why Chicago?"

"I don't know," said Dr. Liefhaecker. "I'm intrigued by the arctic winters. I have my eye on one of those big biodiesel all-weather performance jeeps. That, and they just seem ready for what's coming."

"It's true," I said. "So how am I doing? When can you do my upgrade?"

Dr. Liefhaecker was a neuropharmacologist. He made a great living helping people enhance their neural performance. I had been talking to him for six months or so about a series of cocktails that could give me like a twenty percent edge in processing power—just what I needed to make the most out of the next five years before burnout.

"Yeah," said Dr. Liefhaecker, looking at my electronic records instead of looking at me. "Here's the thing."

"Yeah?" I said.

He sat down across from me, as the rainbow of my color-coded brain rendered itself on the monitor behind him.

"I talked to Dr. Kalki."

"Yeah," I said. "The surgeon you sent me to last week. She is so hot."

Dr. Liefhaecker ignored that. "She confirmed what I thought. To make your enhancements work, first we'll need to cut some manual adjustments. I'm going to send you a link with the full tutorial, but basically, imagine a toggle switch in there. Made of flesh."

He touched my forehead a few times with his big doctor index finger.

"It's an invasive procedure, and a tricky one, but they do it all the time."

"Head shaved and the whole bit?" I asked.

"Maybe," he said.

"Will I be out of commission for long?" I asked. "I can't miss more than a few hours of work."

"We can do it on a Friday," he said. "It shouldn't be too bad. The real trick is we need to get it scheduled right away. Because the regs won't let us do it after your thirty-fifth birthday."

"That's next month!"

"So I saw," said Dr. Liefhaecker.

"Why the cutoff?" I asked.

"After that age, more or less, the tissue has too much trouble adapting to the switch," he said.

"How much?" I asked.

Dr. Liefhaecker showed me the quote on his handheld.

"Euros?"

He nodded.

"Fuck!"

"Look," he said. "I know it's a lot, even for a guy like you. If you can't get that together now, there are other similar things we can try, without the surgery."

"No, no, this is it," I said. "Let's schedule it. I can do it. I need it. I need that chess computer thing I'm missing, to really take it to the next level."

"You really don't," said Dr. Liefhaecker. "Because you have such a perfect brain for poker. That's what they really want."

"How do you mean?"

"Guys like you are the last great American export," he said. "Freelance deal people whose only loyalty is transactional, with highly developed capabilities for guile and indigenous game theory they can't replicate in black boxes." He pointed at a couple of notes on my fMRI display. "Our own variation on capitalism may be looking a little waterlogged, but we still make a mint selling it to everybody else. You guys are like Hessians. But with business calculators."

"Thanks, doc!" I said.

He laughed and shook his head. "You can schedule your next appointment with the tablet on your way out."

3.

That night I got together with my buddies in Austin to watch the vote. They had they're own idea of the pregame.

"Oh, no, I don't want to watch another one of your marionette shows," I said as I plopped myself down on the sofa between Annie and Chaz, in front of the big screen they had flashed on the wall.

Vijay and Clarice were laughing already before I started bitching.

I looked at the scene on the screen. Retail surveillance from the Kaufstraße in Munich. People walking on their lunch breaks or whatever, letting their earbuds and tablets and bluerings tell them where to go and what to buy, waylaid, lured and consensually hoodwinked by hundreds of ethereal proximity bots.

"Santa doesn't like it when you rig the Christmas lists," I said.

"We're the ones in charge of the other 364 days," said Chaz.

Green text, red arrows, and yellow highlights overlaid the scene, revealing the matching algorithms at work.

"Fucking data miners. You're why I have to clean my chips every night before I go to bed."

"We're ambient advertisers, Tony," said Annie. "We match people with the things they want in life. We don't need ethics lectures from investment bankers."

"Look closely," said Vijay. "This new algorithm Clarice wrote and Chaz tuned is amazing."

"Right, but I came to watch it dissect the referendum," I said. "And to have some of Clarice's chicken masala estilo Jalisco."

"I forgot," said Vijay. "It's Kush-Mex night."

Chaz went for the mezcal.

"I just think it's nice to see we still have something on our Teutonic overlords," he said.

"The Frankfurters are the ones with our bonds," I said. "Not the Bavarians. And the pendulum always swings back through equilibrium."

Annie spit out her drink. "Last time I checked, the pendulum came loose from its mooring and knocked over half the remaining banks," she said.

"But we're still swinging," laughed Vijay.

Vijay changed the channel, and the wallscreen quadrupled in size. Vote tallies by precinct and network, detailed issue briefings in video and text on each of the matters up for ballot, four channels of color commentary from different orientations if you wanted it. The votes were monthly, the democracy was direct, more or less, and the exercise of the franchise was still optional.

"Jeez, this is so much work," said Chaz. "I liked it better when you just showed up every few years and checked the box for Coke or Pepsi."

"And had your life run by four-hundred and thirty-five self-aggrandizing geezers wearing identical suits?" said Annie. "Tony's right. We should be doing political work. Help make it easier for people."

"I guess the idea of a new Constitutional Convention is kind of cool," said Chaz. "I just find it kind of creepy the way it's like a combination of a City Council livestream and America's Hot Talent."

It was three years now since the Aftershock. The Aftershock was the economic event that followed, by about eighteen months, the event we had considered the greatest crash in American economic history, when the big bubble on which the city on a hill had been built collapsed like an Oklahoma fracking sinkhole. The Crash was bad, but the Aftershock was what broke the political system, exposing the varicose veins and clotted embolisms hiding under the pancake makeup of the animatronic boneheads left as stewards of the republic 250-plus years after we buried the Founding Fathers. Once we pulled the thread on Uncle Sam's sweater, he got naked in a hurry. Under the new regime that assembled in the following two years of elections, three fourths of the states petitioned for our social contract to be rewritten, in a convention that would be conducted as an experiment in network-based participatory democracy.

Yes, we were kind of figuring it out as we went along.

"Tonight's the part about new legislative procedures, right?" asked Clarice, taste-testing salsa from her fingertip.

"Right," I said. "Rules for minority ratification of votes that would change their existing rights."

"There's like eleven different proposals," said Clarice, holding up her hands.

"And ten times that many guides," I said. "Self-education is the price of autonomy."

"Some days I just want a dictator," said Clarice. "A matriarch."

"Move to Hawaii after next week's re-vote on the rules for territorial confederation," said Annie. "That lady's running for queen."

"Tony's probably providing the leverage," said Vijay.

"I wish," I said. "But I'm landlocked in the desert this week."

"Oh, right," said Annie. "Yodaland!"

"Yodaville," I corrected. "Yuma County, Arizona."

"How's that going?" asked Chaz.

"Not good," I said. "Keep thinking I found the oasis and it turns out it's just a mirage. Which reminds me." I pointed at my ear.

"I told you he looked more stressed than usual," said Annie. "Grey as a ghost."

"Help yourself, Fantomas," said Chaz, opening the door for me to use the home office they shared in productive polyamorous bliss.

There was a small bathroom connected to the office. I linked my earbud to the mirror display over the sink, and checked my messages.

I assured Chaz I was fine when he popped his head in to check on me, having heard me yelling and pounding on his counter. Then I called my lawyer.

"What do you want me to do?" said Scanlan, working in his office after dinner. The reflection of my face lay over the stream of his, which was in profile, looking at the terminal on his desk.

"Put a fucking plug in it, that's what," I said.

"The filings are public, Tony," said Scanlan. "UN-SOV rules. You know that."

"Yes, but our dispute was supposed to turn public opinion against the Texans. Not to ignite a general freakout about the Mexicans."

"You picked the client, not me," said Scanlan. "MundoRed is controversial. A pure push network. Funded with all those prohibition-era narco funds. But their programming is still super popular, and the information just got out there. Let it digest."

A half dozen lines measuring livepolls and keywords unfurled across the screen over Scanlan's prematurely bald head.

"I can read, Dwight," I said. "We're talking about northern Arizonans we're trying to influence here. All the fucking sesquicentenarian old white people who refuse to die. They bankrupted the state government building that monster border wall and running little militia wars, and when they ran out of people to staff the clinics they imported them from South Asia rather than Sonora. The idea of Mexican advertisers taking over the next county is death to our deal."

"I guess," said Scanlan, staring at his anachronistic pencil.

When Chaz came in the second time, I was smashing my earbud on the steel sink with the butt end of his shaving brush.

"When did you turn into such a complete asshole?" said Chaz. "You really need to take a sabbatical."

I looked at the smashed polymers and silicas. Carlos would find out another way to reach me.

"It's complicated, Chaz," I said. "Where's the mezcal?"

4.

Working at home the next day, I flew an imaginary drone through the real-world landscape of Yodaville.

Yodaville was the nickname for the GWOT-era bombing range twenty miles east of Yuma and five miles north of the Mexican border. It was a fake city built by the Army to simulate the Near East well enough to learn how to do a better job of blowing it up. Yodaville was also the name I used to describe the whole county. That was probably a bad thing, but it wasn't because I'm a bad person.

Investment bankers are not all bad people, contrary to the mob opinion of the network. Especially not geopolitical investment bankers. We fund freedom. We leverage self-determination.

People sometimes get sentimental about place, and identity. That's okay. I just wish they could understand that our political subdivisions are constructs, little different than corporate charters. They are all contracts, which need to be rewritten from time to time. And breaking up the existing states into smaller ones, while confederating it all in a new global order, is a good thing. It's certainly the future.

"Abajo el sistema," reads the graffiti on a crumbling wall at the edge of Yodaville. I'm working on it.

Sometimes when I am doing diligence on a new deal, I wonder about the guys who are in charge of the swarms of microdrones that make all the VR maps we take for granted.

I flew around the dome of a fictional mosque, banking into the beautiful profile of the Fortuna Foothills to the north.

I banked back left, over a big bomb crater, and headed toward Yuma city, where most of the county's hundred thousand inhabitants live. I flew under an old bridge across the Colorado. You could see the river bottom easily, glistening in the sun on the day they recorded these feeds. This town was a natural low-water crossing. A place that gave the finger to the idea of borders.

I got an idea.

5.

Gareth was laughing harder than me when we traded notes after it all went down.

"What in God's name did you have to promise Carlos to fund that?" he asked. "Some kind of spa treatment involving crystals and the divination of prehistoric geolocation?"

"I told him we'd get him and the other senior execs in on your Honduran city state IPO, among other things," I said.

"Right, so long as you give me a piece of your bonus on this one. The Sedona spinoff was brilliant, Tony. Divide and conquer! They'll be talking about it for a year."

"It makes total sense, right?"

"You're making a veritable Arizonaslavia, partner," said Gareth. "Well done."

"Thanks," I said. "If you want to park some money in New Yuma, I can hook you up after the closing. It's going to be a nice haven."

"That's the real reason MundoRed put up the capital, I presume?"

said Gareth. "To relocate their corporate domicile."

"Right, and all they really have to do is back the bonds," I said. "The locals are the real ones behind the deal. And the way we hooked them up they get to pay as they go, and it should be paid in a full in a decade. Win-win-win."

"So the tribes merge in to the new state?" said Gareth.

"That's it," I said. "Most of the population are Indians, or Mexican-Americans, or the descendants of 19th century pioneers. Still federated with the US, but on a totally autonomous basis."

"That's a lot of money for a desert," said Gareth.

"Freedom isn't free," I said.

"Oh fuck off, Yankwank," said Gareth.

"Seriously, it's not how much water you have," I said. "At least not so much. It's about how much autonomy you have."

"I guess that's right," he said, flashing live bits from the celebratory locals. "Money is the true sovereign."

"Or maybe we just make it that way," I said. "We'll see what it looks like after we do a hundred more deals."

The appointment reminder for Dr. Kalki flashed on my screen, and I thought about new permutations in the great game of creative destruction.

Even on alien planets,

the downtrodden must take life-altering

risks to find gainful employment.

Miller's desperation carries him

dangerously close to

both hope and loss.

Jump the Black

Marshall Ryan Maresca

he Emigration Offices will be closing in 23 minutes."

The tinny speakers hissed out four alien languages before giving the message in English. Miller only recognized two of them, and only understood a few words in either.

"If you have not had your number called by closing, you will have to return tomorrow. If you are not present when called, you will forfeit your meeting, and rescheduling will be required."

Miller had already spent three days, from open to close, waiting for his number to be called. If he had to, he'd wait another three. Whatever it took.

The Xoninet he had spent the better part of the day sitting next to nudged him, making a few gurgling noises. The dwarven, sharkskinned alien had tried to start up conversation earlier, but the mutual language barrier had proven far too inconvenient. Despite that, Miller responded, "You and me both, brother."

"*Chre-ya-pou!*" a human caseworker called out. Miller had a chance, still. His number was *chre-ya-qeay*. Even if his alien language skills were poor, he could count in Coalition Standard. Only two to go.

The Xoninet pointed to Miller's ticket and gurgled some more.

"Yeah, I'm almost up," Miller said.

"*Chre-ya-pou!*" The caseworker looked around the room, coughing as she called out the numbers.

The Xoninet knocked Miller on the arm, which hurt like hell. Those little guys were strong. "*Chre-ya-pou, keth fa!*" he called out, pointing to Miller.

The caseworker came over. "You're *chre-ya-pou?*"

Miller held up his ticket. "*Chre-ya-qeay.*"

She shook her head, tapping her bony finger on the ticket. "That's *pou*. Come on."

Miller grabbed his application pad and followed after her, cursing himself for looking at a *pou* for three days and thinking it was a *qeay*. At least it wasn't a fatal mistake. She led him to a cubicle in the back of the emigration offices complex, past several other people having translator-aided sessions with alien caseworkers. It was a minor blessing that he had managed to get a fellow human. Miller took this as a good sign.

"Let's see what we have," she said, taking his application pad and laying it on her desk. A display of his various documents appeared, which she cycled through with weary rapidity.

"Hmm, yes," she said. "You're looking for a X-Theta student visa to Carawkai?"

"That's correct," Miller said. "I've got a scholarship —

"I see that," she cut him off. "Yes, that all seems to be in order, good." Of course everything was in order. After four failed visa applications, Miller made sure he'd jumped every hoop perfectly this time.

She scanned through more pages, her eyes never once making contact with him. "You grew up in San Antonio?"

"We spent a few years there when I was a kid," Miller said. Most of his childhood had been a blur of moving around, wherever his father had found work.

"Specifically, you were there in '54."

"I suppose," Miller said. "The year sounds right."

"In '54, San Antonio was reclassified an Orange zone."

That didn't sound right. He knew the jobs his father had gotten usually put them on the edge — there simply were more jobs near the hot zones — but even then, he knew they never lived in an Orange. "No, it was Yellow. We never lived deeper than Yellow."

She nodded, face still buried in her pages. "I'm sure it was Yellow at the time. Unfortunately, everything south of the 30th parallel has been retroactively designated Orange from '54 on."

"Wait — "

She finally looked at him, putting on a practiced expression of false sympathy. "I'm terribly sorry, but spending any time in an Orange Zone flags you as an unsuitable candidate for an exit visa."

"What?" Miller asked. He had never heard that before. "No, that can't be right. I have my medical records there, you can see, my rad levels are nominal, my viral counts are in tolerance..."

"I'm very sorry, sir," she said. "But that is the policy. Many species in the Coalition are far too sensitive to risk potential exposure."

"Exposure to what, exactly?" Miller asked. "I already went through nine rounds of immunization, not to mention — "

"I'm very sorry, sir," she repeated, pointedly. "There's nothing I can do about policy. Emigration is denied."

. . . .

Power was in brown mode when Miller returned to his tenement. That meant waiting until the elevator was at capacity — seventy humans — before it would ascend to his block. It was midafternoon, and very few people were returning home. Those with jobs wouldn't be back until nightfall, and the rest either stayed in or were out in the thoroughfare shaking their hats.

Fifteen people sat in the elevator. Miller's blockmate, Emile, sat closest to the doors.

"You have a day?" Emile asked when he saw Miller.

Miller joined him on the elevator floor. "The day had me."

"I told you, brother, I told you. They don't let you off the rock for nothing."

"It's not right," Miller said. "I've got the scholarship. I did *everything* right this time."

"What was the hustle they gave you?"

"Time in an Orange Zone."

"You lived in an Orange Zone?"

"No!" Miller said. "That's the guff of it!"

"That's what I told you. They'll always spin some hustle at you. What did you have? Bug? Crab?"

"Not even. She was human!" The whole business wouldn't have stung as bad if it had come from an alien.

"Traitor," Emile said, his voice weary with contempt. "The whole business with that office is a joke, I told you. You see that now?"

"Yeah," Miller said. He had tried the right way. He had done everything like he should have, and it did him no damn good. He glanced about at the rest of the folks in the elevator: the usual crowd of shiftless blanks, just like him and Emile. No one to be worried about. He leaned in close to Emile. "So, let's do it your way."

Emile nodded. "You wanna Jump the Black?"

"No work, no schools, and staying here will kill us one way or another." Dad died at thirty-eight. Mom only a couple years older. Every blank in the elevator had the same story. "Gotta get off the damned Earth. A better life isn't gonna start here, you know?"

"I know," Emile said.

"And there's no other way, is there?"

"Nope. But that ain't much of a way, either." Emile had gone to Jump the Black three times. So he said. Miller always wondered how far he had really gotten.

"It's a way." A few more people wandered into the elevator and slumped to the floor. They were all used to brown mode. "Worst case, get caught, end up back here again, right? Like you?"

Emile looked at him sideways. "That ain't the worst."

"But you're gonna try again, right?"

"Gotta try," Emile said. "Or die trying." Emile's wife and brother had both gone and Jumped the Black. Were working — actual, honest work — on some ship or station or something.

"So," Miller said. "I'm in."

"It's your legs and lungs," Emile said, getting to his feet. "All right, then. Let's go."

"Now?"

Emile gave a nod to the whole elevator. "You got something better to do?"

Miller knew full well the answer to that one. "So, what's the plan?"

"We're gonna go see a bug."

· · · · ● · · · ·

Hj'x was a Lestari — insectoid alien, like a praying mantis, were it bright red and the size of a tiger. Something about him gave Miller the sense the bug was old, not that he had any idea how Lestari aged. But Hj'x moved as if his exoskeleton hurt, giving Miller thoughts of arthritis.

"Space exists for my next run," Hj'x chirped. The translator around his thorax seemed top of the line, a strong contrast to the seedy shipping office on the outskirts of town. Reeking of sickly sweet steam, the whole place made Miller's skin crawl. Maybe that was just being this close to a Lestari. "How are you fleshlings riding? For twenty, or forty?"

Emile put a hand up before Miller could speak. "We've got thirty-eight for the two of us."

This wasn't true. At most, Miller had fifteen. "Not much." Hj'x said. "But I can fit you, so it is fine. You get something, I get something, better than we both get nothing. Hj'x is reasonable."

"Glad to hear it," Emile said.

Hj'x pointed his antennae at Emile. "It is because I know you, fleshling. You keep trying, I like that. Will. And since you know how we do this, you tell your friend, save me time. Worth the discount."

"So, are we set?" Miller asked.

"Deal, it is made," H'jx said. He tossed a handpad to Emile. "You'll be sent a location at *hge-ix-na* tomorrow. Be there in twenty minutes, or miss your ride." *Hge-ix-na*. About three in the morning. Hour of the wolf, as dad liked to call it.

. . . ● . . .

Nothing was packed. Nothing could be packed. They were riding the twenty-fare, at a discount at that, so that meant only five kilos in a small satchel. Emile told Miller not to bring anything more than extra clothes.

"And sell your reader," Emile had said.

"Why?" It was Miller's only possession of even the slightest value. He was the only one on his floorblock with one.

"You can get at least twenty for it," Emile said. "We need that for our fares."

And there it was. Miller didn't argue the point further.

"Not like you want to carry a lot for the jump."

Sleep had been impossible, at least for Miller. He paced and fretted. Emile had dozed on the block floor, the rest of the blockmates pointedly pretending not to know their plans. Several said "good night" with a sense of finality, but beyond that, no acknowledgement. Around two in the morning, they went to the street to wait. The message came, just when it was supposed to. A junkyard a few blocks from them.

There were several dozen humans milling about in the yard when they arrived. Miller thought the whole thing smelled ripe for a raid. A bunch of people hanging around in the middle of the night? Easy pickings. Though maybe Emigration Patrol didn't bother with anyone who hadn't gotten out of the gravity well.

A large vehicle quietly landed, no running lights. Two aliens — Miller didn't recognize the species — came out and opened the back doors. A few waves of their graspers, and all the humans climbed in. Doors shut again, and they were in the dark.

Minutes of bumpy ride passed. No one talked to each other. Miller didn't even talk to Emile. The vehicle came to rest, and the doors open.

Hj'x and the two other aliens stood there. "All right fleshlings, come out. Quickly."

Humans pressed their way out, into a dim warehouse. The place was filled with shipping containers, most prominent were the six in the middle of the floor: large clamshell cases, hard plasticate.

"Here is the run of things," Hj'x announced. "My associates will go around the lot of you. You will give them the money. They will give you an injection. You will strip off your garments — all of them — and give them to my associates. Then pick a container and get in. Eight to a container, so do not be shy. And do not waste time. Your muscles will stop working shortly after the injection. No one will put you in a container if you do not get in yourself."

"Muscles will what?" Miller whispered to Emile.

"Strip, quickly," Emile said. "The injection works very quickly."

Miller took off his clothing. "But what — "

"It's Para. For beating the scans," Emile said, already naked. "Lifesigns would trigger a search. Scan blockers would trigger a search. But for a produce shipper like Hj'x, non-living biomatter gets waved by. Usually."

An alien came up to them. "Money?"

"This is for both of us," Miller said, giving the coins to the creature.

"Not enough."

"Hj'x and us made a deal," Emile said.

The alien turned to Hj'x and barked something out. Hj'x hissed something back that wasn't translated. The alien shrugged and pushed his hypo into Miller's arm, and then into Emile's.

"Gear?"

Miller shoved his clothes into his satchel and handed it to the alien.

"Get in now."

Miller's legs were already jelly, so he scrambled over to the nearest clamshell, Emile right behind. It already had six people in it, shivering and shuddering. Eight people in this thing was a very tight fit, Miller quite aware his flesh was pressed against several strangers. He tried to shift his arm, be a little more comfortable, but his body was limp.

"It's almost like stasis, they say," someone muttered. "Sleep the whole way."

Miller couldn't even make his lips move.

"It ain't," Emile said.

Then the clamshell shut.

. . . • . . .

Miller didn't breathe. He didn't feel his heartbeat. He couldn't move a muscle. His body was dead.

Except every sense was exploding. Someone's knee was crushing his groin. Another body part was jammed into his back. They were pressed into the clamshell, tighter than a fist, skin smashing skin. There was some jostling of the container as it was moved about, probably loaded onto the ships. Miller hoped that's what it was.

If it hadn't been for Emile, Miller would have been convinced this was some elaborate prank. A tease aliens played on humans. Like a kid catching frogs.

There was no sleep.

There was no time.

Nothing but blackness, silence, pressure of flesh and the stink of fear.

It might have been eight hours or eight days. Felt like eight lifetimes.

Light came like a nightmare.

Alien pincers plucked Miller out of the clamshell and dropped him limply on cold ceramisteel floor. Another light flashed in front of him, soft violet. Vibrations knocked his bones. Then everything came on. Heart pounding. Lungs spasming. His stomach spun and dropped down. He puked, pissed and shat all at once, unable to resist his body's need to let everything flow out of him.

The light shifted, a hint of yellow in the violet. Then liquid. Clear, light liquid, like water, bursting out from every direction in a heavy mist. Miller got some in his mouth. It wasn't water. It wasn't bad, a sort of salty-sweetness, but nothing he'd want to swallow. In a moment, the spraying stopped, Miller lay still, clean of puke, piss or shit.

His eyes started to focus as alien paws dressed him, put his satchel on his back, put him on his feet. His head was still whirling before he realized he was standing, fully dressed and in a line with all the other humans, Emile to his right. Were they in space now? Leaving Sol system? How long were they in there?

Hj'x strutted out in front of the line, carrying a large case. He gave a small regard to the assembled line of humans, as if he was making a headcount. "All right, fleshlings," he called out. "It's time to Jump the Black."

<u>Right now?</u> Miller thought. He actually tried to say it, but his mouth wasn't being compliant.

Hj'x dropped the case on the floor and opened it up, revealing few dozen facemasks. "Get ready."

Humans scrambled over to the case for masks. Emile grabbed two and tossed one over to Miller. "This is the hard part."

The mask bounced off Miller's chest and dropped on the ground. Arms were still like jelly, not responding like they should have. "Sorry, what?" he tried to say, but it sounded like mumbles.

"Hurry up!" Hj'x said. "The doors open in two minutes!"

Emile, already masked, picked Miller's mask up and put it over his face. "You don't want to get this wrong."

"I'm still..." Words themselves were hard.

"Christ, you're bad off," Emile said, slapping Miller. "Most people come out of the Para pretty clean, but a few..." He gestured over to another person who seemed in as bad shape as Miller, stumbling and grasping at his gear and mask. He had no one to help him. "Can you walk?"

"I think," Miller said. Emile had gotten his mask on him now.

"One minute!"

Emile guided him near the bay doors. "We want to be as close as we can."

Jump the Black. The reality of what that meant was hitting Miller in the gut. "How far?"

"It's a few hundred meters. Blowout will do most of the work for you."

Blowout? Everyone else in the hold stumbled towards the bay doors, save Hj'x, who skittered to the far exit. "Jump well!"

Emile held onto Miller's elbow. "You're gonna see some lights, and what looks kind of like a spider web, all right? You'll want to — "

Blaring klaxons deadened out any further advice. Emile's grip tightened on Miller's arm, as he pulled him further forward through the pressing throng.

The bay doors sprang open, and in an instant, Miller and several dozen other humans flew out into the vacuum of space.

It wasn't dark or empty at all. Miller was expecting blackness. Instead, the bright blue star blazed in his field of vision. He expected to be hot, even. There was no heat, though. Only creeping chill on his fingers, frost forming on the mask.

What had Emile said? Lights. Spiderweb. Focus. They were hurling towards something larger and looming and covered in flashing lights. Something monstrous. Ship? Space station?

Below the lights, there was a mesh of some sort. Miller thought it looked like jellyfish tendrils. Most of the humans were hurling towards it. The idea crossed Miller's mind to try and grab a tendril as they passed.

Panic gripped Miller. Emile had said "spiderweb" after all. Last thing you'd want to do was get caught in the spiderweb. Maybe <u>not</u> catching it was how it worked.

If he didn't catch it, what else was there? Beyond the mesh there seemed to be sun and open space.

Miss the web, it's just floating into the black.

They were all almost at it. How long had it been? Only a few seconds?

The mesh was retracting back into the station. Miller didn't know what to do.

He tried to grope at the mesh as they approached it, but it was finer than he first thought. His right arm wasn't obeying him at all, and his left hand flailed uselessly.

Then his shoulder wrenched. He stopped hurling through space.

Emile still had his arm, and he had grabbed onto the mesh with his other hand.

Most of the other people had gotten hold of it as they past. Some didn't.

They flew off into the black.

The mesh pulled inside completely. And then there was a great clang. Darkness.

Miller was dragged to his feet. Emile and many other were scattering out of whatever hold they were in.

"Run, come on!"

Miller followed blindly down a nondescript corridor. Green and white lights flashed all around, sirens blared.

"There!" Emile pointed to a compartment panel at the base of the wall. He dropped to his knees and opened it up. Miller stood dumbfounded. Some people were still running. Where *were* they? What system has a blue star?

Emile yanked Miller by his shirt and pulled him down into the compartment, and then squeezed in himself, pulling the panel shut behind him.

"Emile, where — " Miller started. He wasn't even sure what his questions should be.

"Shh!" Emile whispered.

"Are we safe?" Miller whispered.

"For now. Just keep still for a piece."

Another dark tight squeeze. At least he wasn't naked. Quiet and dark, Miller closed his eyes and waited.

. . . . • . . .

W ake up."

Miller hadn't realized he was asleep. "What now?"

His eyes adjusted. It wasn't Emile waking him. Emile was nowhere to be seen. He was being prodded by an alien of some sort — he didn't know the species. Yellow quadruped, scaly skin, smelling of pork and sulfur.

"I was just..." he started.

"Don't care," the alien said. Not through a translator. "Sweeps are coming through here. Catch you. Slap you back to Dirt."

"You mean Earth?"

"Deathplanet you call home, yes. You want back there? You want to stay in the sky?"

"Stay here," Miller said. "But my friend..." Had he been abandoned? Or had Emile been caught?

"You had friend? I see only you, sleeping in a poorly hidden compartment. Pressers left you behind."

"Pressers?"

"Militia. They grabbed many humans, to crew their ships." His hindquarters shuddered. "You'd be better off on your Deathplanet. Come."

"Who are you?" Miller asked.

"Call me Boss, is good enough," he said. "I have many humans work for me. Don't want to get slapped back to Dirt. You with me, or you slapped?"

"With you? But, my friend..."

"With or slap, human?"

"With!" Miller responded, immediately wanting to take it back.

"Good. I have work for humans. You work for me, have security. Sweeps come through station, say you are mine." Faster than Miller could blink, Boss produced a small device and pressed it against Miller's cheek. A sudden sting, slight burn.

"That is contract, human. You work, you stay safe. Earn some credit, in time. Go on your way."

"Wait, wait," Miller said. "What work? You haven't — "

"Did we not have conversation, human? You work, or slap to dirt."

"My name is Miller."

"I really could not care, human. Come."

Miller went where he was led. It was clear he was in a space station now, a massive complex. Boss led him through twists and turns to a large room, where there were about twenty other humans. All of them had some sort of tattoo on their face.

"Here is new friend," Boss announced to the room. "Get him settled. He starts work next shift."

Boss slapped Miller on the back and left.

One woman approached Miller. "You just Jump?"

"Yeah," Miller said. "I'm still confused."

"Come here," she said, leading him behind a partition to a bunk. "This rack's empty, so it's yours."

"Did someone have this before?" Miller asked.

"Contract up," she said. She pointed to her tattoo, which was a series of swirls, the top part blue, the bottom orange. "I've got about two months left."

"And me?"

"New contract is one of Boss's years. Around seventeen months."

Another woman came in carrying a bowl. "Thought he'd be hungry."

Miller realized his stomach was empty. He took the bowl happily and started eating. He had no idea what it was, but it was warm and tangy, and that was good enough. "What is the work, even?" he asked.

"We run the station's waste reclamators," the first woman said.

The second chuckled. "Fifty different aliens shit fifty different ways. It all comes here to us." Miller had read that alien stations recycle and resequence waste proteins, usually for low-grade food.

"Is that what I'm eating?" he asked. It really wasn't bad, though.

"It's what we do," the first said. "Get some rest. Shifts are seventeen hours long." She got up and left the partition.

"How bad is this?" Miller asked the remaining woman.

She shrugged. "The job is disgusting, but it's honest and safe. Boss is fair, fair as you could expect. It ain't fistwork or smutwork, so that's something."

"Thanks." Miller took a few more spoonfuls. Other humans got grabbed for different jobs up here. Emile, maybe. "Boss said something about Pressers?"

She gave a sad nod. "They're usually right on top of a new Jump, to 'recruit' some new crew, take them out to whatever front they're fighting on. Were you with someone?"

"Jumped with a friend. You think he…" Miller let it hang.

"Some people make it back, I hear." She took the bowl, staring at her boots. "See you before shift." With that, she left him alone.

Miller but his pack and shoes under the bunk and laid down. The mattress was hard, but he could take it. He's slept on more than his share of concrete floors on Earth. Hell, this little partition might be the most private space slept in for who knows how long.

He was off the damned Earth, and he had work. Honest work.

It wasn't much of a better life. But it was a start.

Vera receives a strange letter in this

kooky alien abduction story that only

Neal Barrett, Jr. could conceive.

Timeout

By Neal Barrett, Jr.

Vera Lea drops out her nighty-sling, slips on her weedsack, steps in her dawgs. Pops a raven feather on her head. Makes her way quick past Mudd past Winkit past Dread. Hits the Tangles hits the Badds half an hour past dawn. Stops near *Go.* Makes a sign double-ten-does-it-once-again.

Damn fool trick. Walkin' in the dark while the devil's having tea. Fall in a hole, get friggered by a snik. Then where'd you be, Vera Lea?

"Don't make sense gettin' somewhere fast," she tells herself, "somewhere you don't want to get to at all."

Comes on an Oldie, shakes her left foot, does the words quick — *Wood says dip it Water says nip it turn two-'leven-come-around-seven.*

Stops by DryDead, watches the bloodsun blister through the trees. Thinks about the letter. Second one she ever got. Says you got to be there, says you got to go. That's the part riles her, gets her face hot. Isn't no one in Trawly Flat goin' to make Vera Gates do what she don't *want* to do at all.

Hunches low, moves quick through Rustle, holds a scarf atop her head. Wasn't a week when a Curly dropped down on poor Mary Freed. Sucked her dry 'fore she hit the ground dead.

Knows she's getting close, Rhoad coming on fast. Steps off the path takes the long way 'bout. Makes sign quick not even looking back.

Same as Ma told her, her's afore that. *Vera Lea Platt age seven near eight stands right flat on it, stands where Daddyoak split the blacky road that wound through the World 'fore time come to be. Hops off quick lest the creebies pull her down...*

. . . . • . . .

Time she gets to Addie's got her mind made out. Won't do it that's that. Spit-on-your-hand-don't-even-look-back.

Addie's got a pole, got two ends tacked on a tree. Pole's got a shelf hanging down. Shelf's got leeks, got a bowl of fat acorns, got a skinny mudrat hanging by its tail. Got a sack of sugarflies catches Vera's eye.

"How old's that bugger," Vera wants to know. "Think I saw it Tuesday week."

"Didn't see any such thing," Addie says. "Ever dead critter's going to 'pear about the same." Looks right at her then, nods to one side. "Stranger's down there a ways. Been here since dawn."

"Know he is," Vera says. "'spect I can see good as you." Stands there thinking, not moving anywhere at all. "I'll take those sugarflies, Addie. What you want for 'em?"

Addie reaches up, gets the sack down off the shelf. "Won't take anything today, Miss Vera. See you next time you stop by."

Vera's never cared much for Addie, can't meet his eyes now. Tucks the sack in her pocket, looks the other way. "That's kindly," she says, and turns off down the path.

. . . . • . . .

Man's some shorter than any she's ever seen 'afore. Shaves his face, shaves his head. Suit's tight, suit's green. Looks like a frog been dead about a week.

"You would be the Vera Lea Gates," he says, doesn't look at her at all. "I am the Jones. If you are ready, I've got transportation down the draw."

Vera's never heard of a *transbors*, doesn't want to see one now.

"No, sir," she tells him. "Don't want to go nowhere, don't want to do whatever 'tis you want me to. Have to get you somebody else."

Jones seems to think about that. "You received our letter?"

"Did. What I'm sayin' is —"

"You have it with you, Vera Lea Gates?"

Vera takes the letter from her pocket, hands it to the Jones. Jones lets it fall. Reaches in a pocket brings out something shiny, something new, something bright. Something Vera Lea's never seen in all her life.

"Vera Lea Gates," he says, "in the event of a recipient's refusal to abide by the orders so received, I am authorized to perform liquidation."

With that, he raises the shiny thing and points it at Vera's head.

"Hey, mister — " Vera's heart skips a beat. "What you aim to do with that?"

"You may turn around if you like, Vera Lea Gates. There will be no pain at all..."

. . . . • . . .

One look at *Transpors* Vera throws up. Outside's awful, inside's worse. Somethins' not real, can't do a picture in your head. Passes out wakes up gets sick again. The Jones makes her drink something sweet. Doesn't help a bit 'cause she's *Outside now*

and the Rhoads are all real...
real and long
real and dark
real and dark
long and flat
long and
flat and
tarry black —

. . . . • . . .

Just sit up now, Vera Lea Gates. You will presently be all right. I must tell you that your stay here will differ from anything you may have experienced in your ordinary life. You will appear to be frightened and ill at ease. Nausea, spasms and the occasional stroke might seem to occur. You are likely to feel you are losing control of your bladder and your bowels. However, you will scarcely notice any of this at all. We have given you something to block all discomfort from your mind. From your expression, I see that our treatment is working fine.

"Do you understand what I have been saying, Vera Lea Gates?"

"You're a woman," Vera says. "You sure ain't a Jones."

"I am a Sarah. I will be your guide and companion while you're here."

Vera blinks. Looks the woman over, takes her all in. Same froggy suit. Short, skinny, got no tits no bottom at all. Worse than that, hasn't got a hair atop her knobby head.

More'n likely ate somethin' dead, Vera figures. Left a winder open, let a fog critter in.

"I will be bringing in your dinner, Vera Lea," the Sarah says. "After that, you will lie down and have a nice nap. We have a big evening ahead."

Vera looks the Sarah in the eye. "Don't want no dinner, woman. Don't want no *nap,* neither."

"Yes, you do, Vera Lea."

"Darn sure don't."

"I feel you surely do..."

Vera feels a yawn coming on, figures how supper and a nap would be just about right. Like the Sarah says, need to rest up for the big whatever up ahead.

. . . . ● . . . .

Vera Lea's scared out her ever-lovin' mind. Wants to scream wants to cry wants to lie down and die, knows it won't do any good to try. Truth to tell, why, everything's fine.

Standing on the long black Rhoad that don't have an end at all, she watches as the sun goes down, watches a big shiny ball settle quiet on the ground. Watches as it swells as it trembles as it writhes, watches as something starts oozing, spilling, slopping down its sides, pink stuff, purple stuff, slicky coils of bile, something, Vera thinks, like a hog split open its innards rolling out. Watches, then, as it all stands up, shakes a little, tossin' slime aside, looks at Vera Lea says: "Hi, Feerah-Lhee. I Grii."

"Pleased, I guess," says Vera. "Like to scream, like to toss up lunch. Stuff they give me won't let me do that."

"Mee-too. You bee mos-awfuul-site Grii ever see. Whyy wee bein' here, yu know dat? Godda ledder inna mayel. Don' knows whata leeder be. Usin' alla wurds theys gimmi in my head, sos I getsa tawlka yu."

Vera can't say how, but she knows the thing's crying, knows it's awful scared. Knows it don't belong here, knows it got a letter, too.

"They be a 'wantin' something, don't know what," Vera says. "Maybe we can talk on it some, figure what they're up to. Tell me some about you, Grii, what kinda work you do back home? Me, I do a little fishing, make a little bog jam 'fore winter sets in. So what kinda place you from? Like 'fore you was here."

"*Don' havva playce*
Don' be havva wurks
don' know whatsa doin' *here*
Feerah-Lhe!"

* * * ● * * *

Vera Lea finds a spot off the Rhoad, sits by a tree. Grii's making sounds like a whole pack of DewBears shittin' in a stream.

Isn't no use makin' talk. Clear as can be me and it don' have a lot to say.

When this is all over, she decides, might be good to start lookin' for another place to be. The Jones and the Sarah know where she lives now. Had a notion, they could get a letter off again. Sure don't want to take a chance on that...

Figures she's dozed some, light's near gone and dark coming on. Out on the Rhoad, froggy suits chattering, scurrying about like a herd of baby squirrels. One of em's setting up half a dozen chairs, one's raising big shiny globes atop a pole. Vera watches, wondering what it's all about, when the globes come alive in a blaze of blinding light.

"*Lectricals!*" Vera cries, closing her eyes against the glare. Slaps the ground twice, says the words trice. Seen the devil lights before, high up in the night, looked away quick 'fore they burned out her sight.

"Stop that, Vera Lhe," says the Sarah, suddenly appearing out of nowhere at all. "Get up off the ground. We're starting right *now*."

Startin' what? The look in Sarah's eyes tells Vera she maybe don't want to know that.

Someone's drawn a square. Grii on one side, Vera on the other. The Jones sits in a chair, the Sarah by his side. Another man sits off by himself. Hasn't got a froggy suit, wearing white and black.

"Who's that?" Vera wants to know.

"Shhh. Be quiet," says the Sarah.

"Don't talk," says the Jones.

A few minutes later, something hums, something clatters, something lumbers up the Rhoad. It's a *transpore* is what, and Vera gives a shudder at the sight.

Something gets out. Waddles and jitters, jerks to a stop, just inside the square. Vera shakes her head, tries to make it out. Looks like a pile of rusty buckets, barrels, cans stuck together like a man.

"Pleasant greety to you all," it says in a shiver in a quaver in a squeak. "I am Monitor Man. Coming together we are on this sad occasion. Have to, way it's got to be. Stats tell it all, know what I mean. Drassik and Earth been at it now nine-hundred-sixty-two-years. Earth population down seven-seven-six. Drassik eighty-three. Got to quit got to stop. Got it signed, got it sealed, got the treaty right here."

Bucket man looks at Vera looks at Grii. Looks at the man in the black and white suit. Turns, squeaks, walks to his *transpore,* hums away quick.

"I will be your Referee," says black and white man. "Grii, you will stand here. You will face the west. Vera, you will face the east. This coin," he says, drawing something shiny something from the pocket of his suit, "this coin will determine the outcome of this event."

"Just what event's that, I'd like to know," Vera says.

"Whatsa we du, whereas me at?" says Grii.

Referee sighs. "Are both sides ready? May we please begin?"

"Fine. Vera Lea, as you have adequate hands, you will toss the coin. Grii, as visiting contestant, you will say "heads" or "tails" while the coin is in the air. If the coin lands on the side you call, your world will remain intact, and Earth will proceed with voluntary annihilation. Or, on the other hand, Drassik will do the same. Vera Lea, here is the coin. Ready, Grii? Ready, Vera Lea? When I raise my hand, you may begin."

"Don' wantsa du thiss," Grii shouts, ripping the air with fearsome flatulation. "Is baad iss whasa is!"

"Goes for me too," says Vera Lea. "You folks flat outta you heads is what you be."

Referee looks at the darkening sky. Glares at the Sarah and the Jones. "You got these folks all set up straight or not?"

"Of course we do," says the Jones, "how dare you ask us that."

"You apologize," the Sarah says. "You take that back."

"Uh-huh. Just like I thought," Referee says. "Didn't tell 'em a friggin' thing, did you, now?"

Then, before anyone can blink, Referee brings a shiny brass weapon from his vest, triggers it twice. The Jones and the Sarah sizzle, fall away in ash.

"Monitor Man hears 'bout this..." he mumbles to himself, and turns on Vera and Grii. "Toss it, and call it, folks. Let's get 'er done *now*."

Vera flips
coin dips
"tayuuuls" says Grii
"Aw shiit," says Vera Lea...

. . . • . . .

Have to say this 'bout the most dis-gusting thing I ever seen," says Vera Lea. "I am flat shamed to be part of it's what I am."

"Iss baad," says Grii, "baad's what it be."

"That all you got to say?" says Vera, "don't have to keep sayin' it again."

She looks back at the square, all abandoned now, poles and lights and chairs all carted off and gone. Wonders how the toss came out. Wished she'd had the nerve to ask. When she glances back at Grii, he's ambling up the Rhoad, dripping a trail of nasties behind.

"Oh, sure, you got that shiny thing, somewhere to sleep," she mutters to herself.

Not about to start walking in the dark. Don't know the woods, don't know they brought me a hundred miles or ten..

Settling back against her tree, thinks what she'll tell them back home. Might be nothing, best to let it be. Tossing around, getting settled for the night, finds the sack of sugarflies crumpled in her pocket. Thinks about saving 'em for morning, on the way back.

Remembers there might not be any morning, eats the whole sack. Closes her eyes, lays back. Says the words for dark of night —

bless the roots
bless the sap
when I wake
may the devil
take a nap...

．．．．．．．．．．．．．．．．

The crew of the Carpathia *transport a*

strange rock, whose secret rattles even the

more experienced space travelers.

．．．．．．．．．．．．．．．．

Pet Rock

Sanford Allen

Noor Sayed knelt beside the *Carpathia's* airlock and peered at the specimen that had ripped her away from family and downtime.

The rust brown chunk of stone on the other side of the Atmoscarrier's duraplastic window was no bigger than a newborn infant. No colorful veins ran through it. No ancient carvings or face-like crevices embellished its surface.

The stone certainly didn't seem special enough to warrant she and three other crewmembers sacrificing a promised month of R&R at the station.

"Didn't SeleMine just spend forty billion on remotes to do these kinds of collections?" Noor asked.

Palacios, the *Carpathia's* science officer, popped the helmet of her vacsuit. She and Kirby, the ship's engineer, had ventured onto the planet surface for the specimen.

"They wanted it stowed in an atmospheric chamber for the ride home." Palacios jerked a thumb at the airlock door. "None of their remotes is equipped to replicate the weird hydrogen blend outside."

Kirby turned sideways to navigate the narrow hall in his bulky suit. He flung his helmet into the equipment locker.

"Babysitting a chunk of sandstone isn't your idea of a good time?" he asked.

Noor stood. "Not when I could have been on a shuttle back to Earth. I wanted to see my brother and his family for Eid."

Captain Xiu's voice sounded behind them.

"And don't think I'm not grateful for your sacrifice, navigator." He sauntered into the hall from the direction of the bridge. "Believe me, I played it up to SeleMine when I talked them into paying us a double rate."

"No complaints here." Kirby stepped out of his suit. Its metal articulation bands rattled on the floor grate. "I'd scoop up fossilized dog turds for that kind of money."

Xiu took his turn kneeling beside the Atmoscarrier. He squinted inside and shrugged.

"Way I figure, it's a pet rock," he said.

"Pet rock?" Noor raised an eyebrow.

"You should have paid attention in History of Pop Culture class," Xiu said. "Last century, a smart businessman figured out how to sell people rocks they could find in any riverbed. If SeleMine wants to overpay us for this little thing, I'm happy to do my entrepreneurial duty."

"I'd still rather be Earthbound," Noor said. Her empty stomach rumbled. She always got cranky at the end of Ramadan.

"When you get your check, you can fly your whole clan station-side and put them up in the best suite," Xiu said. "Tell them SeleMine picked up the bill."

"Why's the company so interested in these stupid rocks?" Noor asked. "Excuse my ignorance, but twelve hours' notice didn't leave much time to read the briefing."

"They move." Palacios, now free of her suit, picked up the Atmoscarrier and started for the science bay. "They crawl around the planet surface."

. . . . • . . .

The crew watched over Palacios' shoulder as she tapped at the controls to the science bay's laser cutter.

Servos whirred and the laser's robot arm extended, aiming its photon gun at the smooth stone. The rock seemed tiny at the bottom of the transparent atmospheric tube.

"I don't see any legs," Noor said. "So when you say 'crawl,' I guess you don't it mean literally."

"They're probably like those moving rocks in Earth's Death Valley," Palacios said, looking up from the controls. "That's the result of wind or ice. The remotes tracked some of these buggers moving a few meters a year — enough there's a small chance they could be life forms."

"If that's the case, SeleMine's got to pay for impact studies," Xiu said. "Hell, they may even need to figure out how to negotiate drilling rights."

"Negotiate with rocks?" Kirby shook his head. "Good luck with that."

Noor crossed her arms. "So if your pet rock is intelligent life, does that make us kidnappers?"

Palacios looked up, visibly annoyed the discussion had distracted her from her work.

"We've never encountered intelligent life out here," she said. "And the air on the planet is such a toxic soup there's almost no chance of any evolving."

"The company's covering its bases," Xiu said. "It's a mission for the lawyers."

The laser pulsed inside the atmospheric chamber, filling the room with its ghostly green glow.

. . . . ● . . .

On the bridge, Noor slipped into her chair and lit up her control array. A picture of her brother Amir and his wife smiled up from the desktop screen, between them the two young children Noor had never met.

She'd last seen her brother in flesh — not just as ones and zeros in a holoconference — at his wedding. At the feast, he urged her to come back home, give up deep space for a job shuttle jockeying to Mars and back.

"Money blows away like sand," he'd said, quoting one of their father's favorite parables. "Family is a solid rock."

She pulled up the *Carpathia's* coordinates and a three-dimensional model of the star system spun to life in the navigation globe. The ship had broken out of the planet's atmosphere. A flashing downward arrow icon signaled that artificial gravity had kicked in.

"Back to the station in six days," Xiu said from the bridge entryway. He carried a mug of steaming tea in each hand.

"Looks like it." Noor scanned the route data and Xiu slid a mug in front of her.

"Black Oolong. Tell me what you think. Way better than the ersatz stuff we had in the mess last time out."

"It'll be Eid in two hours," she said, touching the cover of the Quran she kept by her workstation. "Then I'd be happy to try it."

"Still fasting?" Xiu shook his head. "I don't think sunup and sundown mean much out here."

Noor sighed. "It's almost over. I don't suppose we've got a feast waiting in the mess at midnight? Lamb biryani maybe?"

"I'm sorry we pulled you away from family time." Xiu blew steam from his tea and sipped. "It's just that when SeleMine waves eighty grand—"

Palacios' face flickered onto the view screen.

"Captain, I need you down in the science bay." Her brow wrinkled in concern. "I think you need to see what our specimen just did."

. . . . • . . .

Metal tools clattered under Noor's boots as she and Xiu entered the lab. Its floor was strewn with medical instruments, measuring tools and myriad other gadgets she couldn't identify.

A dozen metal storage drawers lay scattered at the base of the atmospheric chamber, bent and misshapen. Their slots on the opposite wall smiled back empty.

The worn brown stone sat in the bottom of the tube, unmoved from when she'd last seen it.

Palacios swept an arm around the room. "I went to my cabin for a few minutes and came back to this mess."

Kirby picked up a dented drawer.

"Our specimen did this?" he asked. "How?"

"It's magnetic." Palacios cocked her head toward the atmospheric chamber. "The sample I lasered off contained iron oxide, nickel, zinc. All stuff you'd expect to find in ferrites, in magnets."

"And it pulled the drawers out of the goddamned wall." Xiu shook his head.

"Why didn't it stick to the bottom of the Atmoscarrier?" Noor asked. Palacios had slid the stone into the science bay tube with ease.

"Been thinking about that," Palacios said. "My nearest guess is the rock is only magnetic when it releases some kind of energy burst. Stone can store energy, so it stands to reason it can also release it spontaneously."

"So it becomes an electromagnet," Xiu said.

"Exactly," Palacios said. "A powerful electromagnet. Probably explains how they move around the planet surface."

"Any danger to our memory storage?" Xiu pointed upward to the bridge.

"The *Carpathia's* old, but this isn't the Dark Ages," Palacios said. "Our systems are pulse shielded."

"Screw the memory," Kirby said. "This whole ship's metal. If this rock — or whatever it is — can send drawers flying across the room, who's to say it won't do worse next time. Like pull the rotors out of the engines."

Noor eyed scalpels and sharp-tipped probes amid the mess. Palacios' departure had been well timed. She'd narrowly missed a skewering.

"I don't think it's big enough to generate a charge of that magnitude," Palacios said. "Just the same, I'll pull together some supplies and build a Faraday cage to contain it."

"Fara-what?" Noor asked.

"Faraday," Kirby said. "It's an enclosure of conducting material. Blocks out electrical fields."

"Or, in this case, seals them in," Palacios said. "I can solder one together in a few hours using the scan mesh from our chemical analyzer."

"Alright then." Xiu clapped his hands. "Let's clean up so our pet rock doesn't turn this place into a whirling hall of knives."

. . . . ● . . .

Noor leaned against the back of a chair in the mess, waiting for the Cuisinier to dispense her bowl of lamb korma. Her stomach grumbled in anticipation.

The korma seemed like the most celebratory offering the machine had to offer. Somehow, it felt wrong starting off Eid with miso soup or buckwheat fettuccine.

She reminded herself to record a video greeting to her brother and piggyback it onto the next transmission back to the station.

It would arrive late, but he'd understand. He always had.

The Cuisinier's door slid open and Noor extracted her order. The steaming contents of the white plastic bowl wafted up rich and spicy, but she was hard pressed to spot the advertised lamb in the golden-hued sauce.

She carried it to the table, sat cross-legged and shoveled a spoonful into her mouth. Its warmth felt good in her belly. Fast long enough and even ship food becomes tasty.

Kirby entered. He walked to the fridge and extracted a beer.

"You think that thing in the science bay is alive?" he asked, popping the can.

"I'm not sure." Noor wiped the corner of her mouth with a finger.

"I don't think *any* of us — not even our science officer — can make that call." Kirby sucked down a long pull of the beer and shook his head. "Given our rookie status wrangling ETs, I don't think we should be messing with it."

"SeleMine wouldn't have thrown us this mission if they thought we were dealing with intelligent life. We're a glorified tug with a science lab."

"Maybe, but that thing makes me nervous. Who knows what it could do to our engines, to the hull, while Palacios sits in her cabin tinkering with the Faraday cage."

Noor swallowed another mouthful of korma. She shrugged.

"Pulling a few drawers out of the wall is different from compromising the engines," she said.

"If it's alive, maybe it was just messing with our heads," Kirby said. He emptied the beer and hurled it into the recycling tube. "Maybe next time, it does something worse."

· · · · • · · · ·

A crash, metal on metal, jarred Noor awake. She pulled on her jumpsuit and stumbled into the hall.

Kirby and the captain stood in their open cabin doors.

"Science bay?" Kirby, shirtless, blinked his eyes, adjusting to the hall lights. "That where it came from?"

"Sounded closer," Xiu said. "This deck, I think."

The captain pounded on Palacios' door. "You in there?"

No response.

"You think she went down to the lab?" Noor asked, rubbing sleep from her eyes. She took a few steps toward the ladder well to the lower deck.

"At 3 a.m.?" Xiu pounded the door again and got no response.

The captain slid his entry card into the panel. The door hissed open and he stumbled back, jaw hanging like someone had punched him in the stomach.

"Jesus," Kirby said.

Noor jogged toward them. Xiu extended an arm to keep her away.

"You don't want to see," he said.

She pushed past.

He'd been right. Palacios' severed head lay on the floor beside her desk in a spreading pool of blood.

Her decapitated body slumped in the chair, a pen-sized soldering torch still clutched in one hand. Strips of silver mesh — the unfinished Faraday cage — scattered the desktop.

The steel panel from the room's air-conditioning duct lay detached behind the corpse, a makeshift but perfectly lethal guillotine.

.　.　.　●　.　.　.

"I found these on the floor beside Palacios," Kirby said, rolling four long metal screws onto the mess table. "They're not broken or stripped. Your goddamned pet rock, captain, was smart enough to unscrew that panel. And it had enough control to drop it with deadly force. It needs to go. Now."

"It's hazardous cargo," Xiu acknowledged. "But we've also got a contract to fulfill. I messaged SeleMine about our situation and demanded an expedited response."

"'Expedited' can't come fast enough." Kirby pounded the table. "That thing understands how the *Carpathia* is put together and it can direct magnetic energy like telekinesis. It's going to tear this ship — and us — to shreds while we wait."

Noor's eyes fell on the mess shelves, loaded with metal cutlery. She shivered.

"We wait an hour, and if there's no response, it goes out the airlock," Xiu said. "But we need to show we at least asked for guidance. We get sued, *I'm* the one who loses the ship."

Xiu's arguments always possessed a cold logic, the mathematics of credits and contracts. That's how he'd convinced Noor to forgo her vacation.

Not this time.

She stood and walked to the door.

"You could lose a ship, but we *all* stand to lose our lives," she said. "I'm getting rid of the rock. If you've got a problem, cut me out of the contract.

She tramped toward the science bay. Two sets of footsteps echoed behind her.

"I can also have the station guard cuff you for mutiny when we land," Xiu called.

Noor ignored the threat and threw open the equipment locker. She ripped the lid from a plastic detergent bucket and dumped its contents.

Kirby appeared behind her. He grabbed a plastic and foam mop and swung it, apparently testing its heft as a weapon.

"If SeleMine comes after my ship-" the captain began.

"This is about covering all our asses, not just yours." Noor said.

The captain exhaled. He yanked a rubber mallet from its wall bracket. "Let's do this then."

Noor opened the science bay's sliding door and the three entered. They circled the atmospheric tube in silence, improvised weapons at the ready.

The rock inside lay still, innocuous-seeming as when she'd first seen it in the Atmoscarrier.

She scanned the room for unsecured metal and saw none.

An icy worm of fear wriggled at the base of her spine. She wondered if their captive could tear off frangments of the deck and launch them like shrapnel.

Kirby gestured toward the robot arm of the laser cutter. "Why don't we carve up the bastard?"

"You know how to use that thing?" Noor asked. "I don't think we have time to pull up the tutorial on the ship computer."

Xiu squatted by the tube's access panel. He punched a code into its keypad.

"I'm evacuating the gaseous contents through the exhaust port," he said. "We open the door now, it's lethal."

Noor nodded and crept up beside the captain. She readied the plastic bucket. Kirby extended the mop, his knuckles white around the handle.

"As soon as we get this thing in the bucket, we run for the starboard airlock," Xiu said. "Get rid of it before it sets off another charge."

"What if it sticks to the airlock?" Noor asked.

"Then we pray like saints it's not stronger than the vacuum." He poised a finger over the control panel. "Ready?"

Kirby nodded.

Noor gnawed her lip, waiting for the rock's defense mechanisms to kick in. The bucket was slick in her perspiring hand.

Xiu mashed the code into the key panel and the door slid back without a sound.

Kirby thrust the mop into the opening and hooked the rock. He yanked backward and it tumbled into the bottom of Noor's waiting bucket.

"Got it," she said, snapping on the lid.

She fastened the seal and ran for the door. The footsteps of the other two rattled the deck behind her.

Noor made it halfway down the hall when a scream echoed behind her. Xiu.

She spun. The science bay door pinned the captain across his chest. His right arm and head extended into the hall and a grimace of agony contorted his face.

Kirby, frantic, jammed a finger at the door's control panel.

Noor took a halting step toward them. The bucket in her hand suddenly seemed like it had taken on weight, tugging downward.

"Get it out the airlock!" Kirby shouted.

He slammed the panel with the heel of his palm. Xiu groaned and his head rocked back. Blood slicked his bared teeth.

Noor sprinted around the corner.

She hung the bucket's plastic handle over her elbow and punched in the airlock's entry code. The thick steel door hissed, starting its slow slide open.

"Come on!" she yelled. The handle dug hard against the crease in her arm. She pushed her shoulder to the door and tried to speed it along.

Glass shattered behind her.

She instinctively twisted to the side and metal slammed the hull where she'd just stood.

A dented red fire extinguisher rattled to the floor, gushing foam. A fan of glass lay on the ground in front of its empty case.

Realizing the door had opened just wide enough, Noor hurled the bucket into the waiting airlock.

She mashed the red "Evacuate" control with her shaking hand. Klaxons rang through the hall. The inside door reversed its path and slid closed.

Through the interior door's window, she saw the bucket laying capsized, lid peeled away. The rock sat two feet away.

Did the lid come off when she'd thrown it? Or had the rock freed itself?

Noor's heart thundered in her chest as she waited for the exterior doors to open. She gritted her teeth, bracing for another salvo of flying metal.

Finally, a narrow band of black showed between the parting doors. The bucket and lid shot across the chamber, splintering as they sucked through the too-narrow opening.

But the rock adhered, even as the doors yawned wider.

Of course it would. It wouldn't give up that easy. What if it just stuck there, tearing panels from the exterior hull as if peeling an orange?

Noor beat the "Evacuate" button with the back of her fist.

"*Just go,*" she pleaded with the thing. "Stop killing us and go."

It clung defiantly, hanging for what could have been ten seconds or a lifetime.

The lock opened further, frosting the edges of interior door's window.

"Go," she said again.

The rock slid backward, perhaps a few inches, then a foot.

It skittered the rest of the way across the deck and out the open lock, disappearing into the void.

"Allahu Akbar," Noor said.

She closed the outside door and slid to the deck, shaken and spent.

A single set of footsteps sounded behind her. Kirby joined her in the hallway. Blood soaked his tunic.

"Xiu?" she asked.

Kirby shook his head.

. . . . • . . .

Noor and Kirby trudged silently onto the bridge. The view screen flashed the arrival of a transmitted message. Its origination read "SeleMine Prevention and Loss Dept."

She fought the urge to hurl something at the screen. The captain and Palacios were dead. She didn't need permission for what she'd done. She owed no explanation.

"Christ," Kirby said, leaning over the captain's control panel. The glowing instruments bathed his face with splashes of red and blue. "That can't be."

Noor's stomach sank. "What now?"

"The engines have been idling all night. Our little friend was powerful enough to mess with the counter-rotors."

He punched at the controls and cursed. "I can't get them to fire. Says we need to switch them off and do a manual restart."

Noor slunk into her chair and pulled up their trajectory. In the navigation globe, the *Carpathia's* icon glided toward the upper reaches of the planet's atmosphere.

· · · ● · · ·

The planet's rocky surface came into excruciating focus on the view screen as the ship plummeted. The heart-clenching descent vibrated the hull as if it could pull apart any second.

Noor yanked backward on the yoke, clenching her teeth. Like the computer controls, it was useless to stop their free fall.

Kirby threw himself into a chair and snapped into its landing harness.

Noor released the useless control stick and followed his lead. She strapped on the harness and dug her nails into the seat's padded arms. The drop wrung her stomach like a wet sponge.

She closed her eyes and prayed.

Then a bounce. A feeling of upward momentum, as if the *Carpathia's* reverse thrusters had fired, breaking the fall.

Noor opened her eyes.

Rusty pillars of rock jutted into view onscreen. The ship hung a few hundred feet over the surface, but its drop had slowed.

Touchdown was gentle, delicate as if she and Xiu had been at the controls.

Dust cleared and the *Carpathia's* exterior cameras flickered the surface image onto the view screen. Delicate stone spires fifty or more feet high circled the ship.

"Those can't have pulled us down from space," Kirby said. "They're not big enough."

The stone spires stared back from the screen, looking down in silent judgment. A chill of recognition crept into Noor's bones.

"They didn't pull us down," she said. "The whole planet did."

"What the hell does it want?" Kirby asked. "We gave back the stupid rock."

"No, we vivisected it and shot it into space. We're not just kidnappers, we're murderers. We tortured and killed its child."

Bolts clattered to the floor and metal panels popped from the walls. The bridge's main screen exploded, showering diamonds of shattered plastic.

"I'm sorry, we didn't know," Noor said. She touched her Quran. "'Whoever kills an innocent soul...it is as if he killed the whole of mankind.'"

The cabin's support beams groaned and the *Carpathia* closed around her like a cold metal fist.

. . . .

In a Texas where dinosaurs roam,

Baxter and his dog traverse dangerous

terrain to deliver packages in

Mark Finn's wild science fiction

adventure littered with guns, bikers,

and lots of action.

. . . .

Take a Left at the Cretaceous

Mark Finn

The last seven miles of Mexico Highway 85, right outside of the New Larado border crossing, are the worst. Everyone calls it "the gauntlet" because of the high number of dinos that like to suddenly dart in front of you on the road, or worse, decide that you're just the right size for a meal. I'm not talking about the big suckers, mind you. Mostly, it's the runners and the egg-eaters who got lost off of the game trails coming out of the low hills in Nuevo Leon. The biggest of them can get up to eight feet at the shoulder, and that's more than enough to screw up your ride if you plow into one going forty miles an hour.

I don't have that problem, not really. Cee Cee is one of those surplus humvees that was just laying around after the Gulf War. Armored everywhere but up top. A good-sized chomper could step on any given hummer and bite right down into the driver's seat, like peeling open a can of sardines. I fixed all of that on Cee Cee. Kept the front armor package and added a Turtle Shell on the back for more cargo space. I don't know what they were originally used for, but it makes damn fine protection against a ripper pack. Changed the power plant, stripped out the unnecessary armor on the bottom, and now she can get up to about seventy five miles per hour on an open stretch. More than enough to outrun the stompers and chompers.

Where was I? Right, on the road to New Larado. On this particular run, I was hauling six cases of medicine to Texas for a private citizen with deep pockets. Well, as deep as Texas pockets get these days. There was also a case of mescal, under a tarp, but right up front, for the inevitable bribes I'd need to clear the border. Truthfully, the rangers weren't going to care one whit for the cheap painkillers and rubbing alcohol, but I'd been stopped before, and detained longer, for less. A case of mescal was a small price to pay to ensure a smooth border crossing.

Right now, the rangers at the checkpoint were the least of my worries. Highway 85 wasn't particularly pristine before the gate opened, but now it had thoroughly gone to shit. Somehow a herd of runners, carrion eaters or maybe eggers from the looks of it, were all bunched up and picking the roadside clean. Some other driver had startled them and they were now in full flight mode, running down the road, darting left and right, going in the same direction as me. I couldn't shoot any of them because they'd fall right in my path and make the road a bloody mess to get over and make me even more late than I already was. It was getting dark, and even seven miles out, no one hung around after the sun went down. All I could do was honk at the bastards, which only aggravated them further. So I'm driving, literally, in the middle of a flock of these things, at about twenty miles per hour. I can't get them to move out of my way, and they keep banging into my left and right side panels and squawking that I won't give them the road. To them, I'm just another runner. Stupid dinosaurs.

Steve was going nuts. He stood, rigid as a statue, in the front seat, his nose trembling with indignation as he barked wildly at the runners who were in his space. If he'd had a tail, it would have been wagging like a windshield wiper. I was tempted to let him out, but these things were a little big for him (not that it would have stopped him in the slightest) and he didn't have his armor on. No fear, that dog. He was part pit bull, part dogo, and part something else, probably Rottweiler, from the size of him. That would also explain the lung capacity. His barks were deafening in the cab, and I was sick of hearing it. We were both miserable at this point; something had to give.

And give it did. The runners abruptly made a sharp right turn, and suddenly, I was free of them. I hit the brakes and cut the engine. Steve was still barking and I grabbed him and scratched his ears as I searched for the predator. How a Rex can be so big and yet so hard to spot is one of the most irritating things on a long list of irritating things about dinos.

Steve had just settled down when I felt the footsteps up through the floorboards and saw it, trotting across the road about a hundred yards in front of us. The Rex gave Cee Cee a passing glance, but was much more interested in the bite-sized snacks that were actively running away from it at that moment. It broke into a gallop, and Steve strained against his collar, but only somewhat. He knew I'd never let him out to chase a tyrannosaur. Damn fool dog. I think if I ever let him, he'd actually take a run at one.

Steve relaxed and licked my face. "Okay, boy," I said. "Thanks for scaring them off for me." He panted and grinned in that way that bulldogs do. I fished around for a dog biscuit and gave him one. As an afterthought, I had one myself. Mexican made. All natural. They don't use cows anymore. Cows are extinct.

When the tremors subsided, I put Cee Cee back in gear and we slapped leather for the border.

. . . . • . . .

It was pitch black when I rolled into the queue, behind a couple of crawlers carrying military supplies from the looks of them. They were waved over by a group of rangers that promptly swarmed over the vehicles in their haste to unload them, and then it was my turn. I pulled up between the concrete pylons and rolled down my window. As an afterthought, I rolled Steve's down, as well, and he happily stuck his head outside to sniff the air.

Ramirez was on duty and he smiled as he saw me. "Baxter, ain't nothing eaten you yet?"

"Close," I said, handing him my manifest and my passport. "I was all the way down in Victoria."

Ramirez nodded as he looked the manifest over. "I heard it's crazy right now. Storms are brutal."

The wind and debris pouring out of the gate was straight from the cretaceous and it regularly played merry hell with the gulf stream. "It's never so much the storms as the dinos it churns up. They had a stampede the day I left. Goddamn bloodbath." He didn't say anything, so I added, "And you probably already know this, but you've got a young adult Rex about seven clicks out, not far from the road."

"What do you want, a fucking reward?" Ramirez thumped his clipboard. "Lucky sonofabitch, Baxter. You left." He paused and asked, "Anything on this sheet I don't want to know about?"

"Not this time. Medical supplies. I'm traveling light. I need the speed."

He smiled, not believing me. "So, no iridium bricks in the sidewalls?"

"Ramirez, you wound me. The only other thing back there is a case of mescal, that I traded especially for you and Carlton. Three bottles each." Ramirez didn't react to Carlton's name, but it had the desired effect. He handed me back my paperwork and said, "Fine, go, but let me grab the case, first."

"Of course," I said, thumbing the release on the back hatch. Ramirez disappeared behind Cee Cee and I held my breath for thirty seconds. Then the back hatch slammed shut and he appeared with the case under his arm. He waved me through and I pulled in and around to the Texas Ranger station, now back on Texas soil.

It was the mirror image of the bunkhouse on the other side of the border. A low, dull pillbox of a building that was jammed full of communications equipment. There was a barracks off to the left and an armory beside that. It looked less like a border crossing and more like a military base, which it was, technically.

Steve jumped out of the cab and immediately ran into the nearby bushes to relieve himself. I waited for him to finish and when he'd rejoined me, I went inside to see Carlton. Steve led the way, pushing past me and the other surprised officers who gave him the lane. He was a dog with a mission. I followed along behind.

Steve trotted into Carlton's office and jumped into Carlton's arms, rocking him back in his chair. "Hey, Buddy," he said, as Steve licked his face. "Dammit, Baxter, are you using him for smuggling now? He's friggin' huge."

"He eats better'n me. How you doing, Carl?" I said, taking the chair on the other side of his desk.

"Get down, boy," said Carlton, and Steve obligingly sat and looked at the man with clear adoration. "Food shortage, my ass." To Steve, he said, "I got something for ya." He pulled open a desk drawer and brought out a package of beef jerky. He opened it and Steve made a warbling sound in his throat. "Can you sing for me?" The warble became a throaty yowling thing. Carlton laughed and flipped the beef jerky into the air. Steve leapt up and caught it and retired to the beat-up couch to masticate his reward.

"You're going to spoil him rotten," I said.

"Says the guy who brought me a case of furniture polish."

I spread my hands. "I'm merely expressing my appreciation for all of the good work you do keeping us safe at night."

Carlton blew air out through his cheeks. "You're about the only one who thinks that right now."

"What's going on?"

He picked up a sheaf of papers and handed them to me. "There's an infestation, is what's going on. Therapods. The big ones. All over the state. The army's having a hell of a time with them. They've killed two so far, but it's cost them."

I studied the reports. It was mostly incident alerts, up and down the central part of the state. "Any civilian casualties?"

"Eighteen and counting," said Carlton.

I gave him his papers back. "How's the perimeter holding up?"

Carlton lit a cigarette. "Same as ever," he said. "We've got infrared all over it, satellite tracking, all that shit. But these fuckers are somehow bypassing all of that."

"How?"

"You tell me."

I rocked back in my chair, lifting the front two legs up. "I got no idea. They're big, they're striped, they're pretty dumb, once you figure them out."

Carlton ignored my oversimplification and tried again. "Did you see anything weird on the Mexico side?"

"The storms are moving the dinos around, but that's about it." I added, "Nothing out of the ordinary."

"I hate that word, 'ordinary.' I'm old enough to remember a time before the gate opened up and turned the world into a dinosaur refugee camp."

I was old enough, too, but I didn't feel like bringing it up. Twenty years ago, the Yucatan Peninsula literally erupted in wind and fire and ash and a shitload of dinosaurs. Tidal waves and earthquakes followed and the weather was insane for months. When everyone could get close enough to the blast site, they found a tear in the fabric of reality. That's what the physicists called it. Eventually someone came online and explained that the asteroid that struck the Earth during the cretaceous period that eventually caused the destruction of the dinosaurs also punched a hole in time that just happened to open up on our end of things. Two weeks later, three more holes had opened up. Fall out from the same asteroids. After the oxygen levels stabilized and the flash fires were under control, Martial Law was declared, and we never really got the civilian government back. Texas seceded, and used its position as the gateway to Mexico to guarantee some economic sanctions in return for agreeing to stop the dinos and the big ass insects before they made it up into the rest of the country. It was a boomtown all over again. All over the state. The wild pig population dried up virtually overnight. A lot of stupid rednecks got eaten. My father and mother disappeared. I tried to find them, but either the army or roaming bandits had forced them out of their home with no forwarding address.

Carlton snapped his fingers. "You still with us?"

"Yeah," I said, grateful for the distraction. "I'm just tired."

"I need you to do some scouting for me. If you don't mind," Carlton said.

I looked away. "I'm in the middle of a run, man," I said.

"So do it on the way," Carlton said. "This is a big deal. The bounty is up. I can offer you fifteen percent. Can you still tag and paint?"

"My uplink is on the fritz at the moment. But I'll get it fixed if you make it twenty percent." Carlton called me a name, and I smiled. "You're only asking me because you know that Cee Cee's the fastest hummer around. I can get in and get out fast. And you know I'm accurate."

"Fine, okay, twenty percent. But I expect you to find me some carnos, Bax. No fucking around. Every city-state is on high alert." He handed me a magnetic sticker. "Consider yourself deputized. Welcome back," he added.

I stood up. Steve jumped off the couch and joined me, his stump tail wagging. I could just rest my fist on top of his stubby, broad head. "Great. Another goddamn turkey shoot. This is why I left, you know."

. . . • . . .

Outside, I affixed the magnetic sticker to the outside of my windshield, over the driver's side visor. It would allow me to breeze in and out of the cities without being detained at the gates. That's mostly why I took the job along with the money. It was eight hours straight through to Dallas. If I had to stop in San Antonio, Austin, and Waco, it would be a two day trip.

So what if I had to keep my eyes peeled for dinos along the way? I was going to have to do it anyway. This way, I could use the tracking system in my roof turret to lock onto any big monsters I saw, and send the coordinates up to the satellite, and back down to the rangers, who would share those coordinates with the army, and who would send out a squadron of men with very big guns to blow the shit out of it. Best of all, I got a finder's fee for any dinos that were harvested after the fact. It was a win-win.

But first, I had to get my gun turret fixed. I left the ranger station and drove out to Cooter Kahn's.

Originally, Cooter Kahn's had been a Seven-Eleven, a Super 8 Motel, and a Jiffy Lube, all clumped together in a row on the edge of town.

Cooter Kahn loved to tell the story of how he "acquired" each piece of property in a poker game, a knife fight, and one protracted stand-off with a biker gang. It was all bullshit. After Larado was overrun, the abandoned stores and shops were there for the taking. Cooter Kahn had enough sense, and enough cousins, to lay a claim to the whole lot and slowly, over the course of several years, tied the businesses together so that it was a one-stop shop for anyone traveling cross-country.

Personally, I hated the sonofabitch, but Cooter Kahn was the only guy in three hundred miles who could fix my gun sights and my uplink. He gave me a big smile when he saw me drive in. Steve growled, but kept his seat. I rolled down the window.

"Cooter Kahn," I said. "How's business?"

"Baxter, you sour-faced bastard," he said. "You've been avoiding me."

"Naw, I've just been taking jobs far and wide out of necessity."

"I got a cousin, saw you in Matamoros last month, playing cards with a bunch of pirates."

At my last running count, Cooter Kahn was up to twenty-five cousins. I shrugged and said, "I don't have a choice, man. I have to go where the job takes me. But I'm glad I stopped here, because I really need your help."

He preened and stood back and gestured into an open bay in what was once the Jiffy Lube. I drove slowly in and let Steve out. "Stay," I said. He sat down, but didn't look happy about it.

Cooter Kahn came around Cee Cee, saying, "So, what you need, a better paint job than this shitty—" He stopped short when he saw Steve. "You keep that bow-legged cannibal away from me, Baxter."

"Steve's fine," I said. "Stay," I said again, and Steve laid down with a harrumph. I handed the keys to Cooter Kahn and said, "I need fresh tires, fresh oil, and a tune-up. But more importantly, that goddamn Soviet surplus targeting system you sold me last year is acting up again. When it works, it's a champ. When it doesn't work, it's a waste of ammo. I need the uplink fixed, too. I've got targets to paint."

"No problem," he said, all smiles again. "You need ammo?"

"Yeah, top me off, and give me an extra belt, too."

"I get you a great deal on fifty caliber rounds," he said. "You know, I wasn't kidding about the paint job."

"You never are."

"At least let me camouflage it."

"No," I said. "I like red. It's a threat color for predators."

"That's a lot of bullsheet, Baxter. Everyone knows Rex are color blind."

"Twenty years ago, everyone 'knew' dinos were extinct. No body knows shit, Cooter Kahn. Least of all about dinos."

"I know this work order gonna cost you plenty," he mumbled.

"For once, I've got the money," I mumbled back. "Call me when it's ready. I'll be in the bar. C'mon, Steve."

As we walked out of the bay, a young man wearing vintage leather and sitting on a bio-diesel Smart Hog nodded at me. I gave him the once over: bad enough that he was riding a motorcycle that costs as much, if not more, than Cee Cee, but he'd modded it out with bones and a skull. The empty sockets of some medium-sized ripper stared, slack-jawed, at me and I felt a pang of sympathy. I nodded in return and kept walking, but he took this tacit adherence to the social contract to start a conversation.

"Hey man, is that your hummer?" he said.

I stopped and considered the smart ass answer. But I was tired, hungry, and I'd left my shotgun, so instead I said, "Yep, sure is."

"She's a beaut, man," he said.

"Thanks. She gets the job done." I turned with a smile and a nod, sure that we were done, but the dino-punk had something else in mind.

"You know, she reminds me of therapod, man."

"How do you mean?"

"Well," he said, smirking, "the way she's brown on the top, on the hard top, and on the hood, and then it's all dark red on the sides, and then black at the bumper and wheels. Looks exactly like the Rexs, especially the males." He nodded again and crossed his arms.

Steve was alert, just waiting for a sign from me. I couldn't see anyone else in my peripheral vision, but dino-punks rarely traveled alone. I forced myself to relax and made my grin a rubbery thing on my face.

"You don't say? I wondered about that when I bought it. Therapod, huh? Well, that's something, ain't it?"

The dino-punk gave me a humorless smile. "Yes, it is."

"Have a good one," I said, and started walking.

"You too," he said to my back. Grateful that the encounter was over, I pushed it into my "Weird Shit that Happens to me on the Road" file and walked over to Cooter Kahn's Take 'Er EZ Cantina, formerly known as Seven-Eleven, and bought me and Steve our first solid meal in two days.

***

I spent the night in Cooter Kahn's, mostly to get a hot shower and a chance to stretch out. Being on the road, jarred this way and that on jungle ruts, and clenching the steering wheel as you drive for your life to avoid charging trikes can really screw your body up. Even though the pit stop was knocking most of my expense money out, I sprung for a solid breakfast. Steve thought he'd died and gone to heaven. Biscuits and gravy. Shit. I made sure he popped a squat before we hit the road. Bad enough I'd have to endure his egg farts for eight hours.

Pulling out of New Larado, I was grateful to see the town get smaller in my side mirrors. I tried the Soviet Common Remote Operated Weapon System and the twin fifties on the roof chattered, splitting a helpless mesquite tree in two. Gorgeous. Cee Cee was rumbling along, smooth as you please, and I nudged her up to sixty miles an hour. Any faster and I wouldn't be able to steer around the massive holes and divots in the road, even though I knew them practically by heart, now.

I should have been in a good mood, but I wasn't. Something didn't feel right. Maybe it was that dino-punk from the night before, or something else I couldn't put my finger on, but I was antsy and keyed up. Steve felt it too; ordinarily, he'd turn around three times and lay down for a snooze, but he stayed up, nose pressed to the window, alert. He even ignored the Mexican dog biscuit I offered him. "More for me, Steve," I said, crunching one between my teeth. He looked over his shoulder at me, disdainful, as if to say, "I know what you're trying, and it won't work," and then he went back to watching the road.

Once we got out onto I-35, away from the border, I was surprised at the number of dinos I spotted. Big ones, stompers, mostly, but there was an actual herd of honkers taking water by the frontage road. I always liked the big prong-head dinos. They sound like trumpeting hell when they're agitated; that thing on their head makes a sound that'll vibrate your sternum. But for all of that, they are pretty even-tempered. Reminds me of cows. I miss cows. Anyway, I painted them with the auto-targeting system, which registered their heat signatures. My onboard computer's ID tracker told me they were parasaurolophuses, which I already knew. Then I uploaded the coordinates to the satellite, where it would bounce down and show up on the Ranger's mainframe, flagged by all of the regional hubs and local outposts, and analyzed for threat assessment. Based on what the computer models said, a squadron of rangers would be dispatched to deal with them, or if it was something bigger, the army would send out an armored helicopter to blow the monsters up. I watched them out of the right side mirror as I shot by and hoped they'd leave the honkers alone.

. . . . • . . .

I was an hour outside of San Antone when Steve suddenly went nuts, barking like mad, his hackles up. I was baffled. We were alone on the road. I swung over to a wide spot on the shoulder that was relatively free of debris and stopped. The gunsights were empty. I gave them a full sweep, just to make sure. Steve was watching me intently, his eyes big and pleading. "You need to go, buddy?" He made a noise in his throat. I popped the locks, pulled out my Ithica, and got out of the hummer. I smelled the air, and figured out what Steve was barking at. There was something around here. A former nest, a carcass, something, because it stank to high heaven. Against my better judgment, I let Steve out of the car and he immediately lifted his leg and peed, marking this turf as his.

The terrain around the interstate was nothing but grassy field. Perfect for rippers, but anything bigger than six feet tall would stick out a mile. Just past the shoulder was a low, sloping embankment made of dirt and gravel and a vast accumulation of trash and rubble; two decades of bad weather and accidents and no one to clean it all up. Off to the left, about a half a mile away, was the burned out hulk of an old school bus. I pulled my pistol and looked through the scope, checking for movement. I wasn't expecting to see anything, and so when the human head popped up and then back down again, it startled me so much that I dropped my sights.

Then I heard the crack of what sounded like small arms fire.

"Let's go, Steve," I said, running around to my side of the hummer. Steve jumped in and I followed, and I floored Cee Cee. She skidded around in the gravel for a minute before grabbing the road and catapulting us forward. Steve was barking frantically, but I was too busy driving to deal with him. Turns out, I should have listened.

The road exploded on my right, and I watched as the mud and the grass rose up, like a giant ribbon of earth, moving right alongside the hummer. As it moved, it took on a more familiar shape, and I understood a number of things all at once. I knew how the theapods were crossing the border, and I knew they were being helped.

The Rex was big—huge—one of those thirty five footers with the horned ridges over its brows—and really pissed. It was literally sprayed down with a layer of mud and crap and what looked like camouflage flocking. More than enough to disguise its heat signature for the infra-red scanners. Someone, or a group of someones, had somehow managed to knock this big fucker out and stealth him, for no other reason than to create a weapon of mass destruction.

The Rex had been laying in wait by the side of the road, and I just stuck my ass out in the wind. Now it had my scent, and Steve's too. I was standing on the gas, but Cee Cee wasn't built for rapid acceleration, and the tyrannosaur was more than able to match my speed. It roared, a sub-sonic scream that was designed to scare prey into bolting. It was working.

I idly wondered who those assholes in the bus were, but I didn't have time to dwell on it. The CROWS was locked up in a futile attempt to target something. I disengaged the paint program and manually spun the guns around and opened up. The overhead chatter was reassuring. I wasn't helpless. I saw the Rex disappear, dropping back, and I had a brief, fleeting thought that I'd survived the encounter. Then the roof thundered, bent inward, and then the bastard was on top of Cee Cee, trying like hell to get to me.

I swerved to get it off, but Rexs have sharp claws, strong feet, and a firm grip. I heard Steve yelping as I wrenched Cee Cee around into a skid, hoping that my rudimentary understanding of physics would serve me well. Sure enough, the weight of the carno was enough to send it forward even as the hummer went sideways. The only problem was, the Rex refused to let go of my roof. There was a lip where the tortoise shell joined the chassis and I heard it rend and pop. Cee Cee tipped, pulled down by the weight of the dino, and went tumbling over as the Rex rolled down the road.

Steve was whining and I was trying to get my bearings. Upside down, I saw the Rex right itself and regard us with alien hate. It roared a challenge, crouched, and then I lost sight of it for a second. Then it landed on the exposed underside of Cee Cee and I cursed the day I took the belly armor off. The Rex was ripping through the transmission, scrapping the humvee in huge bites. I couldn't see or hear Steve. This was bad. It wouldn't be long before it would punch through the floor, and then that would be that. I undid my belt and fell heavily on my shoulders. I still had the Ithica and my pistol, but neither one would be much good against the Rex.

Behind my seat was the Remington VK. Twelve rounds in the magazine, fifty caliber, incendiary. Capable of stopping most anything without armor. I yanked it free and held my breath. I had one chance, and I had to time it just right, or that was the end of my run. It seemed to take forever, but finally I saw serrated claws punch through the floorboard, and then sunlight and the meaty stink of carno flooded into the cab. I waited until I saw its head lunging in and I rolled out of the window and popped up, barely a dozen feet away. Its head was still inside the ruined humvee, seeking me out. I raised the Remington and fired once, twice.

The bullets were designed for long distances and large prey. The Rex jerked its head free and roared at me. I put a third bullet into its open mouth and saw the mist of blood spray out at the base of its skull. The Rex stepped off of Cee Cee and staggered towards me, wobbling on unsteady legs. The damn thing was huge. I didn't take any chances. One more shot into its ribcage and the Tyrannosaur veered off, into the ditch by the side of the road and fell forward.

"Sonofabitch," I said. It was very quiet in the wake of the attack, and I heard a ruckus off to my left. I was more or less parallel with the bus, and I could see men running out of it, getting onto bikes that were laying down in the grass, and riding away. I recognized one of the bikes with the skull on front, and I raised my rifle to fire, but pulled my shot when I saw the streak of white knock the rider off of his expensive toy.

Steve made it out of the crash, after all. By the time I covered the distance between the road and the burnt-out bus, the dino-punk was a bloody mess. I whistled for Steve, and he detached himself and ran up to me, wagging his tail and grinning proudly.

"Good boy," I said as he ran over. "Good boy." The dino-punk was moaning and crying for help. The rest of his crew had scattered, already way down the road. I plucked the sat-comm off of the bike and called for help on the Ranger emergency channel, using their numbered code to more or less describe what had happened. I was told that an evac team was en route. Then I turned to the bleeding dino-punk.

"You bastard," he said. "That goddamn dog nearly killed me," he howled.

"Shut up," I said, leveling the Ithica at him. "Your little liberation project nearly killed me. I'd say we're even."

"Those creatures are beautiful and deserve to live their lives without interference," he said through gritted teeth. "You're the monster, not them."

I spat on the ground. "But now that you're bleeding out, you wouldn't mind a little civilization, right?"

"Hey, I'm human, too, asshole!"

"The jury's still out on that," said. "Come on, Steve."

"Where are you going?" he yelled.

"I've got Rangers coming in the next half hour. If you're still alive by then, we'll see about getting you patched up. But here's an interesting fact you may not know," I said, scanning the rolling grass. "Those big Rexs have their own ecosystem of sorts. For example, there's almost always a crowd of little biters that follows them around, living on the scraps of its kills. Carrion eaters. Great sense of smell."

I watched him go pale. "Don't leave me here alone, man!"

I put the Remington on my shoulder. "You got a new bike, you bought the jacket, probably found the skull, and suddenly, you're an activist. You don't know shit. My hummer's trashed. You nearly got me and my dog killed." I turned away. "We're more important than them."

I walked back to Cee Cee, Steve trotting along beside me, so proud of himself. I surveyed the damage. It would cost a hell of a lot to fix, but the reward for bringing down the Rex, plus the extra information about how the dino-punks were getting the carnos over the border, would fix her up, better than new. Maybe.

Behind me, the grass was rustling and making little scritchy sounds. The dino-punk started screaming. I didn't turn around. Steve barked once, and but he didn't leave my side. Good boy, Steve. Good boy.

. . . .

Jessica Reisman's imaginative

coming-of-age tale introduces a truly

alien society. Sebira, a mind reader in a

traveling show, fears for her future as her

abilities go awry.

. . . .

The Chambered Eye

Jessica Reisman

Sebira! Wake up!" Gilley's voice called me out of sleep that morning. Peering out the semiperm window over my bunk, I saw her standing by the seatrain car where I lived with Ben and Hassif and Mika, my pod, with whom I'd been born and raised in one of the sector crèches.

I pulled on pants, a skirt, tunic and vest, all bright and clashing, and came out, stepping down onto the long dock. Our seatrain, bellied up longwise to the dock slip, rocked slightly with a low hum all through it as it recharged, taking in farmed krill through feed vents all along the undercarriage.

Gilley was tall and gangly back then, her long pale hair shining in the dim. A follow-cart hummed behind her, lights blinking in the dawn. It was Gilley's special cart; she'd painted extravagant, soulful eyes on one end, affixed a rag of rope tail to the other, and named it Wulf.

"Supply run for Zadey; you said you wanted to do the shill," she said. Zadey is the show's owner, boss, cook, and Gilley's mum. Gilley comes from a real family, that rare thing. Most of the rest of us, the aerialists, tumblers, duelists, and dancers, musicians, and reader-tellers like me and the others in my pod, we all come from the sector crèches.

The Gamboges Vivant, the show with which we all lived and traveled, was still mostly asleep, our old seatrain and the grounds beyond shrouded in rain and mist off the sector's inlet. The vivid orange yellow, lemon yellow, and old sunflower gold of the tents and canopies, all the signs and the glint of the gearwork of the rides dimmed and slumbering. I love the show like that, quiet and ghost-like.

Our seatrain, an old Doysen maglev skimmer, the distributed neural net of its light, flexible ceram-steel body latticed with manta ray and bowhead whale code, pulled in late the afternoon before, from another sector. It had been some other sector before that, all of them so alike they tended to blur. Most sectors are built on artificial sandbars in the endless sea, pressure sand made from centuries of refuse. Each sector rises out of the sea plains, a proliferation of towering garden-terraced structures. All of them laid out mostly the same, with a water conversion plant and a market at sector's edge, and then the seatrain yards and docking slips.

Between these hubs of human life, there was only sea and the web of float tracks on an endless beading of amber bladder bubbles, stretching in all directions. The sectors — they had names, but I generally couldn't remember one from another — were strung like gaudy baubles on the lace ribbon of tracks around the world. Except where there was no sea at all, just dust and the empty; they say there's towns there, too, and nomad bands, but it's just what they say.

For the nine and some years of my life since Gamboges adopted my pod when we were five years old, that was the world: horizons of sea, deep color in sky with the wink of stars in the nights, the float tracks an endless stitching from sector to sector, joining it all together, my pod of four and the folk of the show, our family.

It was a rainy, sweet-throated morning. At the sector market there were pussy willows, lilacs, and morels like tiny pale brain trees in trays: wondrous things. While Gilley moved to the more prosaic stands to trade for vegetables, fruits, honey, seaweed flour, and spices, I picked a spot near the lilacs — the smell makes people happy — and did the shill.

My flash gear earned looks. I wore colors that ached in the peripheral vision, mirrors and holo-bead designs in my layered rags; the show performers all made sure to be a walking advert for Gamboges Vivant when we hit public places.

A woman walked by me with her gaze down, a worried expression tightening the lines of her face. "It will be today," I said, easy and just ever so singsong. I can't really tell you what else I sensed, but I sensed, and I read what I sensed. "Today — and in your favor, don't worry." Her wary expression dissolved into a smile as she took in my appearance and what I was saying.

"Tell him," I said next, to a tall, thick man in the coverall of a maintenance tech, "tell him that you love him." He colored over and ducked his head.

"Guys, a seer!" a boy called to his pod and three of them gathered round me. Seers is what people call reader-teller performers. We don't see, though, we sense, and then interpret. I found something in each of them, in their bearing, and in the things that connected them, and gave them the happy news that the fourth member of their pod, back in crèche for tests, would be fine and with them again soon.

Readers, we only read what's there to be read, but isn't by most folks. We should just be called understanders, or interpreters, or something. Calling us seers is just to make us grand and magic for the show.

I read a bunch more folks, singles and pods, as they came by, spreading the word about the show as I did. When Gilley came to collect me I was starving and euphoric.

It isn't like that for every reader. Some get sad, or so tired they have to sleep. I love it. Hassif's like me and Mika gets sad, but in what she calls a luxurious way, so she kind of likes it; Ben, though, always sounds a little insane. It's like he thinks he's reading the world, or the air. We use it in the show, but it makes the rest of us nervous.

There are stories about readers — one member or an entire pod — that've gone wrong, their genesets a sequence off from stable. Mad, ill, broken — taken back to a sector crèche and never heard of again.

Reader pods weren't common; the geneset was, at that time, one of the most experimental.

Gilley handed me a spiced fish bun. The Wulf-cart, loaded with vegetables, oil-paper packets of fish and seaweeds, sacks of grain and spices, and a big jar of honey, rolled behind her with its rope tail swaying.

Something pale swam through the corner of my vision, like a fish tracing a figure in the currents of the air. I brushed a hand over my eye, pushed my hair back, but my hair is dark, not pale, so it wasn't my hair I was seeing from the corner of my eye. It came again, a graceful creature of lace and almost-there color describing a figure that tried to say things to me, in that place between my forehead and the back of my shoulders where reading happened.

Then it was gone and I dismissed it as we walked back through the train yard, a maze of inlets, docks, float tracks and seatrains, great hulking supply movers and sleek but ornate hotel cars from out of the east, coral frames and cuttlefish skins, all festooned with seabirds, the sky above full of their flight and cries.

We were coming around one of the scuffed heavy supply engines, rocking slightly at its mooring, when pain pulsed through me, just below my stomach.

I made a noise and Gilley said "What?"

"Hurts," I said, pressing a palm over the pain.

"You ate too fast," Gilley said.

"I always eat fast," I said; another sling of pain down through my middle and into my thighs made me whimper.

By the time we got back to the show grounds, just beyond the main train yard, my thighs and arms were trembling. The show was bright and alive with activity in the full morning light, the sea an endless shifting beyond.

I ignored everyone and everything and headed along the dock to my pod's train car. Hassif was still there and I just mumbled something to him, feeling like I was going to die as I dove for my bunk and curled into a tight knot.

It didn't help. *Polyps and mollusks*, I cursed in my own head, *what is wrong with me?*

Then, of course, crèche-fed knowledge surfaced and I knew. Hassif's voice had been cracking and changing; Ben had started growing facial hair. Mika had begun to fill out her skirts and vests with curves.

I dragged myself to the car's commode and confirmed.

So, I knew what to do. I made a pad out of a clean rag and went to the dispensary for supplies, including a patch to take care of the pain and shakiness. I pleaded my case to Gustus, the show foreman, and went back to my bunk to let the patch work.

Curled into a ball, I stared out at the sea, a landscape of crumpled silk and sheen. That thing I'd seen earlier, the angel fish speaking in figures at the corner of my eye, I saw again. A dark one this time, with the luminous glow of a red tide cresting in a train's wake. It wound through my peripheral vision.

Maybe this was a side effect of reader puberty never mentioned in the crèche knowledge feeds?

No, I didn't think so, either.

Ben's lunatic pronouncements when he read came to mind, and with that a chill like damp clothes and sea spray.

Eventually, I slept, the gentle rock and gulp of the train a familiar lullaby. When I woke, afternoon light fell gold and laden with dust-motes across my bunk, the car quiet and empty but for me. The cramps and trembles were gone; the angel fish, too, my sight clear of things extraneous to reality. Feeling tentatively pleased with my body's new maturity, tall and strong as I stretched, I pushed the strange corner-of-the-eye visions from my mind.

That evening as the show lights were kindled in the seaside gloam, as gears began to turn and mesh in the rides, the scent of hot sweet buns to fill the salt air, and sector citizens to arrive, my pod and I circulated to hand out tokens, cheap but glittery moon coins good for a telling.

Hassif, a mysterious story prince in spangled vest and slim silk pants; Mika beautiful in layers of gilt and mirror-embroidered, fire-colored silks; Ben, beard coming in, dark eyes kohled and solemn, wearing midnight velvets studded with sequins; me in antique jodhpurs, embroidered slippers, and my favorite green overvest patterned with rhinestones in all the shades of the sea, a bright scarf twisted and braided through my hair, making it a crown; this hair arrangement felt heavy and regal on my head and always made my neck feel longer, my bones elegant.

When we came all together and processed, some of the tumblers leaping before us, a small crowd trailed us like wake to the Fortunate Pavilion. The pavilion was set up to one side of the main show tent. It has an onion dome of parchment and yellow striped canopy with lengths of drapery and holo-beadings through which a cosmos moves, an occasional shooting star flicking through the beading across tent panels.

Inside the pavilion, our set is a cave grotto, walls rough and seamed with silver and gems glittering in the incandescence of biolume lamps. The stage is low, painted dark and sprinkled with more glittering gems, and wends like a tributary stream a fair way into the audience.

We have our own little band, an older pod of three, on balalaika, squeeze box, and tabla. They played a barcarole, low, rhythmic and mysterious to underscore the act.

Mika stepped out with a flourish, flame-colored silks vivid. She strolled along, slowly gathering the audience's attention to her before she stopped, lifted one hand in a sweeping gesture, and said, "Join us, lovely guests, in an exploration of the shadowed paths and vistas of the possible, the probable, and the imminent."

"The world went to sleep beneath the sea," Hassif said, stepping forward as he intoned the Apocrypha of Cephon, "and when we woke, in the crèches, in the sectors, by the sea, some of us had been traced by the salt and kissed by the cephaloi, given the eyes to read the many paths — into this evening, into tomorrow, into the future." The Apocrypha of Cephon is a hagiography, a poetry of the change time. It doesn't tell a history truth, but another kind.

I made exaggerated swimming motions behind him, like a loopy fish. Laughter loosens patterns, makes them easier to read.

Mika focused on one of the people who laughed loudest, an elderly woman whose grey and white hair had been augmented with metallic strands woven through.

"You'll get the news you've been waiting for tomorrow," she said to the woman. "It will seem to be the wrong thing for you and your pod at first, but it will open a new field of inquiry for the work you do."

The act unfolded, Mika and Hassif flamboyant and charming. I provided plainspoken predictions and comic counterpoint while Ben was reserved and mysterious.

We did our freeform segment, taking turns reading out what we sensed for this or that person, then took tokens from those who had them, with requests for specific readings.

You have to be careful with the specifics, because patterns shift, and what we sense are potentials and probabilities projected by the subjects themselves — by their own sense of their lives and relations — not fate or inevitabilities.

It was while answering one of the specifics — a man asked why a woman he still loved had left him, the worst of questions — that the fish and swirls and symbols came back, building through the air around the man. Suddenly I was no longer sensing, I was *seeing*, in the most literal sense of the word. My gaze followed a spiny sea urchin as it traced glowing symbols in the air, and I faltered. With a look out the side of his eyes, Hassif swept in front of me to take over.

I lost track for a while then, of the show, of myself and the world, as figures, motions, pale sprites etched my vision in waves. The world yawed wide around me as I was caught on a current that affected only me. I was distantly aware that Hassif, Mika, and Ben moved around me, shuffled me slowly to the back of the stage, into the shadows.

When the clamor of sprites, sea creatures, and symbol faded and I emerged from my abstraction on a shuddering, sudden breath of awareness, Ben was finishing his segment of the show. The lights were low and smoky.

"The waves sing of a sweet wind and all the sector's beings breathe together," Ben said, his rich-timbered voice carrying, though it seemed quiet and low. "Like the children of luciferase, deep in the deepest depths of the sea, our breath is a phosphor lighting the heaviest of times." He spun a quarter turn, hand out pointing — though it wasn't clear at whom. "Heavy times, the weight of loss and despair," he went on, "it comes on us all — one time and another, and for some of us, it comes soon."

Mika and Hassif shifted, ready to intervene if he got too dark and doomy — sometimes he did; other times he seemed to self-implode and fall to distressed silence. But he finished now, "It comes fast as furies, but hold to the song of that breath and all will come well." Not one of his more alarming readings; looking back I see it for the anodyne it was, but that night my mind was too disordered to know that Ben often softened his readings and purposefully made them less specific; it was only when he couldn't suppress himself that he made insane-sounding pronouncements.

This was our standard set list, a shot of fey and sometimes sinister with Ben, then a reassuring pageant of what we called fizzies — he or she does love you, don't doubt it; the business can be saved; you will succeed — then we bowed as the musicians played the audience out.

I slipped out the back while my podmates did the fizzies, unwilling, unable, to hear or answer their questions.

Out in the dark behind our tent, rain-specked sea wind ruffled my hair and clothes familiarly. Music drifted from the ride nearest, mixing with the patter of rain on canvas. The lights of the nearby rides and the midway's many lanterns glittered and gleamed on the yellow and parchment of the tents throughout an otherwise shadow-strung tangle, the night architecture of the Vivant, familiar to me as the faces of my podmates, the sound of their individual breathing in sleep.

Suddenly feeling hollow as a scoured-out clam shell, I followed the smell of savories to Gilley's food booth. She gave me a packet of smoked fish wrapped in marinated cabbage leaves, greasy with spicy oil. I ate it too fast and washed it down with a sweet-water, watching Gilley gribble and kibitz with the customers.

Was I a defective, more broken than Ben? I thought of tales told in the crèches, of those whose genesets failed, whose integration of traits hit tragic snags. They would recall our whole pod — between Ben and now me, clearly we were defective.

Watching Gilley, my head filled with questions and panic like a drum with bees, I scanned her and the customers closest for readings — the habit of it as old as my small store of life.

A set of tentacles, ghostly octopod of extra limbs, writhed about one man, stretching through the rainy air toward Gilley. Without considering what I was doing or why, I gave Gilley the sign for *watch* — *hinky* with a flick of fingers in the man's direction. Gilley acknowledged with a dip of chin to chest.

Then — it was like every nerve in my body seized, the fear was so strong. What was I doing? I backed away. My vision was empty of extraneous bits — now that I was deliberately trying *not* to read anyone. Would I have to stop reading, abandon the act? Would that keep the strange hallucinatory scritchings of the air away? My head echoed with questions; panic twitched and tightened in my muscles, made my overfull stomach queasy.

I faded back into the shadows between tents, the little alleyways and dark offsides that the show's structures create.

Smell of sandy ground and the shift and feel of it under my slipper soles. Snatches of music and shouts and laughter, as fragmented as the lights of the rides. My head was filled with panic and my breath came short.

One of the ride operators, taking a break for a bite of food behind the octometron, the show's largest gearwork, said my name as I went by. He was no more than a suggestion of mustache and teeth in the shadows. I waved and didn't stop.

I thought about what I'd seen around that man in the audience. Little figures and symbols, like the figures I'd sometimes seen scribbled in the dark above me when I was little, lying in my bunk. Meaningless. Stick figures, a chair, a spoon, a seatrain car, a school of fish. Around the man, the figures had swirled. A fish chasing a bubble into the branches of a tree and emerging as a bird. The sea urchin writing words. A bird, flying with a school of fish, had carried, trailing from its claws, a ribbon of symbols.

I'd rather have to interpret my sense of a person's potentials; I knew how to do that, had spent my life to that point doing it. If that swirl of scratching was trying to tell a story, it was one I didn't understand.

Didn't want to understand — was terrified of understanding.

Clear of the show's structures and lights, beyond the inlets and docks of the seatrain yards, I came out to the dunes at the outer tip of the sector headland. Below the marram grass-stitched sand hills, waves curled in and laced over the beach, over and over.

The world's breath we call it.

The shush of steps through the sand came sometime later and I realized I'd just been standing there, staring out, but not seeing anything.

Ben came even with me and we both stood there for a while more, watching the waves, breathing with the world's breath.

"You're shaking," Ben said, quietly. He took my hand and I realized I was trembling; scared, in shock, not cold.

Ben's hand was warm, grounding. Ben, the least grounded of us.

"I'm seeing…things," I said.

"What kinds of things?"

I gestured with my free hand, clutching his hard in my other. "Childish drawings in the air…it started in my peripheral vision, but tonight, when I was sensing the patterns for that man…it was just there, in the air all around him."

"You're evolving," Ben said, like it was a simple, good thing.

I drew in a breath on a slightly hysterical gasp. "Devolving, broken is more like it. I can't read the things I'm seeing. They're — silly, meaningless."

Ben grunted. "Seb," he said, "I've never sensed patterns and futures the way the rest of you do. I hear them. I hear music, and voices, and other sounds. They tell me different things than what you all sense. I know they sound…mad…but they've been borne out just as often as yours or Mika or Hassif's readings. What I hear…it's of…I don't know, wider, or another level? Or, just different…

"But here's the point, Sebira: I had to learn to interpret them. At first — it was just noise, cacophony."

He wasn't looking at me. I stared at his profile. "You've never… never said." As close as we all were, I couldn't quite believe it, couldn't encompass his keeping such a big secret.

One of his brow's rose as he did look at me, a wry twist to his mouth. "For the same reason you ran away instead of telling any of us you'd started seeing things, I'd guess. I didn't want to be recalled to the crèche, or be the reason the whole pod was recalled, labeled defective."

Those stories, whole pods disappeared back to crèche because one of their members was broken. He'd been protecting us, all of us.

"You all already thought I was…broken, a little, Seb. But I'm not — we're not. Not broken, Sebira."

"Ben, I can't--"

A sudden flood of figures and motions filled the air — hugely — above one of the inbound seatrain tracks. A cartoony line of sharks, nose to tail, looped through the air into a confused knot, then exploded out in all directions until, momentum expended, the sharks flopping over with x's for eyes.

Great huffing mollusks, I remember thinking, *what does that mean?* Because whatever it was had urgency.

Ben's hand clutched at mine.

"I hear screams. And--" he shook his head and shut his eyes for a moment. "A popping sound and trainsong" — the magnetic song of maglev skimmers — "broken and stuttering. I think. What do you see?"

I told him. "Should we--"

"We need to tell the station master," Ben interrupted. "Now."

He started at a lope toward the station, still holding my hand and dragging me with him.

"But--" there was no train in sight and I didn't know what I'd seen.

I tripped after him, slipping up and down the sand dunes.

The station master sat in her geodome shack, playing dice and drinking with another woman — Zadey, our boss; I remembered Gilley mentioning her mother was long-time friends with this sector's station master. The panes of the geodome were mostly opaque from the outside, only a little light spilling from the structure, but from inside the panes provided a panoramic view of the rail yard inlets, coastline, ocean, and, currently, the lights, tent domes, and rides of the Gamboges Vivant.

Zadey and the station master had seen us coming and were paused in their talk and play, looking at us expectantly as we came through the hexagonal door.

"Ben, Sebira?" Zadey surveyed us. Her long, sharp-planed face got longer and sharper. "What is it?"

"Seatrain accident," Ben said. "Or, the track, I think — some kind of failure of the float beads."

The station master, a woman as old as Zadey but softer, with a genial quirk to her brows, frowned.

Zadey made introductions, her own frown curious. "Jadlen, Ben and Sebira. They're two of our reader pod."

"Readers read people, not tracks and ocean," the station master said.

"Gene sets evolve," Ben said; it was the wrong thing to say.

Zadey's expression turned worried, the station master's puzzled with an edge of — pity, that I shuddered to see.

"Sebira?" Zadey said.

"It's," I said, and fell silent, twisting my fingers together, my thoughts twisting with them. That moment never fails of pain in its remembrance, shame fresh in its hollows. I said nothing, only looked away from the station master's pity, Zadey's concern, from Ben as his earnest expression gave way to disbelief and anger.

So Zadey made her own assessment and sent us away, over Ben's protests; I heard her apologize to her friend in a low voice as I pushed Ben out the door before me.

It was Ben who was trembling then, and he turned on me when we were clear of the geodome, "Do you know what you've done?"

"Kept us from being reported to the crèches as defective, I hope."

"Seb--" he shook his head, kohl-lined eyes mournful.

"We can't convince them, Ben," I said, "and I don't even know — I don't."

He looked off distractedly, a gesture I recognized and now I knew what it meant: he was hearing something. I turned my own gaze down and closed the door to my own reading.

I left him there and went back to the show grounds.

As I wandered in a fog through the drifts of crowd and lights and color, Gilley found me.

"Seb," she said, grabbing my arm. "Thank you — that man, he tried to attach a data siphon to the show's chit stream through my cart's terminal, but I was on the look-see cause of your high sign, so I caught him."

I looked at her, blank, and then remembered the man with the octopod arms.

"There was a bit of a fluffle, but Gustus got him booted. So, thanks." She squeezed my arm once and went on her way.

At that moment, away beyond the show and the train yards, a seatrain hove into view over the ocean horizon, its leading lamp a sudden comet.

Suddenly nauseated with fear, I ran all the way back to the train master's dome. Ben sat on one of the shack's steps, dejected. I grabbed his hand and pulled him after me.

"Sebira," Zadey said sharply as we burst back in.

"It's true, what Ben says — I saw, I saw something, too. It could be — is there any way to check the float beads?"

"Full track inspection of the whole local network was completed just weeks ago — a long process for the tech dive team," the station master said. "Failure of the float bead bladders is highly unlikely. And we'd have to call the divers back out," she shook her head.

Seatrains travel at high speeds. The incoming train was close now, the low music of its magnetics already audible, light and reflection from windows all along the passenger cars flying over the water.

And then the station master's highly unlikely failure happened — the oncoming train was diving, ocean closing over it as the rest of the train followed. The track had given out under it.

A beat of silence thick with horror, then the station master tapped the table she and Zadey had been playing on and brought up a console in the air, tapped her ear and started speaking fast and urgent while her other hand continued working the console.

The train's backup floatation deployed, but the front portion stayed under; what was left on the surface drifted, tilting, like an abandoned toy in a giant bathtub.

Several hovwheels were coming across the sand plain from the sector proper, lights whirling. Before they had fully stopped, rescue workers poured out of them and began snapping pontoons into the air to inflate.

The pontoons swarmed onto the water with high beam lights cutting across the dark ripple of ocean. People were pouring out of the Vivant's grounds — customers, performers, vendors, and operators — to aid in rescue operations. Before we went to join them, Zadey leveled us a look that said we would be talking.

Hours later, in what would have been the dreg-time, the show shutting down, emptied of all but the most looped or forlorn of customers, the Vivant's midway and main yellow-gold tent were still lit, our tumblers and musicians entertaining rescued train passengers while the rest of us ran among them delivering food and drink behind the official medical workers administering treatment for minor injuries and shock.

The worst of the injured had been taken to sector care. The fatalities…the bodies…had been taken away, too. Twenty-one in all, I heard someone say. The diver techs had been sent for, too late; a section of the bladder beads had taken ill with bio-mange. At least it would be kept from spreading.

If I had stuck with Ben, if we had pushed…maybe the accident could have been averted, the train advised to deploy its backups earlier.

There was no time to talk to Hassif or Mika, but there was time to think, while waiting on the next basket of fish buns.

Among the rescued passengers, I saw shivering, looping eels and crude ziggurats, connecting, disconnecting, describing things I didn't understand. Yet. Shadows of things invisible to the human eye. But not to mine.

*　*　*　●　*　*　*

In my memory, now, the pungent scent of Zadey's cigar mixes with the sea wind as our train slips fast across the ocean, down the long tunnels of time, the passage of years.

Foretokens braid and pattern the air in my vision still.

I learned, over the years, to read them.

After the bomb dropped at Hiroshima,

the United States, led by President

George Washington, and Texas, led

by President Sam Houston, rest on the

precipice of a cold war in this startlingly

different vision of the mid-20th century.

Best Energies

Josh Rountree

The King

The day after the war ended, King George took breakfast in his office. Black cherries, toast and Coca-Cola. He relished the simple act of eating. No matter how many years he lived, he'd never shake the memory of those wooden teeth, and he thanked Providence that his immortality had carried him to such an advanced age. What the young took for granted, George appreciated for the miracles they were. Reliable false teeth. Automobiles. Modern medicine.

And, of course, the atomic bomb.

The morning edition of the Times announced the Japanese surrender, but it had been a foregone conclusion for the last week. What else would the enemy do in the face of such suddenly overwhelming odds?

The phone calls began while he was reading the comics section. George was scanning the page for the Dick Tracy strip when his secretary's voice announced that the President of California was on the line. George took his congratulations with the proper mixture of false modesty and unquestioned power. That call was followed by countless others, friendly nations eager to claim their places in the new world order created by Hiroshima, and old enemies making transparent attempts to claw themselves back into George's good graces.

He took pleasure in every call, but his delight doubled when his secretary announced that the President of Texas was holding on the line. George waited a full minute, then lifted the handset.

"Sam!"

Sam Houston released a weary sigh and spoke in an irritable drawl. "Morning, George. I suppose you're in a fine mood today."

"I will admit the air smells a bit more like freedom this morning."

"To some, I suppose."

"Not to worry," said George. He slipped a Camel between his lips, struck a match and lit it. "You still enjoy the protection of the United States of America." George inhaled deeply, enjoying the burn of smoke in his disease-proof lungs.

"The Republic of Texas does not need outside help in guarding our own interests," said Houston.

"Sam, I don't like to touch on unpleasant matters, but it pains me that you haven't shown me any inkling of respect in the last hundred years or so. I'd think you'd feel some kind of debt to the man who shared immortality with you."

"Most days I wish to Hell you hadn't."

"Yet you'd have me open the gates and let anyone drink who cares to. That's why you've called isn't?"

"I certainly didn't call to help you plan the victory parade."

"So you'd have me hand that kind of power over to the savages?"

"It was theirs to begin with, wasn't it?"

"That's a matter of some debate," said George.

"Well, I disagree with your take on things."

"So because the savages were here first, the United States must cede everything we've built to them and call it a day? I suppose then you'll be handing over that city they named after you to the Mexicans. Or the Spanish?"

"This is different. That kind of power shouldn't be confined to one nation."

"Damn you, Houston. Here I am celebrating the liberation of half the free world and you can't even choke back your pride long enough to admit I've done you a favor. Instead, you choose this day to call and pursue the same tired matter that you've been carping about for more years than I care to remember. The Immortality Pool is on U.S. soil and that makes it mine to use as I see fit. Now that we figured out how to harness it for other uses, I'm even less willing to share it with those who are disinclined to support American interests."

"That's the main point of my call. What the hell did you do? Those bombs you made; you can't tell me that's not a product of the Pool's magic. I knew you'd managed to do some heinous things with that water. I've heard of the Special Forces you sent against the Germans. But now you've passed well beyond the borders of national interest."

"Yes I have. We are a magnanimous nation. We're protecting the world. You Texans and all the savage nations should be thankful. The whole continent is better for my actions. The Nazis ripped a hole straight through Europe. Do you think they'd stop there? Certainly not. So while you were unwilling to pick a side, we knocked the fascists and their Japanese whipping boys down so many pegs that they won't be capable of starting new trouble any time soon."

"I'm not arguing the Nazis weren't a threat, and we would certainly have responded in kind had our interests been threatened as yours were. But you cannot tell me you wouldn't have steered clear of that war if you'd had a choice. Any sane country would have."

"Or any cowardly one."

Houston remained silent for a few seconds before speaking. "George, I've called to ask you one more time to allow others access to that pool. That power should be shared. This is something you need to do."

"Do I sense an ultimatum in your tone?"

"What you sense is a demand."

"Goodbye, Sam." King George dropped the phone in its cradle and fumed.

What a mistake it had been to let Houston drink from the Pool those many years ago. Sam had been a good man once. He'd served under General Jackson and killed his fair share of savages, and the General himself had recommended the young man for immortality. Yet not a month after Houston tasted that glorious, wondrous

Water, he'd been convicted of nearly killing a man and fled to the wastelands they called Texas. The deserter had been nothing but a thorn in his former nation's haunches ever since.

Simply organizing dirt farmers and rabble rousers into stealing land from Mexico did not make a man presidential. Yet Houston had taken that title with little protest. A few years later, he'd been succeeded by one of his staunchest detractors. That was the limitation of Houston's form of government. The man wasn't old enough to remember when the United States had toyed with the idea of limited term presidencies, and thus never knew the folly of turning one's best laid plans over to someone who does not share the same dreams. George had learned quickly what a mistake that was.

Of course, being long-lived, Houston found himself elected again and again to the Texas Presidency, and each time he regained the title, he bucked against the United States' rightful place as their continental superior.

A painting of the Immortality Pool hung opposite the King's desk in the Oval Office. It showed the Pool as it had been when Captain Smith and his men had claimed it for England. That Spanish fool de León had wandered half of Florida, following trails conjured by lies and false legends. Had he turned his eyes to the north, past those miserable swamps and tangled nests of cypress, he might have found what he sought in Virginia. But to the great detriment of Spain, he never had.

George pushed back his chair and crossed to the painting. He was often drawn to it, and he ran his fingertips over the familiar bumps and swirls of oil on canvas. The artist had captured the Water's elusive shade of silvery-pink, and George could almost feel the cool kiss of dogwood flowers on his cheeks and the soft wind that blew from the Pool like holy exhalations. Now the Pool was surrounded by metal fences, barracks and processing plants. But George still remembered it as a peaceful place.

And although he'd only had one drink of the Water, he'd never forgotten the taste. Earthy, sweet and utterly pure. Drinking it was like embracing the divine.

George hated men like Sam Houston who would see that place overrun by fascists and savages and communists who'd sooner piss in the Water than worship it with the reverence it deserved. George had no idea how the Pool had formed, but he knew God's hand had played a part. One tiny sip and you'd live forever. After all these years, that miracle had never paled. But it was so much more than that. The Water had other uses, uses beyond count. And though they'd graduated a succession of alchemists from government sponsored programs, none had ever managed to harness the Pool's full potential until they'd enlisted the foreigner.

Einstein was an alchemist without peer. Spinning the Water into gold was an old trick. This man could spin all of that magic into power.

The phone rang again, and George returned to his desk, eager to put Houston and his petty concerns behind him for the morning. According to his secretary, the new interim Chancellor of Germany was on the phone, and that was not a call he intended to miss.

The Statesman

President Sam Houston felt every one of his one-hundred fifty-two years. He stepped into the war room, still fuming from his conversation with Washington. The assembled Secretaries of This and That, Joint Chiefs, Vice President Ferguson and various other advisors stood as one. Sam closed the door behind him and took a seat in the empty leather chair at the head of the table.

"Sit down, all of you," he said "Still never figured out how standing up just to sit down again is necessary every time I walk into a room."

Sam hated ceremony, absolutely loathed it. He'd been president far too many times to have people bowing and scraping just because his name was on the door to the big office and his face was on the dollar bill. He had to constantly remind himself that although these men and women seemed of an age with him, they were comparatively young and regarded him with an inordinate amount of respect and awe. It was just another of the countless things that irritated him about being immortal. He wasn't just President Houston, he was the Sam Houston, the last living Father of Texas, hero of the Battle of San Jacinto, and all those other titles he didn't care to remember. Texas was a country that took a great deal of pride in its own mythology. Being a living architect of that mythology was a unique and uncomfortable burden.

"Can we assume by that sour milk expression on your face that King George hasn't yet built a public diving board at the Immortality Pool," said Vice President Ma Ferguson with the trace of a smile.

"He's as stubborn as ever," said Sam.

Ma nodded. Sam knew she was intimately aware of King George and his fanaticism. She'd served as president some years back and done a fine job of it, but she'd had no more success in her attempts to wring common sense and decency from the immortal monarch than had any of her predecessors. "So we move forward with Operation Floodgates?" asked General Eaker, Commander of the Texas Ground and Air Corps. His face was solemn but Sam could see the excitement in his eyes. War wasn't something to be wished for, but Sam understood how the General felt. He wasn't the only person in the room that wanted to take George Washington down a few pegs.

"I will go on record again to urge caution in this matter," said General Nimitz, Supreme Commander of the Texas Navy. "We can't win a war against America, Sam. Mr. President. Even a war of conventional weaponry, which we know this will not be."

"This will only be a war if Operation Floodgates fails," said Sam. "And I'll admit we stand little chance in that case. But if we succeed?"

"If we succeed, we don't know what will happen," said Nimitz. "We have only the theories of a mad scientist to go on."

"Mad alchemist," said Eaker, humorlessly.

Nimitz scowled. "Whatever you call him, we have no proof that the man is capable of doing what he says he can do."

"I'd say the Japanese would vouch for the man's capabilities," said Ma. The room grew silent. Even Nimitz could not argue that point.

What had once been the miracle of everlasting life had been changed. Altering men into mindless killers, heedless of pain and injury. Powering silent flying machines that were faster than airplanes and capable of launching payloads of unquenchable fire and infectious madness. Some reports stated that the aircraft could fly backwards through time. If the US Army Air Corp lost a battle, they'd simply rewind and start again. And again if necessary, until it turned out in their favor. There was no tangible proof of this, but a few spies had reported it to be true, and even Einstein confirmed it for them in his cryptic way. The man's reports were maddeningly vague, but he'd smuggled out what knowledge would be necessary to their plan.

A few encoded transmissions. Engineering plans received in stages. Everything needed to build Bluebonnet Betty. It was an obscenely innocuous name for a bomb, but Sam took some small comfort in the fact that their bomb would be nothing like the one George had unleashed on Japan. Though they were created by the same man, Bluebonnet Betty was not technically even a bomb. If a description must be applied, Sam preferred to think of it as an agent of change.

"The device is finished?" Sam asked.

"Betty's fully constructed," Ma said. "Along with a backup shell just in case we need it. All we lack now is the ignition element."

"I just can't see how this plan is in the best interest of the Republic," said General Nimitz.

"The Ground and Air Corps is prepared to follow the orders of the President," said Eaker. "Chester, are you sure you're not just bucking on this plan because the Navy isn't involved. We'll get you in the history books somehow. Don't worry."

Nervous laughter filled the room. Sam knew they were old friends and that Eaker enjoyed pushing his colleague's buttons even more than he loved tweaking King George. But it was a bad time for humor and the President cut off any potential retort with a pronounced cough.

"I have no doubt that Chester holds the fate of Texas above all other considerations, particularly personal gain," said Sam. "His dissent is noted and welcomed. None of us are certain we're following the right path, but our options are few. Washington is flush with pride right now and he's only going to get stronger. We can wait around for him to turn his eyes our way and figure it's time to annex us, or just to blow us off the map and start fresh, or we can take a proactive stand. In light of the destructive power unleashed on the latest of George's enemies, I think we know what the outcome would be if our nations ever came to blows. Even with all the Native Nations, The Republic of California and Mexico behind us, we couldn't fight back against magic. We would die, and our country would die."

"But if we had magic," said Ma, "the shoe would be on the other foot."

"But we don't know for sure we'll have magic," huffed Nimitz. "That's the whole point of my argument, Madame Vice President. You may be in charge of all these spies of ours, but can you really vouch for the motives of the man who enabled the United States to build the Atomic Bomb?"

"Tread carefully," said Ma with a feral smile. "I might take issue with a man who questions my capabilities."

Nimitz blanched. Ma was a formidable ally but she was an even more capable enemy. Not even a man in Nimitz's position could afford to rub her the wrong way.

"I'm not questioning your capabilities," he said in a lowered tone. "I'm questioning this alchemist. He claims to serve our interests but he ends up building the most horrible weapon the world has ever seen. You've said in the past that he must continue to advance the goal of the Unites States is small ways in order to keep his position and appear loyal to their cause. This is necessary in order to advance our own goals, and I understand the need fully. But he's created an unstoppable force. He's forged the key to world domination and placed it right in George's palm."

"I do regret that," said Ma. "But the man didn't know how powerful that weapon would be. Even for skilled alchemists, magic is a tricky thing to manipulate."

"Exactly!" said Nimitz, slapping the table. Those assembled around him jumped. "He didn't have a full understanding of what would happen when that bomb exploded. How can we know that Betty will perform as he says she will?"

"We can't," said Sam, cutting off any further argument. He'd listened to the exhaustive opinions of every man and woman in the room on numerous occasions, and truthfully he'd made his decision the second he'd finished his call to Washington. Once Einstein arrived with the last piece of the puzzle, Betty was going to fly.

Sam shared Nimitz's doubts, but they had little choice. If Betty performed according to spec, she'd be dropped into the Immortality Pool by a shiny new Boeing B-29, and would create what Einstein describes as magical fission. Whatever force was binding the magic to the water, to that place, would come apart and it would flow into the world. Sam had spent time with some Cherokees in his younger days who swore the magic in that pool had been trapped there by an ancient warlock, and it screamed for release. If that was the case, Sam intended to be its liberator.

What would happen when all of that magic returned to the universe was something no one could guess. Whatever the result, Sam had a strong suspicion it would be something preferable to being bullied and beaten by an increasingly mad, two hundred year old petty tyrant.

"This is a matter of faith," said Sam. "And I will take responsibility for the outcome."

"Then Operation Floodgates is a go?" asked Eaker.

"On the President's order I'll send word through the channels," said Ma. "It's time to retrieve the alchemist."

The Alchemist

Defecting from the Unites States wasn't the easiest of tasks, certainly not for a man as recognizable as Albert. He'd shaved his mustache and cut his wild hair into a short and messy patch with his pocket knife. He'd done so in a gas station restroom somewhere west of Memphis after being recognized by a poultry truck driver who'd given him a ride from Nashville. The man had let him off at the station with few questions and little trouble, so either he hadn't been listening to the radio or had somehow missed the alerts airing constantly for Albert's capture.

Albert trudged along the side of the road, cursing the damned Ford that he'd left smoking alongside the highway a few hundred miles behind. He finally receives the call to put the plan in motion and the car picks that day to die. As far as signs went, it wasn't the most promising.

He'd left the Pool Compound mid afternoon the previous day. Better to make it look like he was leaving for some quick errands than sneaking out in the middle of the night. By supper time the reports of his flight had already reached the press, and King George's propaganda experts were earning their money. Albert had woken a national hero and by the time he'd slept, half the country thought he was a murderer. Killed two men and stole state secrets. Tried to pollute the Immortality Pool. It was nothing but lies, but that wouldn't matter if he was caught.

Albert had expected this sort of thing, but not so quickly. Technically he wasn't even a citizen of the United States and could come and go as he pleased. But he had no more personal freedom than a prisoner. Albert knew far too much about the internal operations of the Compound, and about the Water itself, and he knew how the King would react if he simply disappeared. Better to cut his losses with his pet genius than let that sort of knowledge fall into foreign hands.

The King had never trusted him; Albert doubted there was a man on earth he trusted.

Albert heard the gray pickup rattling before he saw it appear over the rise. He stuck out his thumb, and pulled his hat down a bit, hoping the lack of mustache would be enough to disguise his true identity. The locked steel briefcase he was carrying wouldn't make him any less conspicuous.

The truck stopped and the driver pushed the passenger door open. "Get on in."

Albert climbed into the truck and put the briefcase between his feet in the floorboard. The cab smelled like liquor, and the driver looked as if he was quite familiar with the stuff. He was handsome, and had a better shave than Albert, but he was rail thin and wore only a stained undershirt and worn pants and boots. He had a crooked sort of smile that made Albert a little nervous, and his eyes seemed to be staring at some point just beyond the horizon. His hand jumped slightly when he offered it to shake and Albert wondered if he might be affected by something more than just alcohol.

"Name's Hiram," he said. "Where are you headed?"

"Austin, Texas," said Albert. "I have family there I plan to visit."

"You don't sound like a Texan. Don't really sound like an American either. Where are you from?"

"Switzerland," he said. He doubted the driver would know the difference in the accents, and choosing Switzerland was a safe bet.

"What are you doing all the way over here? The Nazis didn't run you out did they?"

"No, the Nazis never marched on Switzerland, thank goodness. My family left before the war and have been living in Texas since. You can imagine, I'm eager to see them again."

Hiram dug a flask out of his pants pocket and held it out to Albert. "You thirsty?"

Albert shook his head, pleased that the man hadn't pressed him on his invented family, but leery of riding too far if he insisted on drinking more.

"I just need a nip," said Hiram. "Hope you don't mind. My back hurts like the devil. Does most days."

"You're a young man," said Albert. "Have you injured yourself?"

"No, I was born with pain. Haven't figured out how to chase it the hell away yet, but I'm working on it." Hiram drank from the flask for several seconds then left it in the seat between them. "Tell you what, I'm heading to Texas too, though I'm going to Dallas. I've got a show there in a couple of days on the radio. I'll drive you as far as I can."

"Radio?" said Albert. "Are you an actor?"

"No, I'm a singer. I've sung on enough radio stations in the south that I've lost track of how many, but I ain't never sung for foreigners before. This should be something, shouldn't it? I figure them Texans are pretty much like southerners. I mean, they speak English and all. And they ain't got no love for Washington. We'll get along just fine."

"You don't agree with your president's politics?" asked Albert. It was a subject far too close to the truth of things, and he was a fool for pressing the point. But he'd so rarely met someone who'd speak out against the government in front of strangers, he was fascinated.

"I don't agree with a man who hordes power. And what else is that damn Pool he's got but power? He makes all his buddies immortal and lets everyone else just go to Hell. You think if I knocked on his door he'd give me a sip of that Water? Hell, no. He'd run me off and then go make a speech about responsibility and how he's single-handedly taking care of us all. Like he knows better than we do what's good for us. No, sir. I do not care for that man. I'm sorry if you're offended."

"No apology necessary."

"So what do you do for a living back there in Switzerland?"

"I'm a scientist." It was the truth, for what little that was worth, though he'd let ambition twist it into something less noble. He'd gained worldwide fame for his theories of mass-energy equivalence and the particulate nature of light. He'd even won the Nobel Prize. Albert had a way of looking at the world from angles others hadn't discovered, and when King George had offered him a chance to apply his mind to the mysteries of magic, the very antithesis of everything he'd ever known, he could not turn it down. He'd secretly come to believe he'd reached the limits of what he could achieve without violating the fundamental laws of the universe. But the Pool was without limits, a grand mystery that defied physics and called into question even the most ironclad beliefs of the scientific community.

Upon his arrival at the compound, Albert had been astonished at all the things Washington's alchemists had managed to do with the Water: simple mind reading, pain relief, and brief moments of enhanced speed and agility, all from ingesting drops of the Water mixed with various compounds. Albert immediately set his heart to the task of finding new uses for what proved to be nothing more than a previously unknown element, bound in an unchangeable liquid shape, sizzling with electromagnetic force. Within weeks he'd learned more about the Water than the Americans had in several hundred years, and within a few more years, he could do absolutely anything with the Water. Anything.

Not that he had free reign. All of his research had to benefit the American good, and he was thankful to King George for allowing him access to what was surely to be his life's work. So much so that he even shared his suspicions that the Nazis were working on a nuclear fission weapon, a monstrous bomb capable of untold destruction. George had laughed and told him he'd better get to work on magical fission, and so of course he had.

By the time he realized what kind of fury he was set to unleash on the world, it was too late to reverse his research.

It was his own guilt that had driven him to spy for the Texans; even before the bomb was finished, he knew that he would have to seek redemption somehow. The Texans offered it to him, and he seized it. They had sought to stop the manufacture of the bomb, but by that time it was out of Albert's hands. So they settled for making a weapon of their own, and Albert gave them the intelligence they needed. The fools wanted to release the magic into the world so that everyone could gain access to it. Hadn't they seen what that Water could do? It was madness, and when Albert had heard of their intentions, he'd almost laughed.

No, the Texans would have their weapon. They had great faith in him. But it would not function in exactly the way they expected.

"A scientist?" said Hiram. "You know, you look like a scientist."

Albert laughed nervously. "I think I always have. Even as a child I knew this would be my profession."

"We're alike in that," said Hiram. "I've never been good at much but singing, but that suits me fine. Say, you think we're close enough to pick up any Texas radio broadcasts? I'd like to know if they got any singers there can give me a run for my money."

Hiram switched on the truck's radio and Albert suppressed a gasp. A preacher shouted through the tinny speakers, urging them off the lost highway to sin. When the news cut in with an announcement that the famous alchemist and Nobel Prize winning scientist, Albert Einstein, was still at large after magically murdering half the Immortality Compound and trying to destroy the world's supply of Water, Albert reached instinctively for the handle of his briefcase and put his other hand on the passenger door knob.

Hiram grinned. "Settle down, doc. I'm not an idiot and I read the papers. I knew who you were the second you jumped in the truck. I just didn't want to run you off. I have a notion that you ain't done none of that stuff they said you did. More of the King's bullshit, I'll wager. I'm just going to keep on driving, and you don't have nothing to worry about from me. Okay?"

Albert nodded thankfully, still clutching his precious cargo. "You are a good man, Hiram."

"No, I'm a sight worse than most. But if you took off you probably got a good reason. And I can't imagine it makes old splinter teeth too happy. Any man willing to spit in his eye is a friend of mine."

Hiram stuck his hand out again; Albert released the grip on his case and shook it.

The Hell-Raiser

Hiram's world was a dark blur of asphalt and pine trees awash in threatening yellow headlights. Fresh pain born of hours on the road lanced through his back and he resisted the urge to sip some more whiskey. He was drunk enough as it was, and he didn't intend to kill such an important man as Albert Einstein.

Besides, they didn't have much farther to go. The Republic of Texas was coming up fast.

"I appreciate your help," said Einstein. "But please don't feel compelled to risk you life for mine. You can stop and hand me over and they'll make you a hero."

"The hell I will. We're twenty miles from the border, and getting into Texas is easier than getting into Mexico. Those old boys behind us may be bold over here, but they won't follow you into another sovereign country. Washington just finished up with one war. I reckon he ain't looking to start another."

Hiram hoped he sounded more confident than he was. The identical black Packard's had caught up with them about an hour back, and they'd been pressed up nearly to his bumper ever since. They'd fired a few shots in the air but it hadn't taken a scientist to figure out they weren't shooting at Hiram's truck. If they had been, they'd have hit it. And besides, they wouldn't want to kill the greatest alchemist the world had ever known. They needed that man.

"You have Water in that briefcase," he asked, fear and adrenaline finally stripping away his manners. He'd been waiting for the man to volunteer the information but he wasn't much for conversation unless you prodded him a bit.

"Yes, but it won't grant you immortality. It's been converted into a Water Uranium suspension with a --"

"I don't care to be immortal," said Hiram, guiding the groaning old truck around a corner. "I just thought maybe you could use it against them." He motioned behind him with his thumb and the Packards seemed to sense it. They revved their engines and pulled close again.

"The suspension in this case has only one possible use."

"Well it was worth a shot. They're supposed to have them airplanes can fly back in time. Wish they'd fly back to when these yay-hoos didn't know where we were."

"You may get your wish."

"What's that?"

"If we get to Texas alive, I'm going to turn all of this back. The whole war. Everything. What do you think of that?"

Hiram would have thought any other man in the world was crazy, but he knew Albert was serious. Reading about the Eighth Air Force's Rewind Missions in the magazines was one thing; best as he could understand, those time reversals were localized occurrences. They wouldn't affect anything more than a mile or so from the aircraft. But it sounded like Einstein was talking about something more dramatic, and that scared the hell out of him.

"How do you intend to do that?"

Einstein studied him with that famous face, the one he'd recognized immediately, even without the wild hair and mustache. His eyes were wet with sadness or fear, and he held onto his briefcase with both hands like a child with his blanket.

"Hiram, you're risking your life to get me to Texas, so perhaps you should know what you're risking it for. The Texans are going to build a bomb."

Hiram nearly swerved off the road. "What kind of bomb? If you mean to build another of them atomic bombs, then maybe I will just pull over and let you walk."

Einstein shook his head. "No, not one of those. Never one of those. It's more of a time bomb, though that's not exactly what the Texans are expecting. I've been sending them the plans, sneaking out bits of information at a time. I simply want to make amends for my part in the atrocity that is Hiroshima. The Texans, they want to free the magic so that everyone in the world has an equal share, but that would only exacerbate the problem. We don't need more people making weapons, we need less."

"So why are you helping them if you don't see eye to eye?"

"They are manufacturing the bomb to my specifications. I could never have built such a thing under the King's thumb." Einstein patted the briefcase. "Once I put this inside it, the device will be functional. But that's where our paths diverge, hmm? These Texans, they chase one goal and I chase another. Let them believe that this Bluebonnet Betty of theirs will free the magic. I know what it will really do. It will turn back this world, all of it. Not too far, mind you. Violating history is not something to be taken lightly. But if time were to reverse to a point before I joined my efforts to the Americans, I am confident they could not discover magical fission without my assistance."

"That's all well and good," said Hiram, "but who's to say you don't just join up with old Georgie again? If time goes backwards you ain't gonna remember none of this."

"That is where science and alchemy must bow to faith. When time reverses, I believe nothing will be exactly the same. I must hope this new version of me will be less prideful. Perhaps he will see the dangers inherent in such unchecked power. And if he does not, then I hope he has the opportunity to do all of this over again."

Hiram's head was hurting as badly as his back, and he wished to hell those boys chasing them would give them some room to breathe. His mind reeled at the thought of years of history being wiped away. When had Einstein come to America? He couldn't remember exactly, but it was when he was a kid. Life hadn't been wonderful and he wasn't entirely sure he wanted to live it all again. But putting the alchemist out now would be the same as sentencing him to life in prison. And though Einstein's plans weren't comforting, they were far less worrisome than what business the King would put him to if they drug him back to the Compound.

"My life hasn't been much to write home about," said Hiram. "I don't think I'd care to go through it all again. Besides, I'm starting to get a little success. A little money. There's a feller out in Nashville told me I got a million dollar voice. I might be somebody famous one day, like you. I hate to turn back now."

"You are right. Things will not necessarily follow the same path. But perhaps you could have a better childhood this time. And if you are the musician you claim, then I expect you will be so again. Admittedly our experimentation has been limited, but certain aspects of people's nature do not change. If there is music in your soul, it will remain there."

Hiram drank the last of the whiskey in his flask and fished in his pockets once again for pills he knew weren't there. They'd been gone before he left Alabama. He clenched his jaws together, waiting for the worst of the pain to pass, and he wondered what he'd done to be born with a bent to hell spine.

"How far are you planning to turn back time?"

"As little as possible," said Einstein. "I came here in the thirties. Some time before that."

"How about nineteen twenty-three?"

"Why would you suggest that year?"

"It's the year I was born. In September. I ain't in the best of shape in case you ain't noticed. There's plenty of reasons for that but mostly it's cause of my back. I was born with something wrong. It's all bent up and causes hellacious pain more often than not. I throw back some whiskey and pills, and it don't make everything better but it helps a little. If you were to go back before I was born, is there a chance I might come out right? I mean, be born without this problem?"

"There is certainly a chance, though there is an equal chance you will retain your affliction."

Hiram nodded. "I don't care for the idea of messing with time. But if you got to do it, you go back that far at least, would you?"

"I think nineteen twenty three would be an ideal year," said Einstein. "Life was fine then."

Lights flooded the highway ahead, and for a second Hiram thought the sun had risen early. Then he realized he'd reached the border and the Texans were bathing them in floodlights. Armed soldiers stood atop several guard towers, and three tanks emblazoned with the Lone Star insignia idled alongside the highway ahead, guns directed straight at them. A contingent of U.S. border guards manned their own towers, rifles pointed at the sky. The way west was unobstructed, but the road back in from Texas was gated and heavily guarded. The men on the towers watched the cars approach with casual interest. They apparently hadn't gotten word that the great fugitive Einstein was headed their way. Another man wearing the same stiff blue uniform peeked out of a booth and waved at Hiram so he might slow his approach.

No doubt sensing time had run out to capture their escaped alchemist, one of the Packards rammed into Hiram's back bumper. Metal screamed and the truck shuddered, but he kept it riding the center stripe. They slammed into him again, and then fell behind as

Hiram pulled within firing distance of the soldiers. The Packards braked, and Hiram shot across the Texas border with a whoop of triumph, the loose bumper clattering against his back tire and the engine whining from the strain of the chase. Once he'd passed, the tanks pulled into the road and the soldiers hurried to drop a striped crossbar over the highway, shutting off entry through the Texas half of the emigration station. The U.S. border control agents finally realized that something was amiss, but they had no intention of testing their rifles against the Texas tanks.

Whoever was in charge over here had known they were coming, and Hiram was damn thankful. He doubted his old truck would have held out much longer.

He eased it to a stop, removed his shaky hands from the wheel and wiped them on his pants. Blood thundered in his head and he wore a wild grin. He hadn't realized how worked up he'd become. The engine ticked and Einstein breathed heavily. Hiram started to laugh.

"Welcome to Texas, Mr. Einstein."

The Vice President

Vice President Ferguson stood in the far corner of the hanger, watching as Einstein and the crew of engineers he'd been assigned put the finishing touches on Bluebonnet Betty. Men pulled and tugged at a proliferation of levers and dials sprouting from the bomb's surface, a process that was, according to the alchemist, just as vital to the bomb's proper function as the Water they'd already inserted into the fission chamber. Unable to contain her excitement, Ma crossed the hanger, her footsteps echoing off concrete and steel, and she took up a supervisory position just off Einstein's left shoulder.

"You're sure everything is in order?"

Einstein sighed. "Your engineers have done a fine job. I've told you this bomb will function as planned. What more do you want from me?"

"The United States won't sit around waiting for us to move. I'd be shocked if they haven't already sent a squad of their Special Forces freaks across the border to track you down and bring you back."

She thought she saw Einstein shudder at the prospect and suppressed a smile. She didn't care for the man, but he was a necessary evil. Wasn't he responsible for elevating King George to an even greater threat than he already was? It had been a coup to win the traitor to their side, but that didn't mean she trusted him.

"They will come or they won't," said Einstein. "Either way, this device must be properly calibrated. Else this entire endeavor has been a waste of effort."

"Then please finish."

"Another few minutes should suffice. Just have your men ready to leave."

She'd already seen to that. The B-29 waited outside the hanger, belly open to receive its payload. A squadron of P-51 Mustangs, ironically purchased from an American defense contractor, were ready for escort duty. Their pilots smoked cigarettes and traded nervous jokes. The Pool was in Virginia, and there was a lot of airspace between there and Texas. But the United States would never expect such a sudden attack, even in the wake of Einstein's defection. It was entirely out of the Republic's character, and that would be their chief advantage.

Flying low to the ground would hopefully allow them to avoid radar, and if they were spotted by civilians, they'd likely be mistaken for American aircraft. If the military got wind of them, then their only shot was for the Mustangs to keep the enemy at bay long enough for the bomber to release its payload over the Immortality Compound. When Betty blew, all bets would be off. Einstein said it would release whatever power was binding the magic in place, and nobody knew what would happen then.

Whatever it was, it would be preferable to that miserable man in Washington holding all the cards. Ma only wished she could see his sallow face when he learned that somebody had pissed in his sandbox.

"When this is done, I'd like to keep you in our employ," she said.

Einstein pushed a confused looking young engineer out of the way and turned three of the knobs a fraction of a turn. "We'll need you to help us harness all of that free magic roaming the countryside."

Einstein turned a tired scowl her way. His frustration and impatience was etched into every wrinkle on his face. The man didn't even have the decency to hide his dislike of her.

"I thought you Texans wanted to liberate the magic, not usher it into another prison cell."

"We do want to liberate it. But only to make it available for everyone. Do you expect us to gain access to the magic and then turn our noses up when it comes our way? Oh, Houston's a little idealistic, I'll grant you. He likes to think sending all of this magic into the world will empower mankind and help it all come together. But I don't think he has a real understanding of human nature.

"It puts everyone on equal footing. That's for sure. That's the goal. Take away America's advantage. But once it's a free for all, you can damn well bet I'm going to put Texas in a position to succeed. If I did any less, I wouldn't be worthy of office."

Einstein studied her for several uncomfortable seconds. He scratched his stubbly head and leaned against Betty's side, as if the air around him was too heavy for a man of his age. He licked at parched lips, then turned away from her and tapped a fingernail against one of the device's gauges. "This isn't exactly right. Look, you need to dial it in to thirty. No, move please and I'll show you."

Einstein did not speak to her again again until the B-29, with Betty in its bomb bay, lifted off with its compliment of fighter planes. They stood together on the insufferably hot tarmac amid a host of ground crew and government officials. Grim-faced General Eaker barked commands. Einstein's inscrutable gaze followed the planes until they were nothing more than tiny black blotches against the darkening skies. His eyes were red and wet, and he looked as if he'd aged ten years in the last twenty-four hours.

"If you'll kindly excuse me, I think I'll retire to my quarters," said Einstein, never taking his eyes off the horizon. "I think I've had quite enough of this world."

The Scientist

lbert slid beneath the blankets, and closed his eyes for the last time. He relished the cool feel of the pillow against his cheek, and the clean smell of bleach on the sheets. He tried to take it all in, to hold it to him somehow. These were likely his last hours, and though he was too tired to spend them doing anything else, he wanted at the very least for his last sensations on earth to be pleasant.

He would not die; not technically. But he would be gone. All of them would. Possibly far enough gone that they'd never exist again.

The Vice President's intentions had shaken him to the core, and he cursed his own naiveté. He wasn't playing on the level with the Texans, so why had he expected them to be any less duplicitous. They didn't want the magic free at all. They wanted it for themselves. The moment she'd spoken, a host of alternate futures had exploded into life in his mind, and none of them were any better than the one he planned to eradicate. As long as that sort of power existed, there would be someone willing to exploit it.

It wasn't the Pool's fault, it was his. By itself, the Pool was nothing more than a wonderful gift from Creation. But with tampering, his and others, it had become something it shouldn't have.

In those last moments, in the choking heat of that hanger, Albert had performed a few small changes to Betty's calibration. A few degrees here, a pressure adjustment there. Now all of his mistakes could be erased.

Betty would still be his salvation. She would turn back the world to a time before he'd hired his brilliance to such an unworthy cause. But not to a time when he might once again be tempted to turn from science to alchemy. Nor to a time when he might still grow to become a person of such reckless pride. Time would be turned back far enough that such temptation might never occur, at least not to him. Far enough, perhaps, that the Pool could have a good long rest without worrying about the presence of humanity.

There was a real possibility, if Betty did her work, that Albert Einstein would never be born. Or any of the other wolves who chased immortality and power through the forests of human weakness.

That would not be such a bad thing.

Albert turned on the radio, not quite ready to fall asleep forever. He tuned in a fuzzy station and was delighted to hear Hiram — or Hank as he called himself professionally — speaking in his southern American drawl.

"Thank y'all for letting me play for you. I've got one more, and I'll dedicate this one to my scientist friend. Maybe this is the last one I'll ever play, at least in this life."

Hiram sang a low mournful tune that brought tears to the scientist's eyes.

It was the sort of melancholy that the end of the world deserved.

"There is no greater satisfaction for a just and well-meaning person than the knowledge that he has devoted his best energies to the service of the good cause."
—Albert Einstein

Appendix A
The Essential Texas Writers

To make this list, we need to define a Texas writer. This is hard to clarify. To some, it is a person born and raised in the state. That definition knocks out many of the famous Texans in history — David Crockett, Sam Houston, Howard Waldrop, and many more. Perhaps it is someone who once lived in Texas. Many others fit that description but perhaps it is too wide a definition. Samuel R. Delany lived in Texas for a while, working as a gulf coast shrimper in the late '60's while working on one of his novels and I don't think of him as a Texas writer (though we would be more than happy to claim him). Do we include those raised in Texas who soon left? This would include folks like Gene Wolfe who went to school in Texas attending Texas A&M University but soon left and was drafted into the Korean War. He later returned and got a degree from the University of Houston before heading north. I included him in my all Texan anthology *Cross Plains Universe* and was happy to have him.

What about those born and raised elsewhere who managed to move to Texas as adults and made their home here for a long while. This would include authors such as Chad Oliver, Michael Moorcock, Walter M. Miller, Howard Waldrop, Bradley Denton, and a host of others. Ultimately, Texas is a state of mind and attitude, hard to define, but easy to see.

There is an old joke that says "Never ask a man if he is from Texas? If he is, you will know it by the way he acts and talks. And if he isn't, you'll just embarrass him."

In 1976 George W. Proctor and Steven Utley edited *Lone Star Universe*, a collection showing the current state of Texas science fiction. It featured stories by the two editors, Chad Oliver, Neal Barrett, Jr., Robert E. Howard, Howard Waldrop, James Sallis, Lisa Tuttle, Bruce Sterling (whose story was printed with paragraphs out of order), Robert Lory, Tom Reamy, T. R. Fehrenbach and more. Published by Heidelberg Press of Austin, TX (who counted future thriller writer David Lindsay among its ownership), a warehouse flood shortly after publication created a scarcity of the much sought after book. The cover by Mike Pressley featured two aliens wearing Stetson hats leaning against a Cadillac with longhorns attached.

In terms of science fiction, Texas boasts one of the earliest short stories. In 1865, the *Houston Tri-Weekly Telegraph* newspaper published a short story by Aurelia Hadley Mohl entitled "An Afternoon's Nap, or: Five Hundred Years Ahead" describes a far-future utopia and briefly mentions air travel, radio, television, and colonies on the moon and various planets. It is one of the first American science fiction short stories written by a woman. In context, this was the same year as Jules Verne published From the Earth to the Moon and it precedes Around the World in Eighty Days and Twenty thousand Leagues Under the Sea.

As modern science fiction began to take shape during the pulp era, Texas writers took a strong role in the field. Jack Williamson was raised in far west Texas and as a young 20 year old college student at West Texas State Teachers College in Canyon, TX near Amarillo he sold his first science fiction story "The Metal Man" to Amazing Stories where it appeared in the December 1928 issue. He sold several more stories to Hugo Gernsback before leaving the school. Williamson is more generally recognized as a New Mexico writer.

Neal Barrett, Jr.

His idiosyncratic and unique tales mark Neal Barrett, Jr. as a truly different writer. His masterpiece *The Hereafter Gang* wherein Doug Hoover takes a trip across Heaven (or maybe Texas or Oklahoma, it gets confusing) with the ultimate sweet young heartthrob carhop/ sex goddess to find Nirvana, the fantasy series featuring the swashbuckling pig Aldair out to save the princess, the short story "Winter on the Belle Forche" with its literary mashup of Liver Eatin' Johnson and Emily Dickinson, and his countless other works all have a quirk that is hard to describe and even harder to forget. After more than 50 years of producing unusual and acclaimed stories, the SFWA honored Barrett as an Author Emeritus in 2010.

Bradley Denton

Born and raised in Kansas, Brad Denton has been on Texas for more than 20 years. His novels *Buddy Holly is Alive and Well on Ganymede* and *Lunatics* use Texas settings. *Lunatics*, in particular, deals with the unique moon towers that illuminate Austin. His short fiction collection *The Calvin Coolidge Home for Dead Comedians and A Conflagration Artist* won the World Fantasy Award. The story "Sergeant Chip" won the Theodore Sturgeon Memorial award.

Charles Harness

Despite four Hugo and two Nebula nominations, Charles L Harness remains largely unknown to most fans. His novel *The Paradox Men* (aka *Flight to Nowhere*) has been hailed as a classic space opera. Though celebrated throughout the UK when published in Authentic Science Fiction in 1953, the novelette *The Rose* did not appear in the US until 16 years after its initial publication. NESFA Press published a collection of his short fiction (*An Ornament to His Profession*), a collection of novels (*Rings*) and a standalone novel (*Cybele, With Bluebonnets*) The Science Fiction Writers of America in 2004 recognized Harness as Author Emeritus.

Robert E. Howard

Perhaps the greatest of all the pulp writers, Howard lived in the small west Texas town of Cross Plains, located near Brownwood and Abilene. His series characters include Conan the Barbarian, Kull of Atlantis, Bran Mac Morn the Pict, Solomon Kane the Puritan wanderer, Sailor Steve Costigan, and El Borak. Writing only a few novels, Howard concentrated on short fiction. Many collections of his works exist with *Skullface and Others*, *Kull of Atlantis*, and *Red Shadows* among the finest. Howard only penned one science fiction tale, *Almuric*, a sword and planet novel which rivaled some of the work of Edgar Rice Burroughs and Otis Adelbert Kline (who was Howard's agent that sold the story to *Weird Tales* following Howard's death). The strong story telling that typified Howard's writing influenced a variety of science fiction and fantasy writers. Two biographies (*Dark Valley Destiny* by L. Sprague and Catherine Crook deCamp and *Blood and Thunder* by Mark Finn) present sharply contrasting images of a great writer and enigmatic person. The film *The Whole Wide World* focused on Howard's relationships with his family and his girlfriend during the final years of his life. (As a side note, the de Camps later moved to Plano, TX north of Dallas following the sale of their library and personal papers to the University of Texas. They remained there until their deaths in 2000 about six months apart. It is tempting to include them here but the majority of their work had been long completed before the move and they never truly embraced their inner Texan).

Joe R. Lansdale

The prolific Joe R. Lansdale started off, like his friend Lewis Shiner, writing detective stories in *Mike Shayne's Mystery Magazine* (*Detective Fiction As You Like It* collects the Lansdale and Shiner solo and collaborative efforts). He soon graduated into the dark horror and western fields. For his over 500 short stories, some 40 novels, and numerous comic scripts, Lansdale collected a variety of awards including the Edgar Award from the Mystery Writers of America for Best Novel, the British Fantasy Award, eight Bram Stoker Awards from the Horror Writers of America, the Grinzani Cavour Prize for Literature, and the American Horror Award. He accomplished all this while developing an original martial arts style called Shen Chuan, which eventually landed him in the Martial Arts Hall of Fame as both a performer and as an instructor. While rarely dabbling in science fiction, some of his better works including *The Drive-In* series, "Tight Little Stitches On A Dead Man's Back," and the steampunk novella "The Steam Man of the Prairie and the Dark Rider Get Down: A Dime Novel" are undeniably science fiction.

Ardath Mayhar

Noted for her strong characters, Ardath Mayhar quietly exploded onto the science fiction/fantasy scene in the late 1970's with a series of fantasy novels with titles such as *How the Gods Wove in Kyrannon*, *Exiles on Vlahi,* and *Seekers of Shar-Nuh*n that evoked Andre Norton and Lord Dunsany. Mayhar produced the first authorized sequel to H. Beam Piper's *Little Fuzzy* series: the entertaining *Golden Dreams: A Fuzzy Odyssey*. As a contributor to *Writer's Digest*, she helped beginning writers hone their own style. Mayhar wrote fantasy, science fiction, western, and other novels over the years. Perhaps the pinnacle of her career, *The World Ends in Hickory Hollow* is now considered a classic of post apocalyptic fiction. Mayhar was named an SFWA Author Emeritus in 2008. She passed away in 2012.

Cormac McCarthy

El Pasoan Cormac McCarthy would probably be shocked to be considered a "genre" writer of any sort. But *The Road*, his Pulitzer Prize winning novel is post apocalyptic and can only be classified as science fiction. Parts of *Blood Meridian* are astoundingly horrific and the character of the Judge can be viewed as supernatural.

Elizabeth Moon

The award-winning Elizabeth Moon works in both the science fiction and fantasy fields. *The Sheepfarmer's Daughter*, the first of her

Paksenarrion series won the Compton Crook Award for Best First Novel. *The Speed of Dark* won the Nebula Award in 2003. A former Marine, Moon's science fiction works often contain military and space opera themes. An avid fencer, she is a member of the SFWA Musketeers.

Michael Moorcock

Since the mid 1990s, the legendary Michael Moorcock spends half his year in Texas, dividing the remaining time between Paris, London and Spain. Winner of countless awards including the Nebula, World Fantasy, and the British Science Fiction, he additionally garnered a SFWA Grand Master and received the Life Achievement Award from the World Fantasy Convention and the Horror Writers of America.

Author of over 100 books, Moorcock's works feature a panoply of characters such as Elric of Melnibone, the Eternal Champion, Dorian Hawkmoon, and Jerry Cornelius. During the 1960s, he edited *New Worlds* which served as one of the boiling pots of the New Wave and featured the work of Moorcock, Thomas M. Disch, John Sladek, Norman Spinrad, J. G. Ballard and many others. Among some of his best work is *The Best of Michael Moorcock, Mother London, The Final Programme, Gloriana*, and *The War Hound and the World's Pain*. His studies of fantasy — *Wizardry and Wild Romance and Fantasy: The 100 Best Books* (edited with James Cawthorn) — display his vast knowledge and individual opinions of many works of fiction.

Chad Oliver

Writer, teacher, and friend to all, Chad Oliver influenced a generation of authors as the Dean of Texas science fiction. His novels, among the first to feature anthropological themes, predated the better know works by Ursula K. LeGuin and Michael Bishop. Oliver's juvenile novel *Mists of Dawn*, an early effort, featured a time travel story of early man. *Shadows in the Sun*, his first adult novel, starred a tall, pipe smoking Texas anthropologist which one reviewer found improbable. He obviously never met Oliver who used himself as a model.

Tom Reamy

Part of the Big D in '73 WorldCon bid and the Dallas Futurian Society, Tom Reamy produced the multiple Hugo nominated fanzine *Trumpet*. He began writing in the early 1970's and was a member of the Turkey City Writers' Workshop. His novella "San Diego Lightfoot Sue" won a Nebula Award in 1976. Reamy also won the John W. Campbell Award for Best New Writer in 1976. A collection of his short fiction (everything except his story for the infamous *The Last Dangerous Visions*) appeared the following year as *San Diego Lightfoot Sue and Other Stories*. Reamy died in 1977 of a heart attack before the publication of his only novel *Blind Voices* which has been compared to Ray Bradbury or Clifford Simak if they had been writing *The Circus of Dr. Lao*.

Lewis Shiner

Originally writing detective stories for places like *Mike Shayne's Mystery Magazine*, Lewis Shiner quickly moved over into science fiction. His presence in Austin and discussions with Bruce Sterling led him to be closely associated with the cyberpunk movement. The Sterling edited fanzine *Cheap Truth* provided a forum for Shiner and others to decry the state of science fiction and to give rise to many of the concepts incorporated into cyberpunk. His World Fantasy Award winning novel *Glimpses* deals with classic unreleased albums of rock and roll such as The Beach Boys' *Smile* and The Doors' *Celebration of the Lizard*. Short stories offer perhaps the greatest showcase of Shiner's talents. *Collected Stories* features his finest tales. New Shiner works appear only sporadically, with only seven novels appearing since 1984. Now located in North Carolina, his most recent novel is *Dark Tangos* (2011).

Bruce Sterling:

Futurist Bruce Sterling began his writing career with a sale to Harlan Ellison's *The Last Dangerous Visions* (recounted in Ellison's introduction to Sterling's first novel *Involution Ocean* [1977]). His early short stories, set in his Mechanist/Shaper universe, showcased the conflict between computer and genetics based technologies. These stories spawned the collection *Crystal Express* and the novel *Schismatrix*. Sterling's samizdat/fanzine *Cheap Truth* which he edited as Vincent Omniveritas criticized the moribund state of science fiction and helped to usher in the cyberpunk movement. His association with other cyberpunk writers William Gibson, Rudy Rucker, Pat Cadigan, and Lewis Shiner as well as the ideological nature of his articles led to him being dubbed "Chairman Bruce." The Sterling-edited *Mirrorshades*, one of the best selling anthologies of all time, is the Bible of the cyberpunk movement. Sterling won two Hugos for novelettes "The Bicycle Repairman" and "Taklamakan". His novel *Islands in the Net* won the John W. Campbell Award for Best Novel while *Distractions* won the Arthur C. Clarke Award.

Lisa Tuttle

Guest of Honor at the 2007 World Fantasy Convention, Lisa Tuttle was one of the founders of the Houston Science Fiction Society. She won the John W. Campbell Award for Best New Writer in 1974 (in a tie with Spider Robinson). Tuttle's novels frequently focus on gender issues and feminism. Her *An Encyclopedia of Feminism* is a basic text in the movement. An early graduate of the Clarion science fiction program, she has taught at it and at the university level. In a controversial move, she refused the 1982 Nebula Award for her short story "The Bone Flute" because of what she felt were unfair advantages gained by some writers when their editors sent their work out to all members of SFWA when not all publications could afford to do this practice. Her novels include *Familiar Spirit* which is set in the Austin house and neighborhood in which she lived. Since 1981 she has lived in the UK.

Howard Waldrop

Though born in Mississippi, Howard Waldrop got to Texas as fast as he could. His unique stories, often born out of the Texas tall tale, frequently dabble in alternate histories Works such as "Ike at the Mike" where Dwight Eisenhower gets distracted on his way to West Point and becomes a celebrated jazz musician or "Custer's Last Jump" where Little Big Horn features airships and paratroopers typify Walrop's output. Collections *Things Will Never Be the Same* and *Other Worlds, Better Lives* from Old Earth Books offer a great retrospective of his best work. Who else would try to incorporate such diverse ideas as the H. G. Wells Martians invading Texas or John Bunyan and Izaak Walton fishing for Leviathan in the Slough of Despond? The last of the dodos story "The Ugly Chickens" won Waldrop the World Fantasy and the Nebula Awards in 1981.

Gene Wolfe

Named a Grand Master by SFWA in 2013, recipient of the Life Achievement Award from the World Fantasy Convention, member of the Science Fiction Hall of Fame, and winner of multiple Nebula, World Fantasy, British Science Fiction, Campbell, and World Fantasy Awards, Gene Wolfe created the celebrated works *The Book of the New Sun* (which includes *The Shadow of the Torturer*, *The Claw of the Conciliator*, *The Sword of the Lictor*, and *The Citadel of the Autarch*). Wolfe went to high school and college in Texas. Wolfe's prose is dense and frequently features hidden depths and allusions that become apparent only upon re-reading. Award nominations include 20 Nebula nominations (2 wins), 13 World Fantasy Award nominations (5 wins) and nine Hugo nominations (but, alas, no wins). His short fiction can best be seen in *The Island of Doctor Death and Other Stories and Other Stories*, *Storeys From the Old Hotel* and *The Best of Gene Wolfe*.

Appendix B
Other Texas Writers You Should Check Out

Lou Antonelli

One conversation with Lou Antonelli will reveal that he is not a native born Texan. Raised in Massachusetts and New York, he moved to Texas in 1985. A journalist by trade, Antonelli writes short fiction with a Texas setting, frequently with a twist ending.

Bill Baldwin

Former NASA contractor, Bill Baldwin is a fan of old fashioned space opera. The *Helmsman* series has been described as if Horatio Hornblower had grown up to become the Gray Lensman and had sex. The series also features talking Soviet bears who work as space engineers.

Damien Broderick

Australian by birth, Damien Broderick currently lives in the San Antonio area. He has won the Ditmar Award (the Australian Science Fiction Achievement Award) five times for novels *The Dreaming Dragons*, *Striped Holes*, *Transmitters*, *The White Abacus*, and the non-fiction title *Earth is But a Star: Excursions through Science Fiction to the Far Future*.

Melissa Mia Hall

The masterful short story writer Melissa Mia Hall sadly languished in obscurity. Though she tried her hand at novels, Hall never quite got one to the point of publication before her sudden death in 2011 at 56. Her stories frequently appeared in the Shadows series edited by Charles Grant. Hall regularly reviewed science fiction, fantasy and horror for *Publishers Weekly*.

Katherine Eliska Kimbriel

Fire Sanctuary, the first of her three *Nuala* novels earned Katherine Eliska Kimbriel a John W. Campbell nomination for Best New Writer. She has also written two novels featuring Alfreda Golden-Tongue, starting with *Night Calls* as well as short fiction

Jay Lake

The child of a Foreign Service officer, Jay Lake grew up in Nigeria. A Writers of the Future winner in 2003 and Campbell award winner in 2004 for Best New Writer, Lake has produced 11 novels and six short story collections while also editing 12 titles. His *Mainspring* novels (*Mainspring, Escapement*, and *Pinion*) are set within a steampunk society.

Joe McKinney

San Antonio policeman Joe McKinney writes police procedurals masquerading as science fiction and horror novels. The sf novel *Quarantined* deals with a medical emergency requiring the total isolation and eventual destruction of San Antonio. *Flesh Eaters*, one of his *Dead World* zombie novels, won the Bram Stoker Award for Best Novel from the Horror Writers of America.

Henry Melton

Wire Rim Books publisher Henry Melton now occupies the spot vacated by Robert Heinlein of providing action science fiction novels with strong teenage characters. The first novel *Emperor Dad* won the Darrell Award for Best Novel. His books fall into several general grouping such as *Small Towns, Big Ideas* (presenting characters from a rural background facing big problems; each book is a standalone) and *The Project Saga,* a large cast multi-generational space epic.

Warren Norwood

Viet Nam vet Warren Norwood started out writing space opera with *The Windhover Tapes* (4 novels between 1982 and 1984), earning him nominations for the John W. Campbell Award in 1983 and 1984. He wrote 13 novels before retiring to teach writing and play music. Norwood died in 2005 from liver disease and kidney failure.

George W. Proctor

Educator and writer, George W. Proctor co-edited *Lone Star Universe* with Steve Utley in 1976 as well as *Science Fiction Hall of Fame, Volume 3* with Arthur C. Clarke. He wrote in a variety of fields, including fantasy and westerns. Among his science fiction novels are *The ESPer Transfer, Starwings,* and *Stellar Fist.* Proctor died in 2008.

Joe Pumilia

One of the driving forces behind the Houston Science Fiction Society and its magazine *The Purple Obscenity,* Joe Pumilia wrote short stories. He and Bill Wallace created the Lovecraftian imitator M. M. Moamrath, the fictional author of "The Next to the Last Voyage of the Cuttle Sark," "Curse of the Kritix," and "Riders of the Purple Ooze."

Chris Roberson

Called one of the new writers to watch by Garner Dozois, Chris Roberson won the Sidewise Award for stories of alternate history twice, once for his short story "Oh One" and once for his novel *The Dragon's Nine Sons* and was a finalist for the John W. Campbell award for Best New Writer on two occasions. He received three World Fantasy Award nominations: one each as a writer, editor and publisher. Monkey Brain Books, Roberson's publishing venture (with his wife Allison Baker), has published non-fiction, science fiction, art book, and comics.

Steven Utley

Poet, artist, and author Steven Utley co-edited with George W. Proctor *Lone Star Universe*. A prolific short story writer, collections of his works include *When or Where, Ghost Seas,* and *The Beasts of Love*. Utley returned to his native Tennessee in 1997, where he died of cancer in January, 2013

Martha Wells

Nebula finalist for the fantasy novel *The Death of the Necromancer,* Martha Wells writes of the fantasy world Ile-Rien. Her three science fiction novels dealing with the shape changing Raksura began with *The Cloud Roads.* Wells also penned two original *Stargate Atlantis* novels.

Appendix C
The Essential Texas Artists

Berkeley Breathed

Bloom County and its denizens Opus the Penguin and Bill the Cat made Berke Breathed into a household name. The political content of that daily newspaper cartoon strip earned him a Pulitzer Prize in 1989. Breathed began his cartooning career at the University of Texas newspaper *The Daily Texan* with his daily strip *The Academia Waltz*. Science fiction themes were abundant in both strips and in the Bloom County successor, *Outland*. Breathed retired from comic trip work in November 2008. Breathed has since concentrated on illustrated children's books such as *Mars Needs Moms*.

R. Cat Conrad

Former industrial chemist, R. Cat Conrad combines his love of classical art, comic art, and science fiction art into his paintings and illustrations in a style he refers to as Surreallustraton. An award winning artist, he lives with his, fantasy writer Rachel Caine in Ft. Worth.

Brad Foster

Earning a record Hugo Award for Best Fan Artist eight times, Foster's iconic line art has appeared in virtually every fanzine. A publisher as well as an artist, his Jabberwocky Graphix showcases his work as well as more than 300 other artists.

Teddy Harvia

Four time Hugo winner for Best Fan artist, Dallas area resident Teddy Harvia's (an anagram of David Thayer) cartoons frequently feature a group of alien creatures with a weird sense of humor dubbed the Wing Nuts. His other characters include the sabertooth Chat in the U.S. fanzine *Mimosa*, the goddess Opuntia in the Canadian fanzine of the same name, and Enid the Echidna in the Australian fanzine *Ethel the Aardvark*.

Rocky Kelly

Award winning artist Rocky Kelley's work incorporates science fiction, fantasy, surrealism, and Pre-Raphaelite influences. In 2006 he won the Art Directors Award at the World Fantasy Convention. The David Letterman show once highlighted Kelley's work as have Nieman Marcus and Spiegel which used his designs in their Christmas catalogs.

Stephan Martiniere

Frenchman Stephan Martiniere moved to Texas in 2008. For his international appealing work Martiniere won a Hugo, two Chesney's from the Association of Science Fiction Artists, two British SF Awards, and three Spectrum Awards. His future vision achieved cinematic immortality as he provided concept art for, among others, *I, Robot*, *Red Planet*, *Star Wars: Episodes II* and *III*, and *The Fifth Element*. The books *Velocity* and *Quantumscapes* showcase the variety of Martiniere's art.

Clayburn Moore

Striking action poses on anatomically precise figures are the hallmark of sculptor Clayburn Moore... His typically resin or bronze statues garnered him four Chesley Awards in the Three Dimensional category. CS Moore Studios operates in the Dallas area.

Real Musgrave

The Dallas-based Real Musgrave created his first pocket dragon character in the 1970s and incorporated them into drawings and paintings. Musgrave along with his wife Muff created the pocket dragon figurine line in 1989 releasing more than 400 individual figurines. The whimsical creations even starred in their own cartoon series in 1996. A full time artist and sculptor for more than three decades, Musgrave was been honored as the official artist for the Texas Renaissance Festival for 14 years and later three years for the Scarborough Faire festival.

John Picacio

San Antonio artist John Picacio has a shelf full of awards including a Hugo (for Best Professional artist), four Chesley Awards, one World Fantasy Award, and two International Horror Guild Awards. He is the only artist to have won all four awards. Trained as an architect, he created the comic *Words and Pictures* with Fernando Ramirez in 1994. In 1997 he began doing book covers starting with the 30th anniversary edition of Michael Moorcock's *Behold the Man*. Picacio's beautiful *Cover Story* contains many comments on the creation of his art with examples of his creative process.

Don Punchatz

Based in Arlington, Don Ivan Punchatz produced numerous covers and interior illustrations for magazines such as *Heavy Metal*, *National Geographic*, *Playboy*, and *Time*. He created iconic paperback images for Asimov's *Foundation* series as well as *Dangerous Visions* and employed the painting for Philip Jose Farmer's *A Barnstormer in Oz* as the promotional poster for his studio TexOz. Judged the second greatest cover of all time by Game Spy, Punchatz's work for the video game *DOOM* influenced game promotion for a generation. He died in 2009 of cardiac arrest.

Vincent Villafranca

Artist and sculptor Vincent Villafranca has won the Chesley Award for 3D art three times and has received awards three times at the World Fantasy Convention art show. He designed the base for the Hugo Awards to be presented at the 2013 World Science Fiction Convention in San Antonio. Villafranca also designed the Bradbury Award given by the Science Fiction Fantasy Writers of America for the Best Screenplay.

Author Biographies

Sanford Allen, at various times, has worked as a newspaper reporter, a college journalism instructor, and a touring musician. He currently divides his creative energy between writing tales of horror/ sf/dark fantasy and his band Hogbitch, which wallows in the murky swamp between doom metal and space rock. He lives in San Antonio, Texas, with his wife Tracey. Visit him at *www.sanfordallen.com*.

A lifelong Texan (born 1960 in Corsicana, reared all over the damned place, and settled in the Austin area), Aaron Allston is a *New York Times* bestselling author. Best known for novels set in the *Star Wars* Expanded Universe, he has also written original science fiction, fantasy, horror, nonfiction, role-playing games, and screenplays. He is a member of the Academy of Adventure Gaming Arts & Design Hall of Fame. His recent work includes *X-Wing: Mercy Kill* (Del Rey Books), *Plotting: A Novelist's Workout Guide* (ArcherRat Publishing), "Big Plush" (in *Five by Five*, WordFire Press), and "Epistoleros" (in *Shadows of the New Sun: Stories in Honor of Gene Wolfe*, Tor Books). Allston is visually impaired, ethically pedantic, and morally bankrupt. Visit his web sites at *www.aaronallston.com* and *www.archerrat.com*.

Neal Barrett, Jr. has published over 50 novels and numerous short stories. He has been named Author Emeritus by the Science Fiction Writers of America. Subterranean Press has recently published Barrett's "career-spanning" short story collection, *Other Seasons*.

Matthew Bey is a writer and editor living in Austin, TX. He has succeeded in attaining editor-at-large status for many quality publications including *RevolutionSF*, *The Drabblecast*, and his own zine *Space Squid*, which gives him plenty of padding for anthology bios but no actual responsibility. He blogs about hotdogs, fishing, and Bollywood movies at his site *MatthewBey.com*.

Chris N. Brown (aka Chris Nakashima-Brown) writes short fiction and criticism from his home in Austin, Texas, where he is an active member of the Turkey City Writer's Workshop, as well as a practicing lawyer. Brown is the co-editor, with Eduardo Jiménez, of *Three Messages and a Warning: Contemporary Mexican Short Stories of the Fantastic* (Small Beer Press, January 2012). A complete bibliography of his work is available at *chrisnbrown.net*.

For more than 40 years Scott A. Cupp has been involved in the Texas science fiction scene as a writer, fan, convention goer, editor, ape fan, and all around geek. Primarily a short story and essay writer, he lives in San Antonio with his wife, two cats and many books and movies. Most recent among his works are the essay "The Four Color Ape" in *The Apes Of Wrath* and "Splash" , a round robin story written with Don Webb, Richard Lupoff, Michael Mallory, Michael Kurland, Paul DiFillipo, and James Patrick Kelley which appeared in *Lore Magazine*. Weekly reviews of Forgotten Books and Forgotten Movies appear at *www.missionsunknown.com*. Other details of his life can be seen in the memoir within this volume.

Bradley Denton and his wife Barbara moved from Kansas to Texas in the spring of 1988, which now makes them naturalized Texans. In the twenty-five years since that move, Brad's novels and stories have been nominated for the Nebula, Hugo, Stoker, and Edgar awards — and have won the John W. Campbell Memorial Award (for *Buddy Holly Is Alive And Well On Ganymede*), the Theodore Sturgeon Memorial Award (for "Sergeant Chip"), and the World Fantasy Award (for *A Conflagration Artist And The Calvin Coolidge Home For Dead Comedians*). And now, after a decade in development, it looks as if the motion picture version of *Buddy Holly Is Alive And Well On Ganymede* is finally about to go into production. We'll drink a Shiner Bock to that.

Nicky Drayden is a Systems Analyst who dabbles in prose when she's not buried in code. She resides in Austin, Texas where being weird is highly encouraged, if not required. She's the author of over 30 published short stories and you can see more of her work at _www. nickydrayden.com_.

Rhonda Eudaly lives in Arlington, Texas where she's worked in offices, banking, radio, and education to support her writing She's married, with dogs and a rapidly growing rubber duck collection. She likes to spend time with friends and family, movies, and reading Her two passions are writing and music. Check out her website _www. RhondaEudaly.com_ for her latest publications and downloads.

Mark Finn is an author, actor, essayist, and playwright. A renowned Robert E. Howard scholar, Finn's _Blood and Thunder: The Life and Art of Robert E. Howard_, was nominated for a World Fantasy award in 2007 and is currently available in a new Second Edition. He is the author of two books of fiction, _Gods New and Used_ and _Year of the Hare_, as well as hundreds of articles, essays, reviews, and short stories for The University of Texas Press, RevolutionSF, Greenwood Press, Dark Horse Comics, Wildside Press, Monkeybrain Books, Tachyon Publications and others. Current projects include _Dr. Zombie_ for Monkeybrain Comics with longtime friend and collaborator John Lucas and a short story in _Tails From the Pack_ from Sky Warrior Books . When he's not lecturing or performing across Texas, he lives in North Texas with his long-suffering wife, too many books, and an affable pit bull named Sonya.

Derek Austin Johnson was born in Springfield, Massachusetts, in 1968 and lived in Chicago during the Democratic Convention riots before spending his formative years in Houston, Texas. His reviews and criticism have appeared in _Nova Express_, _His Majesty's Secret Servant_, _RevolutionSF_, _Moving Pictures_, and _SF Signal_. He produces the ongoing monthly film and media column "Watching the Future" for _SF Site_, and has written erotic romance under a pseudonym. He currently lives in Central Texas with the Goddess. You can find out more at his website at *http://derekaustinjohnson.weebly.com.*

Joe R. Lansdale is the author of thirty novels and numerous short stories. He is Writer in Residence at Stephen F. Austin State University, a member of The Texas Literary Hall of Fame, and has received many recognitions for his writing, among them The Edgar for Best Crime Novel, The Lifetime and Grandmaster Award from The Horror Writer's Association, and is the founder and Grandmaster of Shen Chuan, Martial Science. He lives with his wife in Nacogdoches, Texas.

Stina Leicht is a former Campbell Award nominee. Her debut novel *Of Blood and Honey*, a historical Fantasy with an Irish Crime edge set in 1970s Northern Ireland, was released by Night Shade books in 2011 and was short-listed for the 2012 Crawford Award. The sequel, *And Blue Skies from Pain* is in bookstores now.

Marshall Ryan Maresca is a fantasy and science-fiction writer, as well as a playwright, living in South Austin with his wife and son. His plays include *Slow Night at McLaughlin's, Cinco Cenas, Danger Girl's Night Off, Last Train Out Of Illinois, Entropy* and *Slept the Whole Way*, as well as producing the award-winning sci-fi stage serial *Flame Failure*. His micro-story "Reminder" appeared in *Norton Anthology of Hint Fiction*, and his story "My Name is Avenger Girl" was featured in Paige Ewing's anthology *The Protectors*.

One of the first professional Texas women journalists, Aurelia Hadley Mohl (1833–1896) contributed articles, essays, poems, and even fiction to various publications including the *Houston Tri-Weekly Telegraph, Houston Post, San Antonio Herald, Waco Examiner, Dallas Commercial, Dallas Herald, Youth's Companion of Boston, New York Examiner, Philadelphia Times*, and *Chicago Standard*. A suffragette, she served as the corresponding secretary of the Women's National Press Association and later as vice-president of the Texas branch of the organization. She helped to found the Texas Women's Press Association. In 1893, Mohl attended the Women's Suffrage Convention, which lead to the creation of the Texas Equal Rights Association. In 1900, the Federated Women's Clubs commissioned a monument in her honor, the first by Texas women to commemorate a Texas woman.

Michael Moorcock has lived in Texas for about 20 years. When asked why he moved to Texas he explains he was on the dodge. Born in London in 1939, he edited *New Worlds* and wrote some SF and fantasy novels mostly featuring his Eternal Champion, a recurring character whose job is to maintain the equilibrium of the multiverse. His current novel is *The Whispering Swarm*. A new uniform edition of all his genre fiction is being published by Gollancz beginning 2013. Titan are currently republishing in the USA his proto-steampunk *Nomad of Time* series beginning with *The Warlord of the Air* and his *Hawkmoon* omnibus recently appeared from TOR.

Lawrence Person is a science fiction writer living in Austin, Texas. His work has appeared in *Asimov's*, *Fantasy & Science Fiction*, *Analog*, *Postscripts*, *Jim Baen's Universe*, *Fear*, *National Review*, *Reason*, *Whole Earth Review*, *The Freeman*, *Science Fiction Eye*, and *The New York Review of Science Fiction*, as well as several anthologies. He also runs Lame Excuse Books and reviews movies (frequently with Howard Waldrop) for *Locus Online*. He owns a very large library of science fiction first editions. He also makes a mean batch of salsa. His blog is at *http://www.lawrenceperson.com/*.

Jessica Reisman's stories have appeared in magazines and anthologies. Her first novel, *The Z Radiant*, was published by Five Star Speculative Fiction. She was a Michener Fellow, owns a large collection of Hong Kong movies, and finds inspiration and solace in books, movies and television, good friends, animal life, and rain. She lives in Austin, Texas with well-groomed cats. Some of these facts are not related. For more about her fiction, visit *www.storyrain.com*.

Josh Rountree is a sixth generation Texan, a descendant of Texas Rangers, horse thieves and other shady types. His short fiction has been published in a variety of magazines and anthologies including *Realms of Fantasy, Electric Velocipede* and *Polyphony 6*. His short story collection *Can't Buy Me Faded Love* is available from Wheatland Press, and his first novel, a collaboration with Lon Prater called *Alamo Rising* will be published by White Cat Publications in 2013.

Bruce Sterling, born in Brownsville, is a Texan science fiction writer and sometime "Visionary in Residence" at various design schools.

Don Webb has over 40 stories on Year's Best Lists in the last 24 years. He teaches a Writing Science Fiction class for UCLA Extension. His latest fiction is from Wildside Press — half space opera/half vampire fiction — *The War with the Belatran/A Velvet of Vampyres*. He is a regular at Armadillocon and has written many nonfiction books about the occult.

About the Editor

Professional reviewer, geek maven, and optimistic curmudgeon, Richard Klaw was the co-editor of the groundbreaking original anthology of short fiction in graphic form, *Weird Business*, editor of the acclaimed *The Apes of Wrath*, and co-founder of Mojo Press, one of the first publishers to produce both graphic novels and prose books. He also served as the initial fiction editor for *RevolutionSF*. Over the past decade, Klaw has written countless reviews, essays, and fiction for a variety of publications including *The Austin Chronicle*, *Blastr*, *Moving Pictures Magazine*, *San Antonio Current*, *Geek Dad*, *Conversations With Texas Writers* (University of Texas Press), *The Greenwood Encyclopedia of Science Fiction and Fantasy* (Greenwood Press), *San Antonio Business Journal*, *King Kong Is Back!* (BenBella Books), *Farscape Forever* (BenBella Books), *SF Site*, *Science Fiction Weekly*, *Nova Express*, *Steampunk* (Tachyon Publications), *Electric Velocipede*, *Cross Plains Universe* (MonkeyBrain/FACT), and *The Steampunk Bible* (Abrahams). Many of his essays and observations were collected in *Geek Confidential: Echoes from the 21st Century* (MonkeyBrain).

Klaw can often be found pontificating on Twitter (*@rickklaw*) and his award winning blog *The Geek Curmudgeon* (*revolutionsf.com/revblogs/geekcurmudgeon*). He lives in Austin, Texas with his wife, a large cat, an even bigger dog, and an impressive collection of books.